Ancient Decree

Path of Lazy Immortal Book 10

A.P. Gore, Patricia Jones

Sign up for my Wuxia Sect to get latest update, and sneak peeks and an extended epilogue of the other books.

Patricia's Xianxia Sect

Contents

Chapter 1

Prologue

On a landscape far away from the Mortal World, a man with a short beard opened his green eyes, shooting a red light toward the jade-coated roof of his secluded cave. The rocky bed he slept on crashed under the immense pressure his body released, but the man didn't fall. Instead, he floated in a relaxed position, with his arms crossed behind his head, a few feet above the rocky ground of the cave.

"The Primordial Blood Palace has been lost. I can't let that happen. I wanted to save it for the escape, but this is more important." He pulled a hair from his head and blew on it.

The hair floated upward until it reached the ceiling. The man shot a beam of light from his eyes, and it exploded in the ceiling, giving the hair a rare chance of escape before the ceiling repaired automatically. Once outside, the hair turned into a copy of the man in the cave and laughed. A blue pendant rested on his chest, and a strange power rushed into him and enveloped him completely before turning him invisible.

In the room, the bearded man coughed a mouthful of blood. The last strike had used a lot of saved-up energy, and he would have to cultivate a few decades to gain it back. But it would be worth it.

Chapter 2

Sun Nuan's Dilemma

Sun Nuan sat on her petal-shaped flying artifact, floating toward the signal color in the sky. The color had changed to light umber in the last hour. The closer she got to it, the more excited her heart became. In fact, a couple of times, it became louder than a drum, and she feared Elder Deimu might get distracted.

However, the elder remained sitting on the flying tool. She bet it was because of his condition. He was on the verge of death, and she wasn't sure how she could save him. The poison he'd sucked from sister Ki Fei had affected his core. His cultivation level had dropped to Heart Blood Realm, and he had aged into a hundred-year-old and looked completely different.

Even his aura had changed. When she'd met him, he smelled like herbs, but now he smelled of death and rot. The feeling crept into her mind and made her taste the bitter taste of death, which she was quite familiar with. Whenever Sun Nuan sacrificed her age to see into the past—touched the shadows that shouldn't be touched—she felt death coming for her. And it wasn't a good experience. Big brother Wei had forced her to take a vow to not use the skill until her life or his was in danger.

Sighing, she focused her attention on the small forest on the horizon. It was made up of gray-and-brown trees, and she spotted big brother Wei sitting at the base of one, sipping tea from a golden ceramic cup. She had gifted him that the last time he'd come to the Five Firmament City, and seeing him use it made her heart flutter like a butterfly.

"Big brother Wei." She leaped off the flying tool and ran toward him.

Smiling, he got up and wrapped his arms around her. He'd done that since he came from the other world. He'd told Sun Nuan that one of his friends had said that was how good friends greeted each other in that world. She was his good friend, and he was her—well, everything.

Resting her head on his head gave her a peace she'd never had in her life except while hugging him like this. His arms were her world, and she would never stay away from him.

"Nuan'er. It must be hard on you." He touched her hair softly with his fingers, his hot breath brushing against her ear.

Her arms tightened around his back.

"Is that your girlfriend, brother Wei?" someone asked.

Nuan jumped out of big brother Wei's embrace and looked at the bald monk who had spoken. He was ugly and chubby, and his eyes scanned her like an object. She didn't like him at the first glance.

"This is brother Shaya, a monk from the Buddha Vasta Kingdom."

"Did I meet you before?" Sun Nuan asked, stepping close to Big brother Wei.

"Mahataba, I've never met you before, Princess Nuan. But I've heard a lot about you from a few of my brothers, and one of them described you as a fiery, unruly princess who toppled the mightiest auction house in the State of Zin."

"Aha. I know why I feel this way. You bald monks all look the same. I met one detestable fellow in the auction, and he even fought with me for a treasure."

"Nuan'er." Big brother Wei shook his head, suppressing his laugh.

"Big brother Wei, I've news about sister—"

Suddenly, a little tree appeared on big brother Wei's shoulder and looked at her pitifully with big eyes embedded in the middle of its trunk.

"Hey, how did you come back?" Big brother Wei frowned as he pulled the tree down by its branches.

"Big brother Wei, what's that? Please don't hurt that child," Nuan said. The tree looked like a child, and she couldn't bear to see the tears rolling down its trunk.

"It's a Forest Elemental, and it's in pain. Young man, these are holy emissaries of the forest, and you don't enslave them." The elder, perched on the flying tool, coughed intensely, his body withering in pain.

"Who is that with you, Nuan'er?" Big brother Wei stepped toward her flying tool and scanned the elder.

"It's related to that, elder." Sun Nuan didn't know what to say here.

"He's been poisoned. Is he a good man, Nuan'er?"

"He is."

"Then let me help him." Big brother Wei pressed his palm against the elder's back, and the poison slipped out from the elder's head in the form of green-and-black smoke. It made an angry face at big brother Wei before dissipating in the air.

"Brother Wei, that was a nasty curse poison. How did you cleanse it?" the bald monk asked, his face full of disbelief.

"Big brother Wei can nullify every poison in the world," Nuan said proudly. "If you stay with him, you'll understand how mighty he is." Then she realized that if big brother Wei had been present, sister Ki Fei wouldn't have suffered. If he could cleanse the Elder Deimu's poison, then he could cure her as well.

"Big broth—"

"I couldn't cleanse it. I could only drive it away," big brother Wei said. "But he will be fine afterward and might even regain his cultivation."

"Young man, thank you," the elder said in a weak voice. "If you give the elemental to this little girl, I can help her to enhance her wood powers."

Big brother Wei looked at the small tree.

The tree jumped from his hand and leaped onto her shoulder, covering her neck with its branches. "I like this big sister more. If you aren't going to refine me, then I'll take a heaven-and-earth vow that I'll serve her until time comes to an end."

"Will you really do that?"

"Yes. I feel an affinity toward her," the tree said, his branches caressing her earlobe, and a tickle ran down her neck.

"Then do that."

The tree swore an oath among the rumbling clouds, and then big brother Wei removed his soul marker from it. The tree rubbed his head against Nuan's cheek and turned into a rough scarf that wrapped around her neck. He must have learned that from the way Purple wrapped around big brother Wei's neck.

"Big brother Wei, I've bad news." Nuan couldn't hold it inside anymore.

Big brother Wei raised his palm, his face turning stone serious. "Nuan'er, I think a little fox is in trouble. When is the army from Divine Fragrance Palace arriving at the Old Martial City?"

"Seven days, according to my spies, but I've moved everyone related to the Li clan into the Five Firmament City. So there won't be any danger even if they arrive earlier. The place is like a ghost town now."

"That's a good thing. Take this. You know what's inside?" He tossed her a pouch, and just by the feel, she knew it was a new bottle filled with the godly liquid. "It's four times more potent than before."

She gasped. Two-thousand-year-old herbs would be common in her alchemy chamber going forward.

"Go back, and prepare to defend the city. They might head to the Five Firmament City afterward, and I'll be back there soon." He grabbed the bald monk and flapped his wings. "Nuan'er, how is the army preparation going on? I trusted Xue Qi's pills, but I regret doing that now."

"Big brother Wei, I don't know what's wrong between you and master, but the pills master produced with your special recipe are outstanding. Most of the people are already in Heart Blood Realm, one realm higher than we anticipated."

"In both the paths?"

"Yes," she said proudly.

"Good." Big brother Wei floated higher, staring at another direction as if he spotted someone else.

"Big brother Wei, I have to tell you something. It's important. It's about—"

"Later, Nuan'er." Big brother Wei flashed into the air and vanished over the forest. "Please take brother Du with you."

"Ki Fei is fine. I can sense her vitality. It's not improving or declining," Elder Deimu said, sounding better. "If you told Wei this now, he would face the dilemma of saving one over another, and that's not a good way to be, child."

Sun Nuan rubbed her nose. The elder's words had truth, but by not telling big brother Wei about Ki Fei, she felt like she'd betrayed him. But if she'd told him, he would have a dilemma, as the elder had said. She was trapped between a hard place and a mountain, and she had no idea what to do.

Chapter 3

Lines of Fate

Hui Ma knelt in front of her master, who sat on the lotus in the middle of a pond filled with blood. Her master, despite being a thousand years old, looked to be in her thirties. Gracefully, the master lifted her chin from her palm and looked at her, making Hui Ma feel as if she were hearing music. Everything her master did exuded dao. She had unfathomable powers, and no one in the Martial Realm dared to go against her.

"Ma'er, I called you here for a reason. There is a great test ahead of you." Her lips moved under the blue veil she wore.

Hui Ma felt like asking her to remove it. She was the most beautiful woman Hui Ma had ever seen in her life, though she had seen her master only once, when she was a little girl. Hui Ma was the only one who had lived even after seeing her master's face.

Her master was a devil, a killer for the others, but for Hui Ma, she was like a mother. Since Hui Ma had woken up in this world, she'd only seen poverty, brutality, and torture. Only after meeting her master had she learned the meaning of life, the meaning of killing.

"Master, you've prepared me for everything. I'll do anything you ask."

"Ma'er, the fate lines are not clear. The Gatekeepers are moving, and the world is going to enter a time of chaos."

"Chaos is good." Hui Ma smiled. "I like chaos. I can kill many."

"Child, this is nothing to be happy about. I wronged you by raising you to be an assassin. Fate lines were already not in favor of that." Her master sighed hard.

Hui Ma shook her head. "Master, you raised me to be a fine assassin, and I don't believe you were wrong."

Her master practiced a strange cultivation art that allowed her to read fate lines, but Hui Ma had never believed in them. She believed in her own heart and her master. When she was eight, Hui Ma's father had sold her to a brothel, where she was trained for dancing, singing, and whatnot. However, before she was forced to sleep with a slimy man, her master picked her up and killed everyone in that brothel. Later, Hui Ma underwent the master's training and, as a first mission, killed her father, who was nothing but scum. After that, she'd vowed to never let a man touch her in her life.

"Child, what will you do when your husband wants peace? This hot temper of yours will be the death of him."

"Why would I marry a man, master? I'm dedicated to killing, and even if I marry, I'll marry a killer."

"Because your fate intervenes with a man. I can see the lines. If I could, I'd stop you from taking a step outside of this place, but the sect wants to send you, so I can't do anything."

"Master, please don't worry. A man who can touch me hasn't been born yet. So there is no fate between me and a man.

"And what if this man touches you?"

"Impossible," Hui Ma said confidently. "They have tried it a thousand times, but not even the King of Speed could catch me once."

In recent years, she had challenged everyone who mastered Wind Intent, or any form of Intent that helped cultivators in speed, but no one could catch her. In fact, even the old fogies in the Houtian Realm who could perform Spatial Bending couldn't touch her. She was untouchable.

"Child, fate is not constant, nor is it perfect. If there is a fate between you and a man, nothing can stop it, and if it isn't there, nothing can start it."

"Master, if a man can touch me four times, I'll sow a fate between us. But if the man can't even touch me four times, there is no fate between us." Hui Ma shook her head. "I'll take a heaven-and-earth vow right here that I'll marry the man who can touch me four times. Not even fate can stop me from marrying him."

Chapter 4

Little Fox in Trouble

When the sky-piercing trees blocked his vision, Li Wei flipped metal wings, turning winds into gales that lifted him so high that the air turned bitter cold and a layer of ice formed on his wings. With a thought from Wei, a thin layer of fire covered them, expelling the icy breath of the heavens. It had been long since he'd risen so high in the sky. Fei'er had always wanted to fly with him, but she was missing, and he was missing her.

High winds slammed against his wings as he rose higher, but with a flip of his wings, everything was pushed back. Like a dragon's roar, they flapped, cutting through the punishment of the skies. These were called Astral Winds, and no one dared to fly so high, but he'd stopped caring about them after learning the Intent of Wind in the Ancient Constitution trials. And he couldn't care less about them when Little Fox was in danger and the Sky-Piercing Banana Trees restricted his divine sense, forcing him to fly. With only his soul pointing him, he had a general idea of where she was, and he was heading there.

"Brother Wei, mer..." The roar of the wind prevented Kai Shaya's words from reaching Wei. He was hanging by a rope wrapped around his waist, with the other end tied around Wei's waist.

All Wei could see was the pale face of Kai Shaya. A little layer of ice had formed on his thick brows, and the dim sunlight reflected off his bald head. A Heart Blood Realm qi cultivator should have been able to survive this much cold.

"Brother Shaya, I can't hear you. Speak louder. Or perhaps speak once we reach the destination. It's not far away from here."

Squinting, Wei looked ahead, trying to see the end of the banana trees, but the gray fog that tasted like salt and mud covered the horizon. Any other time his divine sense could cover miles and miles, but this strange forest of Sky-Piercing Banana Trees had blocked his divine sense. A silent cry echoed in his ears, and when he looked down, the ice had covered Kai Shaya entirely.

"Damn." Spreading his Heart Essence Aura, he opened Kai Shaya's mouth and tossed a Fire-Toad Apple into it. This type of apple had explosive fire properties, and Little Fox liked it, so Wei kept some on him.

A large piece of leaf slapped his face while he talked with Kai Shaya, leaving a foul taste in his mouth. This was the opposite of a regular banana tree. The leaves smelled like rot, and they tasted like thousand-day-old meat left in the open. Wei bet even a piece of junk would taste better than this. He'd accidentally licked one of the leaves because of Kai Shaya, the stupid monk.

He understood Kai Shaya's emotions. He had to be worried about brother Bai Muja. But what could they do? Either they could win and leave their life in the hands of a maniac black coin and a betrayer Xue Qi, or they could take control and let Bai Muja have a fifty percent chance of life.

"Don't worry. Brother Muja will come back stronger than before," Wei said.

Despite not trusting Xue Qi anymore, Wei believed she wouldn't kill people wantonly. He hoped there was still a hint of humanity left in her.

And he had a gut feeling Bai Muja would safely deliver whatever was in that storage ring to his family.

It was a bummer that Wei couldn't kill all of his enemies. "Nai Fang, I'll take revenge for you, and when I'm done, there will be no Destiny Mirror Sect or Gatekeepers in this world. I will make sure of that."

"Do you think you can go against the Gatekeepers?" Blood Parasite asked in Wei's mind. "They are more powerful than you can even imagine. If they could threaten a Time Emperor, you've no chance of surviving against them."

"Not even your Blood Emperor had a chance against them?" Wei teased the old man, Blood Parasite. After Xue Qi's betrayal, Wei only had one friend left inside him, and it was this guy, Blood Parasite.

"Blood Emperor was long dead before the Gatekeepers arrived, or he never told me about them. Anyway, they are too big for you."

"They might be too big for me to handle," Wei answered confidently as his wings cut through the thick bushes that covered everything in front of him. Without divine sense, he felt what it meant to be a mortal. The divine sense had been with him since he'd been reincarnated as his old self, and he had been using it to his advantage for months. "Yet if they are so big, why aren't they attacking the world and taking over the Incursion Artifact?"

"They can't send their powerhouses to the Mortal Realm. They aren't ruling the world, so I guess they have to act within the rules. They might be bigger, but their fists might not be the biggest. Even in their prime, emperors were bound by the laws of the world."

"What kind of realm do these so-called emperors have? What is beyond Violet Palace?"

"It's too early for you to know about it," Blood Parasite replied. "You should focus on reaching the Houtian Realm first and comprehending the Blood Houtian Trials."

"Blood Houtian Trials? What's that?"

"Those are the trials you have to go through once you reach the Houtian Realm."

"Wait. I heard nothing like that."

"Because you met no one practicing Heaven Grade Cultivation Art. These cultivation arts have different rules, and you will evoke a Houtian Trial from the heavens. It will be brutal. Only ten percent of people survive it."

Wei rubbed the back of his neck. This was something new. "Well, I've a long way to go before I reach there. I've enough problems ahead of me, and saving Little Fox is the one I've got to tackle."

Something stirred inside him, and three clones of him jumped out of him and fell from the sky.

"Fuck! Why did they come out already? I still have a minute left before the merging will be rejected." Wei dropped through the sky to collect his clones before the banana trees slapped them to death.

"Kid, you're nearing the Houtian Realm, so let this old man pass on the actual truth behind the Blood Sword Divinity Art," Blood Parasite said nonchalantly.

"Actual truth? I've already achieved the initial completion in the Blood Sword Tearing through the Skies, and I think I understand the profundities of the divine art." He accelerated to peak speed to save his clones.

"What you know is nothing but the brute force. The real truth is very different from what you think it is."

Blood Parasite's words made Wei curious. However, it was time to save his clones, and if he didn't move fast, they would be dead in no time.

Chapter 5

Trouble of Clones

Icy winds battered Li Wei's face as he dropped from a few miles high. The giant forest, covered in scary gray shapes, closed on him. His three clones descended like stones stone with no wings, and all they could do was slow their descent by covering themselves in qi. He had to catch them before they disappeared into the shadow of the banana trees that looked like a monster ready to gulp down its prey.

With a thought from Wei, the three clones used qi to form wings. However, the qi wings couldn't act as real wings, and they failed to slow the clones down. If they hit the ground from this height, they would turn to a pulp. They didn't have Wei's body cultivation, nor were their bodies tempered by the void. They were like squishy melons that could burst into pieces on the slightest impact. Especially the one with the Refinement Realm cultivation base.

"Fuck. Intent of Wind Travel." Wei used the Intent and rushed like an arrow, the air crashing against his eardrums like a roar of drums.

The rotten smell of banana trees nauseated him, threatening to force him to throw up everything he'd eaten in the morning. Pushing those thoughts away, he caught the first clone in his arms. The next one was close enough, and he used his Heart Essence Aura to loop around him like a rope and pulled him closer. But the final one was too far, and he couldn't reach it.

The taste of defeat wrapped around his tongue. If the clone crashed into a tree and died, he would have to start from the start, and that would be troublesome. He thought of the rope and brother Shaya.

"Brother Shaya, please be a cushion for my clone." After cutting the rope with his fingers, Wei tossed Kai Shaya toward his clone. The bald monk seemed to say something to him, but Wei couldn't hear it. "Save him. Do whatever it takes!" Wei shouted, hoping the monk had gotten the gist of his intention.

The monk shot like a mortal shell used by noncultivators in the war. Kai Shaya threw his arms around the clone, and then a giant buddha flew out of him, covering them both in a shallow energy. The giant buddha crashed into trees, destroying everything within a few hundred feet. A mushroom cloud rose in the air, turning the already dark forest darker.

Wei couldn't see anything. Had they survived? He landed on his feet and dashed into the cloud of dust and splinters.

Thank heavens—the clone was battered but safe. However, he couldn't say the same about Kai Shaya, who looked like a pig stuck in a war between elephants.

"Brother Wei, why did you...?" Kai Shaya coughed blood before dropping unconscious.

"Damn it. I guess the qi cultivators are too squishy." Shaking his head, Wei collected Kai Shaya and tossed him toward one of his clones. Another clone picked up the battered clone, and they headed toward Little Fox. She was close enough, but getting there would take at least a couple of hours by foot.

After retrieving a healing pill from his storage ring, Wei tossed it into Kai Shaya's mouth. Then he poured some water into Kai Shaya's mouth so the pill would go down his throat. His injuries were minimal, and he should wake up in a few minutes at most.

"Blood Parasite, my clones—why did they come out earlier than expected? Any theory?"

"How would I know, kid? You can try asking that bitch."

Wei ducked to avoid a sharp branch coming from a small tree. The forest mainly contained Sky-Piercing Banana Trees, but it also had some different flora and fauna that could be fatal for weak people, and all his clones were weak. He cut through a few branches so the clones would walk without worrying about poison or stray attacks.

"I wish I could choke her and get that information." Wei sighed and drank a mouthful of fresh water. The cold liquid seeped into his body, providing him with much-needed calmness. "I don't have a way to merge the clones back into my body, so I don't know how I would reach the Boiling Blood Realm with three clones. Would I need a new clone, or would one of these clones raise their cultivation to the next level? This is frustrating." Although he had reached Heart Blood Realm in body cultivation, losing the power of qi meant the loss of his battle powers.

"Kid, there is something at your right that would allow you to unlock the next seal on the Primordial Blood Palace. It's a Blood Orchid Beast, and it would help you synthesize the Essence Blood of Chu Tunzi."

"We'll get it once we save Little Fox."

"I think your friend is in trouble because of it. The Blood Orchid Beast has an allure to any wind type of beast. Its core can help them comprehend the Intent. If she learned the Intent of Wind, she would directly break through to the Houtian Realm."

"Is there a thing like that?" Wei asked.

He'd been friends with Rual'er, the beast princess, in his previous life, but they'd met when she was already at the Houtian Realm, so he didn't know anything about her previous cultivation methods. The interesting thing was that she, too, was a wind cultivator, but her lineage came from a scary beast called Fei Lian, a One-Winged Dragon. With her wind powers combined with the archery, Fei Lian was a harbinger of killing.

"But she doesn't need to go through the ordeal. I have some Wind Source Stones I got from the other world that could help her advance." Wei closed his eyes and sensed the connection with Little Fox. It lay there next to his connection thread with Xue Qi. "You're right. Little Fox is in the same direction, and she doesn't seem to be in trouble anymore. We should reach her in a couple of hours. I just have to plan the clone merger."

The clones were Wei's big problem. They could merge with him at most for ten minutes, and then they had to stay out for ten minutes. But if he kept them out of him for longer, the merger time increased as well. It was a big nuisance. Having them or not having them both proved to be problems.

"However, you need to learn the truth behind Blood Divinity Sword Art before you face the Blood Orchid Beast, to subdue it properly. To get the core out of it without killing it would be difficult, and only this art can suppress it."

"What are you talking about?"

"There is a Giant Demon Tree on your right," Blood Parasite said. "You can practice the divine art as I guide you."

Wei checked on the little fox. As he got closer, he didn't sense any fear or call of urgency from her. It seemed like she'd managed the situation well, so he could spend a few hours practicing this skill.

"Give me a drop of the Violet Palace Blood Realm cultivator you obtained," Blood Parasite said. "I'll show you a hint of what you can gain from activating the next upgrade of the Primordial Blood Palace."

Wei froze. Violet Palace Blood Realm cultivator's essence blood was quite powerful, and he wasn't sure if he could trust Blood Parasite completely. Although he'd helped Wei a lot, after Xue Qi's betrayal, Wei didn't feel the trust for everyone that he used to have.

Chapter 6

Giant Demon Tree

A giant tree sprawled horizontally over the ground like a sleeping woman, full of curves and shapes, in the middle of a hazy, isolated area. A unique aroma covered the entire area, attracting living things under the Houtian Realm. It was a deathly zone for any living being, and if one dared to step within a mile's radius around the giant tree, they would be caught in illusions and miss the Giant Demon Tree roots piercing into their bodies, sucking their vitality away.

It was a vicious cycle, and every Giant Demon Tree had countless deaths associated with it. The one that had taken root among the Sky-Piercing Banana Trees was a sapling of only a few dozen years, so it had only cleared out one mile area around it, turning it barren, waiting for someone to step in so it would devour them.

"Brother Wei, why did you change the route?" Kai Shaya stepped out of the shadows of the banana tree, his eyes glazing as he tried to look at something inside the hazy area. "It's so beautiful. The wine, the beauty."

Shaking his head, Wei slammed Kai Shaya's neck to wake him from the illusion he was caught in. Without divine sense, no one could avoid the alluring illusions of the demon tree.

"I'm sorry." Kai Shaya rubbed his sparkling bald head.

"Drink this. It will keep you alive when I'm cultivating." Wei handed him a leather skin filled with a medicinal liquid. He would need to spend time in the Primordial Blood Palace to test Blood Parasite's words, so he had to make some preparations.

Wei stepped into the haze of mist, and an aromatic dream enveloped him, but with his divine sense covering him, the illusion didn't affect him. A rustle attracted his attention, and a tiny strand of a root shot out of the ground, penetrating his shoes, but his Heart Essence Aura stopped it instantly. He leaped back. He'd just wanted to experience the strength of the illusion, and he bet anyone without divine sense would be caught inside it easily. It had been a good decision for Wei to mix the Illusion Warding Medicinal Mix and hand it to Kai Shaya and his clones before he went into seclusion.

"Brother Wei, this thing tastes bland," Kai Shaya complained.

"It's a medicinal liquid, not wine, brother." Wei chuckled. "And aren't you supposed to be a righteous monk who doesn't touch wine or ale?"

"What is this thing, brother?" Kai Shaya asked, changing the topic.

Wei sneered inwardly. "This is called a Giant Demon Tree. It's a death sentence for anyone less advanced than the Houtian Realm. The tree attracts living things and then sucks on their lifeline by pulling them into an illusion."

"Why is this here? Why didn't anyone cut this demonic thing?" Kai Shaya asked.

"Because it is useful for wood cultivators." Wei sighed. "This tree is special. It will produce a Giant Demon Heart every hundred years, which is useful for wood cultivators. It can help them comprehend the Wood Intent before entering the Houtian Realm."

"Does such a thing exist in this world?"

"Didn't you learn a few Concepts in the Ancient Constitution Trial?"

Kai Shaya nodded.

"If you practice the Intent involving those Concepts, I bet you will grasp a couple before breaking through into the Houtian Realm." After going through the Ancient Constitution and learning so many Intents, Wei had an inkling he could help others, as well, in mastering the Intent.

"So someone is raising this tree here intentionally?"

"Yes. The Destiny Mirror Sect. I killed a few of their disciples while coming here." If anything belonged to the Destiny Mirror Sect, Wei wouldn't let it continue. And he didn't have to worry about waiting for the Giant Demon Heart to mature, as he had his own ways to get it done in seconds. Although he hadn't sought this tree, now that he'd laid his eyes on it, he would definitely get it for Nuan'er. She was a wood cultivator, and this demon heart would be crucial for her to grasp the Intent of Wood.

"Brother Shaya, step into the haze, and let me see if the medicinal mix works."

Nodding, Kai Shaya stepped into it. He walked out, after a moment, with sweat dripping from his forehead. "Mahataba. What a vile piece of root." He stared at a bloody hole in his leg.

"So the medicinal liquid is effective. That's good. I'll cultivate in my secret chamber now." Wei retrieved a concealing formation disk. "Stay inside with my clones, and you should be fine, and if you can't defeat something, just run and bring along my clones."

Saying this, Wei entered the Primordial Blood Palace Ten-Day Time Chamber. It was time to use the Violent Palace Realm cultivator's blood essence. Thanks to Chu Tunzi, he'd gotten his hands on this blood essence, and he had enough for a few tries inside the Primordial Blood Palace.

A bloodred figure walked out of the metal corridor of the blood palace. A black mask covered his face, and he wore a dark-green robe.

"Why hide your face? I've already seen how ugly you look," Wei said, handing him a drop of blood essence.

"I look uglier in this form. Only in my divine-sense form can I show my true face."

Wei chuckled. "I'm trusting you, Blood Parasite."

"Don't call me that."

"Then tell me your real name, Sword Saint."

"I can no longer be called that. I've shamed myself by letting you know a secret of mine."

"Then just tell me your name. What's so difficult in that?"

"I can't, kid. Not unless you become another Blood Emperor. Anyway, let's not waste time. Let me show you what awaits at the next level of the Primordial Blood Palace." The blood essence in his palm vanished into the metal corridor, and a door opened.

System: Information interface detected. Temporary access to Primordial Blood Palace Level Three is granted to the host for twelve hours.

"I only have twelve hours' access," Wei said.

"Oh, that thing can read the Echoes of Ancients as well? That's interesting."

"Let's go." Wei stepped through the metal door, and a world opened itself to him.

Chapter 7

Secret of the Primordial Blood Palace

The metal door led into another metal corridor with two doors at the end, one more than the previous level. The environment felt the same—stiff, lacking any sense of vitality—and stank of old books left rotting in a wet place. To get rid of the smell, he would need to burn a dozen incense sticks once he opened the rooms for use. Maybe he should try the sandalwood scent Nuan'er loved.

"What do those rooms do? Are they more auxiliary rooms? Is there a tea room? That would be so awesome." Wei's voice came out strange. "Why do I sound like this?"

"We haven't opened this place in the intended way, so we are foreign people and only have limited time."

"How does that affect our voices? It makes little sense." Wei brushed the metal corridor with his finger, trying to pick up the dust, but he felt like he was moving his fingers through a sticky liquid. "Our bodies aren't present inside this space, are they?"

"You saw through it. They are still in the first level. We're here with our divine sense and souls. So don't use your voice, but use your divine sense to speak."

"And I thought you wanted to speak like a human."

"I'm a blood slave, not a human," Blood Parasite replied with a hint of sorrow.

Wei sighed inwardly. Someday, he would get to the root of this old man's pain—dig out his problems and then solve them. They'd known each other for so long, but Wei only knew a little about him that he'd learned by accident. Blood Parasite used to be a Sword Saint, and had been captured and turned into a blood slave by the previous owner of the Primordial Blood Palace, the one who called himself Wei's cousin and had left him the pendant. Until today, Wei hadn't known what the former owner of the blood palace wanted from him.

"Once you open this level, you will get access to two chambers, and your Ten-Day Time Chamber will be upgraded to a Hundred-Day Time Chamber."

Wei's mood shifted to good—no, awesome. "A Hundred-Day Time Chamber? Really? Fantastic. I'd love to cultivate here."

The Ten-Day Time Chamber allowed him to spend ten days inside that were the equivalent of one hour outside, and it had saved him in many situations. A hundred days inside for one hour outside—nothing could get better than that. He could cultivate many things, concoct pills, do alchemy, or even practice some defensive arts he'd never had a chance to get to because of time constraints.

"It's not that important. The second level has the Chamber of Intent."

Wei frowned. "Chamber of Intent? What's that? Do I get to learn new Intents inside?"

"It's a blessing and a curse. Inside this chamber, you can comprehend any Intent you want to try out. You want Water Spraying Intent? You'll find it there. You want Molten Lava Flow Intent? You'll find it. If you want to learn the Time Pause Intent, you'll find it. You just need to sacrifice some of your blood essence, and you can learn anything. But there's a catch."

"What is it?" Wei asked, his core burning with excitement.

"You can learn any Intent, but you can't advance on the path."

Wei paused, collecting his words. "So you mean I can't reach any Concept associated with that Intent?"

"Yes."

Wei shuddered. "This is a dead end. I once heard that the path never traveled is the path one should travel, and the path fully traveled is the path of the dead end." He'd seen those words on a wall of the Ancient Vault in his previous life. They'd exuded a strange aura, and Wei had remembered them, but he hadn't been able to make any sense of them and had pushed them to the back of his mind.

Today, the words made sense. If he learned the Intent that had already been explored, he could never move beyond that. But if he learned the Intent on his own, it would be the path less traveled.

Holy heavens. It totally made sense.

"So it's a trap."

"Not really," Blood Parasite said. "If your path is of wood, and if you learn a few Intents of Time, it shouldn't cut your path of wood."

Wei nodded. It could work if one chose carefully, but all the daos came from one, and if a single path was cut, could he really walk the other path to the end?

"There is another way. You can always strengthen your current Intent by studying it further," Blood Parasite said.

"So if I know Intent of Wind Travel and Intent of Wind Force, I can use it to comprehend the Concept of Harmonious Flow, which would allow me to travel as fast and unbridled as wind."

"Forget about all of that. You'll understand it once you enter the room with your body. You can use the room to comprehend the true form of the Blood Divinity Sword Art."

"Are you saying the Blood Divinity Sword Art involves an Intent?" Wei asked.

"No. It involves the Will."

Wei's breath quickened, and his jaw almost fall to the ground. "What the heck did you say? Will of the Sword? Is that even possible?"

Chapter 8

Will of the Skill

T he world was filled with happy accidents, and Li Wei couldn't believe the words himself. Will of the Sword. Like the Intent preceded by Concept and then Fragment and then Codex, the sword had its own realms—Sword Image, Sword Flash, Sword Ray, and Sword Intent. And then came the Sword Will. It was the highest form of understanding of the sword. There had been a rumor in his previous life that one who understood the Sword Will could rule the world without cultivating a single realm.

"Are you really talking about the legendary realm, Sword Will?" Wei asked, his voice shaking. If this room could help him understand the Sword Will, he might not need to learn anything else. Just thinking about the world under his feet gave him goose bumps.

"Don't be a fool, kid. Even as a Sword Saint, I couldn't reach the Sword Intent. Do you think you can comprehend Sword Will in this life?" Blood Parasite said, pouring cold water on Wei's mood, instantly turning it brittle.

"But you said Will of the Sword." Wei brushed his fingers through the metallic wall, reliving the feeling of moving his fingers through sticky liquid. Although he knew he couldn't wipe the dust off it, he still tried. It was better than hearing the dream-killer tune coming from Blood Parasite's mouth.

"I only said Will. There is a Will of the Skill. When a creator pours everything they know in a skill, it can manifest as the Will of the Skill, and it will give you power beyond Perfect Completion."

"You mean Breakthrough Completion."

"No. That's a different path of advancing. Will of the Skill gives the skill a different path altogether, one not possible if you walk an old path."

"Like a path less traveled?"

"Something like that. I don't know. I only know that some skills have a Will of the Skill, and you can awaken it if you find a master who has already done that."

"Doesn't that mean it has to be inherited from the creator of the skill?"

"Right. Or you can search for it for your self-created skills."

"Can I create a Will of the Skill for my Wood Sword Tornado? That's my own skill."

"Why not?"

"So, where would I meet the Blood Emperor? You said the Divinity Blood Sword Art came from the Blood Emperor, right?"

"Give me your sword."

Wei retrieved the bloodred sword. It was just a soul version and not the actual sword. "I hope you won't kill me with it." Sneering, he handed it to Blood Parasite.

"I won't." Blood Parasite walked into the second room, and Wei followed him.

The room had an unending desert. Sandstorms roiled around it, hot sand slapping against his face. Wei instantly covered himself with Heart Essence Aura.

"Is this real?" Wei reached with his arms, letting the sand slip through them. The scorching winds burned at his soul, and the smell of intense heat stuck into his nostrils.

"It is, and it is not. Watch me carefully." Blood Parasite raised the blood sword in the air, and the surrounding sand moved in a circular direction. Blood aura slipped from him and covered the sky, which then condensed into a sword identical to the blood sword. The swords pushed against each other and exuded a pressure that surpassed anything Wei had seen from this move.

Wei gasped. "How is that possible?"

It was only the first move, Blood Sword Tearing through the Skies, yet it felt like a completely new one. Was this the Will of the Sword that Blood Parasite had talked about?

"That blood aura. It was your blood essence, wasn't it?" Wei asked.

"This is the first form, Tearing the Sky. Now the second form, Tearing the Earth."

The blood aura slipped into the earth, and the earth swirled, rotated, and rose around Blood Parasite. It wasn't just the blood essence but, rather, the Intent of the Earth—specifically, the Intent of the Rising Earth. Wei had already seen it before.

"I don't know the Intent of Rising Earth."

"It's not about what Intent you use but that you use one of the Intents of Earth."

"So, you're mixing your own blood essence into earth essence, using the Intent." Wei clapped.

This was genius thinking. Learning Intent was like understanding nature a little and manipulating it, but one couldn't do that as easily as one could manipulate their own blood essence. This was especially true for a blood cultivator. However, one could only have so much of the blood essence, and in comparison, earth essence was unlimited. If one could mix them both, the power they could harness would be tremendous. Not unlimited, but limitless for the user.

"You grasped it quickly. Good. In this place, you can harness as much Intent of Earth as you want, and you can then master the first two levels and awaken your Will of the Skill."

"This is interesting." Excitement rushed through Wei's voice. "I wonder why no one told me about this Will of the Skill before."

"You'll understand it once you break through the Violet Palace Realm. Only a skill that is Heaven Grade or higher has a chance to develop a Will when it is birthed."

"You mean...?"

"Yes. The Blood Emperor snatched that chance from the heavens. Each level has been precisely crafted by him and imbued with his own will. The first one will be easy for you to understand. Just will your blood essence, or blood pearls, to go into the sword and the sky."

"Why didn't you tell me this before?"

"You weren't ready. Your qi cultivation bound you. This is not a martial skill, kid, but a divine art, and only pure-hearted body cultivators can understand the heart of it."

"I'm still a qi cultivator."

"No, you are not. You got rid of your qi cultivation, so you can inherit this Will of the Skill from me."

"Good to hear, but in the future, I'll merge my qi clone back into me. Do you still want to teach me this?" Wei rubbed the back of his neck. "Let's just forget about it. I don't want to hurt your feelings, but thanks for telling me about this. I really appreciate it." Wei didn't mention Blood Parasite's stubbornness about body cultivation. Everyone had their own path.

"Don't worry. You can still use it. It has nothing to do with the path you travel, but your qi cultivation would have muddled your blood essence, so I couldn't tell you and let you bring a half-assed skill."

"Oh." Wei got it. "What about the second skill, Blood Sword Piercing through the Earth?"

"Just use your Intent of Earth. In this place, you can practice it as much as possible because you won't be overdrafting your own soul."

"That's good." Wei willed his sword to come back to him. This was going to be interesting. "For the first skill, all I need to do it pour my blood pearls into the air around the sword," Wei muttered, willing his blood pearls to slip out of him and merge with the air surrounding the sword. It didn't work.

"Feel the Will of the Skill, kid. The name is the heart."

"Name is the heart." Wei closed his eyes and felt the dry wind around him, the earth, the heart and the sky.

The sky. Yes, the name was Tearing through the Skies.

Blood pearls poured out of him, flooding the skies around the sword. Technically, it was just a higher level than the sword, but everything was sky. Suddenly, he felt a deep new connection with his blood sword. It hummed with a metallic sound, and he felt the blood pearls merging with the sword.

A thick hum emerged from it, and Wei felt an unprecedented aura rising from the sword. In all the times he had used this skill, he'd never thought something so profound would be hiding inside.

"This is powerful. I can right away use this."

"I bet you can." Blood Parasite chuckled. "Now, try the second skill, and enjoy the feeling of the Intent of Earth." His chuckle deepened, and Wei's laughter mixed with it.

These twelve hours were going to be fun.

Chapter 9

Destroying the Giant Demon Tree

"**I** wish I could cultivate my clones to the highest levels." Li Wei made a mental curse as he avoided the whip attack from the Giant Demon Tree root.

The roots were thicker than his waist, and they hit like a barbed club with those thick, inches-long, sharper-than-daggers barbs. They pierced the skin and cut through the muscle underneath. Unfortunately, he'd gotten lazy, and a tree root had grazed his arm during the previous attack, leaving bloody scrapes and torn flesh. The wounds throbbed with a searing pain reminiscent of the feeling of dipping one's hand into a pit of molten lava. Although Wei healed the wounds using his blood pearls, the memory of lava was still rooted in his mind. Especially as he had done that exact thing in his previous life.

"If I had three more helpers, this could have been easier." He glanced at the six clones, each engaged in a fierce battle with tree roots in different locations, providing him with much-needed assistance and helping him avoid being overwhelmed by multiple attacks.

A sneaky tree root shot out of the ground behind one of the blood clones and tried to stab the clone through its spine, but Wei had already detected it with his divine sense. On Wei's command, the blood clone swung back on his leg and cut through the root, leaving a stinking cloud of smoke behind. After breaking through the Heart Blood Realm, Wei's divine sense had grown to three miles, fifteen thousand feet, and he'd covered the entire Giant Demon Tree with it.

His sword cut through another root, and it exploded in front of him.

Fuck. This tree had stinking bombs, and he could barely make his way through them without spitting up his breakfast. Thank heavens his blood clones didn't have a sense of smell as strong as his. Otherwise, they would have run away, ignoring his commands.

"You can't make any more clones. That bitch has sealed their cultivation to certain levels," Blood Parasite replied without him asking it.

Wei spat a mouthful of black blood to exhale the poison the last tree root had left inside him. Even his Yin Poison Pill Clone didn't like it and only forced the poison to accumulate in one spot in his stomach. He was spitting it out every few seconds. The poison wasn't really toxic, but it increased the effect of the illusions. Without divine sense, he would have fallen prey to the effect easily.

Swinging his sword, he cut a few more tree roots while rushing forward as fast as he could, but he couldn't use a stronger attack because he didn't want to waken the core of the tree. Currently, it was sleeping, and the roots defending themselves on their own.

So far, he'd advanced a few dozen feet from the edge of the forest. Once he was near the core, he would have to use the strongest attack he had to cut the tree down in one shot. Otherwise, the tree would shed its shell and escape in the ground with its core, and no matter how fast his Earth Escape was, he wouldn't be able to chase it. The tree had an innate Earth Concept built into it, and it was too fast.

Of course, he could have set up an overarching array formation—every sect that grew this tree did that—but it would take a lot of time, which he didn't have. So he could only act as a sheep ready to eat a tiger and use the direct approach. However, so far, he'd only gained a bad taste of the poison in his mouth and bruises all over his body. The tree itself had a gravitational effect, so he had to use the Intent of Earth to counterattack it constantly.

"You shouldn't have fallen in her trap and just disposed of your qi cultivation. Body cultivation is the best."

"Stop trying to convince me with that bullshit." Wei stabbed the sword into the next root, retrieved another sword, and used the Ten Sword Strike. After learning Reverse Sword Flash, he'd used this skill less and less and relied more on the body cultivation skills, but he kind of missed this pure sword skill—it had the dao of a sword cultivator, and he loved swords. After he'd lost his qi cultivation, he'd grown distant from the sword skills, and he regretted that, so he just used it to keep the feeling alive.

A bad premonition struck him, and when he focused, he spotted a bunch of roots coming for his metal clone. Despite the roots only acting on instinct, they had somehow targeted his metal clone.

"Damn it." Wei changed his path and dashed toward the metal clone.

It couldn't handle so many roots at a time. Then an idea struck him, and he threw the Essence Origin Cauldron at his metal clone. This cauldron could be enlarged or shrunk with the help of wood qi, which he could use thanks to his Yang Wood Pill Clone. The cauldron was made of a metal stronger than anything he'd seen in the Martial Realm, so he hoped it would be enough.

The metal clone caught the cauldron and then used it like a turtle shell, hiding inside. It was a funny sight. Wei sensed Kai Shaya chuckling at him from the edge of the forest.

"Bastard!" Wei shouted at Kai Shaya while cutting a few roots that were coming at him.

The bunch of roots that had ganged upon his metal clone clashed with the cauldron and sent it flying toward the main body of the tree. With a deafening hum, the cauldron tore through the roots as if a colossal bull was demolishing wooden walls. The metal clone spun and twirled within the cauldron, like a bouncing ball. But other than some bruises, it suffered no serious injury.

"I can use this." Wei dashed toward the metal clone, jumping over the roots that attacked him. With the cauldron, he had a way to reach the core of the tree without awakening it faster.

In a few quick sprints, culling roots as he went, Wei reached the metal cauldron and slipped inside it. By this time, the metal clone looked as if he were drunk on a strong ale, ready to pass out. The continuous tossing and turning seemed to be too much for him.

"Merge." Wei absorbed the clone and then used his sword to damage a few roots to provoke them.

The roots didn't have any consciousness, and they acted on instinct, which forced them to attack the cauldron from one side. Wei had angled his attacks so they would push him toward the tree. Soon he was riding toward the trunk. The only downside was the constant rolling, but with his Heart Blood Realm body cultivation, it felt like a kid punching him. It worked fantastically, and after just three minutes, and lots of bumping and crashing inside the cauldron, he reached the main body of the tree. It was time to unleash a full-fledged attack.

"Don't use the Will of the Sword right away. Slam the tree with the cauldron, and force the core to awaken and attack you with its full force," Blood Parasite said.

"Why?" Wei couldn't make any sense of his suggestion.

"When it's attacking you, it can't run away, and the cauldron doesn't pose a major danger to it."

Wei smiled. It made a complete sense. Spreading his wings, Wei rose to the height where the roots could barely reach him. Previously, he hadn't flown because the core would have sensed it and run away, but now he was going to attack the core head-on.

"Smash." Wei smashed the Essence Origin Cauldron on the main body of the tree.

Even with ten of him, he wouldn't be able to cover it completely, so he made the cauldron as big as he could and bashed it against the tree continuously. Each hit chipped a little off. The damage to the tree was minimal, but just like a child constantly hitting someone's head, the attack quickly became annoying, and the main branches moved slightly. They tried to shake the cauldron away, but Wei dodged them and continued hitting the trunk. After twenty minutes, the trunk finally reacted, and all of its branches shot for the cauldron.

"Time for some boom." After retrieving some of the Fire Runes he'd gotten from Allen Ming, Wei tossed the cauldron into the branches and lit up the runes.

The branches had entangled the cauldron, attempting to devour it, but the blast scattered them. A blood sword appeared in Wei's hand, and he sacrificed twenty percent of his blood pearls and poured into it. A giant sword image arose over his head and slashed down on the tree. A deep grumble echoed from within the tree. Maybe it was trying to shake him away or begging for mercy, but the sword's attack continued and descended on the trunk, cleaving it in two.

A tiny heart-shaped patch of wood tried to escape, but Wei was ready and caught it, using his Yang Wood Pill Clone. He dropped it into his storage ring. If he hadn't, the wood pill clone might have devoured the delicious heart-shaped snack.

The trunk shriveled, and the roots sank into the ground. The illusion vanished, and the place instantly became an empty patch of barren land.

"Let's go," Wei said after retrieving the cauldron.

Even after so much smashing and tossing, the cauldron didn't have a single scratch. He could definitely use it as a weapon in the future. They were just starting out, and the fights were not done.

Chapter 10

The Secret Information from the Destiny Mirror Sect

Sun Nuan was in a daze when she entered the Five Firmament City through the secret tunnel built by the Earth Golem. Only she, Sonja, and her aunt knew about this thing. Even her aunt's husband, Kang Suan, wasn't aware of this tunnel. Sun Nuan's aunt had taken a vow of heaven and earth, so Sun Nuan could trust her in this matter.

Anyway, it didn't matter, as the Kang Kingdom was over. The Destiny Mirror Sect had gulped it down, and only three kingdoms had remained on their side of the Guinshin River: State of Zin, Buddha Vasta Pagoda Kingdom, and Crimson Moon Kingdom.

As soon as she walked out of the secret tunnel, she advised the servants to take the elder Deimu to the alchemy house. After big brother Wei had cleansed himself of poison, he'd regained his health, but he still suffered from some side effects and wanted to concoct some pills for himself, so she sent him to the alchemy house right away.

"Princess, Elder Yen Poe is waiting for you in the main hall, and he is looking impatient!" her maidservant called as soon as Sun Nuan entered her palace through the secret tunnel.

Nodding, Sun Nuan headed to the main hall, where she met the other people and saw Aunty Sun Liang and Elder Yan Poe sitting with grief-stricken faces.

"Now what?" she asked, taking her seat next to the main chair, which was kept empty for big brother Wei. She would kill anyone who dared to sit there.

"There's bad news," Elder Yen Poe said, his shoulders shaking a little.

"Elder, just once, deliver good news." Sun Nuan sighed, tired of everything.

"The Crimson Moon Kingdom has declared allegiance to the Destiny Mirror Sect, and they have created a new kingdom called the Destiny Mirror Kingdom and are launching an attack on the Buddha Vasta Pagoda Kingdom."

"Have they gone mad?"

"They haven't. My spies told me the Destiny Mirror Sect has gained many Houtian Realm cultivators. They sent a big army, and the Crimson Moon Kingdom gave up after a brutal fight."

"Damn it. This means they've divided us from Buddha Vasta Pagoda Kingdom, and we can't even help them."

Yen Poe nodded.

"I met a monk recently. I wonder if he knows about the predicament his kingdom is in." The bald monk had looked like a pig compared to big brother Wei.

"There is more bad news."

"Don't tell me that Buddha Vasta Pagoda Kingdom has fallen already..." Sun Nuan rubbed her heart. She felt like a tiny frog at the bottom of a well.

The State of Zin was a small kingdom to start with, and now the entire world was against her. If it weren't for the Five Firmament City, and she and big brother Wei guarding it, the State of Zin would have already fallen to the Destiny Mirror Sect's clutches.

"No. The war hasn't started yet. But the Blue Pagoda Sect has conquered the Tang Kingdom on the other side of the Guinshin River. I had to extract my companions and the Tang clan's royalty in haste. They'll join us soon and seek for shelter in the Five Firmament City."

Sun Nuan nodded. It was the least she could do, and she had a connection with Tang Sia, the princess of the Tang Kingdom who had joined the Divine Fragrance Palace.

"There's good news as well. My pupil from the past has arrived, and I want to give him access to the puppets from the Three Treasure House." Yan Poe smiled.

"What pupil?"

Yen Poe sighed. "He's the only remaining member of the Ancient Puppet Sect, and he was doing some research in Tang Kingdom. His name is Wang Purang."

"If you trust him, then please do as you see right." Sun Nuan nodded before getting up. "If you have nothing else, then I have to attend to an elder. Aunt, increase the pill supply to our army. I think a war is coming, and we have to prepare for it. Also, send a request to Father to gather his army in a city near the Five Firmament City. We may have to defend the maximum area around the Five Firmament City."

"Elder Yan, any news about the Heavenly Firmament Sect? If things break loose, we can't protect their nodes forever."

Yan Poe got up. "Don't worry, Princess. I've established a contact inside the sect, and they are fighting their own war. If things get worse, they can send a few people to help us, but those will be only at the peak of Heart Blood Realm."

"It will be fine as long as we get some help."

Chapter 11

Meeting Rual'er Once Again

An arrow stabbed the ground in front of Li Wei, blocking his advance out of the forest. The golden shaft half-buried in the ground warned him not to proceed. A white feather waved on the gentle wind flowing from the open area next to the forest of Sky-Piercing Banana Trees and bringing relief from the rotten smell of the banana trees. The smell stuck to Wei's nostrils, and he bet he wouldn't be eating anything for the next few days because all he would taste would be rot and decay.

"That was fast. I didn't even see that arrow," Kai Shaya whispered.

"It was fast." Wei looked up at a tree a few hundred feet away from the forest.

The arrow had come from the tree so fast that it had stabbed in the ground before his danger sense could pop up and warn him. The winds generated by the arrow had cut through his robe over the leg and left a white scar on his shin. Squatting down, Wei picked up the arrow. It had a slight texture added to it, and it shone in the bright light of the sun, reminding him of a golden arrow he'd seen in his previous life.

No. It was the same golden arrow. The mark of the dragon on the tip of it confirmed it. Why had a golden arrow appeared here? It was one of the signature arrows of Rual'er's Winged Archer Force, which was famous throughout the Martial Realm.

His heart palpitated, not from fear but because he had a chance to meet an old friend—a friend he'd let go of, which he'd regretted after reincarnating. As he gulped down his curiosity, his divine sense spread toward the large tree where the arrow had come from, unleashed like a tidal wave. He couldn't wait to see who'd attacked him.

"Aiya. What a powerful divine sense!" someone cried out, followed by a woman in a green dress leaping down from the tree and arriving in front of them. She had a long oval face, eyes sharp as a knife, and a dress that fit too tight around her shapely figure.

"She is powerful," Kai Shaya whispered, his body taut.

Wei nodded. This woman was a layer-three Houtian Realm cultivator—a body cultivator—and she exuded the familiar aura of a beast. A One-Winged Dragon. She was part of Rual'er's race.

"Respected Winged Dragon race elder, may I know your name?" Wei cupped his hands and bowed a little.

The Winged Dragon race, though infamous for their quick tempers, were not without reason. If you treated them with respect, they would reciprocate it. Even in human territory, everyone respected them for their attitude.

"Aiya. You know my race." Her thin lips curled into a smile. "Which sect did you come from, human junior?" She lowered her bow but didn't relax the drawn string It was at least an Earth Grade weapon, a lethal weapon in a Houtian Realm cultivator's hands.

Wei smiled. "Junior came from a very unremarkable sect, and the senior might not be aware of it. This one is called Li Wei."

"You can call me Wi Vastira. One of my juniors is fighting with an arrogant fox, so stay away from this place."

Wei shook his head. No wonder he'd received a strong danger sense from Little Fox. She was fighting with someone from the Winged Dragon race. These people were powerful.

"Kid, you need the essence blood of the Blood Orchid Beast to unlock the next level of the Primordial Blood Palace," Blood Parasite said in Wei's mind.

"That little fox is my friend, so I'm afraid I have to disappoint you, senior," Wei told Wi Vastira.

"Human, you've got some manners, so heed my advice, and go back. The fox is from the beast race, so we don't have any reason to kill her. Prin—" She stopped. "My junior just wants to get the beast core of Blood Orchid Beast for breakthrough."

Wei shook his head. He, too, needed that Blood Orchid Beast, so he couldn't refrain from attacking.

"Please forgive me for being impudent, but I can't let you have this." A sword appeared in Wei's hand, and he raised it to strike down the woman in front of him. "Blood Sword Tearing through the Skies."

A giant red sword formed above his head, sucking the blood pearls from him. His aura rose rapidly like a tide wave, shaking the ground, forming gale-force winds around him. The first form allowed him to condense energy from his own blood. The second form allowed him to condense energy from the surrounding area. Blood Parasite had once said that if Wei could achieve the Breakthrough Completion in this skill, he could tear apart a Houtian Realm cultivator with ease. Even with five blood clones, Wei couldn't achieve that, so he didn't bring them out. However, Blood Parasite had shown him a way to achieve the Will of the Sword, and this changed the way the divine art worked.

"Interesting. Junior, you are getting serious right from the start. I like it." Wi Vistara shrugged and drew her bow string.

A white arrow of energy formed on the bow and shot toward the bloodred sword. The attacks clashed in the air, bursting out the ground below them, forming a foot-deep ditch. The sword continued forward after dispersing the energy arrow.

"Slightly infuriating now." Wi Vistara retrieved a golden arrow and shot it toward the sword. It passed like lightning and cut through the bloodred sword image, like a knife cutting through a piece of tender meat.

"Elephant Fist of Pain." A dragon elephant formed behind Wei's elbow as he punched hard at the arrow. The dragon elephant clashed with the arrow and shattered it into pieces. If he had used the second level, Blood Sword Tearing through the Earth, he might have injured the woman, but he kept that trump card hidden.

"Aiya, a skill that can shatter a Gold Grade arrow? Not bad, junior. You've got some skills for a Heart Blood Realm junior, but can you survive my full-power attack?" A jade-white arrow appeared in her hand, and the surrounding energy crazily swayed toward it. It had a natural affinity with the wind, and if he dared to take it without using one of his trump cards, then he would be in trouble.

He had to bring his blood clones and use the Breakthrough Completion to finish this fight quickly. If his clones decided to come out of him before it was time, he would be in big trouble.

"I guess I have to get serious as well." Wei smiled, making hand symbols to call out his blood clones.

"Wait, Aunty Vistara. I've captured the wolf and the beast. We don't need to waste our time here." A long shadow appeared in the sky, followed by a huge winged dragon. It quickly reduced itself to a small copy of the giant form.

Wei gulped. It was Wi Rual, a friend from the previous life. He remembered her beast form very fondly. However, Wi Rual had the little fox tied with a rope on her back along with the Blood Orchid Beast.

Wei didn't want to fight, but for the little fox, he could battle with a god or a devil. There was no way he would let his friend get humiliated like this.

Chapter 12

Deal with Rual'er

The small dragon descended elegantly, her single wing flapping like a music note. She was only at the half step of the Houtian Realm, so she couldn't transform into a human form, yet she looked as opulent as a princess could look in a beast form.

"Senior, I'm sorry." Wei paused. "I need the fox and the Blood Orchid Beast," he said, his eyes glued to the Rual'er's dark-brown form.

Her beautiful eyes stared at him like they used to when they traveled together. She reminded him of a coconut—hard outside but soft and tasty inside. She could kill a thousand enemies with a single arrow without blinking, but she could weep at the slightest pain faced by her friends. When he'd asked her to walk away, she'd cried hard, leaving a deep scar in his pained heart.

He'd been a fool back then. Maybe he was now as well. Seeing her like this brought a lot of memories to Li Wei's mind. When they'd trained together, she would take this form sometimes, and they would travel over the sea to catch some exquisite fish kings and eat them while sitting next to a campfire. They'd been on a joint mission, and he'd loved that time. She was one of the most beautiful women he'd seen in his life—beautiful in her heart and beautiful in her attitude. Even in her beast form, she looked as lovely as a heavenly maiden.

"I missed you, Rual'er," Wei said in his mind, his heart thumping like a drum.

Emotions washed over him like the waves they'd floated over during their mission over the sea. Without his consent, tears rolled down his cheeks. Even the rotten taste from the banana trees of the forest couldn't hide the bitter taste of regret in his heart. It was the same regret that he'd felt when he saw Fei'er for the first time after reincarnating into his own self.

"Human, you are breaking my heart. Do you really care about your pet?" Rual'er asked when she landed on the ground.

"She is not my pet but a friend," Wei answered, wiping the moisture from his eyes.

Rual'er sighed. "Have her, then."

"Lady Rual, what are you doing?" Wi Vistara asked, looking shocked. "She can be your stead once you break through. Why let a human mess with a beast?"

"Look at him." Rual'er shook her head, water accumulating over her big eyes. "He is crying for his pet. No, his friend. When did you see a human call a beast a friend? Isn't it heartwarming to see a human crying for his beast? He even went against you. If he was ready to put his life on the line for his beast friend, then I can't take her as my substitute. I can't separate two friends." She waved her wing, and the rope tying the little fox loosened.

The little fox cried in ecstasy before leaping toward Wei. Like a fierce wind, she crashed into him, forcing him to the ground, tears pouring from her eyes.

"Don't cry, Li Wei. I'm fine. I know you care for me, but don't worry. I'm fine." Little Fox wept. "The elder sister went soft on me. Her attacks didn't hurt me at all." Little Fox rubbed her soft head against his cheeks.

Wei's sobs deepened but not because he'd missed this little beast. What was wrong with these two? He wasn't worried about the little fox at all. When she'd appeared in his view, he had already scanned her with his divine sense, and other than a slight injury to her muscles, she was perfectly fine. The tears were for his past, for Rual'er, for their lost friendship.

"Don't worry. I won't leave you ever again." The little fox wept again. "You're my Li Wei, and I'll be your little fox."

She rubbed her fur fiercely along his cheek, almost pushing him into the ground. Although she looked small, she was a half-step Houtian Realm beast. She could kill any human with a swipe of her claw, and she was rubbing her head against him like a giant golem rubbing its head on the mountain.

"Little Fox, let me breathe." Wei grabbed her head and lightly pushed her away. Although he liked her a lot, he couldn't take this much affection from her.

Getting up, he saw Wi Vistara floating toward Rual'er, who was already in the air. They were heading away. Just like that. But he couldn't let them go. He needed that Blood Orchid Beast, and he had something Rual'er wanted.

"Miss Rual'er. I have a thing you need. Can you trade the Blood Orchid Beast for that?"

"See how rude that human is? You let go of his pet, yet he has his eye on the beast you captured. Human, you're a vile character, and I hate you." Wi Vistara drew her bow, the same jade-white arrow appearing on the string.

Wei rolled his eyes. Was something wrong with this woman? He wanted to trade things, and she was treating him like a thief.

"Miss Rual, don't you need a Three-Wind Cicada Fruit to heal the deficiency of your constitution?" he asked, using his divine sense so only she could hear him. Rual'er had told him about this once, along with her fortuitous encounter that had opened up Wind Acupoints on her body and led her to practice archery.

Rual'er froze in the air. "What did you say, human?" she asked, her wing fluttering for a moment.

Suddenly, Wei realized what the problem of her constitution was.

"Did he insult you with his divine sense? Vile human, die." Wi Vistara shot an arrow toward him.

"Damn it, woman. Don't force me to this," Wei said, conjuring his blood clones to counterattack. Some people couldn't be argued with, and they needed beating.

"Wait, Aunt Vistara." Rual'er appeared in front of the arrow, and it changed direction.

The arrow crashed into the forest behind Wei and knocked off a mile of forest. An explosion rang in his ears, and thousands of birds chirped, flying from the forest.

"Do you really have Three-Wind Cicada Fruit, human?" Rual'er asked, her eyes shining like pearls.

"I don't, but I know where you can get it." He'd seen it near the little fox's mother's cave. It shouldn't be a problem for Rual'er to acquire it.

"How dare you lie to the princess?" Wi Vistara drew her bow again.

"Is there something wrong with her? She was fine a minute ago, and now she is behaving crazy. If you need, I can discipline her." Wei glared at the green-robed woman. She seemed to want to provoke him no matter what.

"Aunt Vistara, please." Rual'er turned to face the rude woman, prompting her to lower her bow.

"Rual'er, don't trust a human too much. He might be bluffing," Wi Vistara replied, her tone bordering on rude.

"Don't worry. I'll tell you the location and trade this stone with you. This should be enough for you to comprehend the Intent of Wind." Wei tossed a Wind Source Stone to Rual'er. He'd gotten it from Allen Ming when that guy had visited some distant place. It contained the power of Intent, and he'd planned to give it to the little fox, but he could give her Blood Orchid Beast core instead. They were similar in quality, according to Blood Parasite.

"Aiya. It's a Wind Source Stone. Where did you get it?" Wi Vistara shouted when the stone landed in front of Rual'er. She quickly moved and grabbed it and put it in her storage ring. "Rual'er, I will hold this for you."

"Human friend, do you have more of these?" Rual'er asked.

"Sorry, I only had one, which is in front of you now, and it came from a very faraway place. I don't even know the direction of that place." Instinctively, he stared at Wi Vistara, wondering why she'd taken the source stone instead of Rual'er. That woman gave off a strange vibe.

"What is your name?" Rual'er asked, her voice soft as a feather.

She then tossed the Blood Orchid Beast to him, and he put it in his Pet Storage Pouch. It could accommodate two beasts, and Purple and the Seven Rainbow Void Serpent Beast already lived inside, but Purple came out and wrapped around his neck. He'd sent the fiery panther to Beast Origin Realm, where the little fox was supposed to be. He'd met her briefly in the Ancient Constitution Trial, but he never got to ask about what had really happened and why the little fox was out. There were so many questions, but they could wait.

"You can call me Li Wei," he said, rubbing the little fox's fur. "Little Fox, your core is injured, so you have to wait until I concoct some pills for you. Then you can absorb the core and comprehend the Intent of Wind. I'll help you—don't worry."

"Li Wei, which pill will you cook for me?" the little fox asked. "Are they as good as Xue Qi's pills?"

Pain flashed through his heart. "Little Fox, Xue Qi is gone, so don't speak about her anymore. I'll concoct the same pill I made for you when you were injured first. In fact, I'll concoct a better pill this time." He'd concocted the pill in the Beast Origin Realm. He'd succeeded in making it partially because of the Yang Wood Pill Clone and partially because he'd had no other option to save the little fox. Now that he had a wood qi clone, his Yang Wood Pill Clone had improved a lot, and his experience in alchemy had improved as well. This time, he would concoct the best pill possible.

Chapter 13

Spy of the Human Race?

This human was interesting. He was bold, loyal, and ready to expose his wealth before knowing the opponent, yet he held back a little. Wi Rual had never met a human like this. Especially not a young man of her own age. Was he not afraid of her and senior sister Vistara killing him and stealing all his treasures?

They would never do that, but he should have been more careful. He trusted them too much. He sat there with his back facing them as he worked on a pill. A strange guy indeed.

The guy next to Li Wei gulped a mouthful of water, attracting her attention. He was so bald his head shone like a light stone of the night. Her mother said an average woman could bring an ugly friend with her in order to look beautiful by comparison. Li Wei had to be using the bald guy to make himself look cool and a little handsome.

Senior sister Vistara sent her a divine transmission: "Princess, we should kill him. He knows too much about our race."

Senior sister Vistara had recently joined her as a guard, and Rual had been surprised when the elder had sent her as a guard on this journey. Rual didn't need a guard and only let the woman accompany because the elder had said she should.

"Don't suggest something like that again," she whispered so Li Wei wouldn't hear her. If a person treated her with respect, she would reciprocate it with everything she had. The guy had trusted her, and she would never be the first one to break that trust.

"But, Princess—"

"Senior sister Vistara, can you search for some game in the forest? I'm feeling hungry," Rual whispered. "Maybe search for some honey as well. I need some sweet today."

"I can't leave you with a human. The queen will execute me if she knows I lapsed in my duties."

"Just stay nearby so if I need you, you can come quickly. Don't look down on my battle powers just because I'm not in the Houtian Realm." Wi Rual's tone was calm, but she didn't like the way senior sister Vistara behaved sometimes.

"Please forgive my impudence, Princess." Wi Vistara bowed.

"Also, leave the Wind Source Stone. I need to study it."

"But, Princess, you can't absorb it before your constitution is healed completely."

"Do I look like a fool to you? Of course I won't absorb it. I just want to have a look."

Wi Vistara retrieved the stone and handed it to her before vanishing into the shadows.

"She has tempered the stone, Princess Rual," the human's voice echoed in her mind.

"How can you use the divine sense?" She tried to sense senior sister Vistara but hadn't opened up her own divine sense, so she could only rely on her beast senses.

The human turned back, his blue eyes staring into her soul. "Do you trust me, Princess Rual?" he said, sending a divine transmission.

"I guess I do."

He retrieved a white disc and tapped a Qi Crystal in the middle. A formless energy spread out of it and covered a hundred feet around them.

"A concealing-formation disc? But it can't block the divine sense of a Houtian Realm cultivator." She shook her head.

"It's a Traceless Formation Disc. I carved the formation myself, so don't worry too much. Until your subordinate has reached Violet Palace Realm, she can't eavesdrop on our conversation."

"You can carve formations—that's inconceivable. Forgive me, but I can't trust you," she said.

"You said the same thing that time as well," he whispered, looking into the shadows, lost in his thoughts.

"What did you say?"

"Nothing. Did you notice the Wind Source Stone is tempered and useless for you now?"

She sighed. She had sensed it when Wi Vistara had handed it to her. Why she'd done that, Wi Rual didn't know. She would have to find out sooner rather than later.

"You knew it in advance, and that's why you had that array on it before tossing it toward me," she said.

Now that she thought about it, this guy might have some knowledge of arrays and formations. That was a special array, and she only knew about it because her father had shown her once.

She studied the source stone. "That vile woman sucked half the wind energy out of it, making it useless. If I use this to break through, I'll receive backlash. What a terrible plan. If you knew it would happen, why did you toss it far away from me?" Rage built inside her. Had he done that on purpose?

"I didn't know." He shook his head. A clone separated from him and sat next to the golden cauldron. "I gave it to you as security until I complete our deal."

"That vile woman. I want to kill her." Wi Rual cursed. Rage boiled up, and she wanted to kill her right away, but she suppressed the desire. This conversation was much more interesting than killing that woman. "Do you have another stone? I can pay for it."

"No. That was the only one," he said, tossing a bunch of herbs into the golden cauldron.

One of the herbs exuded a scent of life so dense that she had an urge to eat it right away. It glittered with white light and prompted her blood energy to revolve by itself.

"What herb is that?" she asked, regretting the question instantly. A person didn't ask an alchemist about his secrets. That was taboo. "I'm sorry. I shouldn't have asked."

"Five Petal Life Herb." He tossed a couple of herbs to his clone, who retrieved another cauldron—a shabby one compared to the glimmering golden one Li Wei used—and started processing them. Then he pulled out a large black beast core and tossed it into the shabby cauldron. The fresh air was assaulted with a rotten smell.

"Did you really apply the Null Source Array yourself?" she asked.

He was a strange guy. His alchemy seemed proficient, judging by the smooth actions he took. Could he also be proficient in array? That would be hard, right? Null Source Array was a high-grade array, and she couldn't wrap her mind around the idea that a guy in Heart Blood Realm of body cultivation had carved it on a treasure.

"I did. If everything had gone smoothly, I'd have removed that Null Source Array from it, but your senior sister tempered with it, and it's evident." He extended his arm.

Wi Rual tossed the stone to him. "You keep it. You might have some use for it."

She knew about the array because her father protected the treasures using it. It allowed treasure aura to leak and acted as a lock while treasure was exchanged. Only the one who'd created the array had the key. For anyone else, the treasure would lose half of its effect. Wi Vistara had reached the Houtian Realm, but her status didn't grant her access to the deep secrets of the royal family.

"Tell me, human. How did you know about me being a princess of the One-Winged Dragon race?" It suddenly bugged her. "I can't just trust you blindly."

Was he a spy?

Chapter 14

Pill Tribulation

"Do you think I'm a spy?" Li Wei chuckled. He gulped a mouthful of water from a leather skin. Beads of sweat had materialized on his forehead, maybe due to exhaustion or the heat of the cauldron. Or fear.

Wi Rual took a deep breath. She was reluctant to label him a spy. At least she hadn't felt any hatred from him, and her senses were attuned to detecting hatred from others because of her bloodline ability.

"You also know about my deficiency in the constitution. Only a few people in this world know about it. Don't blame me for not trusting you, but you should give me a proper answer. If you can't, don't blame me for showing no mercy." Wi Vistara had betrayed her, and Wi Rual was already sullen about that, and if this guy also had unscrupulous thoughts, she would lose trust in others.

"Can I say I can divine the future?" The guy laughed, carefree.

He then went on to control the wood qi his clone injected into the golden cauldron. The qi had an exceptional thickness, and she bet she'd be able to collect it in her claws if she reached for it. This guy was a proficient alchemist. Soon the rotten-flesh odor turned into a pleasant smell of flowers and life. Dark liquid bubbled up and floated above the cauldron in the form of a thick gas before vanishing into the air.

"I'm waiting for your answer," she said when he was free from the alchemy for a moment.

"Okay, I know your origin because that stupid woman called you Pri-Pr-Prin so many times that even a dumb person can guess what she wanted to say. Then you also have the symbol of the royal family around your head. I'm sorry. I didn't mean to pry, but I'd like to scan the little fox to make sure she was safe on your back."

Rual giggled. "No wonder everyone called Wi Vistara "Dumb Vis" behind her back. What about my constitution issue? She doesn't know that, so how did you find it out?"

"Your flying has flaws. When you flip your wing, don't you feel pain in the joint that connects it to your back?"

"I do, but every One-Winged Dragon feels the same. Although we are not true dragons, we have their strength, so it's common among us."

"It's different. I don't know why no one noticed it before, but let me show you how my wings perform." He leaped back, and two sparkling gold metallic wings shot out of his back.

They shone in the dim light so beautifully that she wanted to touch them and caress them until she'd had enough of them. Every One-Winged Dragon loved wings. Maybe it was due to them having only one wing, but they had this attraction to two-winged beasts. And this guy had real wings. She could tell they were part of him.

"Are you a beast hybrid?"

He chuckled. "No. It's because of my strange cultivation technique. Watch carefully when I flip my right wing. You'll see a natural curve and fold in it."

He flipped his right wing, and he was right. The wind moved around his wing as it lifted him in the air. With those wings, he was a king of the wind.

A sudden realization struck her. "You practice the Intent of Wind, and that's why your flying is proficient."

He smiled—a confident and handsome smile. "You got the point. But you don't need Intent of Wind to understand this. If you studied the birds and two-winged beasts, you would comprehend the technique of effortless flying."

"Why didn't my father mention this to me before?" In fact, no one had. It couldn't be a secret that everyone hid from her.

"You're thinking too much. They just assumed you would be proficient in the technique as you're a princess. When you flip your only wing, your weight is forced into it. That's the main reason for the flaw in your constitution. Once you spend some time, you'll remove the flaw."

"So even if I ate a Three-Wind Cicada Fruit, I would still have this issue."

"Yes. Only comprehension can save you from this fault," he said.

"Then you cheated me by telling me about the Three-Wind Cicada Fruit."

"I didn't. It might not fix your constitution issue, but it will improve your Beast Core. You should still search for it."

"Are you sure? Why are you sure about this?"

"I can heal your injuries with my pills. Don't worry about them. It might even fix your constitution issue. We just have to see."

"What nonsense," she said. "Don't fool me. My father has consulted many alchemy masters, and there's no pill that can fix my constitution. If there was, it would have been found by now."

"You didn't find it because your father consulted alchemists who excelled in human pills." He tossed another beast core into the cauldron, and a giant fire, which sent a chill down her spine, shot out of his fingers and wrapped around the cauldron.

"You have a Hell Flame. Are you a devil, human?"

"Your father consulted the wrong alchemist."

"Answer my question."

"See the irony? You call me human and then ask me if I'm a devil." He chuckled, sending a burst of qi into the cauldron. "You should have asked an alchemist who excelled in beast pills, but I guess there isn't one in the Martial Realm." He shook his head.

"It doesn't prove your human nature. You even have innate wings, which a human shouldn't have."

"I like you, Princess Rual, but if you keep questioning my integrity, it will become difficult to treat you well." A white qi surged out of him and covered him. "This is pure qi, and a devil can't use it. Does that answer your question?"

She lowered her head. She was ashamed. A devil couldn't use pure qi, nor could it mimic a human like brother Wei.

"Thank you," she whispered. Brother Wei had shown nothing but trust in her, yet she'd suspected him for every damn reason out there.

The beast core in the cauldron exploded, pulling her attention away from her guilt. It exuded a dense scent of medicine, and everything turned silent. It was the time when an alchemist had to be cautious because the pill took a Breath. Although she didn't understand what a Pill Breath meant, she knew it was quite important.

For thirty breaths, nothing happened, and then a small cloud appeared over the cauldron. It turned black, and the energy swirled inside and filled the ten feet around it with crackling energy.

"Brother Wei, your pill is attracting Pill Tribulation. Heavens, you are a Pill Adept Exceptional." The silent bald guy next to Li Wei got up and gazed at the cloud.

She'd heard about that. When a pill reached beyond exceptional quality, it attracted a Pill Tribulation. Who was this guy, really? And why hadn't she heard about him before?

Chapter 15

Killing a Bitch

P ill Tribulation? The dark cloud sent a pulse through his core. A dense scent of heavenly tribulation filled the air, and his Blood Lightning Pill Clone stirred from inside like a beast awakened by prey entering its area of control.

Li Wei spread his divine sense and probed the tribulation cloud. It was different yet familiar. Kai Shaya had attracted it once, and Wei had accidentally sucked it in. It couldn't feed his lightning pill clone's stomach, but it could satisfy the taste buds. Lightning didn't taste good. It made his entire body frizzle with energy. He preferred his Green Fragrant Potatoes or Nuan'er's cooking.

Lightning crackled inside the dark cloud, ready to descend on the cauldron. But why had he attracted a Pill Tribulation? This wasn't the first time he'd seen one. In his previous life, Wei had been friends with many alchemists, some exceptionally talented, and a few times, he'd seen Pill Tribulation descending on their pills. That had been the extent of his knowledge, but after spending a lot of time with Xue Qi, that betrayer, he'd gained a lot of alchemy knowledge. He wouldn't call himself a master, but he bet he could go against any alchemist in the Mortal Plane.

"Pill Tribulation—how is that possible?" Rual'er exclaimed, her voice shuddering.

Wei shrugged. How would he know? Pill Tribulation only happened to the pills that broke the laws of the heavens. When the pill reached more pill lines than it could contain, it brought down the heavenly punishment—Pill Tribulation. It was heaven's means of destroying something that shouldn't exist.

However, his pill shouldn't have brought that. It was only a fucking Silver Grade Pill. The last time, he'd carved a pill line on the pill by accident, almost making it a Gold Grade pill. He'd made it with the help of the simulation function from the system, and it had worked wonders. So with his richer experience, he expected to produce a Gold Grade Pill, and that was why he'd confidently said he would fix Rual'er's constitution problem. And of course, he knew the root cause, and Rual'er had fixed it with a pill in his previous life.

So he was cheating. Cheating by improving the pill and having future knowledge. The pill was supposed to reach Gold Grade.

Wait—had he carved a Pill Matrix accidentally? He couldn't have, right? A Pill Tribulation only descended when one carved a Pill Matrix—four pill lines—on a pill.

Or one could increase the grade of the pill by two levels.

There was no pill line on the pill, so that only meant the pill quality had jumped to Earth Grade. Fucking Earth Grade.

"Brother Wei, are you really a Pill Expert? Did you really draw a Pill Matrix on the pill? Or did you concoct a forbidden pill to draw the heavens like I did?" Kai Shaya asked, his voice full of disappointment.

"Fuck no. I'm not an expert. I'm a dabbler in this, but I know why this had happened." Wei shook his head. This was because of his cheating ability.

He chuckled. Why hadn't he thought of this before? His clone practiced a Heaven Grade Wood Qi Cultivation Art, and it had increased his wood qi quality to the low-tier Human Grade, so he had an insanely high-quality wood qi. Then he had Yang Wood Pill Clone, which raised his wood qi quality further by a tier. So his wood qi quality had reached a frightening level. And on top of that, he'd used two-thousand-year-old herbs. After breaking through the Heart Blood Realm, his Yin Yang Liquid Art had improved, allowing him to age an herb to two thousand years, and he'd forgotten that and used the herbs he had duplicated using Yin Yang Liquid.

Two-thousand-year-old herbs. Who concocted a Silver Grade pill with two-thousand-year-old herbs? Two freaking thousand years. It had broken the balance, and the result was in front of him.

"Brother Wei, please answer, or my alchemic heart will shatter into pieces. Don't be my heart devil," Kai Shaya begged, looking disappointed in himself.

"Brother Wei, even I am curious about this," Rual'er said in a soft voice, stepping close to him.

A warmth spread through Wei's heart when he heard her call him brother, reminding him of his previous life, when she'd roamed around with him, calling him brother Wei. Those were the good old days.

"That." He rubbed the back of his neck. "I accidentally added two-thousand-year-old herbs, and it pushed the quality from Silver to Earth Grade."

"A two-thousand-year-old herb? Aren't you afraid of heaven stealing things from you?" Rual'er trembled, and Kai Shaya flopped onto his ass.

Wei smiled sheepishly. In the entire Martial Realm, only a few sects had two-thousand-year-old herbs. He knew that because he'd seen a war break out between two prominent sects just because of a thousand-year-old herb.

"I got it from my Specter. I don't have many, so don't worry. Let me just take care of this first." The lightning swirled in the dark cloud and descended like a serpent trying to attack its prey.

Wei raised his palm and caught the lightning between his fingers. This was nothing but a snack for his Blood Lightning Pill Clone. He wasn't afraid of it, but he was afraid of the Heavenly Tribulation that would descend when Blood Parasite lifted the Heaven-Stealing Formation from him. After he broke through into Heart Blood Realm in body cultivation, the tribulation hadn't descended because he'd been in Ancient Constitution trials and sealed off from the heavens. Before he came out, Blood Parasite used some means to conceal him from the heavens, saying he wasn't prepared for it. And he'd known he wasn't, because the moment he stepped out of the Ancient Constitution, he'd felt the rage of the heavens. They had been waiting for him.

Four baby-fist-sized pills emerged from the cauldron, shining like a golden sun about to set. The last time, it had been pitch-dark, but this time, it had a shiny golden hue that blinded them. The pills floated for a moment and then shot in four different directions.

"Damn it." Wei wasn't prepared for the running pills, but Kai Shaya reacted faster as four energy hands shot from his back and caught them.

"Brother Wei, you attracted a Pill Tribulation, yet you let them run away. I don't know how I should treat you. Are you genius or a rich young master who has tons of money to waste?" Kai Shaya dropped the pills into a glass bottle, shaking his head in disappointment. "You are an oddity, benefactor."

"Thanks." Wei chuckled. "Little Fox, one is for you, and one is for you, sister Rual. May I call you that?" he asked, hoping for a positive answer.

"Of course you can't," a ragged voice said, and Wi Vastira appeared in front of them, two arrows drawn on her bow, pointing at Wei and Kai Shaya.

She wouldn't listen until he beat her to a pulp. With a heavy sigh, Wei retrieved his sword. It was time to kill the barking bitch.

Chapter 16

Setting a Mutual Contract with Forest Elemental

"Elder Deimu, what brings you here in the morning?" Sun Nuan placed the pill she was appraising down in the wooden box.

The fragrance of herbs coming out of it instantly decreased. The pill had reached the low-tier Gold Grade quality, pleasing her innately. The alchemist she'd groomed in the Li Alchemy Firm had rapidly improved and could already concoct low-tier Gold Grade pills. Well, they had no choice after training under the first batch of alchemists trained by the master Xue Qi herself. Those few people could even concoct midtier Gold Grade pills.

"I envy your alchemy rooms, little girl. They are as good as those of the bastards from the higher planes." Master Deimu picked up a couple of pills and sniffed them. "Excellent quality. I heard you can concoct high-tier Gold Grade pill."

"It's nothing." She shook her head. It was trivial.

"What's nothing? Even those people in the Destiny Mirror Sect can only eat high-tier Silver Grade pills. They have a deep heritage, but even they can't give Gold Grade pills to all of their people, while you are tossing them to every beggar on the road."

She chuckled. This was indeed true. With big brother Wei's godly liquid, she could concoct unlimited Gold Grade pills, and they were quite common in the Five Firmament City. With those pills, her army had made big leaps, and everyone had reached at least the Boiling Blood Realm. Not just that, but they'd seen an overall improvement in their power and constitution. If this was old times, she would have no issue in conquering the surrounding kingdoms with just a few thousand people she had.

"If I didn't know you had a grand alchemist as a master, I wouldn't have believed this, little girl." He smiled, looking much better than he had when she'd found him. The improvement in his condition was mostly because of big brother Wei's help. Without it, she would have had no guarantee of saving the elder.

"Please take a seat. I'll get a servant to serve you a new tea I prepared." She had been researching this tea with the help of sister Li Niya, who had come from the other world. She was a disciple of big brother Wei's and looked like Chen Chi. Only Li Niya and Sonja knew about the tea, and now brother Chen Du. Sun Nuan could only hope sister Niya and brother Du would find solace in each other.

A servant walked in with a tray filled with tea and snacks. Elder Deimu and she enjoyed the warm, sweet tea for a full minute without saying anything. Big brother Wei always said the tea should be enjoyed in silence. Talking only ruined one's dao heart.

"Good tea." Elder Deimu placed the empty cup on the tray. "You have mixed the herbs in a perfect quantity. I've worked with that lass, Ki Fei, and if she'd shown a half as much dedication as you, she would have done much better in alchemy." He sighed, looking like he was reminiscing about the past.

"Sister Fei's talent is much better than mine."

"It is, but she lacks dedication. Half the time, she was knitting these robes for her brother Wei." He retrieved a heap of clothes from his storage ring and gave it to her.

Nuan brushed her fingers over the robe, and she could see why big brother Wei liked these more. They smelled like sister Fei. The ones Nuan had given him had been made by someone else. Unfortunately, she lacked any talent in knitting.

"I'm sure he will love to have these. Did she ask you to give them to him?"

"No. I confiscated them when I got tired of seeing her wasting time on them. But they will go to the intended owner."

"Thank you, elder." Nuan placed the clothes neatly in her storage ring. They were all sky blue, knitted with a precision in a way big brother Wei liked. "He'll love them." A smile played on her lips, but a string of pain rang in her heart.

"Lovestruck fools. Anyway, I came here to help you refine the Forest Elemental."

"What do you mean by refine, old man?" A little tree jumped out of the corner and settled on her shoulder, wrapping his branches around her neck. He'd been like this since they'd met, and she felt a comfort having him around. They'd even established an equality contract, allowing her to absorb him into her body.

"Don't forget, you took a heaven-and-earth vow to help her," Elder Deimu said harshly. "You're a nature-born soul, and your destiny is to get refined by an alchemist. It's the greatest service you can do to her."

"Elder, no. I can't do anything that will harm this child." Nuan shook her head.

"Little girl, don't be foolish. That is no child. He is at least five hundred years old."

"Yes, I'm no child, and I'll help her. I've a Forest Elemental Seed she can use." He extended a branch, and a small sapling appeared on it. The tiny sapling exuded a mighty wood aura, but it had no soul fluctuations.

"What's the use of the sprout? It will take at least two hundred years to grow into a mature Forest Elemental."

"What if I can mature it to five hundred years?" the Forest Elemental asked.

Nuan was taken aback. This little guy had asked her for a drop of big brother Wei's godly liquid, and she'd given it to him after their contract was in effect. However, she'd never known about him having another Forest Elemental with him.

"Would it have a consciousness like you once it matures?" she asked.

The small tree shook his head. "No. The Elementals are basically fools, and they just wonder without sense. Only a few can achieve the consciousness. It was a special case for me, and I was trapped inside an evil spirit tool." The tree sighed, his branches shaking. "Elder, I can mature it to five hundred years. Is that sufficient?"

"Don't kid me." Elder Deimu shook his head in disdain.

"I don't joke around her. I've stolen a Life Elixir from a Forest Deity, and I can use it to mature this sprout." A thick, green drop appeared on one of its branches and exuded a vibrant aura, instantly filling the room with life and joy.

"What is that thing?" Elder Deimu rose from his chair.

The little tree dropped it on the sprout, which instantly grew to a few feet. It was a Forest Elemental, so it didn't grow into a giant tree. A common tree would have broken through her alchemy chamber.

"Why did you waste it, stupid tree?" Elder Deimu's legs shook, and he flopped into the chair. "I could have used it to concoct an Earth Grade Pill."

"I need to sleep now." The little tree shook some of the branches and entered her glabella.

"Little girl, ask him if he has more," Elder Deimu said.

Nuan shook her head with pain. "I don't think so. He's in slumber now. I bet he was refining it and gave it away to appease you," she lied, sounding as dispirited as she could.

Of course, it was big brother Wei's godly liquid, and the little tree already knew about it. He just played along with her to make it seem like something unfathomable from a mysterious forest. Other than her, no one knew about the godly liquid. In fact, no one could know. Even she never dared to use the new liquid, which could age an herb to two thousand years old. She would mostly supply hundred-year-old herbs. She would rarely toss out a three- or four-hundred-year-old herb and complain for days how much she'd had to spend to acquire it from the black market.

"Is this good, elder?" She handed the five-foot-tall tree to Elder Deimu. Although the tree looked the same, it had a dense aura of life and a strange fluctuation.

"Not bad, little girl. If you weren't my disciple, I'd run away with this." Elder Deimu chuckled. "With this, I'll let you know the power of a real alchemist."

His smile widened, and Nuan had a crazy thought of seeing another master, Xue Qi. This old man was as crazy as Xue Qi when it came to alchemy.

"Little girl, this will improve your talent in alchemy. Trust me—you will be no less talented than that lass Ki Fei once you refine it. Once I chanced upon a two-hundred-year-old Forest Elemental, and my alchemy path improved by leaps and bounds, and you will do the same."

Nuan nodded. Although she'd spent very little time with the elder, she had seen him really concerned about sister Fei, and she had gauged his good intentions. Moreover, he was crazy for alchemy, like Master Xue Qi, so she innately trusted him.

Chapter 17

Ancient Decree?

"**H**uman, you've gone overboard, putting my princess in danger, so you ought to die today!" Wi Vistara shouted, her bow string pulled back to the limit.

A white light was shining on the tip of her arrows, and it exuded a mighty pressure for a few feet around her. The ground began depressing as the essence energy poured out of her and entered the arrows. Li Wei shook his head. He should have expected this and acted beforehand.

"Senior sister Vistara, stop it. He is a friend!" Rual'er shouted, putting herself between Li Wei and Wi Vistara. Her figure started growing into her beast form.

A warmth spread through Wei's heart. She was the same as the Rual'er he knew from his previous life. She wouldn't hesitate to put her life on the line for her close friends. Even after knowing him for a dozen minutes, she'd jumped in to take a blow for him. How could he not regret losing a friend like this? He would have been better off if he had accepted her proposal and married her.

"Princess, you're blinded by the human's bewitching techniques, so even if I have to injure you, I'll kill this human," Wi Vistara said, no remorse in her icy tone. "Don't worry—it will only set you back a few years, and your father will understand the situation when I explain."

It was clear that she wanted to hurt Rual'er as well as Wei.

"Wi Vistara, don't make me look down on you. Stand aside!" Rual'er roared, her angry voice shaking the trees behind them. "You're no match for me, so don't make me hurt you."

The peculiar scent of her dragon qi, bitter and calming, spread through the air, covering the entire area. Dragon qi was her race's innate ability, and a One-Winged Dragon only used it in a life-and-death situation. She was going for the kill.

"Ha ha," Wi Vistara giggled, sounding hysterical. The evil laughter flowed like water, sending cringes down Wei's spine. "Princess, you're too naive to think that I'm only at layer three of the Houtian Realm."

The wind around her churned like water vapor twisting in a cauldron. Her essence manifested in the air, and the entire world seemed to listen to her. Suddenly, her aura burst to layer four of the Houtian Realm, forming the shape of a flame arrow. It was her Houtian Essence Aura, and it was strong.

"Vile woman!" Rual'er's explosive shout shook the ground again. "You used my Wind Source Stone to break through. You tried to harm me, so your only punishment is death."

The ground cracked, and the air became electrifying as her dragon qi surged around her. She was pushing herself to the extreme to fight against the formidable opponent. However, it wasn't needed—not when Wei hadn't even used his trump card.

"Sister Rual, don't use your core qi. I can handle this." He stepped forward with confidence radiating through his smile. If Wi Vistara had reached layer five of the Houtian Realm, Wei would have been in trouble, but she hadn't, so he still had trump cards to take her down. He might not kill her, but he could fight her to a standstill, and then Rual'er and Kai Shaya could deal the final blow. "I will tie her down, and you can strike the killing blow. Are you willing to help?"

"How can I do that, brother Wei? You're not even at the peak of Heart Blood Realm. So let me handle this," Rual'er said, turning pale white.

"Winged dragon, don't look down on my Li Wei. He can even kill an immortal," the little fox said, her fur standing up as she prepared to attack.

"Let me try first, and if I can't, then do what is needed." Wei raised his sword.

Five blood clones separated out of him and stood next to him, each holding a sword made of their blood, matching the structure of the blood-red sword in Wei's hand. This was the same sword Wei had found in the Ancient Ruins outside the Old Martial City, but he had yet to discover the material it was made of. He just knew it was a supreme weapon, and he couldn't break it by any means.

"Human, so you want to die? Come. Wind Emperor Arrow!" Wi Vistara shouted, releasing the three arrows from her bow. Wind swished around the arrows, forming a gale that swept over the cracked ground leading toward Wei.

"Blood Sword Tearing through the Earth." A red sword appeared above him, pulling the surrounding essence into the image.

The ground shook, and the air crackled as he attacked. This was the second level of the Blood Sword Divinity Art, and he had awakened the Will of the Skill with the help of Blood Parasite. The earth pulsed as he used the Intent of Pulse to mix his blood pearls and the earth essence, forming an unending tide of energy that charged into his sword. This was the first time he was using his divine art outside of the Primordial Blood Palace, and it had immense power—so much so that his skin cracked and blood flowed out under the pressure.

"That's as much I can handle." Wei attacked, no longer able to bear the impact of the divine art. If he'd continued, his body would have broken down, and this excited him because as he reached further in his body cultivation, the power of this divine art would only grow to new heights.

Simultaneously, five blood clones attacked on their own. They used the same move but with less intensity. However, when all six attacks were combined, a thousand feet area around them shuddered, and a giant crack spread through the ground, extending in all the directions like a spiderweb. Space cracked, and a howling void smashed against the fabric of nature.

"Damn it, kid. The walls of this place are not strong enough to hold that much power. You shouldn't have used it here," Blood Parasite told Wei in a panicked voice.

An intense pain rushed through Wei's hands, fissures spreading across his bones, and the sword image blew up right before it crashed with Wi Vistara's arrow. The evening lit up as if a sun had exploded in the middle of the forest. The devils howled, and ghosts cried. A sense of danger enveloped Wei and his party.

"This is the Ancient Decree!" Rual'er shouted, her face turning paler than white paper.

Chapter 18

Trial of Incursion

The world shifted around them, twisting, shattering, and erupting as if a god's anger had descended upon them. The evening light shifted from dark to bright as the sun and then back to dark, and a huge shockwave spread from the explosion site, sending a tremor through the ground like a giant beast approaching them on earth that couldn't bear its weight.

Li Wei trembled, not in fear but because he couldn't resist the backlash, and ended up coughing a few mouthfuls of blood. The metallic taste lingered in his mouth as he struggled to balance himself with the help of his sword. Kai Shaya was sprawled next to him, his eyes and ears bleeding, and the little fox wasn't in any better condition.

It wasn't over yet. An enormous earth wave smashed toward them. It was so big that the moon, visible a few moments before, was covered up. It was so fast that Wei was sure he couldn't fly over it. Rual'er wouldn't be able to either, as she was in her giant beast form, which was slower than her smaller form. She would require at least a few seconds to transform and fly away. Her one wing couldn't hold her giant weight for a longer period, nor she was a Houtian Realm cultivator who could fly with her qi or essence.

"Sister Rual, shift back, and fly as high as possible. I'll protect you!" he shouted, dashing forward.

"I—"

"Do as I say!" Wei roared, bringing his self-assurance back up. Seeing the giant earth wall traveling toward him had sent a shock through his confidence that he needed right now at any cost. "Blood Earth Force Divine Art. Brother Shaya, bring out your strongest defensive move and support me. I promise you I won't let you die here."

Kai Shaya nodded and pressed his palms together. A sacred chant spread around him, and a golden buddha with dozens of hands appeared behind him, looking down as if the world was beneath him. The buddha expanded exponentially, and dozens of his hands shot forward, pressing against the avalanche of earth heading their way.

The earth shattered, sending pieces flying toward them. Wei leaped in front of Kai Shaya, pushing his Blood Earth Force Divine Art to the maximum so he could protect him. The tiny pieces of shrapnel clashed against his defensive field, trying to break through the blood mist. Some even succeeded and hit him, but he stood there so none could reach Kai Shaya.

The buddha wasn't faring well. The impact of the avalanche had broken many of his hands, and he was crumbling apart, and so was Kai Shaya. His face had turned pale, and he'd coughed a few mouthfuls of blood onto Wei's back.

The situation was dire, but Wei couldn't give up yet. Rual'er had flown a thousand feet high, but a few dozen feet still remained, and he couldn't let her or Little Fox get injured because of this.

"Intent of Pulsing Earth," Wei said.

He used the Intent to ease the pressure on himself, but he couldn't pass through it as Kai Shaya was still behind him, his golden buddha strained to the limit. It was shattering like a house of bricks, and it couldn't hold on for long. Rual'er had reached a few hundred feet above, but the giant earth wave was so high that she was still in the danger zone.

"One more second, brother Shaya!" Wei shouted, hoping Kai Shaya would hear him through the clusterfuck.

He couldn't believe his attack had triggered this, but he knew nothing about it. And Rual'er had spoken about some Ancient Decree when the earth collapsed. Something else had happened, and he could only understand it once he survived the current situation. There was something off about this.

Rual'er flew out of the danger area into the dim sky.

"Blood Water Healing Divine Art. Muxi's Blessing." Wei activated both the skills while grabbing Kai Shaya and using Earth Escape to enter the ground, because above the ground was a complete mess. If he could take Kai Shaya into the Primordial Blood Palace, he would do that.

He could send him instead. He'd done that with Allen Ming. However, he wasn't sure where Kai Shaya would come out, so he didn't take that risk.

"Hold on, brother. We'll get out of this together." He glanced at the pale Kai Shaya, who was in bad shape. Even inside the earth, Wei felt the tremors of the attack passing around him, making it difficult to pass through the ground.

Then the place turned silent, and he found himself in front of a giant dial that moved from left to right, like the one in the clock. Rual'er appeared next to him, and the little fox leaped from her body into Wei's arms.

"Heavens, you're fine. I was scared for my Li Wei."

"I'm fine. Don't worry." He retrieved a healing pill, stuffed it into Kai Shaya, and poured a glass of water into his mouth. It was déjà vu, but this time, Kai Shaya was badly tattered, and Wei felt terrible.

"Thank you for borrowing time for us." Rual'er bowed her head toward him, her voice shaking.

"Sister Rual'er, do you know what this thing is? You called it something—Ancient Degree?"

"I know a little about this. Ancient Decree is the First Pulse of Incursion. The Trial of Incursion is beginning in the Mortal Realm, and the world is about to go crazy." She sighed heavily. "And you can't leave this place. Otherwise, you will die."

Wei's heart thumped harder. This didn't sound like good news at all.

Chapter 19

First Pulse of Incursion

Time flowed like a ripple in the hundred miles of barren land surrounding the giant clock. The avalanche had transformed everything in the area into nothingness, opening this thousand-foot-deep depression in the ground. It was like someone had stamped down a soft area with a hundred-mile-wide metal stamp, creating a perfect trench for battle.

Battle was coming. Li Wei sat on one of the unremarkable gray stones that littered the area around the clock, turning the overall mood of the place gloomy. The dry air didn't make things any easier. It had been two hours since he and his friends had appeared down here, and according to Rual'er, things would take a drastic turn in three hours.

"Blood Parasite, did I provoke this entity with my attack?" he asked.

"I think so. The thing must be hidden in the void near this place, and by opening the void, you attracted it."

"What is this thing?"

"I don't know. The Mortal Plane is not something people like us could pry into."

"What do you mean?" Wei asked.

"Even the figures at the emperor levels weren't able to pry into the secrets of the Dark Forest that run through every Mortal World. If they dared to pry too much, they would be killed."

Wei felt a mountain of pressure on his mind. "Something that could kill an emperor? Wow!"

He was amazed more than shocked. When he'd visited Allen Ming's Mortal World, he'd seen the Dark Forest there as well. The same mysteries had run deep through the forest. He wondered why they would appear there as well.

"Guess I shouldn't look too much into this thing. I've better things to do, anyway," Wei said.

"Don't use the Will of the Skill unless it is the only option," Blood Parasite said.

Wei nodded. That skill was too much for him, and it might be the strongest divine art he knew other than Qicang Fist of Pain.

Taking a deep breath, Wei watched the bright moon hanging in the sky. It reminded him of Nuan'er waiting for him, but he couldn't contact her or check with her from here, so he had to wait for whatever Rual'er said would happen. All he could do was to drink tea while Kai Shaya healed from his injuries.

Another gust of green particles slipped out of the ancient clock. It was made of ancient dark-brown metal and glass, with a golden pendulum hand that rang like music of gods, and stood in the middle of the thousand-mile area. Every half hour, on the swing of the pendulum, these green particles came out of it. They smelled like herbs and pure water. Whenever the scent washed over him, his vitality surged and his blood-pearl count increased. In the last two hours, he'd knocked on layer two of the Heart Blood Realm with ease. He bet he could reach the peak of body Heart Blood Realm in a month if he continued getting these green particles.

Their effect on Kai Shaya had been marvelous. They'd healed him faster than Wei's own miraculous healing art could. These green particles would continue being emitted for twenty-five hours after the start, according to Rual'er, and this was one of the benefits of the Pulse of First Incursion.

Kai Shaya's body shuddered when the green particles entered him, and then he coughed a mouthful of black blood. His face turned a little redder, signaling the further improvement in his health. Wei sipped the Three-Honey Butter tea in silence, watching over Kai Shaya with a solemn heart. The tea tasted best when he had a calm heart, and that state was needed for the next breakthrough in the soul cultivation, which had gone stagnant since he'd opened up his Soul Palace.

"Brother Wei." Kai Shaya opened his eyes, still looking exhausted.

Wei stood up from the stone. He'd already changed into a bright-red robe that Nuan'er had sewn when he'd visited the Five Firmament City a few days ago. Thinking about her, he touched the ring on his finger once again, but nothing happened. In three more hours, he might regain the connection.

"Where are we?" Kai Shaya asked, sounding like a shell of his previous self. His arm moved to check on himself, and he sighed in relief to find all things at their places.

"Rest. I will tell you everything." Wei sat next to Kai Shaya and sipped on his tea. "We are in the First Pulse of Incursion, a giant trial set by heaven knows who. People call it the Trial of Incursion."

This was a bloody game. There were four incursions in Mortal World 44. One was in the Martial Realm. It was won by the Gatekeepers. The second was in the Land of Empires, and it was under the Fourth Pulse of Incursion.

"Pulses?"

"Yes. There are Four Pulses of Incursion and four Ancient Decrees. Some people even call them four nodes. The real Ancient Decree will descend when the winner of the fourth pulse is determined."

"Winner? Is this a competition?"

"Sort of, but at a bigger scale," Wei said. "Martial Realm's Ancient Decree is already won by the Gatekeepers, and many prodigies of the Martial Realm have fallen inside. The second intense competition is happening in the Land of Empires, so the Gatekeepers haven't invaded the Mortal Realm and ruled our kingdoms."

"It's not like they're keeping it shut. Sects under their influence are already in play."

Wei shook his head. This had not been the case in his previous life. "Anyway, how is your injury?" He hadn't scanned Kai Shaya using divine sense but had only checked his pulse and aura.

"I'm much better. Thanks for the healing pills."

Wei shook his head. "It's the ancient clock."

He sipped the warm tea. It had been days since he'd had a nice tea. Although his heart wasn't calm, he was stuck in this place, so all he could do was to enjoy the peaceful moment. Once Kai Shaya recovered, he had planned to open the second seal of the Primordial Blood Palace, and he was looking forward to it. In fact, Blood Parasite was urging him to do it right away, but Wei needed Kai Shaya to awaken, and the strange energy from the mysterious clock had sped up the process.

"This is strange, this area. Are we still in the forest?" Kai Shaya asked.

"Yes and no," Wei said. "This was supposed to be the Sky-Piercing Banana Forest, but the avalanche turned the ground upside down. It has created this hundred-mile ditch for the first pulse."

"What are these four pulses?"

"I know little but what Rual'er has told me. The four pulses together are called the Ancient Decree, and it is supposed to open a path to the real Incursion."

"So there's more to it."

"Yes. The thing is that the real Ancient Decree is hidden somewhere near the State of Zin, and four ancient clocks have descended to initiate the First Pulse of Incursion. First, we have to defend this place. At least, Rual'er said that would be the case."

"Defend it from whom?"

Wei shrugged. He didn't even know what would happen if they didn't defend this place. "I only know the second pulse will be like a treasure hunt, and that's where the actual Void Objects will show up, and we can even invite others to join us."

Tun Hu, daughter of elder Yen Poe, had invited him for this phase only. It made a little sense now. Wei had many more questions.

"So there are four places like this?" Kai Shaya asked.

"Yes. Four powers have been selected to defend the places, and we happen to be the power chosen to defend this place." Wei wasn't interested in playing the role of defender, but here he was—part of the team with Rual'er, Little Fox, and Kai Shaya.

"I don't like this." Kai Shaya rubbed his forehead. "Where are the other two?"

"They're at the other side of the clock, cultivating the pills I gave them."

Rual'er had been in seclusion when the Ancient Decree had appeared in the Martial Realm. A bloody war had been fought, and finally, the Gatekeepers had won the Ancient Decree by holding up against the fourth pulse. Only people less advanced than the Houtian Realm could take part in the Ancient Decree trials, so many prodigies had died in the first trial in the Martial Realm, and when the second Ancient Decree popped up in the

Land of Empires, both powers had had very limited numbers of people. The third Ancient Decree had appeared in the Evil Host Empire, and the Gatekeepers had been fighting on that front as well. That was what Rual'er told him before she'd gone behind the clock with the little fox.

"What do they really want?" Kai Shaya muttered.

"I don't know, but this entire thing smells like a big conspiracy."

Chapter 20

The Battle Commences

Two figures appeared from the other side of the clock, attracting Li Wei's attention. They were, of course, Rual and Little Fox. They looked vibrant, their bodies shining. Although their cultivation hadn't increased, they seemed to be full of life, and their bright smiles echoed their joyous mood.

"Your gains seem plentiful." Wei smiled at them.

"Li Wei, I missed you." Little Fox jumped next to him and rubbed her face against his palm. Smiling, Wei petted her soft fur.

"Brother Wei, please accept my gratitude for that pill. It not only fixed my constitution issue, but it also healed many internal injuries that had accumulated over the years." Rual's little head bowed deeply.

"No need for courtesy, sister Rual. You've called me brother, so I have to help you as much I can."

"Didn't I tell you, dragon? My Li Wei is the best."

Wei rolled his eyes at the way the little fox talked with her. Although the little fox had a bloodline of a Nine-Tailed Fox, the dragons were the agreed kings of the beast race. It didn't matter to him as long as those two didn't fight. One was his best friend in this life, and one was from his previous life. They held equal importance in his heart.

"Li Wei, where's my treat?" the little fox growled, turning hostile instantly.

"I knew you would ask that as soon as you came out of your cultivation." Wei tossed her a few pieces of fruit he'd gathered from the other world. They had a sweet taste that could make anyone addicted to them. "Sister Rual, try these. They're great."

Rual stared at him and the fruit he was offering as if wondering if he was treating her like he treated the little fox. Wei chuckled, offering the same fruit to Kai Shaya, who tossed one into his mouth right away. Wei liked this bald monk because he was straightforward and spoke from his heart. Rual sucked in air, the fruit traveling with it. The little fox behaved more like a human, while Rual behaved the way a real beast would.

"Sister Rual, can you tell us more about the Gatekeepers?" Wei asked, munching on a piece of fruit. He would have offered everyone tea, but after the little fox, Fan Ji, and Fuishui had teased him about it, he preferred not to offer it to any beast.

"I know little." She seemed hesitant.

"You can just tell us general information. Anything known in the Martial Realm would be fine."

"Aren't you from a sect in the Martial Realm as well?"

Wei rubbed the back of his neck. This woman wasn't easy to deal with. "I was, but I came here a few years ago, and I don't have any news about the Martial Realm." He was lying, but what could he do?

"Okay." She sat on a gray stone. "They arrived one day and waged war for supremacy. They attacked multiple sects in a day, and in just a few years, they'd captured half of the Martial Realm."

"Mahataba. Half a realm? Where did they come from?" Kai Shaya asked.

"I don't know. They just showed up."

"They might have invaded the Martial Realm years in advance." Wei sighed. Although he'd reincarnated in the body of Li Wei, the world had changed. In his previous life, there had been no Gatekeepers. Much of the world had been at peace, and he'd died because he'd trusted a bitch. Since coming to this world, he'd only faced bloodbaths and conspiracies.

Whatever. The people he'd cared about in his previous life were all good people in this life as well. The world might have changed, but the people hadn't. So he would protect them all. In fact, he didn't care about the Gatekeepers. All he cared about was his friends and family, and if he had a chance, he would give up on this trial. If the Destiny Mirror Sect hadn't provoked him by killing his friends and family, he wouldn't even have waged a war on them. He'd vowed to live an easy life and walk the Path of Lazy Dao, but he wasn't able to do this because of the things outside of his control.

He poured some more tea for himself. Having a good flame meant he could keep the tea warm forever. Exactly to his liking.

The tea flowed down his throat, sending the sweet taste of honey through his taste buds. He was stuck in the current cycle of the Tea Soul Ceremony and, for reasons unknown, hadn't been able to break through in his soul cultivation after he opened his Soul Palace.

Kai Shaya's soft cry disturbed him, and Wei choked on the tea, which burned his throat. "What the hell, brother Shaya?" Wei asked between the bouts of coughing.

Kai Shaya stood frozen, his gaze glued to the ancient clock. "It's a Buddha Sacred Clock. I have a replica of this clock in my sect. Mahataba." He bent down and bowed to the clock as if bowing to his master.

Wei arched his brows, studying the golden-handed clock. Was there something special about it?

"Brother Shaya, are you sure? There are four clocks like this around the State of Zin. I doubt it has anything to do with the clock in your sect."

"I'm absolutely sure, brother Wei. This thing is called the Clock of Immortality. The rumor is that it can give life to a deceased soul."

"Are you interested in trying this to revive your brother?" Wei asked, probing Kai Shaya. Although they had grown closer as friends, Kai Shaya had never talked about his history of concocting a reincarnation pill for someone close to him.

"I can't tell you that, benefactor. Please forgive me for being rude."

"Pretend I never asked you." Wei chuckled, sipping his tea.

"Brother monk, don't go close to the clock. No one can touch it. If you try, you will be repelled by it," Rual'er said.

Kai Shaya's excited expression died down upon her warning. "Thank you, benefactor. I'll be careful."

"Sister Rual, can you tell us what will happen next? Do we have to defend this place after twenty-two hours?" One more hour had passed, so they'd been there for three hours already.

"Two hours. We only have two hours before the First Pulse will pull champions from the thousand-mile radius. If they are your friends, we will be at an advantage. If they aren't, we'll be at a disadvantage."

"What do you mean?" Wei felt confused.

"This clock..." She pointed at the clock and sighed heavily. "It has stopped time for everyone within five thousand miles. For us, five hours will pass, but for outsiders, only a fraction of a second will have passed. Every five hours for us, the clock will pull anyone within a thousand miles into this place, provided they are above the Boiling Blood Realm and below the Houtian Realm." She gazed at the area around them. "This is our battleground. We will fight with everyone within a five-thousand-mile radius. If they are friends, they will join us, and if they are enemies, they will slaughter us. And if we survive all of it, an enemy will come from outside of this world in the third pulse. It will be an impossible fight."

Wei gulped. Fuck. All he had was enemies. The nearest city was Dabuio, and as Nuan'er had said, his image was plastered everywhere as a wanted criminal. How was he supposed to defend himself from a city full of enemies?

Chapter 21

Dabuio City

A Few Hours Before in the Dabuio City

"Ju Waji, my brother, your death won't go to waste," Ju Dang said furiously as he approached the giant stone walls of the city on the horizon.

A large Three-Winged Parrot carried them faster than a normal flying artifact ever could. These new beasts acquired from the sect were good. They had strong constitutions, and they were obedient to anyone who wielded their Spirit Token. Each inner-sect disciple had acquired one, and after the beasts arrived, the sect had regained its power, which it had lost through an accident a few weeks earlier. That was when Ju Dang's brother had died. Ju Dang hadn't been able to save him as he'd been out of the sect, in the Martial Realm, on a "mission."

"Today, I'll bleed the mayor to death on your grave and let you go to the otherworld in peace." His voice choked as the parrot stopped above the walls. "Ling Wutong, get the fuck out here!" Ju Dang shouted as he descended from the bird, flipping his black metal wings from his back.

The elder from the training realm had given him the wing artifact for his accomplishments. It hadn't been a mission, in reality, but a training of prodigies from various sects handled by the Gatekeepers. The sect couldn't announce that, so they'd called it a mission before sending him, along with forty more disciples, to the Martial Realm.

The wings sent a strong gust toward the stone wall, chipping away at its edge.

"Brother Dang, smash through the wall!" someone shouted.

Ju Dang shook his head. These people from outside of the Mortal Plane treated this place as a backwater. Even he used to do that, too, but when he met others in the training realm, their powers had blown away his mind. There he'd seen people who could kill a Houtian Realm cultivator while being in the early Heart Blood Realm. He had nowhere near their powers. Only after getting the strange artifact that bonded with him had he regained his confidence. So he was a little cautious about the situation in this city. It was better to be that way than to do something he regretted.

"Brother Dang, what are you waiting for? You have the Dark Dragon's Wings!" another brother shouted.

Ju Dang frowned. With these wings, he could have beaten anyone in the Mortal Realm. He had full confidence in them and in himself. He could even beat the sect master, but many elders from the Gatekeepers had come here, along with other geniuses, so he'd had to act cautiously. However, when he'd heard about his brother's unfortunate demise into the Dabuio city, he hadn't been able hold back and had snuck out of the sect along with a few of his brothers.

"Brother Dang, let me destroy this city and fetch him," Luang Jantian said, sounding as arrogant as ever. He came from the other side of the Guinshin River, so he looked down on the Destiny Mirror Sect, but when Ju Waji had won the favor of the elder and received Earth-Grade Artifact Wings, Luang Jantian had no option but to swear loyalty to him.

"Brother Jantian is looking too lightly on this city," Wing Hoto said. "This city has many hidden dragons, and they wouldn't like people like us barging in. The mayor is just a face, but the Wang family manages the city, and I heard their ancestor has performed a blood sacrifice, allowing five of their elders to reach the Houtian Realm a couple of weeks ago. Although we don't have to fear them, we have to maintain some respect." She, too, was from the Destiny Mirror Sect and knew a lot about the area's powers. She was fat and ugly, and people didn't like her, but Ju Dang let her stick with him as he liked chubby women, and she was good in bed.

"This is why you guys are no match for people from the Martial Realm." Luang Jantian shook his head. "Anyway, why are there Houtian Realm cultivators in this sparse qi area? I remember it was just an unremarkable city of this area. There shouldn't be anyone in the Houtian Realm staying here."

"Brother Jantian, Elder said the Ancient Decree will descend in the Mortal Realm, so the qi density and natural destiny flow has increased," Ju Dang said. "People are gaining inheritances left and right and making breakthroughs daily. Didn't it happen with the Martial Realm, too, and one of the elders even broke through into Violet Palace Realm, which was impossible before?"

Luang Jantian nodded. "Yes, it was like that before." He rubbed his short beard, jumping on the city wall. "How about I use my artifact, and we steal him from the mayor's office?"

Ju Dang's face broke into a smile. Luang Jantian had a strange artifact that allowed him to teleport anyone in his sight to the place he wanted them to be. It worked for anyone under his cultivation level, and the mayor wasn't in the Houtian Realm.

"Let's do this. I want to cut him into a thousand pieces and feed his blood to my brother's grave." Ju Dang's smile deepened. It would be his tribute to his brother. Then he would find this Li Wei and kill him.

Chapter 22

Beast Rebirth Cultivation Art

The sky was the same. The moon shone brightly, and the dry air stiffened Li Wei whenever he looked at the golden clock hand. He was like a prisoner waiting for his execution with a clock hanging in his prison cell.

Sighing, he retrieved a golden cauldron from his storage ring. There was only one more hour before the battle commenced, so Wei couldn't delve deep into the Primordial Blood Palace. Although he could use the Ten-Day Time Chamber and try upgrading it, he wasn't sure if that would work in this place, so he pushed the thought away.

Placing the golden cauldron in front of him, he separated his three clones from himself. They sat close to him, each facing a cauldron. Wei retrieved some herbs and tossed them into the cauldron to process them. That way, he could increase his alchemy production by three times. At least something useful had come out of this mess he'd made of himself.

However, not all the clones could concoct Gold Grade Pills. Only the wood clone could do that. Each one could concoct pills using beast fires, but only the wood clone could enhance the quality of the pill, so he was

Wei's favorite. He called the clones wood, metal, and earth. Silly names, but he just used them.

These three were like his avatars. They had his divine sense, so he could share visions with them or even use them to do simple activities with him. However, he couldn't make them fight like him. Despite sharing the divine sense, they did not have his physical constitution or the muscle memory of the fighting stances, martial skills, or even brawling methods. They were only proficient in alchemy. And heavens, they were good at it, thanks to Xue Qi. She'd trained them in a time-accelerated environment and taught them alchemy as if they were her personal disciples. So they even knew some pill recipes he wasn't aware of.

"Brother Wei, why do these clones seem different from you and also seem part of you?" Rual'er sat next to him in an elegant stance. It was hard for her to sit a normal way, so she spread a rich-looking sheet on the ground and lay down with her front legs folded in half. Everything about her exuded elegance and royalty.

Wei poured a cup of tea for himself and offered a glass of wine to Rual'er. She'd loved wine in his previous life, and he hoped she had the same habits in this life too.

"I like wine, but can I try the sweet-smelling tea you keep drinking? I'm curious. If you don't mind."

Wei chuckled. "Why not?"

He poured the tea into the largest ceramic cup he had and pushed it toward her. A nice design of a dragon and phoenix was carved on it, and of course, it was an artifact from the Three Treasure Auction Hall. Others might wonder how she would drink the tea, but he knew she had her ways. Although she was in her beast form, she had her ways to lift the cup, using her essence energy like hands. The golden ceramic cup floated in the air, and the murky brown liquid vanished into her mouth.

"This tea is excellent." She inhaled the smoke before taking a sip, like a genuine artist who studied tea.

Wei had never seen her drinking tea in his previous life. She'd always enjoyed wine. She'd been a free spirit back then—unruly and untamed.

"One of my friends perfected it," he said, thinking about Li Niya, who had improved the tea based on Chen Chi's notes.

After coming out of the Ancient Ruins, he'd met Nuan'er and had sent Chen Du with her. But he hadn't had time to tell him about Li Niya, who looked exactly like Chen Chi, Chen Du's deceased wife. When they met each other, it would be a mess—or a blessing—and Wei could only hope they became friends and found love with each other. Everything else, he had to leave to destiny.

"Brother Wei, why are your clones different from you? They should be your avatars, right? But I've never seen clones performing alchemy before. Doesn't it require your unwavering focus?" she asked, sipping tea.

"They are, and they are not." Wei rubbed the back of his neck, collecting his words. "See, I'm a dual cultivator, but I had to disperse my qi cultivation, and these clones are cultivating it for me. So they are not my avatars but full individuals."

"They are your weakness, brother Wei. You can't lose any one of them, unlike common clones."

Wei nodded. Indeed, they were his weakness.

"Don't worry. I'll take a vow of heaven and earth that I won't divulge this secret to anyone other than myself. Thank you for trusting me, brother Wei."

Wei chuckled. Although they were his weakness, would he be fool enough to expose them in the battle? During that time, they would remain inside him.

"Don't think too much of it. They're not really a fatal weakness. My power lies in my body cultivation." He clenched his fingers, and a cracking sound thumped through the air. After reaching Heart Blood Realm, his arms were stronger than any common metal, and he could easily put a dent in an Earth Grade artifact. After all, those were Yin-Yang Arms, and their powers had reached the level of an Earth Grade artifact.

"Got it," she replied. "You must be practicing Qi Rebirth Art or something."

"What's that?" Wei asked, licking his lips, savoring the taste of honey as his fingers drummed on his thigh.

"I don't know. I was just sputtering nonsense." She smiled. "In fact, I have a Beast Rebirth Art that allows a beast to practice cultivation using clones. For each cultivation level, you have to create nine clones, and they'll accumulate energy and then merge into you, giving you their cultivation. It's fascinating, but it's quite slow because each clone has to start from the bottom, and it takes a heaven's worth of resources. However, it can be useful if you're stuck in a bottleneck."

"That's interesting. Do you have that art? I can trade it with you for a two-thousand-year-old herb."

He had plenty of the herbs, and even if he gave them away every day, he would have enough after a month or two. Rual'er's cultivation art seemed peculiar. It might not help him through his current predicament, but it might show a way or two.

"I have it here," she said. A jade slip floated toward him. "And no, I need nothing in return. I haven't even repaid you for your pill. I can't accept anything from you."

"Sister Rual'er, can't we just offer things to each other?" Wei asked, feeling emotional. This girl had helped him so much in his previous life that he couldn't repay it even if he wanted to. Whenever he'd needed something, she would be the first to help him, and not only for one or two things—she had helped him hundreds of times.

"We think alike. Let's just wipe out all the debt between us, friend." She smiled radiantly. Wei missed her human form. She would have looked beautiful right at that moment.

Sighing in his heart, he poured more tea for her and then placed the jade slip on his forehead.

System: Information interface detected. Downloading Beast Re birth Cultivation Art.

System: The cultivation art has missing pieces that match with the diagrams the host has seen before. Do you want to upgrade it with the missing pieces the host has? Yes/No.

Wait, what the hell? What diagrams?

Chapter 23

First Enemy Appears

"Diagrams? System, what diagrams?"

An image appeared in front of Wei, and he recalled where he'd seen them before. These were from the Ancient Ruins. Those dark winding corridors had held diagrams he couldn't imprint with his divine sense, but the system had captured them. That was why he didn't recall them.

This was part of the Enhancement Module, and it had already upgraded a blood array before. Could it upgrade a cultivation art as well? This was fascinating.

"Yes, do it!" he shouted, and Rual'er raised her brows to stare at him.

"Brother Wei, what do you want me to do?" she asked, her gaze laced with doubt.

"Nothing." Wei waved his hand. "I was just excited about this art. This might help me solve some issues."

"Would it? That's wonderful." She smiled—a beautiful smile even in her beast form. Wei hadn't known dragons could smile. But he again wished she were in the human form so he could enjoy her alluring smile.

Suddenly, his Yang Wood Pill Clone stirred, and a gust of wood qi slipped out of his dantian and through his arm. It entered the cauldron in front of him, acting on its own. After reaching level two, it could do some things independently, and if Wei asked it to trigger the wood qi at a certain time, it could do that. After all, it had a piece of Wei's divine sense.

"Which pill are you working on, brother Wei?"

"It's just basic Blood Nourishing Pill. My Boiling Blood Realm clone hasn't reached the peak of layer nine yet, so I'm trying to increase his cultivation. In fact, there are just two more layers."

"Isn't that a forgotten pill?"

"Is it?" Wei arched his brows. "Well, my mentor gave me the recipe, and she is not from the Mortal World, so..." It was Xue Qi's recipe, and he hadn't kept tabs on what was happening in the Mortal Realm around the pills. Maybe he should have.

"Sister Rual, are you interested in alchemy?"

"Sort of. I, too, dual cultivate in qi and body, and I sometimes make some wine and pills with my wood qi."

Wine. That made sense. But the Rual'er from his previous life had never told him about her pill concoction. Well, there ought to be changes, right?

System: Enhancement complete. Downloading Samsara Clone Rebirth Art.

Samsara - the cycle of death and life is the start of the primal chaos, the very start of the fabric of reality. Spoken in hushed tones among the echelons of ancient masters, the cultivation art is the path of transcendence. It is the silent echo of the endless dance between the life and death.

It would allow a cultivator to send his clones through the path of Samsara, through the primal chaos that defines the very existence of the universe.

Tread this path carefully. The dangers of mortality and immortality lie hidden in the shadows.

Clone Samsara Cycle:

Allow the cultivator to send their clone into the cycle of Samsara. The lower the cultivation of the clone, the faster the cycle of Samsara. Once it has survived the cycle, the clone can be reabsorbed into the cultivator's body to regain the cultivation path experienced by the clone.

Refinement Realm Clone: Four hours for one cycle. Maximum cycle allowed is one. Requires one Samsara Rebirth Pill.

Foundation Realm Clone: Twenty-four hours for one cycle. Maximum cycles allowed are two. Requires two Samsara Rebirth Pills for each cycle.

Bone Realm Clone: Four days for one cycle. Maximum cycles allowed are four. Requires four Mid-Samsara Rebirth Pills for each cycle.

Marrow Cleansing Realm Clone: Twenty days for one cycle. Maximum cycles allowed are eight. Requires eight Mid-Samsara Rebirth Pills for each cycle.

Boiling Blood Realm Clone: Two months for one cycle. Maximum cycles allowed are sixteen. Requires sixteen Peak Samsara Rebirth Pills for each cycle.

Heart Blood Realm Clone: six months for one cycle. Maximum cycles allowed are thirty-two. Requires thirty-two Peak Samsara Rebirth Pills for each cycle.

Houtian Realm Clone: Ten years for one cycle. Maximum cycles allowed are one. Require one Samsara Rebirth Flower and a thousand Peak Samsara Rebirth Pills for each cycle.

Samsara Rebirth Pill

Created from the essence of Samsara, this pill will allow a mortal or a cultivator to go through the Cycle of Samsara. It needs to be

only cultivated with Samsara Clone Rebirth Art. Otherwise, the result would be death.

Red Purple Somandar Flower

Death Poison Grass

...

...

System: Further information is missing.

Wei rubbed his stubble. This was interesting information. The first-recipe pill was simple, and he could easily concoct it with the help of Yang Wood Pill Clone. Even the midlevel pill recipe seemed easier, and he had all the ingredients, but the peak-level pill had a few ingredients he hadn't heard about before. Then there was this Samsara Rebirth Flower.

"Sister Rual, have you heard about the Samsara Rebirth Flower?"

"I have, but it's just a rumor. Do you know where the Nether Gate Valley is?"

Wei nodded. It was one of the forbidden zones of the Martial Realm. He'd heard about it in his previous life. It was a certain-death danger zone.

"Someone saw this flower there. It's rumored that just looking at it makes one go through a cycle of Samsara. It's the only way to grasp the Intent of Samsara."

The Intent of Samsara. Wei's heart thumped as if someone had shown him the greatest treasure of the heavens. Samsara was one of the rarest Concepts of this world. A person who grasped it would be unrivaled in battle.

"Brother Wei, are you aware of the Samsara Intent? How does it feel to have an Intent? How does it feel to have Wind Intent?"

Wei smiled. This girl was curious about her future path. Well, who wouldn't be? He'd been curious about it when he'd first understood the Fire Intent in his previous life. However, he had grasped the Earth Intent while he was in the qi Foundation Realm, and afterward, he'd also grasped the Concept of Earth Escape. So grasping the Intent of Wind Travel and Wind Force didn't excite him that much.

"Is that forbidden to speak about before you grasp it?" she asked.

"It's not. In fact, I can help you grasp the Intent of Wind before you break through, but you might not like the method."

"How? Please help me, brother Wei. If I comprehend the Intent of Wind before I break, I'll wield much more power."

"I can teach you archery," he said, laughing inwardly.

"No. I don't want to learn archery. I hate the thing that vile woman used. Instead, I'd study something else as my human-form skill."

Wei shook his head. "Sister Rual, don't be stubborn just because that bitch tainted it for you. Don't you like archery?"

"How do you know that?"

If she didn't learn archery, the world would miss out on a master archer. The Rual'er Wei knew was a killing machine. She could kill thousands of people with one arrow. She wielded a divine bow that sent a tremor through her enemies. It would be a loss if she hated archery just because of Wi Vistara.

"I saw the light in your eyes when Wi Vistara used arrows. Do you think she survived the avalanche?"

"I doubt it. She must be dead," Rual replied. "Don't change the subject. How would you teach me archery in this form? I can't hold a bow."

"How do you drink tea?" Wei poured more tea into her cup.

"I just suck it in. It's all about power."

"You're wrong." He poured a glass of water and started sucking it into his mouth. The water rose in the air before splashing on his face. Then he used the Intent of Wind and gently wrapped air around the water.

Although he hadn't learned the Intent, he had an elemental grasp of the wind, so he could easily direct the water into his mouth.

"That's genius." Rual'er shuddered, and she sucked in the tea, twirling it like a figure eight before it vanished into her mouth. "Why didn't anyone tell me about this? This is so easy."

"It's not easy. How many beasts from your clan have you seen drinking tea like this?"

"Very few. They just crush wine barrels in their mouths. They're brutes." Her voice had a hint of anger when she spoke about her clan mates.

"How long have you been drinking wine in this manner?"

"Since I was a child." She sipped more tea. "I don't like their brutish methods."

"You grasped it because you've used it thousands of times." Wei sent an herb to his wood clone. He'd already started processing herbs for the Samsara Rebirth Pill. Wei wasn't going to waste any time.

"That makes sense. Thank you, brother Wei. I will practice this more." A light shone in her beautiful eyes.

"Keep practicing it, and when the time comes, I'll teach you a few things to understand the Intent. Wind Intent is just an elemental Intent, so it won't be difficult to grasp, compared to something like the Intent of Samsara."

Could he gather the Intent of Samsara by cultivating the clone rebirth art?

"You're thinking too much about this. Send one of your clones into the Primordial Blood Palace, and eat that pill. Only then can you understand it," Blood Parasite said in his mind.

"Can I really do that—send my clones in?"

"If you do, you can't use your qi cultivation properly. Are you willing to have that happen?"

"Yes, I'm ready. But first, I have to concoct the pill for this."

"Do it in the Ten-Day Time Chamber. Isn't that a better way?"

"Brother Wei, the clock has stopped. It seems the battle is about to start."

The ground shook, and a white light enveloped the surrounding area. Hundreds of people appeared out of thin air. And among the hundreds of people, Wei recognized someone he knew. That person was in a dire state.

"Don't you dare." Wings exploded at Wei's back, and he shot toward the enemy.

Chapter 24

Mayor Ling in Trouble

It was the mayor, Ling Wutong, who Li Wei had detected was in danger. Wei's emotions flared up. If he hadn't sensed the aura before, Wei would have missed him. Mayor Ling was on the ground, half-dead, bleeding from everywhere. Wei's frown deepened as his wings flapped, the wind pushing him forward like an arrow. The cold air didn't affect him anymore as the Intent of Wind enveloped him.

Wei cursed as he saw a tall guy with black wings kicking Mayor Ling in his gut, sending him flying onto a gray stone. The stone shattered with the impact, and the pieces scattered. Mayor Ling whimpered. He seemed in such a bad condition that he couldn't even cry.

Fuck. Wei pushed the wind to the maximum speed, propelling him forward. Those people were too far from him, so he couldn't teleport directly, and he couldn't take too much of a chance with Purple, as she might just teleport him out of this place.

"Mayor Ling, please hold on," he said in his mind.

Mayor Ling had a close connection with Wei's grandfather Shua, and although Wei had spent little time with his grandfather, he loved him a lot. Shua's death had been a big blow. Wei wouldn't let anyone kill his grandfather's friend. Not ever.

"Mayor Ling, hold on. I'm coming," Wei transmitted again when he got closer.

"Li..." Ling Wutong tried to say something, but the guy with black wings stomped on his chest, thrashing him into the ground.

"Stop it!" Wei shouted, flashing through the air.

He was still a few miles away, and people were already shooting attacks at him from the ground. A few hundred people had arrived, and half of them targeted Wei, who was flying over them. It was human nature to attack an enemy without thinking about the power difference, and being in a group gave people false hope. Half of the people attacking him were in the Marrow Cleansing Realm, and Wei could kill them with his Heart Essence Aura itself, but he didn't bother. They didn't know who they were fighting with. First Pulse didn't give them a chance to take a breather. It had forced them into this trial and then announced Wei and his three friends as enemies.

The black-winged guy turned toward Wei. "You want to save him, Li Wei, don't you?" He gave an evil chuckle that could send dread through an opponent's spine. "Did you pause when you killed my brother? Did you even think about his family once?"

Now what? "Who the fuck are you?" Wei's mouth filled with a bitter taste as if he'd gulped down a cup of spoiled-milk tea. This was going to stink later, and he had to finish it soon.

A fireball struck, and fire spread over his metallic wings. The fireball had an earth attribute associated with it, and his wings became heavier the more it spread. Flipping them a little, Wei put out the fire. Any other Heart Blood Realm body cultivator would be in trouble taking that much fire, but he'd faced Hell Flames and developed resistance to the Inferno Fire—the wildest fire of this world—so a fire ball was nothing. It just washed over his metal wings, warming them a little. It might even have cleaned some gaps Wei couldn't clean himself without using his Heart Essence Aura. It was a tedious job that Wei had thought about hiring a servant to do.

"Don't kill him. I'll kill him!" the black-winged guy shouted at the others, and the attacks slowed down.

"How dare you not know about me when you killed my brother like a street thug with the help of this bastard?" The guy stomped on Mayor Ling's thigh, crushing it to the pulp.

"If I killed your brother, he can't be a good guy." Wei bit his lower lip. "If you don't touch this man again, I might let you live. But touch a hair on his body, and you can join your fucking brother in the afterlife!" Either way, the guy was dead. Wei might not kill the guy himself, but he would let Mayor Ling do it.

"I will kill him first and then come for you." A sword appeared in the guy's hand, and he stabbed it downward, aiming for Mayor Ling's heart.

"You were warned. Teleport." Wei rubbed Purple's fur, and he dematerialized, reappearing in front of the winged guy who'd refused to listen. For such bastards, punches worked the best.

The guy's eyes twitched, and he pushed his sword down with force. How could Wei let him kill his friend in front of him? Reaching with his right arm, Wei grabbed the sword and smashed it upward.

The winged guy tried to avoid the hit, but Wei's hand moved so fast that he couldn't. The hilt slammed into the man's nose, breaking it and sending him flying backward. He smashed through a few people behind him and crashed on a gray stone. His black wings bent at a weird angle, but they didn't break, nor did his back. This was interesting. Wei's attack should have broken a normal peak of Heart Blood Realm qi cultivator's bones like a thin bamboo stick, yet he'd survived.

"I warned you." Squatting, Wei picked up Mayor Ling and rose in the air. First he would bring the mayor to a safe place, and then he would go for the kill.

A familiar scent arose behind him. "Give him to me, brother Wei. I'll make sure he doesn't die," Rual'er said, hovering with the help of her one wing.

"Take him to my clone. He knows what to do." Wei placed Mayor Ling on Rual'er's back and turned to face the guy he'd just knocked out. "Now, are you going to fucking tell me your brother's name before I kill you?"

Chapter 25

Wyan Jim's Choice

Wyan Jim sat in the corner, watching the young man he had once met at the gates of Dabuio City fight a devil with black wings. The cool-looking guy also had wings, golden metallic ones, and he looked way better than the ugly black-winged guy.

"Li Wei. I never thought I would hear that familiar surname," he muttered.

When he'd met this Li Wei, Wyan Jim had been the guard captain of the soldiers protecting the gates of the inner city. It was a prestigious job, and he took a pride in doing it righteously. Then one day, this young man, Li Wei, arrived, punching a hole through the gate. There was no way Wyan Jim could have stopped a guy this powerful, but others didn't listen to him, and he'd been demoted, expelled, and imprisoned for the damage done to the city gate.

It wasn't fair, and he knew who'd been behind his treatment—the Wang clan. They had the most prominent cultivators in the city, yet they played dirty. If it hadn't been for the mayor releasing him from the prison for his previous good deeds, Wyan Jim would be dead in the prison, stabbed by Wang clan thugs. They didn't leave any survivors.

And the mayor hadn't received good treatment either. He'd been demoted to deputy commander after a farcical inquiry that ran for a couple of days. It had all been for show, and the Wang clan had made sure the mayor would never raise his head again.

But Ling hadn't experienced the worst yet. One day, this black-winged guy showed up, and the Wang clan handed him the former mayor. Those villains dragged the mayor to the city's main square, and the black-winged one thrashed him. Then everyone had found themselves in this barren land. Someone spoke in their minds, telling them about Li Wei and an Ancient Decree. They could fight with Li Wei as allies or fight against him and win the artifact.

"Brother Jim, whom are you going to ally with?" a man he knew asked. He was a retired guard and depended on others. He'd regressed into the Marrow Cleansing Realm yet had transported here.

"I don't know."

"Aren't you going to save your benefactor?" the retired guard asked.

"I want to, but I have no power, nor can I help the lord mayor. I'm useless." Guilt crept into Wyan Jim's heart, and he couldn't even push it away. The mayor had saved him, but he could do nothing.

"So you're a traitor." The retired soldier drew his weapon. "People like you who eat the Wang clan's food and refuse to help them ought to die. Today I'll kill you. and once that lord kills Li Wei and the mayor, I'll spit on his corpse."

Was he really useless? Maybe he was. If the mayor survived, Wyan Jim would definitely offer his life to him. However, at the moment he could do nothing but watch from the side. But he wouldn't let the mayor's name be defiled by a brute like this.

"Then I'll fight you to death. Although I can't help the lord mayor, I can kill you and make sure you don't get a chance to see his end." Wyan

Jim's weapon swung in an arc, but before it clashed with his opponent's weapon, a woman appeared right next to the retired soldier and whispered to him, turning his ears black and green. The next moment, the retired soldier dropped dead, his flesh rotting and decaying instantly.

"The mayor saved you again. If you'd agreed with him, you'd be dead too." The woman, veiled from head to toe, spoke in a soft, venomous voice before vanishing into the crowd.

Wyan Jim wiped the sweat that had accumulated around his brows. That woman was scarily dangerous.

Chapter 26

Legendary Teaching under Siege

L i Wei felt a gaze scanning him, and when he spread his divine sense, he saw the guard captain he'd met before. Another guy lay on the ground next to the captain, dead from poison. The poison felt familiar. Its smell seemed a notch more intense than what he recalled from before.

Someone he knew was here, and he couldn't be happier. A friend he could trust. Sonja. A voluptuous figure flashed in his mind, wrapped under dense clothes. Well, he hoped she wore many clothes. Otherwise, she might kill just with her looks.

Wei almost waved to the guard captain. Wei was the enemy of half of the people here, and if he waved at the guard captain, it would put him in the spotlight, and he might die even before Wei could say hi to him.

"You bastard! How dare you hit me?" The black-winged guy cursed and then rose in the air. A strong gale below the wings propelled him so that he moved like a bird heading for the sun. Those wings gave him unimaginable speed. And he was rushing toward Rual'er.

"Damn it. Teleport." Wei rematerialized right next to Rual'er, intercepting the black-winged guy's attack.

"Die, you bastard." The black-winged guy slashed his sword at Wei.

A black light surrounded the sword, and a tremendous pressure spread through it, descending on Wei and Rual'er. He felt like he was standing in a mud pool, held down by gravity's pressure. The sword attack had an attribute of gravity, and the black-winged guy was using it to suppress them. Rual'er grumbled, and her body increased in size to resist the force of gravity.

"Rual'er, use the wind," Wei said, flipping his wings faster to withstand the pressure.

"Wind? But how?"

"In some places, even the mountains can float, going against gravity. Why?" Wei asked.

"They use wind-attributed formation."

"Do you think a formation has absolute power in this world?"

"No. It depends on the forces of nature..."

"That's the way to go about it." Wei said. "Watch how your wings flip and how the wind travels everywhere. Breathe wind. That's how you prepare yourself to receive the Intent."

Wei parried an attack from the enemy. This was how he'd learned his first Intent. When he was submerged under the muddy earth water, he'd learned the Intent of Earth by staying there, struggling. Rual'er, in his previous life, was a genius with the Wind Intent, and he bet she would be the same in this life as well.

"Are you looking down on me, Li Wei?" the black-winged man shouted furiously. "How dare you teach her some blasphemous techniques while your life is about to end? Do you think one can attain the Intent by just thinking about it?"

"I'm not looking down on you." Wei punched with his right arm, using the Dragon Fist of Pain, and sent the black-winged guy staggering backward. When his fist met the opponent's sword, he felt his blood roiling backward from the impact of an immense force. "Because I don't fucking know your name. Didn't you say I killed your brother? Are you going to die without even telling me your name?"

"You—I'm going to kill you." The black-winged guy swung his sword and sent a slash of gravity toward Wei.

Every slash cut through his robe and increased the weight of gravity on him. It was exhilarating. The gravity reminded him of his connection to the earth. Although he'd learned the Intent of Wind, the earth always felt like his mother, caressing him, allowing him to learn the intricacies of her nature. Yes, he thought of her as his mother—the mother who'd never bothered to care for him and ran away having affairs with other men.

His mouth turned bitter. This wasn't something he wanted to think about.

"Mark my name, Li Wei. This one is called Ju Dang. Ju Dang will take your life and pay tribute to my brother Ju Waji with your stinking blood."

"Oh, Ju Waji. That name seems familiar." Wei rubbed the back of his neck. He'd heard this name before. "Got it. It's the bastard that looked like a pervert grandpa." Wei shook his head in shame. "Why do you care about him? He had one foot in the grave. Are you sure you want to die just because of that pervert?"

Wait, that pervert hadn't mentioned his brother's powers. These villainous guys tended to try the *brother* thing a lot. "Are you really his brother? He looked like your grandfather."

"How dare you? I was just born late."

"Then why didn't he mention you when I killed him? Don't you villain types want to spout some nonsense about your brother from the sect, your father from the pasture, or your mother from the brothel?"

"Fuck you, Li Wei. How dare you insult my mother and father?" Ju Dang flipped up, his hair turning into a mess as he smacked his forehead rapidly. "I will kill you. I will kill you. I will kill you."

"I know the reason. You're the psycho brother no one wants to talk about. No wonder he died without threatening me. Not that it would have changed his fate."

"I'll fuck your mother, Li Wei. Fuck your dad and then fuck your son." Ju Dang had gone completely crazy.

Wei sighed. That old pervert had been right to break any connection with this psycho. "I'm tired, and as for Ju Waji being a good old man and dying right away, I'll just kill you as well. At least in his afterlife, he won't have to be associated with a psycho like you. Elephant Fist of Pain."

Wei attacked with immense power, bringing a white dragon elephant's silhouette behind him. He was tired of this guy's nonsense, so he might as well kill him.

"World Change to Cotton." A tall feminine-looking guy appeared in front of him, intercepting Wei's attack.

Wei felt like he'd hit a cotton ball, and his power dissipated into the strange palms of the new guy.

"Brother Ju Dang, didn't the elder tell us to fight in combination? Are you looking to die and turn the three of us into a weak party? Are you selfish?" the feminine-looking guy scolded Ju Dang, who lowered his head.

What the heck was that? Wei floated back, spreading his wings long and tall. That feminine-looking guy's defense was strange. When Wei's attack had hit him, his hands had turned into something soft that was almost impossible to move past, and he'd then redirected the power toward the ground. A ten-foot-deep hole had appeared right below the guy, and he was floating with the help of a flying artifact.

A legendary cotton ball?

Chapter 27

She Is My Bitch

Wi Rual felt a tremor pass through her core when brother Wei asked her how the mountains in a certain area floated in the air. It was like traveling through a desert, searching for water, with a water skin tied to your waist. The mountain floated with the help of natural phenomena, or sometimes it was constructed using formations.

And both things used the force of nature. It was the Intent of Nature. Why hadn't her beast brain ever thought about this before? She felt so dumb that she wanted to hide in the earth and never come out.

Well, beasts were dumb. They didn't have wittiness or brains. They only believed in raw power. Which was fine. But she had a human mother, and she'd always believed in doing things the human way, like using swords, bows, and formations. Her father had never allowed her to try those things. He'd been the happiest when she'd taken the beast form.

She would have loved to have had a human form, like her mother. But nature had done whatever it did, and she came out as a human but had reverted to the beast form within seconds. It was weird to think how that had happened, but nature allowed it, so she didn't dwell too much on it.

Anyway, the important thing was the connection she'd never felt before. Now it was like her eyes were opened to the laws of the world—not the real laws, but she'd been put forward on a path, and she could already feel things changing around her. It was so simple that she couldn't believe it. Nature allowed the formations to borrow their power in terms of supporting the mountain with the force of wind against the force of gravity.

"Brother Wei, is it that simple? I can't believe I missed such a small thing. Why didn't you show up before?" She giggled, feeling dumb. Maybe her father's side made her dumber than other humans.

"Of course not."

Brother Wei punched hard at the guy who looked like an ugly girl wearing a man's clothes. If he hadn't had a bulge at his crotch, Rual would have called that man a girl. The way he cast his skills—heavens, he lacked anything that made a man a man. But he was weird. His glove allowed him to withstand brother Wei's full-power attack.

"It's not so simple, sister Rual. If it were, you would have found an army of Houtian Realm cultivators around us." He shook his head, avoiding an attack from Ju Dang. That guy, too, had a pair of wings that controlled gravity around him. "What I told you is only the simplification of the process. Intent is just a start, and then there is Concept, Fragment of Codex. I just showed you a path toward the first step." He flipped his wings, sending the female-male away with the wind. "See? I don't know the Intent of Gale or Intent of Blowing Winds, but I can still use it in elementary form because I believe nature is full of concepts. Feel them with your heart, and you shall find a way."

Rual almost cried. "I understand, brother. I'm glad I met you. I know what I have to do now." Intent with intention. Although her father had never told her the secret of Intent, he'd always said to do anything with intention. She just had to follow his advice and mix it with brother Wei's advice."

"You bastards. Why are you talking shit while we're fighting?" Ju Dang shouted, his sword swinging like a hungry beggar's chopsticks on a bowl of rice.

"Shut up, you moron!" she shouted at Ju Dang. "Brother Wei, please continue. Your words are more beautiful than my father's teachings."

"Bitch, what are you trying to do here? How dare you lay your guard in front of me?" A girl appeared in front of them, standing on a Vibrant Red Sparrow, a low-level beast that had advanced to the peak of Heart Blood Realm. It squeaked at her, but when Rual spread her Heart Essence Aura, it shivered in fear and dropped down.

"What a fool. Have you gone crazy, woman—trying to intimidate a dragon with your peasant beast?" Rual giggled.

The human girl jumped out, fear rushing through her eyes. "What did you do to my beast?"

"Wing Hoto, you are a fool to pull out your beast in front of a Winged Dragon. Do you see any of us using a beast?" A thick, burly guy materialized, sitting on top of a flying rod. "I knew you were chubby, but I guess you grew the same flesh in your brain too."

The girl called Wing Hoto charged up, flaring in flames of fury. Even Rual'er disliked this new guy on the rod. How could he insult a woman based on her looks? If a woman insulted another woman, it was fine, but when a man insulted a woman, she went crazy.

"What nonsense." Rual's wing flapped, and she flew at the guy on the rod.

Suddenly, brother Wei appeared in front of her. "Sister Rual, please help the mayor. If you try to dance here, his condition will worsen."

Rual realized she had a refugee on her back. "I'm sorry, brother Wei. Don't get angry. I'll take him to the other side."

"A girl named Sonja will find you at our side. She's a friend, so don't attack her, please."

Rual'er felt ashamed. Her curiosity had almost made her harm a person brother Wei cared about. "I'll go away. Don't worry. I'll save him." She flapped her wing and shot away from the battle. She would be back, and then she would kill that rod guy for daring to insult a woman.

But now she had to find this woman named Sonja. She hoped she wasn't ugly like others she'd seen. Was she brother Wei's girlfriend? That would be troublesome.

"That woman is a bitch!" Ju Dang shouted at brother Wei, and she froze, waiting to hear how brother Wei replied.

"She is," brother Wei said, and Rual's heart fell to the bottom of her stomach. Did brother Wei hate her for asking too many questions? "But she is my bitch, and no one can insult my bitches."

Brother Wei's aura rose exponentially, and so did the flower in her heart. Brother Wei liked her.

Chapter 28

Blood Parasite's Vow

"**S**he is." Blood Parasite spoke through Li Wei, who felt like he was hearing his own voice through a sound-capturing device. "But she is my bitch, and no one can insult my bitches."

The world turned darker, the air choked him, and the scent of dread filled his heart. Wei lost control of his wings and felt a deep jerk as he fell. To counter it, he pushed his Heart Essence Aura below his legs and stood on it. Fuck, it was hard, and his aura was getting out of control.

"Sister Ru..." He turned back to watch her reaction.

Blood Parasite had gone mad, and he wanted to kill Wei. Yes, that bastard definitely wanted Wei dead. Why would he call a fine lady a bitch otherwise?

"Brother Wei, I didn't know you had this naughty side to you." Rual'er's words floated on the air as she dashed away from him.

Wei rubbed his ears. Had he heard wrong? Was there wax stuck in his ears?

"Blood Parasite, what the fuck was that?" he roared in his mind. "Are you trying to get me killed?" He ducked, avoiding the sword slash from Ju Dang. This guy and the cotton ball guy were like cockroaches who refused to die.

"Li Wei, how dare you look down on us and stand there doing nothing? You deserve a thousand and ten deaths."

Wei arched his brows. "I'll give you only one death. Keep the others to yourself."

"What? I did you a favor," Blood Parasite replied, his voice full of pride. "I like that girl, so it's obvious you'll marry her in the future."

"Fuck! What is wrong with you?"

"You fucker, how dare you tease me for my burly looks? You look down on me too much, Li Wei!" Ju Dang shouted, his fury exploding.

Wei felt rage bubbling in his heart. The tang of metal spread over his tongue, and he sliced down with his bloodred sword while activating the three fingers of the Five Finger Blood Sacrifice Array. The sword merged with the world and cut through the gap between Ju Dang's wings. It left a big gash on his back.

"Brother Dang, are you all right?" The cotton ball guy dashed over and collected the falling Ju Dang.

"I'm fine. How did your sword merge with the world?" Ju Dang asked Wei.

"As if I'd tell you." Wei shook his head. It was Reverse Sword Flash, but he'd failed to cut the enemy in two. This was bad. "Why didn't it work?" Wei asked in his mind, feeling down. "I lack power in my Sword Flash. This shouldn't be happening."

"You've lost the touch with the sword. It was because of losing your qi cultivation," Blood Parasite said.

"But why? It doesn't make sense. Intent of Sword—Sword Flash—and qi cultivation have no connectivity."

"Of course they have. Your Sword Flash came from the skill you practiced after learning qi cultivation. It formed a flaw, and as you lost your qi cultivation, you lost the connection that enhanced it."

"This makes little sense." Even though Wei had merged with the world a moment before, he could feel the lack of power. If he could have, he would have cut the opponent in two. "Blood Parasite, you were a Sword Saint, so you should have a solution, right? I love my sword, and I don't want to lose it."

"You can always practice the Intent of Sword with a cheap sword. Practice a million times, and you might learn the Sword Image once again."

Wei shook his head. He didn't have time for that.

"Kid, you have to marry her. There is no other option," Blood Parasite said, his voice shaking in excitement.

"What the hell are you talking about? Why would I marry her? And even if I wanted to, do you think she would marry me after you called her a bitch, using my voice? I'll be glad if she doesn't slap me when we meet again. Stop treating me like a child, Blood Parasite." Wei cursed, dropping his wings to keep the sword from touching them.

Ju Dang had recovered surprisingly fast, and he was already attacking him again. The latest time that sword touched Wei's wing, he felt like he was carrying a mountain on his back. The feeling was not good.

"Heck, your answer wouldn't fool even a child," Wei added.

"Kid, she has Royal Blood of a Winged Dragon. As pure as your Nine-Tailed Fox concubine. Aren't you due for blood essence consumption? If you can consume her blood essence, you'd get a nice ability. So I helped you in bedding her."

"What? Bedding her?" Wei pushed himself off the ground and leaped toward the cotton ball man, but a fatty on a rod appeared and swung his rod at him.

The rod expanded into a metal pillar and struck him hard on his chest. Wei felt as if a boulder had hit him, and he flew toward the ground like a cannonball falling from the sky. In the blink of an eye, he crashed like a meteor drilling into the earth. After dozens of feet of drilling, he stopped.

"That was nice." Wei flipped into the hole and flew out.

While floating, he brushed the dust and pebbles off his robe. The fall had been avoidable. Otherwise, he could have used the Intent of Earth to avoid the drilling. But he wanted to test his metallic wings, and to his joy, they performed extremely well.

He cleared his mouth of the dry dust then landed and splashed his face with fresh water from his storage ring, instantly feeling refreshed. The frigid water provided a much-needed respite. He sought solace in the stillness of the moment, finding the peace he needed.

After Blood Parasite's cheating, he needed an anchor to remain grounded. Rual'er would be pissed off, and he would have to do everything he could to reduce her fury. It wouldn't be easy. When women held a grudge, they did it for a lifetime. All he hoped was that she wouldn't take him to be a pervert who drooled over beast women. Yes, there were such people who liked to...

Whatever. He didn't let his mind wander to the dark things humans were capable of. Once she transformed into human form, he might think of really marrying her. But for now...

"I'm not asking her for any essence blood," Wei said. "You know my thoughts about absorbing someone else's blood."

"Come on, kid. It's not like you're drinking it. Just use your devour bloodline after you sleep with her. She won't disagree to giving you a little blood after doing so much for you." Blood Parasite snickered.

"I don't have the devour bloodline, Blood Parasite. Wait, what did you say?" Wei felt the world swirling around him. Damn it—was this Blood Parasite a pervert in reality?

"You have it, whether you agree to it or not. You have the devour blood-line, and you can do wonders with it and Blood Essence Body Cultivation Art. You're just acting like a coward, not accepting your fate."

Wei shook his head. This guy blurted a lot of nonsense when he allowed him to, but Wei didn't retort as he used to. Blood Parasite was tough, acted like a dick, and talked nonsense most of the time, but he hadn't stabbed Wei in the back like Xue Qi had, except once when he'd tried to force-feed Wei Wood Source. But in his defense, they'd had no feeling of camaraderie at the time. They'd been like fire and water, each trying to kill the other on every occasion.

Wei sighed. Blood Parasite had changed over the months and years, and Wei had too. Blood Parasite had turned into an ally Wei could count on.

"Blood Parasite, are you still going to take over me once you get the chance?"

"Why do you ask such a nonsensical question?"

"Because you told me you would try that once I broke through into Heart Blood Realm. In fact, you had multiple chances when I was weak, at my wits' end, but you didn't try possessing me," Wei said nonchalantly. He'd forgotten about their conversation until that moment.

"I will," Blood Parasite replied after a brief pause. "Once you defeat that bitch and turn her into a slave, I'll definitely possess you. After all, I can't just let that bastard go who captured and turned me into a slave."

Hate and pain flooded his voice. Whatever Blood Parasite's past was, Wei guessed it wasn't simple, nor was it peaceful. He called himself Sword Saint, yet he was reduced to being the slave of the Primordial Blood Palace. His sadness touched Wei's heart.

"How about I let you control my body and do whatever you want to that bastard? As long as you don't drink blood, I won't say anything. Will that reduce the pain of your heart?" Wei flew away, avoiding the metal-rod fatty.

"Will you let me do that?" Blood Parasite asked, his voice full of hope and shock.

"Of course. You're like my brother, after all," Wei said.

No sound came for a brief amount of time, and just when Wei thought Blood Parasite didn't want to answer, a sob slipped from him—a sound full of deep feeling. The hatred and pain in Blood Parasite's heart echoed through that sob.

"Thank you, Li Wei. You've grown into a true man. I won't say much, but I take a vow of heaven and earth that as long as you, my brother, don't betray me, I will never betray you, nor would I take advantage of you like that bitch did. Even if the yama king came, I would stand in front of you and take him for a stroll."

A strange emotion flooded Wei's gut. In a good way. It was the first time they'd connected like this, and he wasn't used to it.

"Thanks, and don't worry. I'll never betray you. I'll kill you if you force me to do something I don't want to, but I'll never betray you, even if it means I have to fight with a god, devil, or ghost," Wei replied solemnly. This was the oath of a brother, and he would never betray what he believed in

.

"Wing Hoto, are you done playing? Come here and fight with us, and you, too, fatty—Buta. We need to combine our artifacts and beat this bastard once and for all!" Ju Dang shouted, and two people joined him and the cotton ball.

It seemed like they were getting serious. This was finally getting interesting.

Chapter 29

Little Fox Takes Action

L i Wei stretched his right arm and then his left, waiting for the four clowns to finish their preparations. What the heck were they doing—pulling each other's artifacts out? It had been forty seconds, and they hadn't attacked him yet. If he'd wanted, he could have smacked their asses to the ground by now.

"Are you done, guys?" Wei asked, sipping cold water from a leather skin. Rual'er hadn't returned, and he hoped she wasn't pissed off because of Blood Parasite's derogatory comment.

But going by her response, she'd seemed okay with it. Was she into trash talk or something? He shuddered at that idea. Blood Parasite's vile thinking was infecting him, and he suddenly smelled like a bad person to himself.

"Control, Wei, control." He lightly slapped himself.

"Wait, you bastard. We'll kill you once and for all!" Ju Dang shouted, his voice panicked as he couldn't pull off the cotton ball's artifact gloves.

Those gloves looked dirty and too tight for his skinny hands. Had he even cleaned them before wearing them? What if they smelled like their previous owner? It was dirty and unhygienic. If Fei'er were here, she would have a panic attack, looking at those gloves.

"Guys, tell me if you need help, but don't ask me to touch those stinky gloves. I feel like vomiting my morning breakfast just looking at them, and trust me, I had a nice sweet baked potato and heavenly tea," Wei said, rising a little higher to check on them. "Fuck! You're still stuck on those dirty gloves. That cotton ball is useless. You should have picked someone else. He's like a glue stick. No wonder you can't pull the artifact out of his hand." He shook his head in disappointment.

The other three had separated from their artifacts. The fatty had the rod, Ju Dang had the wings, and the girl had ladies' shoes. They were definitely combining their artifacts, and he wanted to experience it and try some of his own moves against it. The cotton ball seemed like the weak link. He looked more like a girl—not that Wei was against girls. In fact, he was surrounded by powerful girls who could give him a run for his money, Fei'er, Nuan'er, Yang Fang, Nai Fang, Sonja, and now Rual'er. But he liked people to either be women or men.

"Cut his hands. Do it fast," Wei said.

"Bastard, shut up, and let us do our work."

"What are they doing?" Little Fox appeared next to him, rubbing her head against his arm.

Her fur had become softer. Wei bet Fei'er would love to cuddle her and sleep next to her. Fei'er loved everything soft and comfortable. Even the clothes she stitched were the most comfortable in this world.

"Where are you, Fei'er?"

"Are you missing her, Li Wei? She must be fine. Don't worry." Little Fox stared at him with pitiful eyes.

"I know. But she should have been with me. We could all have gone on vacations, lunches, dinners. I hate this fighting sometimes." Wei sighed. "Guys, time's up. You have ten more seconds to get done, else I'll attack," he said, frustrated by the foolishness of the four people.

"Li Wei, your other girlfriend showed up," Little Fox said.

"My other girlfriend?"

"Sonja."

"She's not my girlfriend." Wei glared at the little trouble fox. "Don't make up things, or she'll misunderstand. She's just a good friend."

"And what's up with that dragon girl? You can only have one beast girlfriend, and that's me. Get that straight, mister."

Wei's soul almost jumped out of him. "What has gotten into you, Little Fox? You're like my little sister, so don't speak nonsense. I'll find a big bad wolf for you once you transform, and you can have cute little wolf kids, and we'll all play."

"No, I will marry you only. My mother asked me to follow you, and I'll be your principal wife."

Wei coughed. This little fox had her head twisted by bad thoughts, and he would have to put some good things in it. Principal wife? Really?

"Wait there—we're almost done!" Wong Hoto, the girl on the bird, shouted, cutting cotton ball's arms with a sword slice.

She really did that. The cotton ball hadn't expected it, and he wailed in pain, blood leaking from his arms.

"What a pussy. He can't even cut his own hands out." The fatty shook his head and stabbed the metal rod into shoes, then into the wings, and finally into the bleeding gloves.

The four items glued into each other and formed an energy shield around them. Although it looked like nothing to Wei's eyes, he scanned it with his divine sense, and it seemed powerful.

"You motherfuckers, how dare you cut my arms? How am I going to hold hands now?" the cotton ball cried, his hands bleeding continuously.

Wei cringed. Although he'd asked them to cut their friend's hand, he'd been joking. He would never do something like that to a friend. To an enemy, yes, but to a friend, absolutely not.

"You guys have no redemption. Let me send you into the afterlife quickly." Wei retrieved his bloodred sword. With his wood clones away and safe, he could only rely on his body cultivation. "Cotton ball, you made some bad choices in your life, and I pity you." His fingers were clenched around the hilt, his blood rushing toward the Five Finger Blood Sacrifice Array he had carved on the sword. Before, he'd only been able to activate three fingers of it, but now he wanted to try activating four fingers and see what happened.

"Li Wei, wait. Let me show you my new power." The little fox flashed in front of him like an empress. "Just watch how this lady protects her man."

She opened her mouth, and a small ball of a fierce gale formed in it. Gales clashed into each other before settling into a rhythm, and then the ball started growing. Wei arched his brows. That ball packed some real power. In fact, it looked small, but just being close to Little Fox felt like standing in a valley filled with deathly astral winds that could rip apart a devil.

Essence energy swirled and got sucked into the gale ball as the ball kept getting bigger and bigger. Gradually, it took on a golden hue, resembling the setting sun. The gale ball continued to expand, reaching the size of a human head, causing cracks to form in the ground beneath it. Wei's clothes fluttered in the wind, and he regretted not keeping a single clone to himself to form a qi shield to protect them.

As the little fox pushed more power into the ball, it turned deep gold before it matched the gray in volume. The ball turned silent. Stone broke into pieces, and a depression formed on the ground. A deathly silence covered the battlefield. Some people fighting in the distance stopped and turned to look at the battle scene. Wei held his breath in anticipation. It would be the first time he got to watch Little Fox's real power, and he was excited.

"Die, you bastards." Little Fox sent the gale ball flying toward the four people.

Wing Hato grabbed the four artifacts by the rod and coughed a mouthful of blood on them, and they merged into her body, giving her a strange look. The artifacts stuck out of her so she looked like a clown dressed with weird props, but Wei knew it wasn't as simple as that. The shoes on her leg shone with a bright-red light as she got ready to kick the gale ball. Suddenly, the gale ball changed direction and flew toward a bunch of people a few miles away from them. Wei's heart dropped as he saw the guard captain he'd met in the Dabuio city. The gale ball was super fast, and it packed enough power to obliterate anyone below Heart Blood Realm. The guard captain couldn't survive this, nor could the other innocent people with him.

"Little Fox, control the gale ball and send it somewhere else," Wei said.

"I can't!" Little Fox cried. "I don't have control over my attack. I can only send it out."

Damn it. The situation had turned worse. Wei couldn't watch innocent people die like this.

Chapter 30

Blown Away by a Gale Ball

Li Wei pushed his Blood Earth Force Divine Art to the peak and used his Heart Essence Aura to form a few defensive shields in front of him. As the gale ball rushed toward him, he regretted not searching for or practicing any defensive divine art. With the help of his five blood clones, he could have stopped this attack easily. Nor had he prepared some defensive formations. What was the use of being an Array Master in his previous life if he hadn't used the knowledge wisely?

It had to change. Soon enough. At that moment, he couldn't use anything but his own body because the blood clones were fragile little pieces in front of an absolute power like this.

Smoke rose above the ground wherever the gale ball flew over, and Wei had no option but to reach forward with his bare hands and stop the gale ball because he couldn't use any attack to neutralize the incoming attack. If he did, everyone around him would be blown apart.

Was he going to face a defeat like this? Damn it. No. He would not be a sore loser who gave up at the first hint of defeat. He had many trump cards. He was supposed to have one that could still stop this attack.

"Yin Yang Hands, it's time to show what you're made of," Wei muttered as the gale ball destroyed all his defensive shields and crashed against his palms.

A burning sensation spread through his arms as if he'd accidentally put them into a furnace filled with scorching oils. The winds inside the gale ball were rotating at a fierce speed that turned it into a weapon sharper than anything else. Just the outer shell of the gale ball had enough sharpness to cut through Wei's skin and attack the muscles and bones in his palm.

Fuck. A fear rose in his heart. Yes, he was afraid. If this continued, his arms might just blow up. Although he could regrow flesh and muscles easily, or even regrow a piece of bone, he would be doomed if both of his arms blew up. Either it would take an insane amount of time to regrow them slowly, or he might just lose them until he found a pill that was Earth Grade or better.

But how was he supposed to concoct an Earth Grade pill without his hands? A chill ran through his bones as he searched his mind for new ideas, but none came.

"This isn't working. I have to teleport away with the guard captain. Why did I let the little troublemaker attack? Damn it." He turned away to check on the guard captain, who was running away from Wei.

In fact, everyone was running away from Wei's location, but with their speed, they wouldn't survive the gale ball's attack. Wei's curiosity was going to kill many innocent people in the vicinity. But what other choice did he have?

Wei was about to pull his arms back when something moved in them. The threads that had merged with his arms awakened with a strange energy, emitting gold and black. A strength he'd never experienced before broke out of his arms, and suddenly, they felt like someone had turned his blood into the heaviest metal in the world.

"What is going on?" Wei roared in his mind, trying to control his arms so they wouldn't just drop to his sides.

Was this the same rune he'd got from the Yin Yang Divine Worms? It had to be similar. Otherwise, why would his arms feel so much heavier than before? The rune was carved in his divine sense, and it weighed like a world, so Wei hadn't dared to bring it out of his Soul Palace. It could literally crumble his divine sense if he exposed it.

"Blood Parasite, any idea what's happening with my arms? Is it the weighted rune the worms transferred to me?"

"Don't insult it by calling it a weighted rune. It is more than that. This is something else, but it has a connection to those Yin Yang Divine Worms. This is the union of yin and yang. Something that shouldn't be happening in your arms."

Wei used his Heart Essence Aura to support his arms so they wouldn't droop. They were still emitting a gold-and-black aura, suppressing the gale ball easily. In fact, his arms were rapidly healing, as well, without him needing to use any of his trump cards.

"Tell me everything. I can't hold this anymore." Wei was losing his control, and he didn't know what would happen.

"Yin and yang make the world, and they can take any form. The Yin Yang Divine Worms have many powers, but they only transferred you the power of weight to crush heaven and earth because you excelled in the Intent of Earth."

"What the hell? Does it have anything to do with this?"

"Of course. Once your soul learned the power of that rune, the yin yang threads somehow awakened in your arms, and they're using the same power as the original source has given you."

"It makes little sense, but how do I control it?" Wei thought hard but couldn't find an answer.

Wait. He recalled the worms had left something in his mind. They'd said he would forget it once he walked out.

"System, did you record what the Yin Yang Divine Worms left for me? I think my memory was wiped after I left the strange world."

System: The host has received a Divine Art called Yin Yang Thread Divine Art.

"I know that, but there's nothing in there. It just talks about the fate lines or something."

System: The first layer of the divine art revealed itself when the time froze. Does the host want to read it?

"Go ahead!" Wei roared, pushing his Heart Essence Aura to the peak. In only a minute, the innocent people would be out of the gale ball's impact range. If he could hold on, he wouldn't let them die even if he had to take a grievous attack.

System:

Yin Yang Thread Divine Art

Layer One.

A strange melody played in his mind, and he felt a divine power passing through him and enveloping the yin yang threads imbuing his arms. The melody calmed the threads down, and the pressure on him decreased. Then the music stopped, and the weight of his arms increased again.

"Fuck, what just happened?"

"Wonderful. I never thought a divine art could be this powerful. Kid, you are fortunate. Too good. This art is even better than the fourth level of the Blood Divinity Sword Art," Blood Parasite said, sounding pleased for some reason.

"Are you two playing with me? I heard nothing but a musical tune. Where is the divine art?" Sweat dripped down his neck, and the impact of the gale ball had reached the peak.

"Strange, but I know the reason. Your cultivation is too low for you to understand the cultivation art. Once you reach Violet Palace Realm, you'll definitely understand it."

"This is cheating." What the heck was going on? Why was the cultivation art those worms gave him extra powerful? The first one had required him to reach the Houtian Realm, and the second one required him to reach the Violet Palace Realm.

Wait.

"System, can you tell me the first-layer content on the loop?" The music started again, and the heavy pressure from his arms lifted, leaving him with breathing room. "Now we're talking."

Wei smiled as he pushed his palms forward. The threads had made his arms like an impenetrable fortress, and the gale ball couldn't destroy his skin anymore. However, with the pressure, he'd also lost some power, and the gale ball burned his palm because of high friction.

If it ended there, he would be fine, but his arms, which were tiny compared to the big gale ball, couldn't stop the entire destruction, and the ball's power slipped through the gaps, assaulting his chest and mouth. Although it wasn't a full-force attack, and his arms had burned more than eighty percent of the attack, the remaining power was enough to skin him alive. First, the robe vanished from him, and then his skin cracked under the immense pressure before his muscles turned to mush.

"What a fool. Sacrificing himself for mere mortals. It's an irony that he died from his companion's attack," one of the people around him said. Although everyone had left the vicinity, some fools were still watching the show.

Wei's lips, or what remained of them, curled in a wicked smile as he let a small current of wind slip through his arms. It thrashed the person who had opened his mouth and turned him into nothingness. He deserved it.

"Suppress." Heart Essence Aura slipped out of Wei like an avalanche and pushed the wind energy back into the gale ball, easing the pressure on his entire body.

Burning a few blood pearls, he quickly healed the most grievous injuries. And then he focused on the gale ball and suppressed it, using his both hands, until it was squeezed into a tiny ball. Although tiny, it packed enough punch to kill anyone under the Houtian Realm.

"Teleport." Wei flashed to the cotton ball and tossed the tiny gale ball into his clothes before teleporting away.

The cotton ball's face twisted in fear as he tried to push the gale ball away, but before he could do anything, the gale invaded his skin and he exploded into pieces of skin and blood. A giant hole appeared where he'd stood as Wei had pushed the gale ball toward the ground. The cotton ball was just a byproduct of the real attack.

"Now it's your turn." Wei hovered in the air, looking at the trio, who were drenched in fear.

Chapter 31

Killing Ju Dang

"How dare you? How can you kill him?" Ju Dang stuttered, his face flashing through all the colors of fear, shock, and anger.

If he became any redder, he would look like the cherry on the white pie Nuan'er had made for him the other day. That had tasted yummy, and comparing this bastard with Nuan'er's pie was insulting her. No more comparing things to food in the heat of the battle.

"Are you trying to look stupid, Ju Dang?" Li Wei asked, suppressing a chuckle. This was one of the stupidest questions he'd heard that day.

"What nonsense. Just stay there, and I'll kill you."

Wei almost dropped and rolled on the ground, but he feared his new robe would get dirty, and he didn't want to mess up with the soft fabric again. The Heart Essence aura prevented the blood from his skin to dirty his robe, so he was fine where he was.

"Why are you laughing, bastard?" Ju Dang asked.

"I gave you time to finish combining your artifacts into a formation, but that was a mistake. Not again. It's time for you to die quickly."

Wei burned his blood pearls to heal the injuries to his face and chest. After reaching Heart Blood Realm, he could heal surface injuries like these in a matter of moments, using his blood pearls. The Muxi's Blessing and

Blood Water Healing Divine Art were reserved for grievous injuries. Before teleporting, he'd donned a new soft black silk robe, and he guessed he looked like a devil with peeled-off skin. Once again, he missed his chubby features. If he had more fat on his face, he might have looked handsome.

Anyway, it wasn't the time to dwell on this. Once he reached the Houtian Realm, he would just bring all his friends and family away from this place and live a nomadic life. All this fighting and massacring was taking a toll on him. But that was for the future, and he had to kill a few to scare the others.

"Fatty, I'd start with you. I hope you don't smell as bad as the cotton ball there." Wei shifted the five blood clones out of him and attacked with Blood Sword Tearing through the Earth, but he didn't use the Will of the Skill form. The last time, it had almost torn through his bones and brought this Ancient Decree in advance. He couldn't take that risk for a fatty as weak as this.

The blood sword image smashed through the air, sending gales around the sword's path. The fatty with a rod panicked. He coughed a mouthful of blood onto the artifact formation. The combined artifacts launched forward like a war puppet but with one source of energy missing. It lacked its former grace and speed. By allowing these bastards to build the artifact formation, Wei had made a mistake, but it wouldn't happen again. Curiosity wouldn't kill the cat anymore.

Wei sent Heart Essence Aura to lock on the shiny shoes tied to the bottom of the rod so it couldn't kick away Wei's attack. When the shoes flew up to strike the sword, Wei's Heart Essence Aura tied it down, letting the bloodred sword go through and clash with the metal rod. The listless cotton gloves tried to hold back the sword, but they'd lost most of their power with the cotton ball's death, and the blood sword cut through them like a spoon cutting through a tender piece of meat. The gloves fell, their connection with the artifact formation broken.

"Aw, you broke it!" Fatty cried, spitting more blood onto the metal rod. The rod expanded into a pillar, blocking the sword.

The blood sword hit with the metal pillar, sending sparks as thick as lightning bolts shooting around. Ju Dang and Wing Hoto leaped away, their faces full of fear. The blood sword continued pushing forward, suppressing the metal pillar.

"Brothers, help me!" the fatty cried, blood leaking from his orifices as he tried to push back with his metal pillar.

The sword continued surprising him, but no one came to his help.

"Cowards." The fatty chuckled. "Li Wei, you've pushed me to use my trump card. Now you can die in peace knowing that you've provoked someone from the Lightning-Splitting Sect."

Fatty's laugh turned evil. A pair of books flew out of him and formed chains of lightning in front of him, stopping the blood sword. The sword and the lightning chains clashed against each other, grinding the energy from each other, but the blood sword had used a lot of energy already by hitting the artifact formation. The sword lost in the end and dissipated in the air.

"See, Li Wei. I can defend, and now I'll attack."

"Interesting." Wei nodded. Those books looked like a powerful artifact, and his Blood Lightning Pill Clone had stirred as soon as it sensed that lightning. "Did you say you're from the Lightning-Splitting Sect? I know those brutes. They lust after women and are hated by everyone in the Martial Realm."

These people had harems as big as a small country. Wei hadn't encountered them in the previous life, but he'd heard about them, and he hadn't liked them because of their barbarian ways.

"Let me take those books from you and send you to yellow spring." Wei teleported next to the fatty.

"Die, bastard." The books appeared in front of Wei, shooting arcs of thick lightning. "I knew you would try to sneak attack me, so I was prepared."

"Oh, you mean prepared with some lightning? Let me show you what kind of lightning I have. Lightning Emit." Wei chuckled, and a storm of lightning spread through him, enveloping the books and the fatty. This was only a fraction of the lightning he had inside his dantian, yet it instantly burned the fatty to death. It was a super killer move, but Wei rarely used it as it took him too much time to refill that lightning, and he wasn't sure if it could kill a peak of the Heart Blood Realm cultivator easily. He'd only used it here because he didn't want to hurt the book artifacts by using any other move. The books, now ownerless, flew into Wei's body obediently.

"It was fast. The lightning power has increased by a lot. Good thing," Wei muttered.

"It's not that strong, but the fatty had no other trump card," Blood Parasite warned him. "Or he was overconfident in his lightning. These books are Earth Grade artifacts, so study them. They are storing Earthly Lightning, which you would face soon enough."

Wei frowned and sent a divine transmission to his Blood Lightning Pill Clone. It reluctantly let go of the books. If he'd let the pill clone absorb the books, Wei would have regretted it later.

"Thanks, buddy. I'll give them back to you back once I study this formation." Wei scanned the books. They felt thick and contained a lot of mystery. A formation protected them, and small arcs of lightning continuously shook out of it. They couldn't hurt Wei as his skin was already immune to common or tribulation lightning, as long as it was a one-shot event. "I'll have to study these carefully after the fight." It was the one thing that made Wei happy in this entire fight.

"Give it back, bastard. That's brother's Twin-Lightning Book Treasure, and it belongs to the Gatekeepers. If you steal that, the Gatekeepers will hunt you and your family down!" Wing Hoto shouted, her face reddish brown.

Wei could smell the fear radiating from her body from a few dozen miles away. "Gatekeepers?"

"Are you afraid now, peasant?" Ju Dang chuckled. "You should be. The Gatekeepers are not someone you can provoke. They are the gods of the Mortal Realm, and soon, they will rule the entire world. Just give us your head, and we will beg the master to spare your family."

Wei chuckled. It seemed like these newborn babies didn't know about Wei's relationship with the Gatekeepers yet.

"Babies, who is the most-wanted person for the Gatekeepers in the Mortal Realm?"

Ju Dang scratched his nose. "We don't know."

Wei rose in the air, pointing his index finger. "Any guesses?"

Wing Hoto shook her thick head. "Why do you want that information? We asked for your head. Just cut it already. You can't even defeat us, and you want to defeat the most-wanted person in the Mortal Realm. Give up on your thoughts of capturing him and begging your life from the Gatekeepers. That's not happening. That bastard Li Wei is a hell lot more powerful, and we have been given instructions not to provoke that demon master."

"Li Wei," Wei said.

"Yes, I remember his name now." Ju Dang had a look of a sudden understanding. "You two have the same name, but you're no match for him. Give up, and give us your head."

Wei was speechless. Was there someone else named Li Wei?

"It's me, morons." Wei shook his head. These two were really idiotic. How could the Gatekeepers accept such fools into their organization? Wei didn't want to, but now he really looked down on them.

"Impossible. You look nothing like the blood-drinker demon master they spoke about. He has six hands and ten heads. He's as giant as an elephant." Du Jang scratched his head.

"Heavens, I must kill these all bastards, and I should start with you first." Wei flashed toward the duo, aiming to finish this quickly.

According to Rual'er, this battle would last five hours, and then it would be time for the clock to bring more people in. Half an hour had already passed, so Wei didn't want to waste any more time. Although this battle had taken little from him, the little fox's attack strategy had really disappointed him. So he only had three members in his team.

"Li Wei, you killed my brother, so give me your life." Ju Dang charged with his sword.

Wei grabbed it with his right hand and punched Ju Dang with his left. "I'd be worried if you had your artifact on you, but now you're nothing but an ant."

"How dare you, Li Wei." Wing Hoto came charging at him, but Rual'er appeared out of nowhere and smashed into her, sending her away from the battlefield.

"Brother Wei, quickly finish this. We have to make some battle strategies for the next one." Rual'er came back, charging at Wing Hoto.

"Battle strategies?"

"Yes. We have three hundred people joining us, and others are dead. That follower of yours has some nasty poison on her."

Wei smiled. Sonja had shown her real skills, but he felt worried about the conversation he would have to have with her about Xue Qi.

"Keep her alive. We need to get some information from her." He flashed next to Ju Dang and ran his sword through his throat. Wei had had enough of this, and it was time to finish quickly.

Chapter 32

Won Lian's Frustration

"Fuck off, bastard." Won Lian tapped on the earth, creating a fissure that shot a barrage of sharp earth spikes at the guy floating in the air with the help of mechanical wings.

"Don't forget my name. You should tell everyone about me, including your mother, father, girlfriend, son, daughter, nephew, and grandmother!" the mechanical bastard shouted, flying around him like an annoying insect.

It had been ten days since this mechanical bastard had started following him and pestering him, almost making Won Lian cough blood in fury. "What is wrong with you? I can't handle you anymore, so just piss off!" Won Lian shouted.

Won Lian had been casually walking on a road a few days before, trying to comprehend an Intent of Nature, and this guy had shown up, demanding that Won Lian spread his name far and wide. Won Lian had just ignored him at first, but then he'd started hurling curses at him, and Won Lian had attacked.

"Why won't you spread my name? First tell me this."

"Fuck you, mechanical bastard. Did you even tell me your name?" Won Lian connected with the earth at a deeper level and raised a spike from the ground that shot at the mechanical bastard.

"If you agree to spread my name, I will let you go." The mechanical bastard dodged the earth spike.

Won Lian almost flew in rage, but he recalled that he had to practice peace and calm if he wanted to connect with nature. Maybe this was his tribulation, and if he could pass through it, he would comprehend the meaning of nature and peace. Then he would have a place among those freaks who called themselves the Chosen Gold. What a shitty name, though.

Suddenly, he felt an immense danger, and he vanished into the earth, but before he could escape, a dagger cut across his arm, drawing a trail of blood. Earthen armor appeared around him, and gravity pushed him away through the ground. It was his Intent of Gravity, and he'd traveled a few dozen feet using it.

"Who are you?" He stared at the petite girl with brown hair tied in a ponytail. She looked fifteen years old, but she was a Blood-Colored Assassin and a top one among them.

"Hui Ma. I'm your friend, so don't worry."

"Why are you here? And why the heck did you attack me if we're friends?" Won Lian asked, his heart beating faster and faster. Hui Ma—he'd heard about this woman and knew she was absolutely ruthless. It was wise to avoid her.

The girl giggled, wiping the blood from her dagger with a white cloth before tossing it away. "I was just checking to see if you can touch me. Guess you can't."

"Don't provoke me, girl. You might be one of the top five assassins of the Blood-Colored Assassins, but I'm a reserve Chosen Gold, and I can fight with you to a standstill."

"Without your artifacts, you are nothing." She snorted coldly before vanishing into the void.

Yes, she was dangerous because she had comprehended the Intent of Void.

Chapter 33

The Gatekeeper's Plan

Hao Juwan knelt in front of the golden mirror. An elder's image appeared in it, flickering slightly, but Hao Juwan didn't move. Elder Hong was a divining master of the Gatekeepers, and his words were law in Mortal World 44. And after what had happened in the Dimensional Gateway Trials, he didn't dare do anything. A big name had vanished as if it hadn't even existed, and he didn't want his name to be next.

"Junior Juwan greet, Elder Hong." Hao Juwan bowed deeper after he heard the tap of Elder Hong's golden cane.

"Junior, move half of your peak of Heart Blood Realm juniors to near the Five Firmament City."

"Elder Hong, are we going to attack the city? We were still preparing until the main force from the Martial Realm arrived."

"No. Ancient Decree has descended in advance, and it will fetch the Five Firmament City in the third or fourth wave, and we need our warriors to go in and finish them."

"Elder, I don't have enough manpower. All the new people have been sent to conquer the Crimson Moon Kingdom, and they haven't returned yet."

"Send them a message to go near the Five Firmament City quickly. Use the forbidden teleportation formation if needed, but I need them near the Five Firmament City as soon as possible."

Hao Juwan gasped. "But, elder, they have that Demon Killer, Li Wei. He is insanely powerful. He killed half of our people in the Dimensional Gateway Trial."

He thought about what had happened to Elder Juwa, who'd vanished after the fiasco in the Dimensional Gateway Trial. Hao Juwan didn't want to be another Elder Juwa, and he didn't have enough manpower in the peak of the Heart Blood Realm to face Li Wei, who ate Houtian Realm cultivators for breakfast.

"I'm transferring Demon Regression Pill. Choose a hundred early Houtian Realm cultivators, and feed them this pill. It should be enough to kill Li Wei and destroy the power of the Five Firmament City. I'm also calling the Blood-Colored Assassins and tenth batch of the Chosen Gold to hold the Third Pulse against the Outerworld's entity. This is a golden chance to get this Ancient Decree and win this Incursion."

"But, elder, a hundred Houtian Realm cultivators? They're our peak force until the main force arrives. What if Buddha Vasta Pagoda Kingdom attacks us?"

Hao Juwan couldn't believe what Elder Hong was suggesting. The Demon Regression Pill was a demonic pill that allowed a cultivator to regress in their realm without a reduction in power. It had a severe disadvantage, but people could mitigate that by using clones. The pill was mainly used to visit the secret realms that had cultivation restrictions.

"Should we wait for the Chosen Gold to appear? They can finish Li Wei with their left hands," Hao Juwan said.

"Don't worry. There is a Soul Beast wreaking havoc in their kingdom, so they're busy dealing with that. Also, I'll send an auxiliary force to keep them busy. Just do what I tell you to do."

"Junior will carry out the plan." Hao Juwan bowed when the image flickered.

This might be suicidal, but who was he to say anything? It was a good thing Elder Hong hadn't asked him to regress in his cultivation. And for the Buddha Vasta Pagoda Kingdom, it wasn't his problem."

Sighing, he got up and walked out. The pills would be here soon, and he would have to use Temporal Teleportation Formation to transfer the poor souls to near the Five Firmament City. It would be wasting a year's worth of the resources of this wasted sect, but what could he do?

Chapter 34

Infernal Flame Palace

"This was just the first wave. In the next wave, a thousand-mile area will be scourged." Rual'er sat next to Li Wei and Sonja on a soft shawl. Her tail rested against her back, and she leaned on her front legs elegantly.

"Lord, please allow this maid to boil some tea for you." Sonja got up and bowed to him. She was walking away to give him and Rual'er privacy.

"No need. I have tea prepared. Just stay here," Li Wei said. "Your opinion is important as we prepare for the next wave."

He retrieved his favorite tea and set it to boil with the help of his mutated beast flame. It instantly grew in size, enveloping the cauldron, producing a heat that warmed their moods. The fragrance of the honey mixed with butter added a nice touch, thanks to the beast flame which could instantly reach the desired temperature—well, calling it a beast flame would be an insult to it. The thing had mutated into something else after it had gulped down a hell flame. Was it a hell flame? No. Hell flames couldn't be controlled, so it wasn't a hell flame.

"Lord, I might not be any help to you." Sonja stood there, staring at him with her two-colored eyes.

"Sonja, I was busy fighting the four people and protecting others while you swooshed through the battleground and cleared out the enemy. So we need you. Just sit with us, and enjoy the tea." Wei patted the place next to him, and Sonja nodded.

"Then let me massage your back while you talk." She stepped back to him, and her soft fingers rubbed his shoulder.

Wei had to fight hard to prevent a moan from slipping out. Fei'er used to massage his back, and she'd been awesome. Sonja had the same grace and skill.

Little Fox joined them in a moment and sprawled near Wei, keeping her face on his lap as if she owned him. "Li Wei, I subdued the four beasts. They're from the Beast Origin Realm."

Little Fox sent a mental message to Wei. After he'd killed Ju Dang and others, four peak of Heart Blood Realm beasts had flown out of their bodies and tried to attack, but Little Fox had charged at them and suppressed them with her bloodline pressure. Wei frowned, but before he could ask any questions, Rual'er spoke.

"Brother Wei, you have a lot of female friends, don't you? The little fox was telling me about your habit of collecting woman around you," Rual'er said mischievously.

"I collect friends, Princess. Not women," Wei said, annoyed. He didn't like getting labeled like this.

"I'm sorry. I didn't mean to..." She paused when an old man walked toward them. It was Mayor Ling, who looked much better than he had when the Ancient Decree had brought everyone here.

"Sister Rual, I saw many people leaving this site. Where did they go?"

"To another Ancient Decree. There are four like us, and each is five hundred miles apart. People who are brought in waves can choose to go to another decree if they wish."

"So we can go as well?"

"No. We are defendants, so we can't anymore."

"Senior, thank you for saving my life." Mayor Ling walked close and bowed deeply, his face flashing a hint of red. With Wei's pills, he'd recovered to half of his potential in just half an hour.

"Uncle Ling, please don't call me senior or bow to me." Wei got up and helped Mayor Ling stand straight. "Forgive me for not telling you about this before, but I'm Li Shua's grandson. Li Shua from the Old Martial City."

He retrieved a small chair and helped Mayor Ling to sit on it and then handed him a little insignia that his grandfather had given him when he'd asked to go and see the mayor.

"My grandfather asked me to come to you if I was in trouble." He poured the Honey-Buttered Tea into a golden ceramic cup and handed it to the mayor first and then to Rual'er and Sonja. "I assume you had a deep friendship with my grandfather, so let me pay my tribute to his soul by offering you a fine tea."

Mayor Ling's face twitched. "Old man Shua. I knew he was dead when the soul tablet broke, but my promise stopped me from going out for him," the mayor said, sounding lonely at the loss of his friend. "Are you Li Tang's son or Li Jia's?"

"I'm Li Min's son," Wei answered, his words wavering as he thought about his mother.

"Are you really Li Min's son?" He reached out with his palm and caressed Wei's cheeks. "I can't believe the little guy who used to poop in his pants has grown this much. But then, a tigress can't birth a ship, so it's given."

Wei coughed hard before looking at the faces of people around him. Although he couldn't detect any emotion on Sonja's face, he saw a sneer in Rual'er and the little fox's eyes.

Damn it. "Uncle Ling, like every other small kid, I might have done something embarrassing. There's nothing odd about that." Wei forced the words out. What was this old man up to, talking about some shameful things right out of the gate?

"I agree—it wasn't embarrassing. The most embarrassing thing was when you tried to cut your little thing with a knife, saying it stuck out in the morning and made a tent in your pants."

Wei almost coughed blood. What was wrong with this old man? Who said such things in front of girls?

"Uncle Ling, we were talking about strategies. It's good to have an experienced person to put his view forward," Wei said, switching the subject before more *poop* or *little thing* stories came out.

"No, we want to hear more about your childhood." Little Fox gave a mischievous laugh.

"Call me Grandpa Ling. Who is your uncle? Your mother used to call me that when she was little."

"Grandpa Ling, do you really know my mother?"

Grandpa Ling's face twitched. "I know her, and I knew your father as well. Too bad he had to rush away before they came searching for him."

Wei frowned. "Uncle—Grandpa Ling, can you tell me what really happened back then?"

Grandpa Ling looked around. "Let's talk about it some other time. Let me give you something your grandfather left with me for you." He played with the insignia Wei had given him and got up.

"Grandfather left something for me? Why would he do that? I was with him when he sacrificed his life." Emotion choked Wei's voice.

"Child..." Grandpa Ling walked away from the crowd, and Wei followed him. When the little fox tried to tag along, Rual'er pulled her back by the tail. Rual'er was sensible.

"Grandpa Ling, did you want to say something to me?"

"I bet old Shua was hard on you over the years, but whenever we talked, he always mentioned how much he regretted casting you away."

Wei froze. "Grandpa Ling, what does that mean?"

He'd guessed his grandfather's intention, but he could never confirm it with Grandfather face-to-face, and Wei regretted that. Their relationship had gone from hatred to respect to love in a short amount of time, and he missed that fatherly love after he lost his grandfather, who was the only reason Wei wasn't ready to give up on the Li clan, even though they betrayed him constantly.

"I know little about your family's secret, but your grandfather loved you the most. He was in a lot of pain when he had to send you away with your stepfather, but that was his only choice. Don't blame him for that. He was a good guy. He never wanted to do that, but keeping you with him would have attracted trouble for you. You might have lost your life because of a single mistake, and he didn't have the power to shield you from the enemies who came from outside of the Mortal Plane."

"You're making it sound mysterious, Grandpa Ling." Wei chuckled.

"Am I, now?" Grandpa Ling walked to a large stone and sat on it before sipping the tea. "Nice tea, nephew. Your mother used to make the best tea, and she loved the tea made with Three-Butter Honey like you have prepared. It really brings back a few memories."

Wei paused. His mother, that witch who'd run away with a man, leaving him to fend off the world, had also liked the tea. Was this fate or a cruel joke?

"Grandpa Ling, do you know why she ran away with a man?"

"I don't know. I only heard it from your grandfather, but I doubt she ran away. Min'er was one of the most content and understanding women I ever saw in the younger generation. She married your stepfather only to save you from your enemies, but I know she never liked that man or let him touch her. Your grandfather used to praise her for her loyalty to your father."

"Then why did she marry that bastard? Was it difficult to raise me alone? Wasn't she a cultivation prodigy?" Wei snapped. The hatred he'd buried in his heart bubbled to the surface like lava.

"You wouldn't understand her feelings, kid. If she hadn't done that, you might not have survived. Anyway, she'll tell you the truth if you ever meet her in a higher Plane."

"Do you know about Planes?"

"I shouldn't, but by meddling with your family, I got to know a little about the secrets of this world." He chuckled and sipped more tea. "Child, I have nothing to say about your mother or father, but I insist, don't hate your grandfather. He was a nice man, and he loved you dearly. He even left this for you."

A pendant appeared in his palm. It was exactly identical to what his grandfather had given him before.

"Li Wei, that's the Infernal Flame Palace!" Blood Parasite shouted in his mind. "I never thought you would get the second Chaos Genesis Palace. This is an opportunity, Li Wei. Maybe the biggest opportunity of your life."

Wei felt a shiver down his spine. Could such a thing really happen?

"If you put some of your blood in this, it will show you a message from your mother. She might have answers to a few of your questions," Grandpa Ling said, sending another tremor through Wei's spine.

Chapter 35

The Truth about Li Wei's Mother

Li Wei grasped the green pendant in his palm. It had the same cold touch as the first one but had a few engravings that differed from that. Thanks to the system, he could see and compare the pictures despite having the first one merged into himself. The major difference was that this one smelled like blood—his blood.

"Grandpa Ling, before I try this, can you tell me more about the enemies my grandfather feared?" he asked, ignoring Blood Parasite's excitement.

Blood Parasite wanted him to bring the new pendant into the Primordial Blood Palace, but Wei wanted to understand what his grandfather had gone through first. He only had a few memories with Grandfather, and rest of his life was a blank page. The Primordial Blood Palace could wait—the emotions in his heart couldn't.

"Your father came from a powerful clan—one that didn't belong to this Mortal Plane." Grandpa Ling put the teacup down on the gray stone next to him before wiping his mustache. "He came here for a mission, or that's what he said. He said he got injured, and your grandfather found him on his last breath. Your mother was just sixteen, the age for marriage, and your father promised to bring her to the higher Plane for saving his life."

Wei frowned, the lines on his forehead reaching his hairline. "Wait, it wasn't love at first sight between my mother and father, or my mother looked after him, fed him some good food—like the Honey-Butter Tea—and he fell in love with her?"

"What nonsense. She couldn't even take care of her own injuries, so how could she take care of your father?" Grandpa Ling chuckled. "It was a purely a business transaction, and you were born in a couple of years after their marriage. Your mother couldn't cook anything good to steal the heart of a young master like your father. All she could do was roast some meat over the fire and sprinkle some salt and call it a dinner. Once, she called us old men to her house for food and fed us boiled chicken. Can you believe she only had that much food in her house?" Grandpa Ling gave a heartfelt chuckle.

Wei smiled sheepishly. It seemed like his mother wasn't good with worldly matters.

"What happened after my birth?"

"He left when you were little and never came back. After him came the demons searching for him, and they found his trace in your clan."

"Demons?" Wei asked.

"Humans. They called themselves Demon Serpent clan members, and they were here to capture your father. They said he was a criminal of their master's clan, the Yan clan."

"A criminal? But you said my father had a giant clan. Didn't they intervene?"

"No. That's the twist. Your father was surnamed Yan, and the Demon Serpent clan worked for the Yan clan. They said your father was expelled

from the clan for doing some criminal activity. But I know nothing else."
He sighed.

Wei felt like someone had run a dagger through his brain. What kind of twist was this? His father was a criminal of his own clan and had taken refuge here and then married his mother as a business transaction and then ran away from his own clan?

"Then why the hell did he marry my mother when he didn't love her? I bet my mother wasn't a beauty."

Grandpa Ling chuckled. "Min'er wasn't a beauty, but she was a beast in body cultivation. She had a rare physics called Blood Yin Physics, and we later found out that your father cultivated with her to get her yin seed."

"So he was a jerk and nothing else." Wei's heart stiffed. Who knew his father had been a trash person? Even a beast was better than this. How could his father use his mother just for the sake of her yin seed?

"He was and he wasn't. Before he went back, he left a path for your mother to follow him and also covered you with a strange protection charm that protected you from the Yan clan's tracing methods. Do you think you'd be alive if the Demon Serpent clan had found out about your birth secret?"

"Then Li Sua, my stepfather—how did he come into picture?"

"It was Min'er's idea. To prevent anyone finding out about your biological father, she married your stepfather and pretended you were his newborn."

"That meant my mother wasn't a flirt..." Tears rolled down his cheek.

"I won't comment on that. I liked Min'er like a daughter, and she was a strong woman who took on the world for the people she cared about. She took risks to achieve what was hers, and I bet she traveled outside to get your father back. She had a strong sense of possession, and she wouldn't have liked to lose what was hers—your father."

"Do you know what this pendant is?" Wei pointed at the green pendant Grandpa Ling had given him.

"This was a gift from your father to your mother. It had two parts. Your mother gave one to your grandfather and one to me. She only said it would be useful if you were powerful enough to wield it."

"Thank you, Grandpa Ling. This is a priceless artifact."

"Could you open the first piece? Your mother said you could open it only if you reach the Houtian Realm or walk the path of blood cultivation."

Wei pressed the pendant into his palm, feeling conflicted about his parents. Although he hadn't given a thought to his father, he'd literally hated his mother for being a flirt and running away with a man, leaving him, a child, behind to fend for himself.

Everything had changed. Her mother didn't like other men, but his father's action had forced her to marry someone else. Unless he could meet his mother, the mystery of her marriage with his stepfather would remain hidden.

However, that didn't change the fact that she'd left him alone and to go do whatever she wanted to. They both were jerks, in their own way, and if he ever met them again, he would definitely call them that to their faces.

"Grandpa Ling, thank you for your help. Please allow me to hear my mother's message." He lifted the pendant and dripped blood on it.

A storm of blood brewed out of the pendant, swirling around him and bringing him into a golden corridor. It was similar to what he'd seen before in the original Primordial Blood Palace, but this one looked richer than the other. A woman stood at the end of the corridor, smiling at him. She wore a golden dress and looked to be in her thirties. Exactly as he remembered.

"Wei'er, you've finally unlocked the secret of your blood." She smiled.

Despite hating her, he couldn't resist being happy to see that smile once again. She'd left him when he was small, but he still remembered the warmth of her touch, the beautiful smile, and her voice brushing against his ears.

"Mother, I won't say the same to you because you ran away from me. Why did you do that?" Despite wanting to remain calm, he couldn't hold his emotions inside him, and they burst out like the water from a broken dam.

"Did I? Did I really leave the little you?" Sadness lurked on her face. "Then I'll apologize. I can't think of a reason the future me did something so cruel."

"Don't you know the answer?" Wei asked, his rage clashing against his throat, wanting to unleash itself on this woman. "It's you, so you should have thought about this."

"I'm sorry if I did that, Wei'er, but I sealed my blood essence before that must have happened, so I don't have any memories of it. It must be hard on you, living alone in this brutal world. I hope Father took good care of you after I left. How is he doing?"

Wei sighed. It was the memory-sealing method. He'd known about these techniques. One could seal memories for future generations. "He is no more, but he took care of me."

"The age must have been hard on him." His mother sighed, a lone tear dropping from her eyes. "He was always good to me. More than I deserved."

"Mother, why did Father leave us? Was he really a criminal for his clan?"

Her face twisted, the smile fading, and anger flashed through her eyes. "I don't know. We were not that close, but he absolutely loved you. He made sure you would live a happy life if you couldn't cultivate, so he sealed his bloodline's power inside you." She flashed forward and touched his forehead.

A tear fell from Wei's eyes as he savored her touch once again. The warmth and the sadness overwhelmed him. Although he knew they weren't here physically, it seemed so real.

"He hasn't awakened it, mistress. The bloodline remains dormant inside him, and it might be better for him if it stayed that way, as it would invite troubles he can't face right now." Blood Parasite had appeared next to Wei. They were like brothers now, and Wei didn't mind how much Blood Parasite knew about his messed-up family history.

"Sword Saint Sheng, I see you regained your control of your soul. It's a good thing."

Blood Parasite bowed deeply, a mask still on his face. "This lowly one thanks the master who first loosened the threads of fate between me and the bastard who must not be named. Then this kid helped me break the last remaining thread of slavery. If not for this kid's help, I would still be the bloodthirsty blood slave trapped within the first palace."

"You knew my mother and father, and you didn't tell me about them?" Son of a bastard.

"I knew, but a blood oath prevented me from saying anything. Forgive me, brother."

"And yet you were trying to possess me?"

Blood Parasite chuckled. "Kid, didn't that act as a motivation for you? When you awakened the Primordial Blood Palace, I wasn't myself, and I really wanted to possess you. But thanks to your blood essence, I regained my memories, and the inevitable didn't happen."

"Do you think his father would leave you in a child's hands without placing a restriction on you?" Mother said in an icy tone.

"You mean...?"

"If you had tried to possess him, his father's bloodline would have wiped you out." She gave an evil smile. "Anyway, that's not important. Now that you're walking the path of blood cultivation, you can unlock the secrets of the Yin Primordial Blood Palace. Only a pure-blooded blood cultivator can unlock these secrets. I wonder how many demons you devoured using your bloodline. Isn't it exciting to devour powers that could kill you and then make them yours?"

Wei shook his head. "Forgive me, Mother, but I'm not a pure-blood cultivator. I walk a dual-cultivation path. I cultivate both Qi and Blood, and I won't be walking a different path from this."

"No, son, you can't do this. Blood cultivation is the supreme path, and you need nothing else."

"Mistress, I've tried to convince him so many times, but he doesn't listen." Blood Parasite sounded disappointed. "However, please don't blame him. Despite having not awakened his father's bloodline, he has gained a single truth that the world can go mad for—absolute Will. Just having that inside him is as good as having both of your bloodline powers."

His mother's face lit up with a smile, reminding Wei of flowers blooming in the first rays of the sun. "Where did he get it?"

"I don't know. He already had it before he opened the first palace."

"First palace?" Wei asked, feeling confused.

"Yes. There are nine such palaces, and the second one is called the Infernal Flame Palace."

"You mean it has nine levels?"

"No, dummy." His mother giggled, tousling his hair. "There are nine palaces, and each may have one to three levels. It depends upon which palace you found. The second palace your father gifted me was the Infernal Flame Palace. It allows one to enhance their artifacts at level one and enhance pills at second level."

"So they need me to get blood from higher-level cultivators to open them?"

"Of course not. With the second palace, you can open the first palace's second level without a hitch. In fact, you may be able to open the first level of the Infernal Flame Palace using your Violet Realm Blood Essence. We won't be wasting it to open the second level of the Primordial Blood Palace anymore."

"So, are they together called the Chaos Genesis Palace?"

His mother nodded. "We only know its name, and your father said it is a supreme artifact from the Genesis Era. No one knows more details about it, but you have to be careful and not let anyone know about these palaces, or they will bring calamity to you."

"Mother, did...?" He bit into his tongue. Was it really the case?

Chapter 36

Father's Real Crime

"Yes, your father stole these palaces from the Yan clan, but it's not as simple as you might think. There are things I can't tell you right now, but trust your father. Don't hate him," his mother said, her face turning a little blurry. "Or maybe hate him a little. He left us in this world, so hate him as much as you want." She giggled, looking proud of her little t rick.

"Mother, your face—it's fading." Li Wei felt a tug at his heart. He wasn't ready to let her go yet.

"I know. My time's almost over, my little boy." She caressed his face gently. "I only have a minute or two, so ask whatever you want to ask, and I'll preserve some strength to move these memories to the real me."

"Where is your real self, Mother?" he asked, hiding his pain. Seeing her slowly transforming into motes of light broke his heart. "Forget about it. Just let me hug you a little more."

"Come on—hug your mother, and we can still talk." She wrapped her arms around him and tousled his hair like she used to do when he was a little kid.

"I want to know everything. When you were my age, how was your relationship with Grandfather Shua? And tell me more about Father's clan and where can I find him, or you."

If he'd known he had only little time, he would have hugged her from the start, not letting her go away. He'd hated her when she'd first appeared. Even now he hated her, but he hugged her anyway. This was confusing, yet he knew he loved her deeply.

"You have so many questions." Her soft hand rubbed his back, the scent of her motherly love invading his mind as he eased into her embrace.

Wei smiled sheepishly. Although he resented her for leaving him alone in his childhood, he was curious about her. He had no plan to search for her, but he still wanted to keep the door open. And though he hadn't asked anyone else about it, he still wanted to know how she'd been as a mother.

"It will take a long, long time to answer your first question, so ask me once you find me."

"Where can I find you? You know where you'll go after leaving Mortal World 44, right?"

"I don't know. I was searching for your father's information with the help of your stepfather, but I kept meeting dead ends. If I left you, then I must have found some information about your father, and it must have been urgent to make me leave you alone here."

"Don't you know anything about him? More details about his clan?"

"I know little. He never talked about it, and it was fine, as he hated his own clan."

"At least tell me his full name," Wei said.

"Yan Tian. He once told me his clan was one of the major clans in the Planes, but he never told me which Plane. Anyway, my real self must have found it." Her body became thinner as she melted into energy.

"Mother, Grandfather Shua died trying to protect me. I'm sorry I couldn't save him." Tears streamed from Wei's eyes. This was one of his biggest regrets. If only he could have saved Grandfather.

"It might not be the case, my child. The reincarnation cycle of this world is broken, so he might not be dead at all. I can't talk more to not attract the wrath of the heavens, so take care, my son, and I'll pass on your image to current me. I can't sense where she is, but I can sense that she is alive and watching you through me." She turned to face Blood Parasite. "Sword Saint, I entrust my son to you. As the final task for the favor my husband did for you, please look after my son."

Blood Parasite nodded, and Wei's mother turned into specks of light.

"Goodbye, my son."

"Mother!" Wei cried as she vanished into the motes of light and entered him.

"Consider it my gift to you, son."

System: The host has reached layer one of the body Heart Blood Realm.

System: The host has learned the Blood-Sealing Illusion Art.

Blood-Sealing Illusion Art

Divine Art

Grade: Human Grade

Create an illusion with blood that will trigger at a certain condition. The illusion will become a reality for the ones who enter it, and any injury might become real for the ones who enter it if their realm is lower than the creator of the art.

"Mother..." Wei felt like someone had broken his heart once again. It had first been broken when someone told him that his mother had abandoned him. This time, he missed his mother.

"I apologize for not telling you this before." Blood Parasite sighed.

"Sword Saint Sheng, do you know anything more than this that you can tell me about?"

"I prefer that you call me Blood Parasite. I know some things I can only tell you when you leave this Plane. I'll warn you about one thing. Don't underestimate the original owner of the Primordial Blood Palace—the person who enslaved me—to get out of a prison."

"A prison?"

"Yes, he is imprisoned in a secret realm, and he was using this Primordial Blood Palace to get out of there, but he failed because of you."

"If he remains in the prison, why would I need to fear him?"

"Because you're the owner of two palaces now, and he used to own five of them. So when you get in touch with four other palaces he owned, you'll face the Blood Slaves of those palaces."

"We will see when the time comes. I doubt I'd find one of these palaces in the Mortal Realm. Forget it. Let me bind this Infernal Flame Palace with me so I can see what goodies it has packed." Wei felt a little better at the thought of the loot he would soon get out of this entire situation. Although he was a little sad, he knew his mother was alive, and that was enough for him.

Yan Tian. Wei would definitely search for that name one day. There were too many things he wasn't satisfied with, and he would ask this guy for answers.

Chapter 37

Artifact-Enhancing Room

The world turned darker, and stars appeared in front of Wei's eyes as the Infernal Flame Palace sucked blood out of Li Wei like a giant leech. It reminded him of the Primordial Blood Palace's first time. It had almost killed him. The blood loss had been so severe that he'd fainted back then. Unfortunately, that powerless feeling had returned.

"Fuck! Blood Parasite, what's going on? Why is it sucking so much blood?" Wei flopped onto the gray stone so he wouldn't fall down and attract attention. His skin had shriveled, and his arms had turned gold and black, reverting to their original color. He had used a skin-concealing pill, which needed a fraction of his blood to conceal his arm colors, but with his blood loss, that effect had vanished instantly. "This is unbearable at this cultivation level." Wei groaned.

Being at a Heart Blood Realm body cultivation meant he was immune to such things. The closer he got to the Houtian Realm, the closer to nature he was. His body used to exude a thick fragrance that attracted birds and butterflies if he meditated in the deep forest. People called it losing one's mortal air and walking the path of being an immortal—well, for common mortals, a Houtian Realm cultivator would be like an immortal. However, the effect had vanished, and he felt rotten inside his mouth, as if he had regained his mortal air.

"It's nothing. Your blood is your cultivation, so losing it means there will be some unfortunate side effects. Just hold on, kid. It won't suck you dry," Blood Parasite replied, his voice full of confidence and sulk.

What was he upset about?

System: The host has lost 60% of blood. Recommended to burn blood pearls to replenish the blood.

Damn it. Wei had almost forgotten about the basic use of his blood pearls. Had the blood loss made him dumb for a moment or two?

After burning a hundred pearls, the life returned to him. The world turned brighter, and he regained the sweet taste in his mouth. He quickly chewed on the Green Fragrant Potato to top up the taste. Finally, he felt like himself.

"That was brutal." Wei brushed his fingers against the Infernal Flame Palace, which had half embedded itself in his chest. It emitted a warmth. He wouldn't need to worry about the cold ever again. Not that he ever worried after breaking through into Foundation Realm of body and qi cultivation.

"Give me the Violet Palace Realm blood and Purple's blood."

"Why do you need Purple's blood?"

"This is not the Primordial Blood Palace, so we shouldn't waste the Blood Orchid Beast's blood, and you won't give me fox blood, so Purple is the best candidate."

Shrugging, Wei passed a drop of Violet Palace Realm cultivator's essence blood and Purple's blood to him. He kept Purple's blood on him always so he could use the Teleport ability from the Primordial Blood Palace. Purple was the best and gave him blood of her own accord.

System: Infernal Flame Palace has accepted the host's body. Access to the first level is granted.

"Let's go," Blood Parasite said, and Wei materialized in a red corridor the color of the deepest depths of lava. The corridor emitted intense heat, but it didn't bother Wei. He felt like he was in a place where he belonged.

"The Infernal Flame Palace will allow your body to grow closer to the various flames of this world. It's not instant, but over a decade or more, you will slowly gain mastery of the fire."

Wei humphed. Good. He wasn't going to reject a passive benefit.

"What are those?" Wei asked, pointing at the two rooms at the end of the corridor. Although the doors looked the same as those for the rooms in the Primordial Blood Palace, he knew they would have different uses.

"One is Ten-Day Time Chamber, and another is the Artifact-Enhancing Room. The second level will grant you access to flame-cultivation arts."

Wei paused, turning to face the masked old man. "Has the second level of the Primordial Blood Palace opened up?"

"It will once this palace is integrated into your body. It will take some time, but not too much."

"Will I get the Blood Essence Body Cultivation Art's second part? I've no way of breaking through into the Houtian Realm without it."

"It should be there, or you would find enough blood cultivation methods you can choose from. The third room, which we didn't visit last time, has those cultivation arts."

Nodding, Wei headed toward the first door. Blood Parasite tapped on his shoulder and directed him toward the second one. The door opened into a big room filled with many types of equipment that Wei was familiar with. A large forge, made of golden metal, sat in the corner, and an intense fire burned underneath. It was earth fire, the same one present in the alchemy room of the Primordial Blood Palace. However, the intensity of this fire was much higher than the one in the alchemy room. Of course, artificing required a higher degree of heat, so that was given.

Stepping forward, Wei picked up an intricate metal anvil. A dragon's head decorated the metal handle, and the anvil weighed like a boulder. "Good weapon. Reminds me of my old days." Wei swung the anvil and hit the forge, releasing a metal hum that felt good to hear after so many years. "Do I have to craft artifacts myself?"

"I don't know. But this formation should be familiar to you." Blood Parasite pointed at a corner with a formation set up on a large metal floor. Wei rushed forward and squatted next to the formation with tears in his eyes.

"Why are you crying? Have you grown weaker after meeting the mistress? I understand. She is your mother, after all."

"Of course not." Wei brushed his tears away. "You wouldn't understand the heart of an Array Master. You would feel the same if I'd reunited you with your own sword."

"When did you become an Array Master?" Blood Parasite asked, his voice full of suspicion. "I've been watching you since you were an ant, and I don't recall you gaining any tome or secret inheritance on arrays and formations. So how are you this good at them?"

Wei chuckled. "That's my secret. Anyway, this is a long-lost Ancient Formation that I've only read about in books. It's called Dragon Breath Bestowment Formation."

"What does it do?"

"Dragons are the gods of fire and smelting, and this formation brings a dying dragon's breath back to this world."

"Dragons? I know a race of dwarf humans who excel in forging and artifact making. I never heard of a dragon making an artifact. They are powerful but kind of dumb."

Wei shook his head. "I've read about those dwarfs and even met a few, but I've read their ancient records, and they mention a dragon forging god in the ancient history. Isn't it obvious? Dragons are quite old, and they have the purest fire, so it makes sense they had someone capable of becoming a god."

"How do you know about gods?"

"I know nothing," Wei said. "I've only read about them, but I know they would be insanely powerful cultivators. Anyway, this is a good room. Even I wish to have walked the path of forging and artificing after seeing this room."

"Why do you know all this about forging?"

Wei sighed. He'd worked in a furnace room for years when he joined Divine Fragrance Palace in his previous life, and his teacher had a liking for all sorts of forging books. That old man lived on books and forging, and he was constantly muttering. Then Wei had had a few friends who'd loved forging, and they too had told him about a few things. Of course, he wouldn't say he knew everything about it the way he understood arrays and formations, but he had theoretical knowledge about forging.

"I read a lot of books in my free time," Wei said.

"Don't spout nonsense. You pick up girls in your free time."

Wei coughed hard. What was wrong with everyone? Even Rual'er had been saying something like this.

"When did you get infected by those naive girls?" Wei said. "Anyway, let's focus on this. The array formation is the main thing, and other things are just for tinkering."

"What does this formation do?"

"Once charged, it should call upon the dragons' breath, enhancing the artifact by a grade or imbuing it with new powers. Let's test it." Wei retrieved the listless gloves of the cotton ball.

It was an Earth Grade artifact, but Wei's attack had broken it, so he couldn't use it. He tossed it into the corner. Then he retrieved the black metallic wings. These had a weird name—Cang Feather Wings. They were Earth Grade as well, and they gave the wielder an immense speed almost equal to a normal teleportation. It could be used by anyone in the Boiling Blood Realm and above. After placing the wings at the middle of the array formation, he put a Qi Crystal each in three power sources. However, the array formation didn't work.

"Did you not read the manual? It says you need at least three hundred Qi Crystals to upgrade one Earth Grade artifact," Blood Parasite said.

Wei leaped out of his position. "Where is the manual?"

System: Information interface detected. Downloading the cost manual of the Dragon Breath Bestowment Formation.

There were many rows. Upgrading a common Bronze Grade artifact required a Qi Crystal, and upgrading an Earth Grade artifact required three hundred Qi Crystals or an equivalent energy source. Wei didn't even look at the Human-and-above artifacts as it would have given him a fright.

"How am I supposed to use this if it costs this much?" Wei stared at the formation in shambles. Even after plundering so many people and sects, he only had a dozen Qi Crystals on him, and he would not waste them on a damn formation like this.

Had this artifact turned out to be a dud? That would be too disappointing.

System: Information download complete.

Infernal Flame Palace

Grade: Minimum Heaven Grade

Access Level: Level 1

Bound to host (25%).

Detail information missing.

Can be upgraded using blood from other beasts/humans. Next blood requirement: Peak of Violet Palace Realm blood.

Available chambers: Ten-Day Time Chamber. Artifact-Enhancing Room.

Usage:

Artifact Storage:

Can store an artifact inside.

Artifact Purification:

Stored artifacts would slowly be cleansed through internal fire and repaired. Available Slot: 0/3.

Wei sighed in disappointment. The only good thing that had come of this out was the opening of the second level of the Primordial Blood Palace. It would help him a lot.

Wait—why had it said "Available Slot 0/3"?

"System, check which artifacts are stored inside," Wei said.

System: Accessing the interface. Information interface detected.

A list of three items appeared in his vision, and his heart beat like it would jump out of his rib cage and run away. His mother or father had left him a gift. A real gift.

Chapter 38

Mother's Gift

L i Wei relaxed his muscles as he leaned against the stone at his back. The rough surface didn't bother him as much before, when he'd lost most of his blood to the Infernal Flame Palace. After pouring a cup of warm tea for himself, he read the description of the first artifact stored in the infernal palace.

"System, show me the list one by one."

Celestial Hourglass of Time

Quality: Heaven Grade (Broken) (Purification in progress)

In the era of gods, devils, and demons, Celestial Hourglass of Time was one of the thousand greatest artifacts, coveted by the gods, demons, and devils alike. A war broke out, and the artifact was laid to waste. It was broken beyond repair, only to be saved by a wanderer who owned one of the prominent artifacts.

In a few epochs, the hourglass has regained some of its ability but lies broken at the core. Only time will tell if it can be repaired. The hourglass produces Time Sand at a thousand times the speed required in the real world.

Current Quantity: 20,000 Sand Grains.

Time Sand can be taken out from the Infernal Flame Palace level-three vault. If the artifact is taken out, it may crumble forever.

Wei patted his chest. An artifact coveted by gods and demons. Wow. This was beyond his comprehension. He guessed he wouldn't be able to take it out even if he opened the third level of the infernal palace, yet it was fine. The artifact was broken. But he knew that it produced Time Sand, or Time Grains, and those things mattered the most. They charged up his Ten-Day Time Chamber. In the Dimensional Trials, he'd received a few Time Grains, and he was able to use the Ten-Day Time Chamber dozens of times. Then, thanks to Allen Ming, he could extend it a few hundred times. But it would eventually come to an end, and the Ten-Day Time chamber was one of the most useful abilities he had.

Brushing his fingers against the Infernal Flame Palace half-buried in his chest, Wei took a light swig of the honey-buttered tea. "Blood Parasite, I'll soon have two time chambers. Can I use them simultaneously?"

"Yes, you can, but don't send two clones inside. Once they come out, you might have an adverse effect because of the time difference."

Wei arched his brows. "Can I use one for myself and the other for someone else?"

"As long as you have enough Time Grains."

"That's good." Wei sneered. With this, he could train his friends in the Ten-Day Time Chamber, and he himself could enjoy the Hundred-Day Time Chamber.

Myriad Thread Robe

Quality: Human Grade

A masterpiece woven from the life threads of the Myriad Vitality Beast, this robe is unparalleled in its resilience. Imbued with the indomitable spirit of the Myriad Vitality Beast, this robe defies the concept of damage below the Violet Palace Realm.

It protects the wielder not in the real sense of defense, but it helps the wielder to mitigate some damage. Enhanced by an Array Scion, this robe can also conceal the wielder from anyone below Violet Palace Realm, within a certain time limit.

Can be taken out when Infernal Flame Palace reaches level 2.

Wei's eyes almost popped out of their sockets when he read the phrase *Array Scion*. What realm was that? Was it higher than the Array Master realm? Heavens, he'd been stuck at the Array Master Realm forever in his previous life and couldn't move forward because no one knew how to proceed. He and fellow Array Masters searched ancient sites to find a way forward, but they only received defeat after spending decades at it.

Licking his lips, he sipped the tea. Maybe the array was hidden in the fabric, and he might not get to study it. However, just knowing he wore something made by an Array Scion would give him hope for moving forward.

Rubbing the back of his neck, Wei suppressed the urge to tear open the second level and pull the robe out. "Blood Parasite, can we take this item out in advance?"

"No. You've already used Violet Palace Realm blood essence to open the first level, and the blood essence you have is from a low-level Violet Palace Realm cultivator. So you have to wait, and then you need some auxiliary ingredients as well."

Wei sighed. Blood Parasite sounded harsher as he rejected him, but Wei couldn't do anything about it. Taking a deep breath, Wei moved to the next item on the list.

Earthly Broken Treasure Ring

Quality: Human Grade

A relic of the past, the Earthly Broken Treasure Ring contains a Primal Life Space inside which one can store items that can't be

stored in a common storage ring. **Forged by an ancient master, the core of the ring, though broken, retains unimaginable power and is indestructible by anything known to the human.**

Blood bound. Becomes an extension of the master and can be only seen if the master allows it.

Can be taken out when Infernal Flame Palace reaches level 1.

"Blood Parasite, what is this ring?" Wei asked. It seemed to be a storage artifact, but why would his mother leave a storage artifact inside a storage artifact? This made little sense.

"That must be the storage ring Master Yan gifted to the mistress. It is something special. Retrieve it, and see yourself," Blood Parasite replied with a cryptic chuckle. "It's blood bound, so only with your mother's inherited blood could one open it. So it was a gift for you and only you. I wonder why the mistress left it with the mayor and didn't give it to your grandfather."

Wei shrugged. He had no idea. Excited, he retrieved the ring—something his father had gifted to his mother and she'd left for Wei by binding it with her blood. Maybe his mother wasn't a snob after all.

Taking a deep breath, Wei retrieved the broken treasure ring from the Infernal Flame Palace. It was warm to the touch and had a familiar scent. The scent of his mother's love.

He couldn't believe what he saw inside.

Chapter 39

Palace in the Ring - Finding Immortal Dew for Xue Qi

The warmth of his mother spread through the ring into his hand. It had the scent of his mother, or he thought it did. It was the only thing Mother had left him, and he wasn't ready to look into what it contained. It awakened a small set of fuzzy memories of his mother's touch.

Of course, he'd just met her sealed memory, but she hadn't been there in person, nor did the memory have a connection to his mother. So it didn't count. The real thing was his childhood, when she'd still been around him, caring for him, loving him. It was his mother's gift. Sighing, he poured his essence energy into the ring to look inside.

"What the hell is this thing?" Wei shuddered, goose bumps spreading across his arms as if he stood at the edge of an icy cliff.

"What happened?" Blood Parasite asked, sounding like an annoyed child awakened from a deep sleep.

"Don't pretend you're busy with something. See what's stuffed inside it?" Wei asked, almost shouting in his mind. There was a giant palace in the ring. It was real—a palace with thousands of rings that the entire Li clan might fit inside of.

"Kid, for your father, something like this was nothing. This is an ancient artifact and contains a Primal Life Space. I wonder why he didn't fit an entire island inside. He could have even left some rare beauties for you. Don't you like beauties?"

"Fuck you!" Wei said. "Wait, did you just say it can store people in this?" Wei jumped to his feet. "Are you kidding me?"

"What's so difficult about that? Once you reach... beyond the Violet Palace Realm, you can create Primal Life Space inside a storage artifact."

"So I can carry the entire Li clan and my friends with me always." Wouldn't that be awesome? Why would he need to care for other threats? This would bring him to the Lazy Dao he'd always wanted to live. If there was no conflict, he could just enjoy roaming around unbridled.

"If it could be that simple," Blood Parasite said, sounding sad. "You can store them, but you can't carry them around with you. If they were only mortals, then probably yes, but no cultivators can be carried around. Not until you reach beyond Violet Palace Realm."

"That's a bummer. I can't even store them for later?"

"You can for a short period, but you can't move around, teleporting, when they are inside. The ring exposes them to the space around your body. You have a nasty habit of traveling between worlds, and it would kill them. Even a short teleport would impact them harshly. Once you reach the Violet Palace Realm and create a Life Seal inside, you might be able to carry them between worlds."

"Create a Life Seal? Blood Parasite, what is this Violet Palace Realm?" Wei had heard about it, but understanding it was a completely different thing. "You keep bringing this up, but you never told me the mysteries of this thing."

"I can't tell you much, as it will bring Karma of Heaven on you. Knowing too much is detrimental to you. If the Houtian Realm is shedding the mortal body, the Violet Palace Realm is gaining the control over Death or Life."

Wei scoffed. The bullshit of knowing too much once again. Xue Qi used to do the same. "Okay, so this ring is like Pet Storage Pouch but with an ability to store some people inside."

"It's more than that, kid. Look at the back garden of the palace."

Wei spread his divine sense, and the goose bumps on his arms grew by a factor of ten. "A garden with rare herbs. Wait, I don't recognize more than half of them. They don't even grow in the Martial Realm."

"Many of those trees came from distant Planes your father traveled. I pity that bitch Xue Qi. She was asking you for Immortal Dew right? Do you see the plant in the corner—Immortal Orchid? When you water it with pure spring water for ten years, it will produce Immortal Dew."

Wei's focus shifted toward a corner as he identified the plant Xue Qi wanted. Although it was only one ingredient, anything was better than nothing. Phoenix's Feathers, Truth Stone, and Immortal Dew. Those were the things she'd asked him to collect once he grew stronger, but so far, he had found nothing. They were too rare even in the Martial Realm. Sighing heavily, he spread his divine sense into the palace. What he found in the middle room blew his mind one more time.

"I love you, Mother. I love you so much!" he roared in his mind when he saw a mountain full of Qi Crystals. There were so many that he bet even a team of ten people would take months to count them all.

"Mistress must have predicted your needs. She left everything you needed inside. She was a wise person. Too bad she left me in your hands." Blood Parasite appeared in the ring and bowed toward the palace.

"What the hell do you mean by that? Am I a bad master for this ring?"

"Don't tell me you are planning to upgrade every weapon you have using Artifact-Enhancing Room."

Wei smiled sheepishly. That thought had crossed his mind. With a mountain of Qi Crystals, he could do anything.

"Half of your weapons and artifacts are Human Grade and above, and it will wipe this pile in no time. Even if you plan to enhance Earth Grade artifacts, at a minimum, you can't go beyond a few thousand. Is that worth it? Mistress gave you this ring and the stuff inside, and it is a responsibility. Don't waste it on upgrades."

"What other use do they have? I can't cultivate using these, nor can other people. There's a limit to how much they can cultivate using a Qi Crystal. Even if I splurge by spending the Qi Crystals in my arrays or formations, I'll have plenty more remaining after a hundred years."

"Don't forget, you haven't even opened the second level yet."

Second level. Wei sneered. Didn't it say Pill Enhancement Room?

"You're right. I won't splurge with these. I'll only upgrade some artifacts and keep the remainder for future use." The cultivators on his side would definitely benefit from using a large-scale qi-gathering array formation. It could be useful in many ways.

Sighing, he came out of the ring and saw Rual'er standing next to him.

"Brother Wei, we only have two hours, so we should talk about the strategy," Rual'er said.

Nodding, Wei got up and walked toward their previous gathering position, where the others sat peacefully. Someone had cooked food that smelled delicious, and some people were enjoying it with wine, Kai Shaya being one of them. Staring at the bald man, Wei shook his head. He might have committed a crime against the monk ideology by turning Kai Shaya into a wine addict. But who cared? Wine was an excellent drink, and Wei had done something good for his brother.

"Senior Wei, please join us!" a few juniors called him, looking cheerful as if they had come for a picnic or something.

Most of them were in the Marrow Cleansing Realm, and others were in the Boiling Blood Realm. They didn't know the gravity of this situation and put all their trust in Wei. But was he ready to take responsibility and save them from the upcoming doom? There were a total of five waves of enemies, and only one had passed. Each wave would add a few allies and more enemies. Could he make sure everyone here would survive this?

Probably not. Once the arrogant prodigies from the Destiny Mirror Sect arrived, these people would be turned into a cannon fodder. What then?

"Li Wei, there's some bad news from the Beast Origin Realm." The little fox ran to him before Wei had reached the destination.

The world swirled around Wei as he took in the weight on his shoulders. They were putting too much on him, and he felt suffocated. Could he really balance the weight of all the deaths that would be happening because of him?

Chapter 40

Wi Rual's Suspicion

Wi Rual felt the sudden change of mood in brother Wei. Her senses were sharp, and she could sense others' feelings when they were in a bad mood or at a sharp turn in their lives. This was partially because of a bloodline ability that allowed her to do that. However, she wasn't using it here. She'd never used it on friends or strangers because she didn't need to, and it might cost her blood essence and a friend or two. In fact, she knew everyone had a selfish heart, and it was fine up to an extent. As long as they stayed within the limit, she could be friends with anyone. However, if someone had an extreme hatred for her, she would feel it, or if someone felt extreme doubt, love, or hurt, she could sense it in a vague way.

Brother Wei was going through a similar emotion at the moment, and she could guess what the reason was. The doubt in his eyes when he looked at others gave it away. Just standing a few feet away from him made her sense a dark aura that he was emitting, one of doubt and frustration. Her father had had this aura plunged into his heart many times, and she was sensitive to it.

She called it the dilemma of a leader. Her father often confessed to her that he feared he would lead the One-Winged Dragon race to doom, but he never did. He only lamented to her and her mother, while outside he was a great leader who'd even withstood the attack of the Gatekeepers and saved their entire race from extinction. Of course, they'd lost half their territory, but after the first Ancient Decree descended, things had been smoother, and they'd even replenished their army.

That wasn't important. Brother Wei was feeling it because of the upcoming danger, and she had to step in and help him like she'd helped her father.

"Brother Wei, can we talk a bit in private? I've something I need your help with." She bit her lip, pulling him out of the long trance he was in.

"Ah, yes. We should discuss the fate of the people." Brother Wei walked out of the crowd and followed her to a distant corner.

The little fox, as usual, naive, followed him, but Rual pushed her back with her tail. She didn't want a naive little girl messing up their conversation. She had to ask brother Wei to keep his beast friends at a constant distance. She, a princess, was enough for him as a beast friend, and it was only for a few days. Once she broke through, she would be beautiful like her mother, and then brother Wei wouldn't even look at any other woman.

"Calm down, Rual. What the heck are you thinking?" she asked herself when the thoughts went astray. It was all because of brother Wei. Why had he called her his bitch? How could he profess his feelings like this in the open?

Brother Wei paused after traveling a few dozen miles from the others. "Sister Rual, tell me, what do you want to discuss?"

Rual sighed and retrieved a bottle of fine ale. This was made from a Soul-Calming White Ruby Flower, and it had the best effect on her father.

"Brother Wei, please drink this. It has a calming effect and may get you out of your sense of burden." She poured it into a glass and handed it to him.

"Sister Rual, those people. They're following me, but I'm going to send them to their deaths. I should tell them this." His face turned pale as he looked back at the dark silhouettes of the people gathered around the campfire.

"No, you can't." Rual willed the wind energy around him to resist. Brother Wei was a genius, and after just simple advice from him, she'd already grasped the basics of the Intent of Wind.

"Why?" he asked, looking confused. "Shouldn't I tell them my real abilities? I can't save them all. There's no way to protect them."

"Let's drink the ale first. Please," she insisted, and he gulped it down in one go.

Another gulper. She hated it when people drank wine in one gulp. But it wasn't the time to dwell on this, and she couldn't be angry at brother Wei.

"Let's go now."

"Brother Wei, please answer my question."

"Ask it," he said, looking a little annoyed.

"What is the role of a king or a general?"

"Role of a king is to protect his kingdom, and a general needs to win the war, avoiding casualties. But why would you ask that?"

"What is your current position? King or general?"

"What are you trying to do?" His eyes shone with a strange light. He looked quite handsome when he had this look.

"Choose one. Are you a king or a general?"

"I can't choose. I don't want to be either."

His reply stunned her. For a moment, she didn't know how to reply, but her training kicked in, and she laughed. Laughter was a perfect way to break an awkward pause.

"Brother Wei, don't you sense these people have faith in you like an army has in their general? They're looking at you to be their savior."

"You can say that, but it doesn't change the fact that I might push them to their deaths. By following me, they have taken on the world itself."

"Okay," she said, frustration rushing through her nerves.

Brother Wei was difficult. He should have agreed with her, and she would have told him to have a magnanimous heart and ride with the flow, but he was flipping the script. He was difficult to manipulate.

"But think about it. If you give up, what will happen to them? Will they survive the next wave?" she asked.

"They might if they choose another faction. I don't mind them betraying me, and I can be free."

"Can they join the other faction after the faction knows others died and they survived?"

"Sister Rual'er, I get your point, but there are a lot of flaws in your theory. First, they can just say they hid when the others died. With their cultivation level, they can't defeat me, and others wouldn't deny their claim. Second, they can also claim they came here with the others."

Rual'er wanted to smack his head with her tail. Why was he finding flaws in her argument? Even her father didn't do that.

Brother Wei took a deep breath. "Sister Rual, I know what you're trying to do. Although your argument is still a bit far from changing my mind, it has cleared it." He patted her cheeks. "Thanks. Now, as daughter of a king, take charge, and I'll become your henchman."

Wi Rual froze. What had just happened? Wasn't she supposed to boost his morale, and he would say how valuable she was for him? Her father always said that, and the script never deviated. Wait—had her father cheated her?

"Brother Wei, what are you saying? I can't lead them. They don't even know me." Why was he doing this? He had to agree with her, not the other way around. "And you have a problem that we need to work out."

He smiled—an enigmatic smile. "Don't worry. I've a plan. We are going to build a giant defensive formation, and I'll teach you the basics of it."

"What formation? We don't have enough time to build any. Are you already prepared for everything?"

Brother Wei shook his head. "Don't worry about it. I have ten days for that. But tell me, do you trust me?"

"I do."

"Then don't resist when I take you somewhere." Wei placed his palm on her shoulder and then covered her with his divine sense.

She almost resisted, but when he didn't pry into her body, she let him do what he wanted. Suddenly, the world blurred, and she appeared in a giant palace. Built with bricks unknown to her, the palace emitted a thick primal aura. The tower in her One-Winged Dragon race's ancestral ground had the same aura. Her father had said the tower didn't belong to the Martial Realm but came from somewhere faraway place.

"Brother Wei, what is this place?"

"My secret. I have an artifact that will allow us ten days to perfect a defensive formation in one hour's time, and I'll need ten people I can trust. And don't worry. You can teleport out with a single thought."

She sensed that he was telling the truth. She could go out whenever she wanted. "But, brother Wei..."

"Sister Rual, I have a big ask. We need a few people to complete the formation. Can you use your bloodline ability to pick up a few people from the others?"

Wi Rual shuddered, her heart slumping. How did brother Wei know about her bloodline ability of sensing others' emotions?

"Who are you really? And how do you know about my bloodline ability, which only my father and mother know about?" Her aura crashed against her skin, ready to attack Li Wei at any moment.

Chapter 41

Proposing Rual'er for Marriage

L i Wei had anticipated this, and that was why he'd pulled Rual'er into his palace. If he'd been outside among other people, she might have made a scene. He didn't want to spook her, so he'd told her the way out.

However, by bringing her in, he'd also tested how the palace behaved when he pulled someone else along with him. Rual'er was the best candidate because she was at the peak of Heart Blood Realm and could withstand the void for some time if things went south. Thank heavens nothing happened, and they both were fine.

"Trust me—I'm the same Li Wei you know." Smiling, he retrieved a Green Fragrant Potato and munched on it while offering one to her.

Ignoring it, she stepped back, her aura slipping out the ground around her shaking. With his divine sense, he could clearly hear her aura thumping against her skin as if a volcano were ready to erupt. The strange and gloomy noises always made outsiders aware of the danger. Rual'er was shaking violently, reminding him of his limits.

"Okay. I won't keep my ability under the wrap, but I thought you would have noticed it, Princess Rual." He waved his palm, activating Blood Control.

After reaching the Heart Blood Realm, Wei had gained a higher control over Blood Control. Although he couldn't affect a powerful opponent's blood yet, he could slightly shake it inside their bodies, provoking their sense of fatal danger. It was a cheap trick that could be useful in certain situations.

"You—what are you doing to my blood?" Rual'er asked, her front paws tensed like an extra-stretched rope. If he made a single mistake, she would attack him.

"I have a Bloodline Probe Activity. I can sense others' bloodline abilities. When we met, I sensed yours. Your guard had Void Blood ability, didn't she? She must have survived our attack easily, although I'm not sure she survived the entire ordeal." Wei bit casually into the sweet fruit. He was trying to look cool, but he was ready to defend himself at a moment's notice. Rual'er wasn't a weak opponent he could make a fool of. If she attacked, he would have to put everything into defending himself.

"Using my abilities in your name. Good game, kid," Blood Parasite mocked him from inside. "But don't get fooled next time when I tell you about the wrong one."

Wei sneered inwardly. Blood Parasite had mentioned Wi Vistara's ability when he'd attacked her. Heaven knew how he'd found it out, but Wei didn't care.

"Are you telling me the truth?" Rual'er asked.

"Is there any other way I can guess your ability? Are you sure only your father and mother know about this? Can't it be leaked already?"

"Impossible," she muttered, shaking her head in disbelief. "No one knows about this."

"Then that's your answer." Wei shrugged.

He only knew about her ability because she'd trusted him in the previous life and opened her heart to him, and he'd rejected her openly, rudely. Maybe he could have ended the conversation differently at that time, but he'd been a fool trapped in Wang Zia's illusion of love.

Rual'er retracted her aura.

Wei relaxed. "See, sister Rual? I showed you all my cards. I even told you about this artifact, and yet you don't believe me? You're breaking my heart now." He made a puppy face, like she'd hurt him badly.

"I'm sorry. I shouldn't have doubted you." Her face turned pink.

"Kid, aren't you trusting her too much? You even exposed your time-manipulation artifact. Are you going to kill her after this?" Blood Parasite asked.

"Never," Wei said. "She is a dear friend. How can I kill her?"

"Then why are you trusting her with all of these secrets? What if she exposes them?"

"Brother Wei, I'll vow to heaven and earth that your secrets are safe with me, and even my blood family will never know them. If I betray your trust, heaven can kill me with a lightning strike." A rumble echoed in the sky, witnessing her vow.

"See? That's why I trust her." Wei chuckled inwardly.

He knew Rual'er too well. She could do anything but betray her friend. Once she had even gone against an army for a friend—for him—so how could he not trust her? Of course, he'd been a worse warrior at the time. He only focused on arrays, so he was basically a weak cultivator many could kill. And Wang Zia had used his weakness to her advantage.

"Don't bullshit me. How did you learn her Blood Emotion Sensing bloodline ability? I didn't tell you about it."

"I guessed."

"Bullshit. Anyway, she is a rare seed, and you have to mate with her and inherit her ability. This Blood Emotion Sensing can evolve to an ability that can shake the world. With it, she can kill people through their own minds. It's scary."

Wei coughed, attracting Rual'er's attention.

"What happened? Don't you believe me?" she asked.

"Of course I do. That fruit stuck in my throat, so I coughed. Thank you, sister Rual. You didn't have to do that."

"Do you really like me, brother Wei? Do you have those kind of thoughts in your mind?" she asked, turning red, which looked weird on the dragon's face.

"Yes, I do. Why would I trust you otherwise, my bitch? Don't you dare ask me that again," Blood Parasite said in Wei's voice.

Rual'er turned away, shaking visibly.

"Blood Parasite, I'll kill you when you show up in front of me again!" Wei roared in his mind. That bastard had just used his voice again and sputtered more nonsense.

"Sister Rual..."

"Call me Rual'er, brother Wei. But that doesn't mean I will let you do anything with me. You have to get my father's permission after I break through into the Houtian Realm, and you also have to be fast because there are other suitors waiting for my breakthrough." After saying this, she teleported out.

"What the fuck just happened?" Wei rolled his eyes.

What was happening to him? Did he really have the ability to pick up girls? There was Nai Fang, Yang Fang, and now Rual'er. Wait—he knew Nuan'er liked him, too, although she'd never expressed it.

Shaking his head, he teleported out. This wasn't the time to think about romance. He would face it when he had to.

She sent him a message as soon as he appeared outside of the palace. "Brother Wei, you can trust these ten people. I've used my ability twice on them, so there's no chance they will betray you."

Wei sent a divine transmission to the ten people. As expected, Grandpa Ling and the guard captain were among them. "Friends and brothers, I'm going to take you somewhere. Don't resist me."

Wei then covered them in his divine sense to bring them into the palace along with Rual'er. At first, everyone seemed flabbergasted by the small room, but they didn't ask any questions.

"Brother Wei, I've told them about the secret way you found to extend the time for the practice by using the clock outside," Rual'er whispered, nodding at him.

Wei arched his brows. She'd lied to them. By connecting his abilities to the clock outside, she'd given him a way to deny everything if anyone betrayed them. Although he trusted Rual'er, the human heart wasn't as simple as it seemed, and someone might have a treasure to bypass her ability and detect the truth.

"Thank you, sister Rual'er. Friends and brothers, we have found a loophole, and I trust you will keep it a secret, as this is the only way we can guarantee everyone's life."

They all nodded.

"However, before we begin, I want to tell you something." He paused. "I have many enemies, and they will come for me once the next battle starts. So if you want to give up and feign like you were hiding in the first battle, you can speak out and I won't do anything to you. However, if you betray me after we set up everything to protect everyone outside, then you'll be begging for death."

A heavy silence prevailed. Wei expected someone to come forward, but no one did.

"Nephew Wei, tell us what you want us to do. We knew our odds of survival when we were pulled in, and anything you can tell us would be a bonus." Grandpa Ling glanced at the others, and they nodded.

Wei smiled. Grandpa had talked in subtext. He clearly told them that there was no guarantee of their life, but if they followed Wei, they might survive. He was a real leader after all.

After retrieving a few formation plates, Wei tossed them to the group. "You must be aware of the next wave coming in two hours, but because of the loophole, we have ten days in this room, where we can practice a defensive formation."

"Senior Wei, what are you really planning?" the guard captain asked. "Even if you feed them a Gold Grade pill, we won't reach the peak of Heart Blood Realm. Is there really a way to pass this tribulation?"

"I'll speak the truth. I don't have any hopes, but I can't let you die, can I? You and others trusted your lives to me and sister Rual, so it's our duty to protect you all. Although we can't increase your power by much, we can still teach you a way to protect yourselves from anyone less advanced than the Houtian Realm without wasting too much power."

"Can you really do that?" One of them rubbed the Qi Crystal against his nose as if he wanted to inhale its scent, even though Qi Crystals were pure energy, and energy didn't smell like anything.

"I can't, but you can." Wei tossed each of them a Qi Crystal. "If you combine your power, you can even fight a devil or a demon."

"Is this a Qi Crystal?" someone cried.

"Yes, and I will provide you with ten each."

"But we are no cultivators. How can we do this?" someone asked, sounding confused.

"He's right, senior. We know nothing about the formations," the guard captain said, his tone serious.

"Don't worry. My clone will teach you those things." Wei had pulled his three clones into the palace before entering it. "They will teach you Ten-Man-Mammoth Defense Formation. It will allow ten of you to work in a team of two and create a defensive bubble that can easily withstand any attack from a cultivator below the Houtian Realm. All you need to do is stand in the formation circle."

"Just don't compromise your position," Rual'er added. Wei had shared the formation diagram with her.

"Nephew Wei, don't worry. We will give our hundred and ten percent. If we don't, we can only blame our death on each other but not you." He glanced at the others, and they all nodded.

"Good. Then I and sister Rual will activate the loophole, and you can start learning." Wei walked out of the room, and Rual followed. "Rual'er, use this to increase your wind comprehension." He handed her the Blood Orchid Beast's core, which he'd extracted but hadn't used as he'd gotten the Infernal Flame Palace as a gift.

"Brother Wei, don't be partial just because you like me. That naive fox has been following you for so many years, and she is loyal. So give it to her."

Wei froze, speechless.

"Don't worry. I'll look after you going forward. After all, your followers are my followers," she continued.

"Li Wei, your skills in picking up girls are heavenly. If I'd known these before turning into a blood slave, I would have died happy," Blood Parasite said in his mind.

"Just take it." Wei shook his head. There was nothing he could say.

"Fine, if you insist. This is your first gift, and I want a gift every week, okay?" She smiled and rushed into a side room.

"Rual'er, don't break through. Focus on learning Intent."

"Don't worry. Go back, and do your work."

Sighing, Wei flashed out and then instructed Sonja to make potent poison vials and the little fox to control her wind. He didn't give the Blood Orchid Beast core to the little fox, because he was afraid she would break through without listening to him. For her, he had to develop a different approach to training. But it could wait.

After giving a few pills and Qi Crystals to the others, he activated the Ten-Day Time Chamber and entered the alchemy room. For a few minutes, he conversed with the clones in the palace. They were doing well. They didn't feel any discomfort or rejection from the space.

"This is a genius idea, Li Wei." Blood Parasite appeared next to him, hidden behind his mask.

"It feels more like a cheat." Wei poured himself a cup of tea. "Do you drink tea or only blood?" The scent of the tea enthralled his senses. Even in the time-diluted space, the tea smelled and tasted amazing.

Blood Parasite snorted sarcastically. "Why didn't I think of this?"

"It was your idea. When you said the ring would face everything my body would face, it made me think about the time-dilution effect. I knew it would work in the Ten-Day Time Chamber, but I'm not sure it will work in the Hundred-Day Time Chamber. I'll have to test that later." Wei started drawing arrays on an array plate.

"Yes, the conditions would get worse in a hundred days inside the palace. Good work, kid. But why are you making these arrays instead of cultivating? Don't be complacent just because you can defeat powerful enemies. If their number is great, you'll fail."

"I know." Wei sighed, pausing to look at the masked Blood Parasite. "I am making these to save those ten. I can trust them, but I can't trust others. So this will be an extra lifesaving array for them. I'm carving Petrifying Arrays. Anyone who enters the surrounding area will turn to stone for a few seconds. This should be enough for them to save themselves."

"You're giving too much leverage to others," Blood Parasite said. "I would prefer you to focus on your own training. Even the mistress would like that. If you want to meet the mistress in the future, then you should break through out of this Plane quickly."

Wei sighed as Blood Parasite vanished. He sensed that Blood Parasite's emotions had changed, and he more than ever looked at him as his pet project for the mistress, his mother. It was fine either way. Wei considered Blood Parasite a blood brother, so it didn't matter.

Taking a swig of tea, he focused on the arrays in front of him. It reminded him of the time he'd worked like a pig to carve thousands of array diagrams. Could he beat his own speed from his previous life? Only time would tell.

Chapter 42

The Second Wave

Li Wei swayed like a drunkard when he stepped out of the Ten-Day Time Chamber. Everyone else was out already. He hadn't known this earlier, but he could send them out a few minutes before him, and he did that when he felt like the world was drowning him. The array diagrams had chased him from the depths of hell and tried to pull him down, so he'd sent everyone else out of the time chamber and then jumped out himself.

Exhaustion washed over him as he fell to the ground. The world turned darker before turning bright again. He had this weird feeling of looking at himself sleeping in the bubble. It was similar to an out-of-body experience, but it wasn't that. He was looking at himself through one of his clones' eyes.

Five groups of two had spread within a mile's radius, creating a tight array formation. A visible energy bubble covered a wide area around them. Array discs lay next to the ones who'd created the array formation, and the others were instructed not to go within a ten-foot radius around them. Everyone around Wei's clone seemed content and looked at his main body reverently. They'd had their cultivation shot up and defense strengthened.

"Why is he like this?" Rual'er asked one of his clones. "He's been sleeping since he came out half an hour ago. I'm worried."

The clone smiled. "Don't worry, sister Rual. My main body is just exhausted from the horrors of carving all those array plates. Even thinking about it makes me shudder."

"Is array carving so taxing on humans?"

The clone chuckled. "If you try to carve a thousand in ten days, it is."

Wei recalled why he was lying unconscious. The array practice had utterly exhausted him, but his clones were fine because of their separation. Just thinking about it gave him a shiver. It was fucking insane. Why had he done that?

Well, it wasn't the first time. In this strange state of sharing the mind of his clones, he recalled a memory tucked in the depths of his mind. In fact, it had been sealed by him. Once in his previous life, he'd made a bet with his love rival to carve the maximum number of array plates in a week. The opponent went mad after carving four hundred in five days, but Wei persisted and carved seven hundred to prove his love for Wang Zia. His master had sealed those memories so they wouldn't affect his future cultivation.

It had been a crazy time, and he'd attempted it again—a thousand array plates in ten days. How had he kept from going insane? The Soul-Calming Ale Rual'er had given him—he'd drunk that in the time chamber, and it had helped him along with his awakened Soul Space. Interesting. This was indeed an interesting turn of events. Whatever else, he had made a thousand Petrifying Array Plates, and Rual'er and Sonja had taken them from him.

Rual'er walked over to him just before the clock clicked for the second wave. "Brother Wei, just relax. We'll take care of this." Rual'er patted his head.

"Li Wei, just sleep. We'll do the work." The little fox rubbed her furry head against his face.

"Yes, lord. Let this servant take care of things for you," Sonja added.

Wei couldn't even reply. Instead, he used one of his clones to spread his divine sense. The weakest one was sitting next to his main body, and he could use it to anchor the battle if needed. The main body would need some rest, and he hoped he wouldn't have to wake it up to fight in this battle.

Ding Son had a bad feeling when he materialized in a barren place with a giant clock to his left. This was the Ancient Decree battlefield. The first pulse. Why was he here?

Turning back, he searched through the crowd of around a thousand people to look for his teammates, and to his relief, all twelve of them had appeared alongside him, frowning.

"Brother Son, where are we? Aren't we supposed to be heading toward the Five Firmament City?" One of his followers brought his Dark-Blood Peacock close to Son's.

All the prodigies brought from the Martial Realm to the Destiny Mirror Sect had gotten a beast, usually a bird, to ride on. These gifts from the elders had improved their speed tremendously and had proved their worth in the battle with the Crimson Moon Kingdom. Although Son hadn't gotten a chance to participate in that battle, he'd heard about how useful these birds had been.

"I don't know, but it seems like we have joined the battle of the Ancient Decree ahead of the others. We were going to join everyone near the Five Firmament City, but we are the unfortunate ones to arrive ahead of time," he said, spitting out the piece of jerky stuck between his teeth. It tasted good when he was traveling, but here, it seemed to have gathered the foul scent of this place. "Brother Gun, please scan the area."

"Brother Son, what should we do now?" someone asked from behind him.

"We'll wait and see," Ding Son replied, scanning the area himself.

A few hours earlier, Elder Juwan had sent a decree for all the prodigies who had traveled back from the Martial Realm to reach the Five Firmament City. However, Son and his team had been on a mission to obtain an herb from a mountain range, so they'd gotten the message late and had missed joining with the others.

"I don't understand. Why did they send us to the Five Firmament City in the fifth wave?" Bu Judio asked.

"To wipe out the pests from the Five Firmament City," Ding Son replied.

This had been confusing at the start, but one of the elders had explained about the Ancient Decree and their job to defend it until the fifth wave. The sect was going to send one of the Chosen Gold team to fight with the Outerworld creatures in the second pulse, so they had to be the strongest party in the fifth wave. If they could wipe out everyone else, it would be best.

"Chosen Gold team will join all four places of incursion in the second pulse, but before that, we'll get support from a single team in the fourth or fifth wave," Son continued.

"Why not now? If they had joined in the third wave, wouldn't it be easier to win all four Ancient Decrees?"

"They're busy in the Martial Realm, and the sect is teleporting them through a special array." Ding Son sighed hard.

This wasn't something he wanted to do. Those Chosen Golds were the real elites, and they were prepared for the Ancient Decree's descent into the world. They were scary. Even the lowest dragged from their ranks could kill a dozen prodigies who'd undergone the training in the Martial Realm.

Ding Son didn't want anything to do with the Chosen Gold. All he had to do was get out of this fucking place in the second pulse. Even meeting a single team in the fifth wave would bring trouble.

Glancing at the thousand-plus people who had appeared along with him, he gauged their cultivation levels. None of them had a cultivation level higher than peak Boiling Blood Realm. Only twelve of them were in the peak of the Heart Blood Realm.

"Bu Judio, check the others, and see if some of the Blood-Colored Assassins have made it through. I remember the elder said he would be inviting them as well, and they were en route to the Five Firmament City."

"The likes of you don't possess enough authority to talk with us." A dagger brushed against Ding Son's neck before a figure in a red hood appeared.

Behind him, five similar hoods materialized. A black insignia of a dog eating a dragon marked their guild's name. They were Blood-Colored Assassins, a terrifying organization in the Martial Realm, who had allied with the Gatekeepers. They must have been below the Houtian Realm because they had appeared here, but each had battle powers to assassinate people in the Houtian Realm. Ding Son didn't know if these six were the elite Blood-Colored Assassins, but if they were here, that meant they should be quite capable.

Ding Son wiped the blood from his throat with a white cloth. He hated blood, and he hated these assassins as well. "Do you have elder Juwan's message? Do you understand the target's capabilities?" he asked, brushing the icy-cold fear from his spine. If he could keep a cool head in this wave, he would have a higher chance of survival through this ordeal.

"Do we need something like that? We just finished Li Wei, who's holding this position and waits for the Chosen Gold to hand it over." The assassin leader's tone was more arrogant than the heavens. Didn't he fear a lightning tribulation would strike him if he continued being this way?

"Elder Juwan has asked us to warn anyone who is going to engage the target. I've done my duty, so now it's up to you," Ding Son said.

"What a drag. Aren't you a prodigy? Why are you such a pussy? I guess this is why the elder asked us—the elite killers—to do their bidding. The current team is nothing but a bunch of pussies. I wonder how strong the Chosen Gold are. Pussy, do you know who created this weird name, Chosen Gold? What kind of shit is this?"

"I've warned you, so we'll just wait and watch you kill the target. Brothers, fall back, and let the elite killers get the job done." Son signaled his beast to fly back, and his team followed him. The elder Juwan had repeatedly warned them not to engage Li Wei until the Sacrificing Harbingers arrived, so he would just wait for the good show. Although Ding Son believed in his own powers, he wasn't a fool to poke a bear with a thin stick.

"Sit back, and watch us kill them with a wave of our left hands." The hooded assassins vanished and charged at a group of people inside a bubble, which Ding Son assumed was a defensive formation.

"Brother Gun, do you know what that formation is?" he asked Ding Gun.

Gun was proficient in formations and had studied the ancient arts of the formations. His original name had been different, but the clan had forced him to change it to rope him in. He'd studied under a high-level array cultivator, and their entire team relied on him to set up offensive and defensive formations. They'd done better after recruiting him to—or rather, forcing him into—the team. This guy had many artifacts on him, and Ding Son wanted them all for himself. After all, why should a slave of his clan keep those artifacts? Those only belonged to a prodigy like Son.

"I don't know. It is a high-level formation. I assume they have a powerful array cultivator at their end."

"Can you break it?" Ding Son asked.

"I can with time. In fact, I've been studying a Corrosive Formation-Breaking Seal from an Ancient Book. I might be able to use it if you leave me undisturbed for half an hour with that formation."

"That's good. Please start working on the preparation while those assassins make fools of the enemy."

Chapter 43

The Play

Wi Rual's fury shot into the sky when one of brother Wei's clones mentioned the Blood-Colored Assassins coming for them. How dared those blasphemers show up here? Those dogs dared to put a dragon on their insignia. They all ought to die, and as long as a single member of the dragon race lived, they would hunt those bastards. Her wing throbbed to charge out of the formation.

"Sister Rual, don't." Brother Wei's clone stepped in front of her. "Let's just watch what they're planning."

"Don't stop me from killing them, brother Wei's clone. You don't understand what low-level pests these people are," she said, her voice shaking. "Don't you know about our undying enmity with them? How dare they use such a symbol on their insignia? Until my race kills each one of them, I can't sleep peacefully."

"I'm not stopping you, Rual'er. Instead, I want you to use your brain." The clone's voice changed slightly, and he sounded more like brother Wei's main body. She felt the authority in his tone.

"Brother Wei, is that you? Are you awake already?" Her mood turned from foul to good, like finding a sweet core inside the bitter shell of a fruit. But when she turned back, brother Wei was still lying unconscious. "Are you really brother Wei or just his clone?" she asked, suspicious that the clone was using her emotions to stall her.

Brother Wei had been in slumber since they'd exited the secret palace. His clone said he'd done something stupid, but she knew he must have overexerted himself to keep them inside the palace for ten days. He must have sacrificed a lot for them to perfect the array formation, and the guilt had been sucking at her mind for a long time now. If she'd known about this, she wouldn't have allowed him to toil his vitality away to save others. And where the heck was the bald monk? He was missing. Shouldn't he come here and help brother Wei?

"I'm awake in my mind but not in my body. Rual'er, why don't you take a seat and enjoy the play you have set up with Sonja?"

Wi Rual giggled. How could she forget what they'd prepared for the intruders? Those bastard dogs wouldn't understand what awaited them inside the formation.

"Brother Wei, that girlfriend of yours has a twisted mind. I couldn't believe when she suggested this wicked strategy." Rual'er gave a wicked smile.

Sonja had set a perfect trap for anyone who dared to approach the array formation. Not only that, but she'd had the people who acted as formation poles stand far apart, creating an illusion of weakness in their formation, covering them with array plates brother Wei had made for them. She'd even added her poison around them, turning it into a trap. Wi Rual didn't know how it would work, but she could see the evil in Sonja's eyes, and she believed that if brother Wei trusted her, she should as well.

"Do you want to say 'crafty'? She has used poison and something else. I can't even scan it with my divine sense. She is acting mysterious today," Wei said.

Wi Rual nodded in agreement. "She is a genius. She even has divine sense activated already. Brother Wei, why didn't you use her or me as a formation pole? Even that baldy monk is missing. You should trust the people close to you—people who are like your family."

She felt warmth radiating through her neck when she used the word *family*. Once she went back to the Martial Realm, she would have to use the beautification pill to make sure she turned into an attractive woman. But would her father allow her to marry a common human?

No, brother Wei wasn't a common human. He was like the brightest star in the sky.

"You five would have been optimum choice, but I could only use Grandpa Ling, as you guys are needed elsewhere."

"I can understand why you can't use the naive fox, but what about others? Sonja would have been a great choice as well."

"She is more useful outside, and she has enough power to protect herself from any danger, and I put our leader, the princess, as a formation pole. Your father would skin me alive if I used you like that." He chuckled, easing the tension.

Suddenly, a smoke screen rose from the north side of the formation, followed by a loud explosion.

"The play has begun," brother Wei said.

"How did they enter the formation bubble? Didn't you say it's impenetrable by the ones below the Houtian Realm?" she asked, getting up from her sitting position to charge forward. They couldn't let their defense break. Otherwise, morale would plummet, and things would go badly.

"Everyone, sit tight. This is intentional. Don't panic." Brother Wei's voice moved through the crowd, calming everyone with the explanation of the opening and telling them to watch for the next show to unfold.

Wi Rual sat tight. If brother Wei said it would be a good show, then it would be one, and she didn't want to miss anything.

Wyan Jim panicked when two red-hooded figures appeared through a smokescreen and penetrated the defensive bubble. Hadn't senior Li Wei said no one could attack them? Yet two people dressed in dark-red robes walked through as if the defensive formation didn't exist. Had his team missed something?

A message played in their minds, telling them senior Wei's plan. So senior Wei had let the intruders in on purpose. It made sense. Senior Wei could kill these people with a wave of his hand, so he must have wanted to capture them alive.

The hooded figure walked sneakily toward them as if they were hidden, but a fog around them made sure Wyan Jim and his partner could see the intruders clearly. How senior Li Wei had achieved this only heaven knew, but it was effective. Those two sneered as they walked close to Wyan Jim. They must have been conversing about how easily they'd broken the array formation. Those fools didn't know they were walking into a trap.

One of them froze. He'd landed on a pressure plate the senior Sonja had placed around them as a defensive measure. A thick layer of green covered the first one, and he turned into a stone with a grayish hue, as if excavated from underground.

The other one panicked and leaped away from his position, but a tiny dart shot out of the ground and penetrated his chest, turning him green instantly. He'd been poisoned, and the poison was spreading fast. Those fools had just walked in without thinking traps could be spread across the weak points. It seemed like their intellect was nothing more than that of a two-year-old kid. Senior had done something to the pressure plates. Wyan Jim bet she could use poison to kill each of their enemies.

A woman flashed out of the formation bubble, and her sword pierced the two hooded figures before she vanished again. Blood sprayed onto the ground. Wyan Jim gasped. He knew that woman. She was only at the peak of the Boiling Blood Realm, and she'd easily killed two elite-looking assassins.

"Brother Jim, these people are really scary." His partner, an old man in Heart Blood Realm, was holding his sword in the air, ready to attack anytime.

"They are indeed, but everything is under senior Wei's control." Wyan Jim squinted and looked around to see the same scene happening in two more places. Three assassins were killed efficiently. One survived while injuring one person, but the fox alongside senior Li Wei flashed out and saved the old man.

Suddenly, a majestic dragon emerged from of the formation and covered the assassin who was running away. "Dogs of the Blood-Colored Assassins, accept your death." A sharp wind blade rushed out of her mouth and cut through the assassin's head like it was a tofu.

Blood-Colored Assassins? Wyan Jim had heard about them. They were a powerful organization in the Martial Realm. He released his held breath. It had only taken a few seconds, but they'd killed six assassins without much effort.

Would it deter the thousand people who'd appeared on the battlefield, or would they willingly sacrifice their lives in senior Li Wei's schemes? Whatever they chose, they couldn't beat senior Li Wei. He was invincible.***

Ding Son shook his head as he folded down the glass plate. Those assassins had died like chicken on a butcher's plate. Thanks to Ding Gun's ingenious artifact that showed them what had really happened inside the formation, Ding Son had watched the assassins dying like cabbages. The rude one who'd cut across his throat had escaped from the initial attack, but he died to the One-Winged Dragon. Rivalry between the One-Winged Dragon race and the Blood-Colored Assassins was well known in the Martial Realm, so it wasn't surprising to see her taking action.

"Brother Gun, what do you think?" Ding Son asked. "Especially the assassins turning to stone. What kind of skill did they use?"

"It has to be an array or talisman."

"Why can't it be a rune?" Ding Son asked.

"Runes are intricate to craft, and we know these people have a powerful array cultivator. So I guess it's an array plate. They're using it like a pressure plate that can be triggered and petrify the attacker, and then they're killing the assassins with poison. This is an unorthodox method but an effective one. Those assassins were real fools to walk in there without preparation."

"They were jerks who deserved to die. Anyway, do you have a way to bypass those arrays? Why don't you use the artifact of yours?" Ding Son asked, conflicted.

Out of the corner of his eye, he saw a bunch of people heading toward the array formation. They might join the opponent, but they were nothing but cannon fodder, and he really didn't care about them.

"It's possible, but I'd need to study the pattern of activation a little more. I also need more Qi Stones. Can you arrange that?" Ding Gun asked.

His response clear. Was he trying to get away from the Ding clan again? Hadn't he felt the sincerity in Ding Son's heart for the last few months? Or had he caught on to Ding Son's thoughts? Whatever. All the artifacts owned by Ding Gun would be his—Ding Son's.

"Would ten be sufficient? I don't have many Qi Stones. Only fifty. You should get it done with that. I don't have a treasure trove, so you'd better be frugal about this," Ding Son said.

"I need at least a hundred people to test it out for us."

Ding Son sighed. A hundred people. It would put a lot of restrictions on his skill.

"I'll try." Ding Son retrieved an artifact in the shape of an eye and then stabbed it into his forehead. A trickle of blood rolled out as the artifact adjusted into his forehead, forming a third eye. "A hundred, is it?"

Ding Gun nodded.

"Two others will accompany you and protect you while you observe things, but, brother Gun, don't take any risks. I don't want to be a bringer of bad news to the patriarch." He let a note of threat slip into his tone so Ding Gun wouldn't do anything stupid.

Chapter 44

Nether-Reanimating Poison

A hundred cultivators from the newly arrived people walked toward the defensive formation, their eyes shrouded in a strange red light that shone in the barren land. There was a commotion among them, and they were backing down from a group of people sitting over Dark-Blood Peacocks.

Li Wei sat on a chair at the edge of the defensive formation, his divine sense spread like a beam, covering the newly arrived cultivators. One of the guys had a third eye on his head. Using Divine Vision, Wei sensed energies moving from the artificial third eye to the hundred cultivators marching ahead, moving through the barren land in the dim light. His main body could use Void Eyes to confirm it, but he guessed the three-eyed guy was controlling these people through some strange means.

"Why do they look possessed? Their movements are stiffer than stick figures. They must be coming here to test the might of the formation. How stupid," Rual'er whispered.

She was standing next to Wei, watching over the battlefield like a queen. After she'd killed the final Blood-Colored Assassin, her mood had improved, turning her into a chatterbox. She'd even poured a cup of fine wine for Wei's clone. It had a spicy taste, and he hadn't liked it much. Kai Shaya would have loved it, but he'd gone toward the clock to check something for his sect.

"They're being controlled." Wei pointed at the Dark-Blood Peacocks. "There's a three-eyed guy between them, and he's controlling these people."

"I thought cylinder-shaped-mouth guy was their leader." Rual'er pointed at the three men walking behind the hundred people, trailing them as if they were part of the group, though their clear eyes isolated them from the possessed cannon fodder.

Wei scanned the cylinder-shaped-mouth guy and found something interesting. He was wearing a robe that prevented Wei's divine sense from scanning him, and when Wei tried to scan him, the guy stared in his direction.

"I'm feeling itchy. I'll just kill them all." Rual pushed her wings out, ready to fly.

Wei chuckled. This woman had changed into something else after killing the assassin. What had gotten into her?

"Let's wait, Rual'er. We can take action if things don't look good. I can always break their illusion with my divine sense, so we don't need to act. And we should test our team's morale using these attacks. If those people crumble from the inside, nothing can save them."

She sighed. "Why are you so much more battle intelligent than me? Even when I tried to pull you through your dark times, you flipped the script."

Wei chuckled. "I fought too many battles in my life and became like this, and I'd prefer you to remain innocent until the end of our time."

In his previous life, Rual'er had suffered a lot because of him, yet he'd acted like a jerk in the end, rudely rejecting her. Times were different, and he much preferred his friends and family to leave peacefully and let him handle the burdens of this world. "If things go south, I will pull them out of the illusion, but they are not saints. Anyway, how were your gains in the palace?"

Rual'er giggled. "Plentiful. I'll show you when the time arrives."

"I saw your speed had improved when you flew out of the formation. Did you learn something speed related?"

"No, that's just a byproduct. What I learned, brother Wei, will blow your mind." She winked. "I never thought I could do this on my own, but you showed me a path no one in my race has traveled before. When my father was at my cultivation level, even he wasn't as proficient with the wind as I am. Brother Wei, you're like an angel of the wind for me. Why didn't you show up before?"

"Better late than never."

"Yes, better late than never." She giggled.

The hundred people reached the defensive bubble, and then two of them charged at the two people who were working as poles. Those two were husband and wife, and they panicked as soon as the attackers ran forward.

"Don't worry. They can't harm a hair on your heads even if they go all out," Wei told them in a divine transmission, trying to ease their anxiety. However, hearing something and facing a pair of raging monsters with swords in their hands were two different things. The couple could only rely on their wits and courage.

Their faces relaxed after the swords bounced back from the defensive formation, forcing their wielders back from the impact. Skin ripped apart from the attackers' arms, and blood dripped, but they didn't mutter a single word of pain. The attackers charged again as if they didn't feel their broken palms.

One froze and instantly turned into a green stone statue. Two poison darts shot from the ground and penetrated the other attacker, turning him green with poison. The second attacker's body withered under the poison and shattered into tiny pieces that resembled scorpions. They were made of energy. They bared their fangs at the stone statue and instantly devoured it.

"Back down. The poison is spreading," the cylinder-mouthed cultivator cried and leaped back, his pale-yellow robe lit up with symbols forming a defensive armor around his entire body. His clothes looked old, giving him a natural concealing effect. The arrays on his robe defended him not only from the poison but also from his group's stray swords that flew around when the people attacked the poison figures.

"What poison did you use?" Wei asked, his divine sense locked onto the cylinder-mouthed guy, an array cultivator who had carved many defensive arrays on his clothes.

That robe looked familiar. One of the sects Wei had worked with in his previous life had an artifact similar to this, and he wanted to know if this guy had a connection with that sect. Only that sect followed the path of carving arrays into clothes. Wei had thought about it, but the path was time-consuming, and if the clothes lacked quality, the array would be wasted once they were torn apart.

"Nether-Reanimating Poison," Sonja replied.

"Where did you get that?" Wei's shoulders tightened. "Collect it right away, and don't let anyone see what it looks like. It's a forbidden poison, Sonja."

Sonja frowned.

"Lord, this one stumbled upon this, and that's how I ended up coming here. I can control this poison. Lord doesn't need to worry about it affecting our friends."

"No more questions. Just collect it if you trust me." Wei let the gravity of the situation slip into his tone.

Nether-Reanimating Poison was a big taboo in the Martial Realm, and if anyone found out about it, Wei and the others would be hunted down. He didn't want Sonja to be called a criminal. Slowly, he turned to Rual'er, who'd heard everything he said.

"Of course I won't say anything to anyone. Do you even have to ask, brother Wei? You are breaking my heart." Rual'er shook her head.

Those were the same wordings Wei had used on her before. Women—they could hold a grudge for a long time.

"No. I'm just letting you know the importance of this thing. If you speak of it to anyone, even to your father, you'll be implicated as well." This poison came from the Netherworld, and there was a bloody history associated with it in the Martial Realm. Wei didn't want to open any wounds.

"Is it really that troublesome?" Rual'er asked.

"It's more than that. I'll have to assess the situation. Sister Rual'er, can I ask you to investigate our people and see if anyone understands the reality of this? With your ability, I trust you can do that for us."

"I will. Leave it to me."

"Don't force yourself if it's too much for you."

"Don't worry, brother Wei. After my gains in the palace, I've attained more control over my ability, all thanks to you. But then, why should we discuss what's yours or mine?"

"Shall I kill the last one who escaped, lord?" Sonja asked.

"No need. Let's wait for their next move. Disperse the poison, and wipe out all the traces." Wei stared at their enemies, wondering if he should just kill them. He had some trust in the people on his side, and with Rual'er's ability, he would know their exact thoughts, but he couldn't make her use the ability on their enemies.

"Yes, lord." Sonja rushed out of the defensive formation and opened a small pot that looked broken. Instantly, the poison in the affected area gathered inside the pot, leaving no trace.

"That thing smells evil. Are you sure about her, brother Wei?" Rual'er asked, her tone serious.

Wei sighed. After Xue Qi's betrayal, he wasn't sure about anyone following him except Fei'er and Nuan'er. They were his sweethearts, and no matter what, they wouldn't betray him. Well, he didn't doubt Yang Fang and Blood Parasite and his group of beast friends as well. They were loyal too.

"She's trustworthy, and no poison can affect me." Wei's clone glanced at the main body, wondering how the Yin Poison Pill Clone would behave once it was exposed to the nether poison. Would it accept it or seal it instead? That would be interesting to find it out.

Chapter 45

Offer to Join

Li Gun's heart quivered when the surrounding people died like vermin exposed to holy water. They couldn't even open their mouths to cry before their bodies withered. Even the two goons watching over him died like ants. It was a miracle that he'd survived, thanks to the artifact left by his sect ancestor.

He sighed as he reached the group of people he'd come here with. Horror flashed over their faces when Li Gun reached them, and some of them even stepped back. Except Ding Son. He kept glaring at Li Gun.

"Ding Gun, why didn't you save them?" Ding Son shouted, pointing at him from over his Dark-Blood Peacock.

Li Gun wanted to shout back and tell him not to call him Ding Gun. He was Li Gun, and not Ding Gun. That name had been forced on him by the Ding clan, and he hated it.

"You crippled my team." The third eye on Ding Son's forehead pulsed with a strange light, sending a chill down Li Gun's legs.

"Leader Son, aren't you being too critical here? You should be congratulating me for being able to save my life. Instead, you're blaming me. How does that make sense? Do you think that poison was something I could neutralize with my abilities?" Li Gun retorted, unable to take it anymore.

"I don't know. You should have used your arrays to save them. You don't understand how important the team is. I'll be reporting this to the elders of the clan once we go back."

"Do whatever you need to do," Li Gun replied.

"*Ding* Gun, what kind of poison was it? You should at least have some information on it with your tools, right?" Ding Son asked sarcastically.

Fuck him. Li Gun squirmed mentally. Whenever Ding Son wanted to show Li Gun's inferior status, he would use his name as a weapon. Ding Son was a bastard among bastards, and Li Gun wished he could kill him, but with his current battle powers, it wasn't possible.

"Something is happening!" one of their team members shouted.

They turned to look at the defensive formation. Whoever had built it had done an ingenious job. It was as flexible and nimble as wind. Li Gun had studied the art of formations and arrays his entire life, but he couldn't create one using humans as formation poles, and whatever he'd seen was as stiff as metal poles. If he hadn't been bound to the Ding clan, he would have sought out this Array Master and exchanged some pointers.

Ding Son pulled out a formation plate, scanning it for the real-time view of the battlefield. This rare artifact of the Li Gun's now-extinct sect allowed anyone to monitor an area of a hundred miles. Even a Xiantian Realm cultivator would find it impossible to monitor that large an area. It was Li Gun's prized possession, but Ding Son had snatched it under the pretense that a leader needed such an artifact. He'd never returned it to Li Gun.

An image of a busty woman appeared on the formation plate. She walked out of the formation and collected the poison in a small broken pot. It looked quite odd.

"It must be the artifact corpse poison," Li Gun whispered. One of his sect's records had mentioned it. "But that's taboo in the Martial Realm.

Is that person part of the Corpse-Poison Sect, which went underground a thousand years ago?"

"I bet Li Wei is from the Corpse-Poison Sect. No wonder he's so powerful. We can now target them all." Ding Son chuckled.

"I don't think so. I saw Li Wei lying in the middle of the defensive array, unconscious. Although there's a concealing formation around him, it can't hide from my robe," Li Gun said. "I don't think he's the member of the Corpse-Poison Sect, but one of them might be."

Ding Son shook his head. "You are too naive. This guy is the member of the Corpse-Poison Sect. I have to declare this and rally everyone to fight against him."

He turned to face the nine hundred people who'd come with them but hadn't taken any action. Ding Son wanted to manipulate them to attack the defensive formation. He was planning something else, something deep. Li Gun knew Ding Son better than anyone, and whatever he planned wasn't a good thing.

"Ding Son, the sect asked us not to engage Li Wei in battle. Let's just wait until the fifth wave arrives."

"Ding Gun, don't be a jerk. You have an artifact that can save everyone from the poison. Shouldn't you give it to leader Son so he can take care of the vile bastards?" someone from his group shouted.

Li Gun quivered. So this bastard wanted the last remaining artifact of his sect, the Thousand-Secret Robe. It was the inheritance artifact left by the sect master, and it couldn't be given to anyone else.

"Brother Gun, he's right. You should lend me your treasure robe, and of course, I will return it after everything is settled," Ding Son said, a mocking smile spreading over his lips.

"Impossible," Ding Gun said. "This is my sect's treasure, and no one else can use it. If you snatch it away like other artifacts, it will self-destruct."

"There's nothing impossible in this world, brother Gun. There is only absolute power, and you listen to me when I say so. Once you give me this robe and make me a disciple of your so-called sect, it will work for me." A red light emerged from his third eye and enveloped Li Gun. This artifact he'd gotten from the Gatekeeper elder specialized in putting others under an illusion, and it could even work on an array cultivator with a strong mental resistance. Desperation sank through Li Gun's veins. For the first time in many years, he felt helpless.

"Ding Son, how dare you covet my belongings. This is not the deal I made with the Ding clan. You can't use your immoral ability on me."

Ding Son chuckled. "Don't worry—I don't like men, so I won't use it on you for the reason you think I might. Just give me your robe, and tell its secrets. After everything is finished, I'll bury your corpse with the dregs of your sect."

"You killed them." Li Gun felt a heavy mountain on his chest.

Before he'd been saved by the Ding clan, he'd had a senior sister who had groomed him to carry the mantle of the sect forward. Out of a thousand sect members, only she had survived and adopted Li Gun as the future successor, but one day, she'd died mysteriously. The Ding clan had come and saved him from a big monster, and then he'd been forced to swear his loyalty to them.

So this had all been the plan. Those bastards.

"If you join me, I can save you from your enslavement, fellow array cultivator," a voice said, and he knew it was the master who'd created the defensive formation.

Was he giving him a hand just to get his treasure? Whatever it was, Li Gun nodded. Even if he lost his artifact, he wouldn't lose it to the Ding clan.

Chapter 46

An Old Friend?

L i Wei broke into a smile when he spotted the leader who called himself Ding Son using his artifact to control the array cultivator—the cylinder-shaped-mouthed guy, Ding Gun. According to their conversation, Ding Gun wasn't part of the Ding clan but had vowed his loyalty to them.

Interesting. He hadn't heard about the Ding clan before. Where had it popped out from?

"Brother Wei, are you saying something?" Rual'er asked, handing him a grape.

Wei sighed. This girl had given him multiple pieces of fruit in the last few minutes, and she also had a huge wine collection. The bitter wine hadn't even lifted from his tongue before she'd handed him a bunch of golden grapes, a specialty of the area her race lived in. He couldn't say no to her.

"No. Just enjoying your wine," Wei said.

"I've plenty more variety in the Martial Realm. Once you come to speak to my father, I'll let you taste all the thousand different wines in my collection. Even my father hasn't tasted them all."

Wei tapped on the metal hand of the chair, carefully watching the action taking place at the enemy's camp. The conversation was heading in an interesting direction, and he wanted to judge the array cultivator before he made any more moves.

"Brother Wei, why are you smiling smugly?" Rual'er asked, picking up another fruit for him. "Are you hiding something from me again?"

"No, I'm just waiting for a friend to join us." He turned to Sonja. "Sonja, can you check what's happening behind the clock? A few people from the other camp are headed there, and Kai Shaya is also around that place." Kai Shaya had wanted to do some investigation on the clock, so he'd gone behind it, and he didn't want the others to disturb him.

Nodding, Sonja vanished from the array formation.

"Brother Wei, who is your friend, and why hasn't he joined us already?" Rual'er asked. She had a lot of questions.

"Even I am surprised about that." After seeing the array cultivator's pale robe, Wei was trying to match it with a robe image in his memory. They looked almost the same, and the functionality was similar as well. He was ninety percent sure it was the same robe.

The robe in his memory belonged to a friend's sect, and it was a sect artifact that was missing. While roaming through the Martial Realm in his previous life, he'd met this guy named Li Gava in an array competition. Wei wasn't an array master yet, and they hit it off. As they became friends, Wei got to know about his situation. Li Gava came from a small sect with only a thousand disciples and was the founder's son. The sect patriarch always remained in seclusion, and Wei never saw him on his many visits to the sect. The patriarch died after a few years, and the sect disbanded. Li Gava chose to go on a journey to search for the sect's most precious treasure—the Thousand-Secret Treasure Robe. However, he grew older and died before finding it. Li Gava had focused only on array cultivation and neglected his martial cultivation, resulting in the early death.

Wei had been with him until his last breath, and the guy only had one regret—not finding the treasure robe. Before he died, he talked about his father's last dream of finding the long-lost sect artifact. His father had possessed it and then lost to someone, and then he'd reestablished the sect and searched for that robe his entire life, but he couldn't find it. Li Gava had tried his best, but he also failed. He'd wanted Wei to find the robe and bury it in the place where the sect used to be.

Wei hadn't been able to find it, but the image of the robe was marked in his mind forever. So when he saw the array cultivator and his myriad ways of using the robe, he wanted to rush out of the formation and check the robe, but he didn't. Without his main body, he couldn't just let a clone barge out, or he might lose it.

Then he found the chance that could lead him to discover the long-lost artifact. Ding Son had turned on his own friend, Ding Gun. If Wei could get the robe and return it to Li Gava when they met in the future, how awesome would that be? Despite this world being different from his own past life, the future might not be that different. And even if he didn't meet Li Gava, he could bury the robe at the place the sect had been in his old life.

Wei sent a divine transmission: "If you join me, I can save you from your enslavement, fellow array cultivator."

The array cultivator nodded subtly. He didn't startle or jump out in shock, so he must have known how the divine sense worked. It wasn't a surprise that an array cultivator knew about that.

"I can rid of the artifact illusion from your mind, but I can't make your eyes red unless you want to be blind. Can you make your eyes red?" Wei asked. "Move your right index finger once if you have a way and twice if you don't."

Sweat dripped from the array cultivator's index finger when he moved it once, merging into the barren ground instantly. Only a cultivator with divine sense focused on it would spot the change. Adding to the eerie dim light covering the entire battlefield, everyone looked pale as parchment paper, making it difficult for anyone with good eyesight to see Ding Gun's action, which happened in the blink of an eye. Even the array cultivator's pale-yellow robe made it impossible to detect his movements.

"Fair enough. I'm cutting the artifact effect," Wei said, turning his divine sense into a sharp blade that cut through the strange energy coming out of the Ding Son's third eye.

The artifact used energy waves to trap their target in the illusion, so anyone with a powerful divine sense could cut through it. After a person reached the Houtian Realm, it became very difficult to use a common illusion technique on them because of their divine sense. Even a sprout of divine sense gave a Houtian Realm cultivator a natural resistance. Compared to an early-stage Houtian Realm cultivator, Wei's divine sense was like a giant in front of an ant. Even a Violet Palace Realm cultivator would feel pressured by Wei's divine sense, so cutting this artifact's illusion turned out to be a kid's job.

The array cultivator's eyes turned clear for a moment before an array hidden in his robe lit up, turning his eyes redder than a rabid dog. Drool accumulated at the edge of his mouth, and he looked at Ding Son like a dog watching his master.

"See, Li Gun. Even a mighty array cultivator like you fell to my artifact. The elder wanted to give this artifact to you as he thought it would suit your array cultivation, but it would have been a waste on you. Now, make me your sect's apprentice, and give me the robe." Ding Son chuckled, and the other bastards joined him in the evil laugh.

Li Gun. Hearing that word, Wei arched his brow. He'd heard the name before, but he couldn't recall where.

"Come on—do it fast. I don't have time." Ding Son waved his hand, and the array cultivator, Li Gun, walked forward.

"Can you kill them now?" Wei asked. "Tap your finger once to say yes or twice to ask for help."

The array cultivator tapped his finger once.

Wei turned to Rual'er, who was pouring a different wine into his glass. "Girl, are you trying to get me drunk? This clone doesn't have a high cultivation level, and it won't survive your assault." He chuckled.

"I forgot. This little one apologizes." She smiled, blinking. Even in her small dragon form, she looked mesmerizing.

"Rual'er," Wei said, turning serious. "Be ready to charge out. I want to save someone from that group, and I might need your help."

He looked at his main body, which was still sleeping. Purple was wrapped around his neck like a scarf. Little Fox was sitting next to his head, munching on fruit.

"I'll use my new ability if you need my help." Rual'er got up, her hazy gaze turned sharper as she stared at the other group.

"Let's wait and watch first." Wei focused his attention on the drama happening in the enemy camp. If the array cultivator could do it himself, it would be for the best. Otherwise, he would have to rely on Rual'er to save him.

Wei held his breath when the array cultivator walked toward Ding Son, with crazy eyes. They were on the verge of a make-or-break moment.

Chapter 47

Array Cultivator's Might

As if someone had lifted a veil from a dark window, Li Gun was exposed to the bright light of mother nature. Or at least, it felt like that. Whatever the reason, a veil had been lifted from his heart, and he saw the world in its own colors, brutal and disgusting. He'd forgotten the effect of Ding Son's artifact. It turned everything into a murky thought that prevented him from remembering how his senior sister had died.

No more. Now he clearly recalled how desperate he'd been, surrounded by beasts from all sides, weak and exhausted. Ding clan cultivators came to help and saved him. They even offered him a place in the clan, but he had to join their clan and take their name. It was a good deal, so he'd agreed, taken their name, and then married a girl from their clan and even had a son he loved a lot.

However, now that he looked over his entire life, he realized the Ding clan had never accepted him. Many times, he'd been humiliated, suppressed, and taken advantage of. When they'd had to send the prodigies to the Martial Realm, they made him Ding Son's guard, binding him with the bastard.

The man's greed had no bounds. First, he'd snatched a few artifacts Li Gun had managed to keep away from the Ding clan's eyes. Those artifacts belonged to Li Gun's sect, and the senior sister had trusted him with them. And now he'd set his eyes on the inheritance treasure of his sect—Thousand-Secret Treasure Robe. He had to be planning to kill Li Gun and put the blame on the enemy. However, if he thought wearing the treasure robe would be that easy, he was nothing but a big fool. A person who didn't know how to bond with the robe would just die while trying it. The robe was quite vicious, and it fed on the user's vitality if the user didn't provide it enough qi energy.

So Li Gun could easily kill Ding Son by not telling him about the robe's innate properties. But no. Li Gun wouldn't kill Ding Son this easily. That wouldn't be a good enough punishment for the bastard. He deserved a better death. Better pain, better cruelty, and better punishment.

"Hundred-Mirror Array, activate." Li Gun activated a special array inside the treasure robe while walking forward.

For the next minute, the array could deflect any attack a few cultivation levels above his own, and it should be enough to repel the peak of the Heart Blood Realm cultivator. If Li Gun had possessed the same cultivation base as the bastard, he could activate a few more arrays to wipe them out once and for all. There were some midlevel arrays on the robe he couldn't activate with his current qi energy reserve. Anyway, all he needed was a few more seconds, and the Hundred-Mirror Array should give him that time.

"Conscious Piercing Needle, activate." Another array activated inside his robe, turning it into a dimensional portal to thousands of needles laced with poison. With a thought, he could shoot thousands of needles from his robe, killing everyone around him, or at least freezing them for a few moments.

However, his main killing move was the Illusion-Reflecting Array. It was the trump card he'd spent weeks honing, refining with his blood to counter the greedy Ding Son. Although Li Gun had never wanted to use it, he'd felt a keen sense of danger from Ding Son from the start, so he'd prepared this. His senior sister had dreamed of bringing their sect back to glory. There was no way he could let it go to waste.

"Why are you walking slowly?" Ding Son frowned, his face twitching in pain. "Wait, my power. You're draining my power. Bastard. You're resisting my artifact power." He signaled, and three of his teammates charged at Li Gun.

Li Gun chuckled, his eyes turning clear. There was no need to fake anything. All he'd needed was a few seconds to activate the different arrays. Then the game would be over for his enemies.

The two bastards attacked him with physical weapons, one holding a giant sword and another holding an axe. They excelled in their respective weapons, and even a Houtian Realm cultivator would need to be careful facing their combo attack.

But Li Gun just let the attack strike him while he marched toward Ding Son. The attacks clashed against him and bounced back the attackers, cutting across their bodies. Blood spilled like rain, and the attackers cried out in pain.

"Bastard, how dare you injure your teammates? Did you forget we are brothers?" Ding Son shouted, his eyes going red as he watched his brothers bleed and die like chickens.

Li Gun chuckled. "Don't be hypocrite, Ding Son. You will die the same way, but I'll add a twist to it. I'll make your death the most painful. Don't worry. It will last longer than those two bastards', and you'll remember in the netherworld as well. I will make your own illusions devour you."

"You shouldn't tell your methods to your enemy, junior." Senior sighed.

"You're going overboard, Li Gun. You betrayed the Ding clan, so I can kill you without any remorse. Brothers, use your strongest skill, and kill this bastard." Ding Son activated his third eye, and twenty people charged out of the crowd at Li Gun.

Li Gun had expected this to happen. "Senior, please help me get these people out of the illusion," he said.

The senior who had saved him had done it easily and might be able to do it again. If he couldn't, Li Gun would have to push everything he had into the arrays and go for Ding Son's life. It was a gamble he had to take. There was no other option.

"Why not? But don't forget, you owe me two favors now," the senior said.

The twenty people paused, their eyes becoming clear once again. Ding Son coughed a mouthful of blood. The senior had brutally cut through his technique, which gave Ding Son a backlash. Something he deserved.

"Bastard, who is doing this? Come out if you have guts."

"The senior doesn't need to come out. I'm enough for you." Li Gun continued moving forward. In three more seconds, he could attack Ding Son.

"You're forcing me to do this, Li Gun." Ding Son retrieved a square black object and wrapped it around his third eye. "If you hadn't told me about your technique, you could have trapped me, but you, fool, told me your technique, so I've secured my artifact. You can't do anything now." He faced his teammates. "Du Bujio, use the long-range attacks, and kill this motherfucker."

All seven of his subordinates pulled their weapons out and attacked Li Gun from every direction. Li Gun regretted saying his method out loud. He'd become cocky and lost the element of surprise. For a moment, Li Gun was enveloped in many elemental attacks. Ice, fire, lightning, earth, metal—all five elements came for his life, but before they landed, a white crystal dropped from the sky and into his arms.

"Use a Qi Crystal to activate the arrays. Your qi reserve is deficient," senior said, his voice filling Li Gun's ears.

A smile broke out on Li Gun's face. Every array cultivator was bogged down by the use of Qi Stones, and he only had a handful of them, but he'd just been given a powerful energy source.

"Come and die, you bastards." Li Gun chuckled, tapping the Qi Crystal into his treasure robe and activating the arrays at half of their power. This was fun—the feeling of being powerful. He should do it more.

Chapter 48

Going back to the Roots

The treasure robe fascinated Li Wei. The more he looked at it, the more he thought it wasn't the work of any Array Master. The sheer number of arrays carved into that thing would have been impossible even in his previous life. He could only think of one source—the ancient civilization.

Wait—could it have been done by someone beyond the Array Master? An Array Scion maybe? Just the thought sent a shiver down his legs. His breathing became ragged, and a weird taste filled his mouth. The taste of curiosity. Yes, he had to get his hands on this robe to study it further. However, he wouldn't snatch it away from that guy, so he had to think of a way to get it nicely.

Li Gun stepped forward sluggishly. The guy was a good actor, or Ding Son was a fool. Ding Son was at the peak of Heart Blood Realm, yet he couldn't realize that his opponent, who was a few layers below him in cultivation, had broken his illusion.

Sipping tea while sitting in his chair, Wei watched Li Gun activate one array after another while pretending to be under the influence of the illusion artifact. The more arrays he activated, the paler he got. It was a sign of qi deficiency. It became clear that he practiced a low-level cultivation art, as the qi he poured into the robe lacked quality. By comparison, Wei's Earth Grade Wood Qi was like gold. After practicing a Heaven Grade wood cultivation art, his qi had turned a gold-liquid color that was not only soft to touch but exuded an aroma of life. The same was true of his earth and metal qi. In his previous life, he hadn't understood, but the quality of one's qi affected the outcome of everything, even arrays and formations. A difference—a subtle one or a huge one—could be observed by just changing the quality of the qi.

Then Li Gun had outed his plan, and things had turned difficult for him. Although Wei didn't want to help, he had no other choice.

"Rual'er, give him a Qi Crystal." Wei had handed a few to Rual'er.

"Sure." Rual'er floated up.

Wei smiled. Others might think he looked down on Rual'er, a princess of the dragon clan, but they wouldn't know of the bond he and Rual'er had shared in his previous life. Although this life was different and this Rual'er might be different, he looked at her with the same affectionate feelings he'd for the Rual'er in his previous life.

"Shall I aid him?" she asked, rising a little higher.

"Not until he's about to die."

"Why not? That illusion artifact won't affect me. I've my own artifacts to guard against his low-level ones," she said disdainfully.

"Princess, would you stop your soldiers from training for bloody battles?"

"Of course not."

"That's your answer."

Rual'er rolled her eyes and shot into the sky. Her speed had increased, and the wind supported her as if she was the mother of all winds in the world. She had learned the Intent of Wind. It seemed like she was holding her breakthrough, which was a good thing for her.

"Li Wei, I could have gone faster than her. I'm much faster." Little Fox came close to him, munching on her fruit. She'd been acting reserved since the fiasco with the gale ball.

"Little Fox, it's all right. You're a child, so you ought to make mistakes. But don't turn them into catastrophes." He rubbed her soft fun, offering her a piece of fruit Rual'er had given him.

"I'm sorry. I just wanted to..." Her words faded into sobs.

"It's okay." A twinge twisted his stomach.

She was like a little sister, and he hated it when someone close to him cried. It made him question his own resolve to make this world a safe place for his loved ones. In the past few months, he'd gained many new friends and loved ones, and sometimes he felt like a heavy weight had settled on his chest, one he wasn't sure he could withstand for long.

"Tell me what's happening in the Beast Origin Realm. Why did you come out of it? Where is Fan Ji?" he asked.

"I don't know. When we charged in with Fan Ji and the fiery panther, something struck us, throwing me out of the portal. Then I saw these birdies..." She stared at the few giant birds they'd caught from the people they fought in the first wave. "After their owners died, they had turned submissive and didn't fight back. The same had happened with a few Dark-Blood Peacocks whose owners had died. Those came from the Beast Origin Realm. They said a big war took place there. A few powerful cultivators caught them and enslaved them to humans. Millions of beasts have died in that war, and they're only low-level ones. Those strong cultivators captured all the high-level beasts and took them away."

"Where?"

"They don't know," Little Fox answered.

Wei frowned. What kind of war was going on in the Beast Origin Realm? Who was capturing the beasts? Where were they taking them?

"Do they know about Fan Ji and the others? I guess he should be fine. He has a powerful father."

"No, they aren't close to the snake territory, so they are not aware," she replied.

"I don't have a good feeling about this."

Wei glanced at the Dark-Blood Peacocks Ding Son and his team were using. They were not part of the Mortal Realm, and even the Martial Realm had very few species like that. Where had they come from? A gut feeling was telling him they were from the Beast Origin Realm. Had the Gatekeepers had a hand in this?

Rual'er dropped the Qi Crystal from the sky, and no one noticed other than Li Gun. Even the beasts were oblivious to Rual'er's arrival. Wei focused on Li Gun, whose arrays became powerful, and who chuckled like a villain from the stories. The Qi Crystal had instantly upgraded his battle prowess. He was unleashing powerful attacks on his opponents, instantly turning the seven-versus-one battle into seven versus a thousand. The poison needles, especially, kept his opponents at bay.

However, that wasn't what Wei focused on. He was shocked by the way Li Gun was smiling widely. He was like a child given a lot of candies, and Wei related to that feeling. Array cultivators always needed materials and energy sources to use new arrays. It was a rich man's profession, and Wei had struggled with that a lot in his previous life.

"He's doing good." Wei smiled as Li Gun used a rare array, Mirror-Reflection Array, to reflect one of the energy beam attacks, killing his opponent in one shot. Wei had known those arrays, but he hadn't set them up as he'd been too busy with other things. Maybe he had become too narrow-minded lately, and he should focus on dao of arrays so he would find the fun he had lost.

He sighed. There was too much to do, and he had lost his sense of fun along the way. Maybe it was time to go back to his roots.

"What is that thing?" Little Fox asked.

Wei saw a giant Dark-Blood Peacock emerging from behind Ding Son. It was a mutated beast. Where the fuck had it come from?

Chapter 49

Blood Parasite Takes Over

Li Gun lost his wits when the giant beast appeared behind Ding Son.

"Li Gun, you thought you would win by using some underhanded method, did you? You've enraged me, bastard. I'll kill you today, and then I'll fuck your wife in front of others and sell your son to the slave merchants." Ding Son chuckled, his tone changing from amused to pained as his third eye emitted a shiny light that focused on the giant Dark-Blood Peacock.

The Dark-Blood Peacock roared, and his eyes turned red. It had fallen under Ding Son's control. This was bad.

Li Gun sweated hard. He had no option but to seek help from the senior. No, wait. He had something he hadn't ever used before.

"Third-Dimension Beast-Summoning Array!" Li Gun roared, his voice cracking as he poured half of the Qi Crystal's energy into the robe.

The Third-Dimension Beast-Summoning Array roared to power when the Qi Crystal dimmed, losing its white luster. This was one of the midlevel arrays on the robe. His senior sister had told him that until he reached the Violet Palace Realm, he shouldn't attempt to use those arrays, as they were very power hungry, so he'd never tried them before. In fact, he never thought he would be able to try this out, as a Qi Crystal was too costly, and even if he had gotten one, he would have saved it for dire situations.

But it wasn't the time for thinking about any of that. If he didn't activate the midlayer array, he wouldn't survive.

The senior's voice struck him. "What array did you activate?"

"Senior, I didn't have any other option, so I activated the Three-Dimension Beast-Summoning Array."

"Fuck, what kind of beasts have you sealed in?" The senior's voice cracked, and Li Gun suddenly regretted his actions.

He was about to reply, but the ground under him shook, and the first portal opened up. Then the second opened and the third. But the second and third closed instantly, as if there wasn't enough energy to keep them open. The roars of the beasts echoed before the portals closed, shaking everyone around him. Hundreds of cultivators who were watching the fight from the sideline ran backward, and even Dark-Blood Peacocks wailed in pain, blood leaking from their ears.

A cry of happiness slipped out of the portal that was still open. Li Gun could feel it through their connection, but he also felt the resistance to his command. According to the senior sister, these beasts were as old as the treasure robe and the Array Scion who'd created the robe. He had caught the three beasts and sealed them in for his descendants.

When Li Gun heard all of this from his senior sister, he hadn't believed it. The story was overwhelming, and he just couldn't trust her. But after hearing the beasts roar, his doubts vanished like smoke.

A giant beast head poked out of the first portal. It was an elephant head, and the tusks were bigger than a common man's house. Its mad red eyes gawked at him, and then the beast opened his mouth, sending a torrent of white fire at him.

Fudge. Why was it attacking him?

"You fool. Can you even control those ancient beasts with your current power? That's a Dragon Elephant, and it will burn you alive. Cut it now," the senior's voice said.

Li Gun pulled the Qi Crystal from his robe. He should have done it when senior asked him about the array. The portals shrank, but the dragon elephant pushed his head out, tore open its portal, and stepped out of it. Its body was bigger than anything Li Gun had seen before. The beast roared at Li Gun, raised its trunk, and slammed it at him.

Fuck—he didn't want to die.

"Suppress." A giant dragon landed in front of Li Gun and smashed its claw at the elephant trunk.

The two beasts slammed into each other, sending everyone around them flying away. The dragon couldn't withstand the attack of the dragon elephant, and she was thrown away. She crashed into Li Gun.

Li Gun froze. He didn't know what to do. Now he wouldn't die to the elephant but to the dragon. Damn it. He'd wanted to kill his enemy with his move, but he was getting killed instead.

Li Wei couldn't understand how the dragon elephant had torn through the portal. But it was out, and it had a belly full of hatred toward the treasure-robe owner. And its belly was bigger than a dragon. Rual'er had transferred into her original self and tried to suppress it, but she was no match for the dragon elephant. That beast was at the peak of the Houtian Realm, and it was the weakest of the three he had sensed from the portals.

If the other two had stepped out of the portal, he would have said goodbye to everyone, as there was no way they could defeat someone at that power level.

If the beasts were this powerful, how much more powerful was the creator of the robe? Could they really have been an ancient cultivator or Array Scion?

He sent a message. "Rual'er, this space doesn't allow anyone stronger than the Houtian Realm, so the beast will be killed. Can you hold on for a few seconds? If Li Gun dies, I don't know what the dragon elephant will do. We can't take that risk."

Turning back, he stared at his own body. "I wish my main body was conscious." Guilt drove him to be angry with himself. Why the fuck had he forced himself to break his previous record? It had been totally irresponsible.

"Brother Wei, this dragon elephant is the king of the land, and I don't know if I can hold it off. But you asked for that, so I'll do it no matter what." Rual'er's aura shot to the peak, and she transformed into her giant form and clawed at the dragon elephant.

Wei instantly regretted his decision to ask her to hold the beast off. He could have asked her to run away with Li Gun. How could he be so naive even after two lives? Was his main body's unconsciousness affecting him?

Rual'er was no match for the dragon elephant, and it sent her flying back. She cut through the air like an arrow, coughing blood all over the place. The sight of her bleeding wrenched his heart. Because of him, another friend had gotten injured. She was about to fall on Li Gun, but she pushed him away with her tail before crashing into the ground. She disappeared into a bloody pit.

"Fuck, this is insane. I can't let her get injured because of someone's foolishness."

Wei called all his clones and merged them together into his main body. It was time to forcefully awaken himself, and he needed all the help he could get. Otherwise, people closer to him would die. He couldn't let that happen again—definitely not to the person he'd let go in his previous life. However, his main body was still feeling the effects of the exhaustion, and it refused to wake up.

"Kid, it's not going to work. He overdid it, so it will take him a few hours to wake up. Send him into the Ten-Day Time Chamber if you can," Blood Parasite said.

Only after merging with his own body did Wei felt a connection with him. This was odd.

"Why won't it? I'm the main soul, so if I'm awake, then I can't be in slumber, right?"

"I knew something like this would happen if he slept in the darkness like this. Kid, you're nothing but a separated piece of soul. You are hanging there because of his divine sense. Don't think too highly of yourself. Once he wakes up, you'll lose your identity inside him."

"This is impossible. I'm the main soul, and he has no soul." Wei realized he wasn't even a Houtian, so his soul couldn't leave his main body. That meant...

"You mean like Yang Fang and Nai Fang? Damn it. I'm not the main soul, but I certainly feel like one."

"Yes and no. They were yin and yang of the same body, but you both are you. You are in control mode just because he is sleeping. If I were the older demon, this would be the perfect chance to take you over, but I won't. We're brothers, after all."

Wei felt a deep warmth toward Blood Parasite. "Then possess him. You keep saying if I let you possess my body, you can do wonders."

"I can't, kid. You are my brother, or the original soul is my brother, and I can't do it with you."

"You have my permission, brother. Didn't you say I'm different from myself? So what are you worrying about? Just blame it on me. Just take my body for a ride." It felt weird to talk like this and thinking of himself as a separate entity. However, he had to save Rual'er and Li Gun, and if he didn't give this chance to Blood Parasite, then once his main self woke up, he would regret it. "Do it, Blood Parasite. You said I'm in a control mode, so I give you permission to use my body and save my friends."

"Now, that sounds like a good choice. Friends, right? I must save my brother's friends." Blood Parasite's wicked laugh echoed in Wei's mind, and then Wei was rejected along with the other clones. "Dregs of qi cultivation, get out of this body. This master is going to take it for a ride. Remember to convey everything I do today to the original soul once it wakes up."

Wei's original body floated in the air. A bloodred aura slipped out of it, and he turned into a blood demon. Had he made a mistake?

Chapter 50

Blood Parasite's Might

Li Wei sat on the chair. Or should he call himself second Li Wei? Did it really matter? He was Li Wei, and Li Wei was him. In the end, they would be the same. Yet it felt odd. Maybe this was how Nai Fang had felt. He understood her a little better than before. Her death had left a hole in his heart, and he'd always regretted not being able to save her.

"Li Wei, who is he?" Little Fox asked.

"Blood Parasite," Wei answered, staring at his own body floating, emitting bloodred aura.

Blood Parasite had changed Wei's body shape and turned him into something different. The bloodred mask with one hole made it difficult for anyone to identify him as Wei. He even smelled like intense blood. When he looked into Wei's eyes, Wei felt a chill down his legs. Blood Parasite was crazy, and Wei doubted his own choice of letting him control his body.

"I'll use your blood sword," Blood Parasite said before throwing Purple at Wei.

"Do whatever you need to do." Wei caught Purple and wrapped her around his neck. It felt good to have his friend back with him. "Don't let that bastard elephant survive."

"Oh, I've better plans than that." Blood Parasite gave an evil chuckle that sent everyone around them cowering.

Despite his fortitude, even Wei felt like hiding behind something to get away from Blood Parasite.

"Blood Teleportation." Blood aura wrapped Blood Parasite, and he vanished from the defensive formation and appeared next to the pit where Rual'er had crashed.

Her blood still covered the entire place. Wei's heart quivered when he saw it again. No one—not even a beast from ancient times—harmed his friends.

"Beast Princess, I'll borrow your blood to take revenge for your death."

Wei's heart slammed against his rib cage when he heard the word *death*. However when he spread the divine sense into the pit, he found Rual'er's heart still beating perfectly. The dragon elephant roared and slammed its trunk at Blood Parasite as if enraged at Blood Parasite's ignorance.

"Stop it, bastard. It's not your turn." Blood Parasite moved through the blood mist like a bat and avoided the attack easily. The attack sent the earth cracking and covered the sky in a cloud of dust. A few unfortunate souls were killed.

"Who said I'm dead?" Battered Rual'er floated out of the pit in her small version. Her wing had a deep gash that leaked blood, and she looked terrible, sending Wei's mind into a frenzy.

"I was joking. Let me clean your blood from the ground, shall I?" Blood Parasite chuckled.

"Why are you asking for blood that's been shed? Do whatever you want to do," Rual'er said before flying toward the defensive formation. On the way, she picked up Li Gun. He was faring better than the others.

"He would be furious if I didn't ask his girlfriend." Blood Parasite shrugged.

Rual'er froze and turned back. "Use as much as you want. If you want, I can give you more." She clawed her own shoulder, and a stream of blood flew out toward Blood Parasite.

"Blood Parasite, don't go overboard!" Wei shouted, furious. "She is already injured. Stop it already." Every drop of blood his friend lost was precious, and Blood Parasite was making her lose a ton of it. It wasn't acceptable.

"I miss the taste of the blood." Blood Parasite chuckled and waved his hand, and all the blood on the ground and in the air surged toward him like a tidal wave.

What everyone saw was blood waves pouring through the air toward a man with a blood-colored robe and a bloodred mask. The blood bowed to him before becoming one with him. If the title Blood Emperor existed, this would be the first man to claim it. Even Wei, who had known this bastard for so long, felt creepiness weaving through his heart.

The dragon elephant charged at Blood Parasite, but it couldn't hit him as Blood Parasite flashed through the air like Purple would do and avoided all the attacks.

"How can you use teleportation? My body is not at the Houtian Realm," Wei asked, letting the defensive formation open for Rual'er.

"It's not teleportation. It's Blood Teleportation. By sacrificing the blood in the air, I can walk through the Blood Void."

"Blood Void?" Wei asked.

"You won't understand. Now, watch how I use one of the low-level techniques to squash this bastard into a pulp. Blood Sword Tearing through the Heavens."

The blood waves rushed into his body and accumulated around his sword. They formed a deep coating around it, and a life-destroying hum echoed through the sword. The sound was so intense that Wei felt the defensive formation cracking at some places, and every person acting as the formation pole coughed a mouthful of blood.

It was worse for those outside of the defensive formation, who had arrived with the second wave. Half of them died, their brains exploding, and a few powerful cultivators rolled on the ground, holding their bleeding ears. Only a few with defensive artifacts survived. The dragon elephant wailed in pain as the blood streamed out from its big ears. Even Wei felt like his ears would blast apart if he heard the sound one more time.

"Fuck, can't you warn us before you pull something this powerful?" Wei cursed and rubbed the little fox's furry head. She was wailing in pain. "Calm down, little one. It's okay."

"It's just the warm-up. The real strike will happen now." Blood Parasite looked at the sword with pride. "It reminds me of the old days, kid. I wish I could use my signature moves, but I've got to show you the third level. Watch the Will of the Sword. It wasn't only the Blood Emperor who created the Will. I also created my own Will—the Will of the Blood."

The blood around the sword separated and merged into the sword image in the sky. It expanded rapidly, forming a blood world that descended with a thump. Even from behind the defensive formation, Wei felt his blood boiling, and his heart dampened. The dragon elephant wailed like a dog surrendering to an alpha dog after a fierce beating. It couldn't fight the might of the sword.

"Brother Wei, who is that person?" Rual'er gasped as she tossed Li Gun toward one woman. "My blood is getting out of control. It's like what you did before."

She was still bleeding, but from up close, he could see her injuries healing slowly. She hadn't suffered anything critical, and that astonished Wei because she'd faced an attack from an enraged peak of Houtian Realm beast, so she should have suffered more. Not that he wanted her to suffer in any way. She must have had her own trump card.

"He's a friend and is using my body to unleash an attack," Wei said, feeling gloomy.

Because whatever Blood Parasite had pulled was scary as fuck. And he was doing it with the help of Wei's blood cultivation. Wei sensed everything happening in his main body, and it wasn't fine. The skill was burning blood pearls, and strangely, his main body was ecstatic about it. His main body had hidden a blood demon inside it, and he wasn't aware of this. No, it wasn't Blood Parasite but the desire to kill, which he'd suppressed months ago.

"Why didn't you tell me you have such a powerful ally? We don't need to fear anyone if he's with us. With just a blood sword, he has suppressed the dragon elephant. It's unprecedented." Rual'er tone bordered on reverent.

Wei shook his head. "It's not that simple, Rual'er. There's a price to pay for this." He felt it in his heart. If he let Blood Parasite use his body too many times, the blood demon hidden inside his heart would come out and take him over. He had to curb it before it became a heart demon and attacked him while breaking through the Houtian Realm.

The blood sword sent a storm of dust flying away as it descended on the dragon elephant. Before the sword cut through the dragon elephant, Wei saw fear in the beast's eyes. It was afraid of Blood Parasite, and why wouldn't it be? Even Wei would be afraid of Blood Parasite if he were in front of him. The power he displayed overwhelmed anything Wei had seen before.

"Die, you ant." The sword crashed into the dragon elephant, sending a mile-deep crevice through the ground, which gulped down the dragon elephant and left a giant valley behind.

A silence prevailed in the arena.

Wei's main body coughed a bucket full of blood as it fell from the sky. "Kid, come and save this one. I went overboard." Blood Parasite's voice cracked.

A few figures who were hiding underground leaped out to attack Wei's main body.

Chapter 51

Waking up to a Shock

Wind gushed against his face as if he were falling off a cliff. Was he?

Li Wei opened his eyes to the ground rushing toward his face. Wait—no. He was falling like a stone thrown down a mountain cliff. A dark pit surrounded him on all sides, and he was about to taste the blood covering its depths.

What the fuck was happening? He'd been in the Ten-Day Time Chamber, and suddenly, he was falling. A storm of memories flooded him, and he recalled everything.

"Blood Parasite, you bastard. I thought we were brothers!" he roared.

"You gave me permission, and I only used seventy percent of your blood pearls," Blood Parasite replied in his mind.

"Seventy percent? Why didn't you just kill me instead? System, how the fuck did you allow him to control my body?" Wei tried to push his wings out, but they were refusing to operate on his command. If he pushed them further, they might break, and it would cost him a lot to repair them. This was the worst possible condition he could be in.

System: The host's secondary memory fragment allowed the takeover. As per rule 18924, the host can allow a third party to take

control of the body, and the system will not interfere until the host's body reaches seventy percent damage.

System: The host's body lost seventy percent of blood. Hence, the system has booted the third-party parasite from the host's DNA stream.

"This thing pushed me out?" Blood Parasite asked. "Damn it. I could have played it a little more. I couldn't even smell the fear in that brute's mind."

"And kill me along the way? Fuck you, Blood Parasite. You have damaged my body beyond repair." Wei somehow brought his right arm in front of him.

"What nonsense. All your internal organs are fine."

Wei covered his right arm with Heart Essence Aura and used it as a spring board, along with Intent of Wind Travel, to leap out of the dark pit. He crashed on the ground, and it hurt as if a thousand arms had punched him everywhere.

"That's because my Yang Wood Pill Clone protects them." Fuck, he was too damaged. He couldn't even taste the blood in his mouth, and he had enough of that to drown an average human.

"Watch out—five dregs are coming to kill you," Blood Parasite said.

Wei snorted. He knew the five dregs were approaching him. They'd launched a sneak attack on him, using many weapons. If it hadn't been for Wei's divine sense, he would be facing a deadly attack right at the moment he was the most vulnerable.

"Are you looking down on me, bastard? Muxi's Blessing. Blood Water Healing Art." Wei burned ten percent of his blood pearls and healed his back instantly.

The wings shot out and covered him on all the sides. Weapons smashed against his wings and were sent flying. Although Wei didn't have a mirroring array like Li Gun, he didn't need one. His wings were forged from the exotic treasure-grade weapon, and they were part of him, so these attacks felt like someone was trying to hit him with a cloth hammer.

"Bastards, how dare you sneak attack my brother Wei!" Rual'er roared. She landed on the five dregs, crushing them into the ground.

Wei couldn't believe what he'd just seen. A giant dragon of the size of a house had sat on five humans, destroying them instantly. It was an epic scene.

"Brother Wei, are you all right?" Rual'er asked, her tone soft as a feather as she turned into her small form.

Wei had an urge to see if those bastards were stuck to her body, but he suppressed his disastrous thought. "I'm fine. Don't worry." He smiled, blood still leaking from the corner of his mouth.

"Li Wei, are you all right?" Little Fox appeared next to him but stayed a little away, looking at the blood.

"Good enough to beat you in a race back to our formation." He chuckled. "Rual'er, I'm going to enter the seclusion, and I'll take all thirteen of you with me. Sonja can stay outside and clean up the rest." He stared at Sonja, who had come from the back side of the clock.

"Lord, I've killed the fifty people who were harassing your monk friend. There are still a hundred people remaining, and I'll kill them all," Sonja said with a light bow.

"Thanks." Wei nodded and flipped his wings to go back to the defensive formation. The battle was over, but it was a precursor to the upcoming battle, which would be more brutal. The mutated Dark-Blood Peacock and the Dragon Elephant were two of the many variables, and he couldn't predict what others might face.

"Senior Wei, there might be a few good people among them. Do you want to kill them all?" Li Gun asked.

"You are fortunate enough that I don't want to kill you." Wei slapped Li Gun's cheek lightly, his fury about to unleash. This bastard's wrong move had cost him his friend's blood, and he would have killed the man already if he didn't have a connection with the treasure robe from his previous life.

"Kid, wait. Before you enter the time chamber, collect the dragon elephant's corpse. I've a way to strengthen your Dragon Fist of Pain and Elephant Fist of Pain further," Blood Parasite said.

"Don't ask me to drink its blood."

"You don't need to. Just absorb it, using an array, and you should find a power erupting inside your body. Trust me."

Wei sighed. He'd seen what his clone had seen, and he also knew his clone had awakened a consciousness of its own, which was dangerous. Although it had merged with him once he woke up, he couldn't let that happen again. It was his own fault, and he had to be careful what he did going forward.

After collecting the dragon elephant's blood, he covered all of his friends in his divine sense and entered the Ten-Day Time Chamber. It was time to prepare for the next battle, and he had many things to do. This was going to be his longest battle of the life, and it was just the beginning.

Chapter 52

The Path of Qi Cultivation

A mutated fire burned under the Gold Grade cauldron, emitting an intense heat that made Li Wei sweat profusely. The Gold Grade cauldron was showing its weakness. It couldn't contain the heat. The mutated beast flame was too much for it. Since it had absorbed a Hell Flame, it was a given that Wei would need better equipment, but he had no other cauldron his wood clone could use.

Perhaps he could use the Essence Origin cauldron he'd gotten from his adventure in the mirror world, where he'd met Yang Fang the first time. But it was a high-level cauldron, and his wood clone couldn't activate it with its tiny portion of qi. Even when he had his qi cultivation, Wei's main body struggled to use it, so it was only a decoration in this room.

After dabbing the sweat from his forehead with a clean cloth, he tossed a Bristle-Thread Grass into the cauldron. It separated into a thousand tiny grass blades as it fell into the medicinal liquid. The grass was tougher than a metal, and only separated when exposed to intense heat, so if one didn't have a strong divine sense, it would be impossible to process it. This Samsara Rebirth Pill was proving to be a tough pill to process.

"Do you ever taste the shit you throw into the cauldron?" Blood Parasite appeared next to him and sat on a wooden chair Wei had placed in the corner along with a table. It was his tea-drinking table and was used by Blood Parasite now.

"What shit? These are herbs. Don't tell me you now hate alchemy just because your girlfriend betrayed you." Wei stirred the liquid with his Heart Essence Aura, which was separated into a thousand compartments using an array.

The Bristle-Thread Grass had to be melted into a thousand parts before he added the next ingredient. The recipe called for a Thousand-Hand Metal to be used, but Wei didn't have it, so he used his Heart Essence Aura.

"She wasn't my girlfriend. We just grew to be friends after sharing your body for so many months. I would say it was a comradery rather than friendship."

Wei tossed more herbs into the cauldron while two of his clones worked on Metal-Essence Pills in other cauldrons. The third clone was sitting in the corner, eating those pills to cultivate quickly.

"It hurt me as well, but I was kind of expecting it because of all the lies she kept telling me. She never told me about Enhanced Breakthrough or anything like that," Wei said, his emotions stirring like a mercury drop on a smooth metal surface, going from one corner to another.

"I didn't tell you as well," Blood Parasite replied.

Wei shook his head. "We weren't friends but were more like a cat and rat packed into a small room," Wei said. "Anyway, why are you out again? I thought you liked solitude and losing yourself in whatever you do there."

Blood Parasite poured himself a cup of tea and sipped it through his mask. It was weird watching the tea pass through a solid mask, but then, he didn't have a solid body, so the tea didn't even matter. But why was he drinking the tea before it finished boiling? It was Li Niya's recipe, and Wei loved it.

"This tea is nice. Give me one of those Soul-Nourishing Fruits. After I controlled your body, I lost a lot of power."

"So even you agree that you went overboard?" Wei shook his head in disappointment. He would have to start boiling the tea from the start, and this time, he would do it inside the treasure ring in an isolated room so no one would disturb it.

Blood Parasite took another swig and kept looking at the cauldron.

"Guess you're not talking now." Wei retrieved a Soul-Nourishing Peach and tossed it toward Blood Parasite.

With his Yin Yang liquid, Wei didn't have to worry about most of the herbs. As long as he had a single stalk or piece of the petal, he could use the liquid to age it to two thousand years. It was really a miraculous liquid, and of all his heaven-defying treasures, this one would be the topmost one.

"Why aren't you practicing the Elephant Fist of Pain? As long as you reach the Peak Completion, I can let you advance it to Perfect Completion using the blood of the Dragon Elephant. It doesn't break your so-called morality as well." Blood Parasite's tone became sarcastic as he came to the last sentence.

Wei slapped the cauldron, swirling his divine sense into it to swirl the thousand compartments. A small crack appeared at the edge of the cauldron, which worried him. This wasn't a good sign, and he had to find out a new cauldron soon—at least an Earth Grade cauldron. Otherwise, he would break this in no time. Couldn't his mother have given him a cauldron as well?

"I'm going to use Samsara Clone Rebirth Art on my wood clone first. I want to see if I can absorb them into me. And I'm also getting my metal clone to reach the peak of Marrow Cleansing Realm."

"Do you really want to do that? Why not keep them separate and only cultivate the blood body? Are you missing the trivial qi cultivation power?"

Wei shook his head. "I understand your point. Body cultivation is my primary source of power, and I've been using less and less qi cultivation recently, but I won't bail on it. With each of my clones practicing Heaven Grade Cultivation Art, I want to find out how much power I'll have once I absorb them into me. Worst case, I just start from scratch."

"I can't teach an old dog a new lesson. Don't waste your time, kid. Just focus on one thing, and you'll go beyond what you can imagine." Blood Parasite vanished along with the teacup and the peach.

"Damn it. Why did you take my cup?" Wei asked.

"Take it back, greedy bastard." A cup flew at Wei like a dart, and he had to put forward his Heart Essence Aura to stop it from cutting through his skin. The cup shattered after hitting a wall, and an intense smell of honey flowed out, which had been held in by an array on the teacup.

"Fuck you, Blood Parasite." Shaking his head, Wei glanced at the wood clone, who was shaking hard as he separated the Three Life Flower into a powder in another cauldron.

The Three Life Flower, the main ingredient of the Samsara Rebirth Pill, was readily available. People had given the plant this name because it lived three lives before it withered. Other than aesthetics, the flower had no use in the current cultivation world. Wei hadn't possessed any of this flower, but Sonja had, as it had poisonous properties she used for a few of her poison pills. He'd instantly turned a hundred flowers from Sonja into five hundred, finishing his requirement for many pills.

The wood clone sighed when the flower turned into powder, and then he directed it into the main gold cauldron. A silence prevailed as the thousand different compartments mended together, forming a small embryo of the pill. The green embryo flew out of the cauldron, and Wei heard the rumble of the heavens from outside the world. Concocting this pill here was a good idea as some pills were taboo and attracted the heavens' wrath whenever someone concocted them. This seemed to be one of them.

Not that it mattered to Wei. After retrieving a set of books, he used his Blood Lightning Pill clone to stimulate the heavenly lightning. The lightning struck the green embryo constantly, and after five minutes, the embryo flew back into the cauldron.

The silence grew deeper and deeper. The pill was in the final form of its completion and taking the Pill Breath. The quality would be decided based on how many breaths it took.

After a few minutes, a green three-headed serpent flew out of the cauldron and toward the only door. The pill had formed, and it had gained a sentinel, turning it into a Three-Pill Line Earth-Grade Pill. Wei's heart thumped like a drum as he reached out to grab the pill. This indeed marked a success for him along the path of cultivation.

Chapter 53

The First Rebirth - Xue Qi's Motivation

Xue Qi shuddered and hid the reaction instantly so the senior with her wouldn't notice. A Heaven Blasphemy, Li Wei? Really?

Through their thin connection, she could sense his condition a little, and he hadn't done anything to block her spying. Maybe he didn't know about it or didn't care. Not that he could do anything to her even if he knew and wanted to use that connection.

But a Heaven Blasphemy? How daring a mortal could be in this world. Did he not know that he would be whipped with tribulation if he dared to concoct a Heaven Forbidden Pill? Why had she not transferred him the essential knowledge for survival?

There were only a few things one had to do to live on.

A) Don't anger your master.

B) Don't talk shit about the heavens.

C) Don't concoct a Heaven Forbidden Pill.

D) Don't mess up with the Time Immortal Palace.

And he had done two of them already. If it weren't for her and that degenerated soul, Lira, shielding him and Allen Ming from the Time

Immortal Palace's net of scanning, they would have died in that final battle. He'd done something she couldn't understand.

"Xue Qi, you look distracted. Why aren't you focusing on the pill concoction? Are you forgetting how important it is for our freedom from this wretched heaven?"

"Don't shout. I'm doing all I can. I'm not connected to him anymore, so I can't siphon his power."

"You should have killed him. He is a defier of nature, and I hate defiers."

Xue Qi snorted. As if this guy could kill Li Wei. Even demons failed to kill him. That guy's resourcefulness was even superior to hers. If she hadn't siphoned his godly liquid, she would have had no chance of contending in this endeavor.

Sighing, she focused on the cauldron in front of her. "Li Wei, I've given you a chance to fix the issue with your qi cultivation. It's up to you whether you can find it," she muttered in her mind before pulling her attention from Li Wei.

However, she couldn't help but wonder what kind of Heaven Forbidden Pill Li Wei had concocted. Did he have a recipe for such a pill? Even after spending most of her life with the Lord Mayhem, she had half a recipe for a Heaven Forbidden Pill.

Demon Resurrection Pill.

Li Wei's metal clone finally reached the peak of Marrow Cleansing Realm after eating dozens of Metal-Essence Pills. Once again, the pitch-dark metal qi shifted and transformed, taking on a luster reminiscent of mercury.

With a Heaven Grade cultivation art, it was quite easy to upgrade the qi quality of the clones, so why didn't it happen in his main body? Was it because the clones didn't have any restriction of the Spirit Root?

That had to be the reason. With his shitty Spirit Root, it was a miracle Wei could ever break through into Marrow Cleansing Realm himself.

Shaking his head, Wei retrieved the Samsara Rebirth Pill and handed it to the wood clone. His plan was simple. After the wood clone finished his Samsara Rebirth, he would absorb it, and then the earth clone would do the same thing, and then the metal clone would follow. It would take a lot of time, but he wouldn't struggle with making guesses about the path. Perhaps this was better. Even if Xue Qi had given him a path forward, he wouldn't have taken it. He couldn't trust that woman anymore.

In fact, he bet there was no future on the path Xue Qi had shown him. She must have tricked him for her own gain. Only that made sense.

Rubbing his face, he took a swig of the freshly brewed Three-Butter Honey Tea, letting the sweet and earthy taste settle in his throat before heading down into his stomach. In his days in the gray chamber, he couldn't do better than peacefully drinking tea. If that damn bastard Blood Parasite hadn't shattered his teacup and drunk half-boiled tea, that would have been preferable. Anyway...

"Take it," he whispered, and the wood clone gulped it down.

A lustrous aura covered Wei, and he found himself in a shabby hut with holes punched in the ceiling as if someone had practiced a martial skill on his roof. The truth was, his stepfather hadn't bothered to spend any money on him, so this was what he'd gotten.

System: The host has two choices: forget about the real world and wave through the Laws of Samsara, or retain the original memories and walk his own path.

Wei stared at the message for a moment. "I choose the second path."

No reply came back, and his memories of real life remained with him. He guessed the system had conveyed his choice to whoever the message had come from. So he was back at the start. Why hadn't he thought this would happen?

In fact, he wasn't supposed to be here with his own soul. It should have been the piece of divine sense he'd left inside the wood clone, but he was here again—the purple light shining in the depth of his soul told him that. The fighting would never leave his soul.

So was this all an illusion? The Samsara thing— he kind of didn't believe it. How would one gain knowledge of Samsara without actually dying and going through a reincarnation cycle?

"System, are you there?"

No answer came. So the almighty system, which could even capture the arrays in the Ancient Ruins in the Old Martial City, didn't come here. Only the fighting would.

"Break." He pushed his divine sense out and tried to break the illusion, but nothing happened. He was still lying in bed, bandaged over every inch of his skin. Fei'er hadn't learned the basic techniques back then, even after spending a lot of time with Wei.

Pain crept under his skin, but having experienced soul-cracking pain multiple times in both his lives, this felt like nothing.

"Things were so bad back then." He scanned himself with his tattered divine sense while the light shone on his eyes from the holes in the roof, but it couldn't annoy him anymore. For some unknown reason, he was content with this life.

His body refused to move, but he still had his divine sense, which was tattered but usable. When he spread it, he saw Fei'er cooking in the open. She was making a soup with leftovers she'd gotten from other clan houses only for him. He used to love being taken care of by Fei'er because that was the only time he could eat something good. But it felt foreign now, and he wouldn't be drinking that soup at all.

"Fei'er, come here," he called through his divine sense.

He was changing the past, but who cared? This was nothing but a rebirth, and he wouldn't be living the same life again. Instead, he wanted to go back to the roots and form new beginnings.

"Young master, are you awake?" A sweet girl rushed in, a dimple on her right cheek, smiling at him. Her blue eyes looked at him with a care that had been missing from his life.

"Fei'er, come here, and sit next to me."

Ki Fei sat next to him and placed her soft palm on his forehead. "Young master, you're not burning anymore. This is a good sign. I'm cooking some soup for you. Let me bring it to you."

"No, don't. That soup tastes bitter. I can still feel the unpleasant taste in my mouth," Wei replied with his divine sense.

"Young master, why isn't your mouth moving when you talk? Are you feeling hurt somewhere?"

"I'm using my inner voice. Don't worry." Wei chuckled inwardly. "Help me dig in the right corner for a few feet, and once you find a ring there, pour your qi into it."

"Aiya, how did you know I have qi? I only found out about it when the big teacher taught me."

"I'm injured. Please help me dig up the ring."

Fei'er got up and dug out the ring.

"There's some gold inside," he said. "Use that to buy good food, a comfortable bed. Leave the pills in the ring, and take the sword to Wu Xiodia's shop in the market street."

"Why?"

"Please do as I say. Also tell Wu Xiodia if he wants to become an Array Adept, come and meet me tomorrow."

"Young master, shall I buy some healing pills for you?"

"Just let me take rest," Wei said, exhausted by the overuse of his divine sense. He saw Fei'er leaving the Li clan compound before he drifted into sleep.

Something stabbed into his ribs, and when he opened his eyes, he saw Li Sua standing next to him, a mocking smile on his face.

"Father, I'm sorry. I let you down. Please punish me." Wei moved his mouth, but he spoke with his divine sense.

Li Sua's face twitched as if he couldn't understand what Wei had said.

"Father, please let me say thank you for marrying my mother. I have never said this to anyone, but I'm thankful for what you did for us," Wei said, pouring his emotions into his voice.

"Brat, did you hit your head?" Li Sua frowned. "Why are you talking nonsense?"

"I was wrong, and these injuries helped me to understand my errors."

"What errors?"

"I was an unfilial son. I should have been devoted to you, but I failed. Hatred consumed me, but no more. I see the dangerous path you walked for me and my mother and how you saved our lives. I can't be any more thankful than I am right now. Please accept my thanks for all you did."

Li Sua's eyes bore a rare sign of warmth. "As long as you know, brat. As long as you know." He turned away. "Take this pill. It will heal you." Li Sua tossed a pill into Wei's mouth and walked away. "Maybe I was wrong, and this kid can still grow up better than that bitch," he whispered as he stepped out of the room.

Wei smiled. He realized he no longer hated Li Sua after meeting his mother's sealed memory. Li Sua had, in fact, saved them both from the

Serpent clan. Maybe this was how he should have lived after the reincarnation.

Chapter 54

Meeting Wu Xiodia Once More

Fei'er came back along with Wu Xiodia. Seeing the old man made Li Wei emotional. He was one of the first followers Wei had had in this life, and maybe one of the first in this Samsara life as well. This old man was a true array addict and reminded Wei of his own self when he was still learning arrays from his master back then. Those had been the happiest days of his life. He'd had nothing else to do but study arrays, eat, sleep, and study more arrays. What else could be better than that?

"Young master, I brought the food you asked for." Fei'er retrieved a bunch of food from the ring and put it neatly in the corner.

Wei felt his mouth watering when the scent of Little Pigeon Fish slipped out of one of the containers. Fei'er knew what he loved. She was the best.

"Brat, stop drooling. Tell me, how do you know about Array Adept, and where did you get this sword?" Wu Xiodia stepped in front of him and held out the sword, blocking the sun from the main door.

"Old Uncle, my young master is busy. Don't disturb him. Didn't I ask you to come tomorrow?" Fei'er sniffed at Wu Xiodia, trying to shoo him away.

"Old man, she's right. I asked you to come tomorrow," Wei answered, using his voice.

He had healed enough with Li Sua's pill to be able to speak, and he wanted to eat food now, especially the Little Pigeon Fish soup and, later, the tea he would ask her to brew for him. Wu Xiodia could wait. The food wouldn't.

"Fei'er, come sit with me. We'll eat together."

"Young master, I'm your servant. How can I eat with you?" She sat next to him and helped him sit up. Then she retrieved plates to serve him food.

Wei raised his hand with a lot of effort and rubbed her soft forehead. "Who says Fei'er is my servant? She is more than a friend to me. Come on—eat with me. Let's stop this master-servant nonsense. I'll make sure you live the life of a queen going forward."

"Brat, how dare you keep me waiting?" Wu Xiodia complained.

"You want food? Why didn't you say so? Fei'er, get him a plate. It's not good to keep an old man hungry, or he might just snatch our food."

"Aiya, I forgot. Old Uncle, sit here, and I'll give you food. You should say when you're hungry. I won't decline your request. I bought a lot of food, enough for us all for a few days."

Wu Xiodia had a look as if someone had slapped him hard and repeated it ten times. He'd probably never faced two ignorant kids like Wie and Fei'er.

"What are you waiting for, old man? Are you stuck at circles? Why are you carving circles from the right? Start on the left, and draw two half circles. Isn't that easier than the brute-force method you're trying?" Wei lifted a chicken wing and stuffed it into his mouth. It tasted amazing. Just amazing.

"Circles, half circles—what nonsense are you...?" Wu Xiodia froze, his eyes glued to Wei. "Brat, where did you learn this? And how do you know I'm stuck at that array?"

Wei smiled mysteriously and drew a small array in the air, prompting a wild gasp from the old man.

"Old man, if you make such sounds, people will get the wrong idea about me. How would I marry this young maiden if you spread rumors about me?" Chuckling, Wei pulled Fei'er close with his free hand.

"Young master, who is going to marry you?" Red painted her cheeks as she tried to run away from him, but he didn't let her go and rested his head on her shoulder, feeling the warmth of her breath flowing into him. This life, he was going to live differently. With Fei'er around him, he didn't need anyone else.

Not that he regretted building those affectionate bonds with other girls—Nuan'er, Fang'er, and Rual'er—but Fei'er was all he needed in this new life.

"Brat, I have to go back. I don't know how you know my weakness, but if I really break through, I'll come to pay my gratitude."

"Before going back to your cave, just declare you're taking Li Wei from the Li clan as your apprentice. In return, I'll gift you this." Wei handed him a simple diagram of a Silver Grade array, Simple Concealment Array. "This is better than the Cleaning Array I taught you last time."

"What Cleaning Array? When did you teach me?"

"Heaven's guess. Old man, just go and practice."

Wu Xiodia stared at the array diagram, tears accumulating in the corners of his eyes. "Is this really the Simple Concealment Array?"

"Do I look like I'm joking?" Wei frowned.

"You know what? I'll declare that you are my long-lost son... no, my father... no, my brother.... no, my nephew. Whoever dares to point a finger at you will be my enemy." Wu Xiodia bowed to him deeply and turned away to go back.

Wei sighed. This old man wasn't bad. He hadn't dared to make Wei his apprentice. If he had, Wei would have smacked his head a few times to put some sense into him.

"Young master, who is that old man?"

"Our ticket out of this city." Wei pulled her close and inhaled her scent. "Fei'er, will you marry me?"

"Young master, this servant is yours. Why would you even ask? Wait..." Her face turned redder than a tomato. "Marriage? Young master, why are you making jokes with me today?" Her eyes, big and brimming with emotion, released tears that flowed like a gentle stream.

"Why would I joke with you, Fei'er?" He tucked a loose strand of hair behind her ears. "Wait until I give you the biggest marriage ceremony this town has ever seen. Heck, I'll make it bigger than anything this kingdom has ever seen."

A smile played on her lips, and his rebirth became worth all the effort.

Chapter 55

Master Wu's Struggle

Wu Xiodia released a stream of fire through his newly carved Fire Entrapment Array on the sword master Wei had given him, killing the golden-and-black worms. It wasn't easy, but master Wei had asked him to buy a pill from the Herb Fragrance Palace to boost his cultivation for a few minutes, and with the help of array, it just worked. If it hadn't, the worms would have destroyed Master Wei's brain. He couldn't let that happen to Master Wei.

Master Wei picked up those worms and gulped them down as if they were a tasty snack. "Fei'er, now. Guide them into my dantian," Master Li Wei said, and the little lady Fei'er pushed her wood qi into Master Li Wei's stomach.

Wu Xiodia watched Master Li Wei trudge through pain. This was a brutal method, but Master Li Wei had done things Wu Xiodia never thought were possible, so he had no option but to trust Master Li Wei in this. For example, Master Li Wei had made him build a simple array formation using a couple of Qi Stones that killed the entire Du clan overnight. Master Li Wei's techniques and knowledge were beyond the heavens, and Wu Xiodia feared him.

However Master Wei had always treated him like a friend and taught him new arrays and formations Wu Xiodia could never even dream about. In the current state, Wu Xiodia was the strongest array cultivator within a five thousand miles, which was unprecedented. People lined up outside his shop to get an array carved by him, and he turned away most of them unless they were sect elders. Even sect elders visited him many times a month now. Master Wei had transformed him in just six months, letting him reach the peak of Foundation Realm easily with his teachings and money-making techniques.

After eating the two worms, Master Wei sat in the corner, cultivating. He seemed to have some use for those worms, but after five minutes, he coughed them out along with a lot of blood.

"It didn't work." Disappointment leaked through his voice.

What was Master Wei was trying to do? Didn't he like the taste?

"Why didn't it work? Why?" Master Wei slammed his chest and coughed another mouthful of black blood. It was sticky, and it corroded the stone ground in instant, exposing a stink. "The blood cultivation didn't work, and this didn't work either. What am I going to cultivate in this life? Does it have some relationship?" he asked cryptically.

"Young master, are you all right?" Fei'er, Master Wei's future wife, ran toward him. She was very cute and humble and sometimes scary. Other than Master Wei, she listened to no one, not even her father-in-law, who was managing this town's Li clan branch, and everyone, including Master Wei, respected him.

Well, Wu Xiodia didn't have to respect him, and he didn't find him a credible person. He was found mostly drinking and throwing away his life, but as everyone respected Master Wei, everyone gave Li Sua a respect he didn't deserve. But it had nothing to do with Wu Xiodia. All he cared for was Master Wei and his pearls of wisdom about array cultivation. He was the best.

"Old man, cover your arm in the qi, as I taught you, and search for a chamber behind the wall. There is some fruit that would be beneficial for the business," Master Wei said nonchalantly.

Wu Xiodia followed Master Wei's advice and found a few dozen pieces of fruit that smelled heavenly. He handed them to Master Wei. Those were definitely some good things, but compared to the master Wei's knowledge, they were nothing but trash in Wu Xiodia's thoughts. "Master Wei, what were you aiming for here?"

"Just a cultivation technique, but I guess it's not possible anymore." A grave expression covered his face, and Wu Xiodia didn't like it.

Chapter 56

The Cycle of Reincarnation

L i Wei sat on a wooden chair outside of his shabby hut, which was surrounded by a lavish mansion now. Fei'er and Wu Xiodia had insisted on building a mansion for him, but he forced them to keep the hut as it was. It was a run-down piece of wood, but it had the emotional value of his two lives. How could he destroy it for the sake of matching his status in the world?

"Young master, shall I pour you hot tea?" a maidservant asked, pulling his attention out of his rumination.

"No, go back and do your work." Wei sipped the tea. It didn't taste authentic like the Three-Butter Honey Tea he loved to drink, but this was much better than Fei'er's tea. She was a good cook, but her tea was very bland. Nuan'er made a much better one.

A solemn mood hit him as he watched the ducks float around the lotus growing in the middle of a pond built near the hut. It had been Fei'er's idea to turn it into a sacred place no one but she, Wei, and Wu Xiodia had access to.

Two years had passed since Wei had rebirthed into his old self, but nothing had gone according to his wishes. Especially cultivation. That had been easier before and had turned impossible in this life. He couldn't cultivate the Blood Essence Body, nor he could integrate Yin Yang Worms inside his dantian. Instead, he'd suffered a heavy injury, and his leakage in dantian had gotten worse, turning him useless in qi cultivation. So he couldn't cultivate anything that he wanted to.

As a last resort, he'd used a low-tier Human Grade body cultivation method—Thousand Vajra Body Cultivation Art—to make his body tougher, but it was fucking slow. After two years, he hadn't reached the peak of Foundation Realm, and it hurt his pride whenever he watched others break through as easily as eating candies.

A genius who had reached Heart Blood Realm in body cultivation in mere months had been turned into trash. And without the resources he could enjoy with his Yin Yang Liquid, Wei was almost nothing. Well, he could argue that his knowledge had filled in the gaps in his abilities, and Fei'er and Wu Xiodia had been a tremendous help in helping him earn the wealth he'd always wanted.

While he struggled to cultivate, Fei'er had reached the peak of the Bone Baptization Realm. She was faster than anyone he'd seen before, and he once again wondered what kind of Spirit Root she had.

"Young master, what are you thinking?" Fei'er walked into the open space, holding a tray filled with snacks.

Wei smiled and pulled her onto his lap. He kissed her neck, inhaling her sweet-sweet aroma.

"Young master, someone will see." Fei'er was quick to jump away. He couldn't overpower her anymore. And he didn't need to.

"So what? We'll marry in a few months. What's there to be afraid of? Or you don't want to marry me anymore?" he asked in a sad tone.

Fei'er's face turned dark, and tears rolled down her cheeks. She knelt next to him and wrapped her arms around him. "Why would you say that, young master? You are my everything. My husband, my god, and my life. Why would I not want to marry you?"

Smiling, he caressed her cheeks before kissing her deeply. "I was just joking. I won't let you go away from me ever."

She sobbed hard for a few minutes before kissing him on the cheek and running away like a small kitten. Wei smiled before closing his eyes.

Another year passed, and Wei remained at his current cultivation level, but the world had changed drastically. With Fei'er's help, he'd finished a lot of work he should have done in the real life. With her powers and Wu Xiodia's reputation, he brought the surrounding five towns under the Li clan's territory, and Li Sua governed them in name. Wei even established a few array stores in the nearby towns and taught a few promising young saplings, increasing the Li clan's prestige throughout the State of Zin. Along with the prestige came profit and some pests who came to steal everything from him. However, he acted ruthlessly and finished off all the threats to his power.

In all, he was living the lazy life he'd always wanted. He woke up late when Fei'er brought him breakfast and tea. He would then take a luxurious bath and sleep again until Wu Xiodia showed up with some matters in the evening. Later in the night, he would stroll near a lake or take a ride in a boat with Fei'er, enjoying the moonlight and her comfortable embrace.

It was a perfect life, but he had this dread gathering in his gut that something bad was about to happen. His divine sense was declining slowly, and one day, it would be gone forever. Without a soul palace, he couldn't keep it with him, and he didn't have any of the fortuitous encounters he'd had in his real life.

However, it didn't matter. With the lazy life he was living, he needed nothing else. Of course, he missed Nuan'er, his grandfather, and the others, but he didn't meet them on purpose. He just wanted to enjoy this life with Fei'er.

Five years later, he married Fei'er on a fine evening in the presence of hundreds of VIPs who'd come to congratulate him. It was the largest wedding the entire State of Zin had seen. Even princes and princesses didn't get to enjoy such a wedding. All the common mortals under the Li clan celebrated for ten days and ate free food. Even Sun Nuan and Tang Sia came to wish them happiness.

On a fateful morning, Fei'er gave birth to a baby girl as cute as her mother, and he loved her more than anything else. Life was smooth, and he was loving it as it was.

Years passed on, and his power declined slowly. He could never break through into Bone Baptization Realm while Fei'er grew stronger and stronger. On the eve of the fifteenth year, she reached the peak of the Boiling Blood Realm. So far, she had acquired the Divine Fragrance Palace and Sun's royal family for him. If he hadn't asked her not to wipe them out, the two behemoths wouldn't exist anymore. Fei'er was overlord of this area, and no one came to disturb them. Even Heavenly Firmament Palace did nothing about their actions.

Wu Xiodia had also reached the peak of Marrow Cleansing Realm, but it was his peak as well. Without the pills or any elixir, he wouldn't make any further breakthroughs.

Compared to them, Wei had only gotten older. A few years before, he'd lost his divine sense, and his cultivation had stopped completely. The dread was filling his gut every morning, and he realized what it was telling him. His leaking dantian had turned worse after his attempt to stuff the divine worms into it, and he was slowly reaching the end of this life. There was no solution to this, and he had to accept it.

More years passed like a breeze, and Fei'er made her breakthrough into Heart Blood Realm.

"Fei'er, come and sit here," he called when she broke through.

She looked as flawless as before, and the birth of one daughter had only added a hint of maturity to her eyes. While she was more beautiful every passing day, he had aged by a lot in the last thirty years. Gray hair had appeared, and his body had declined a lot from its chiseled state. His stomach had grown, and he kind of liked it. He'd always wanted to have chubby proportions.

"Husband, are you not feeling well? I should visit the Divine Fragrance Palace and demand their patriarch to make a pill for you. If he won't help, then he can't live in this world."

"Don't you hate me for looking like an old uncle? You look like an eighteen-year-old maiden and big sister of our daughter, while I look like this." He chuckled, rubbing his flabby stomach.

"Of course not. You're the love for my life." She snugged close to him, resting her head on his shoulder, but from that touch he sensed her worry about him.

"Fei'er, I want to tell you something serious."

"Husband, you can't die yet. We have only lived together for thirty years, and I want to live with you forever. We only had one daughter, but I want to have dozens of them."

"I'm sorry." Wei kissed her forehead. After he'd lost his divine sense, he'd had lost his ability to make children. It was a side effect of her being too high in cultivation and his inability to guide his seed with the help of his divine sense. "Listen, my days are coming to an end, and I'll soon pass into the cycle of reincarnation."

"Husband, no, you can't go yet. If you go, I'll accompany you."

"Listen, this is not a reality—it's a reincarnation cycle. But trust me, I used my entire heart to live it like a reality, and I've lived it fully and wholeheartedly."

Suddenly, Wei realized why he couldn't grab the opportunities from his previous life. This wasn't an illusion but a reincarnation—a life he was living once again. Although he'd lived with the memories of his past, he should have let them go to enjoy this life to its fullest.

But if he'd let go of his memories, he would have lived his old life, maybe made some different choices, and ended up on a different path. Heck, he liked this way more because he got to spend time with Fei'er on a deeper level. He'd found his love after all these years, and if he had to do it again, he would do the same thing. This wasn't the Samsara he was supposed to live, but it wasn't wrong either.

"Goodbye, my love." He kissed her lips and then drifted away from the reincarnation.

Chapter 57

Divine Abilities of the Blood Essence Body

A jerk shook Li Wei's mind as if he'd been thrown from a thousand-mile-high mountain cliff and then slammed headfirst into the ground. For a few seconds, he felt dizzy and couldn't think straight. He couldn't even recognize the alchemy room of the Primordial Blood Palace he had materialized into, nor could he smell the last whiff of bad smoke coming from the all-burned incense in the corner.

When he regained his composure, the world was dark and scary as if his mother had thrown him into a world unknown. Well, she kind of had, but he hated her no longer. His father had taken her place.

However, what was this feeling of missing something important? Why was he feeling like he'd lost someone dear to him? Had he?

Then memories flooded in—the memories of his reincarnation, Fei'er, and the life he'd always wanted to have but would never choose.

"Fei'er. I'm sorry." Tears streamed down his cheeks, his heart aching with an intense longing for his beloved wife from the reincarnation. If he were given the chance, he would drink her bland tea a thousand more times without complaining. "Fei'er, I choose you, and I'll choose you again." If he were given the same choice again, he would choose to go with Fei'er.

System: The host has chosen to walk a strange path of Reincarnation. The Samsara cycle has been changed. The host cannot learn the Intent of Samsara through the Samsara Rebirth Pill.

System: The host's wood clone has broken through the Foundation Realm into the Bone Baptization Realm.

Wait. What the fuck?

Wei cursed, prompting Blood Parasite to materialize in the room. He looked like the way he always used to. The bloody red mask and the red robe made him look like a cheap villain in a street play.

"Why does this air stink, kid? Can't you maintain this place with some dignity?"

Wei tossed a few more sticks of incense into the corner and lit them up with his beast flame.

"You're the first cultivator I saw using beast flame to light incense. Isn't that an insult to your beast flame?" Blood Parasite mocked him.

"Fuck off. Don't irritate me. I'm not in the mood. And you fucking destroyed my teacup, yet come here acting like nothing happened?"

"Kid, are you going to bicker just because I broke a teacup? In my prime, I could break a mountain of teacups, and no one would ask me for a single reason."

"I don't care how badass you were in your prime, but I know you ruined my perfect tea and broke my teacup." Wei could still feel the bland taste of ruined tea on his tongue. Maybe it was because of the pots of bland tea Fei'er had made him drink in the reincarnation cycle. Again, he missed her deeply. "I'm sorry. I'm just pissed off about something," Wei said.

Reincarnation wasn't a simple thing. He hadn't just lived a life in twenty-four hours. Rather, he'd lived a *complete* life in twenty-four hours. Having lived a life until death had changed something inside him. Or it was just an emotional thing, and he couldn't cope with it.

"I need a good tea and advice on how the fuck this clone broke through." Wei pointed at the wood clone, who lay in the corner, unconscious. The reincarnation cycle had pushed the divine sense within the clone to the limit, and it would take a few hours to wake up.

Blood Parasite squatted down next to the clone and pricked it with a knife. He scanned the blood with his bloodred divine sense. "This is strange. The seal that bitch put on this clone is broken. There is no longer a bottleneck for this clone. You can cultivate it to a higher level without any issue. Even beyond the Houtian Realm."

Wei sat on the chair and rubbed his face. The memories of Fei'er and the reincarnation cycle rushed through his mind whenever he closed his eyes, and he just wanted to sit there and live through them again.

He sent Blood Parasite the message he'd received from the system. "What the fuck did I do? Is it because of the rules I broke? Does it make any sense?"

Blood Parasite stared at him as if he were an odd entity. "Kid, it was a Samsara cycle, and you were supposed to follow the rules of Samsara, and yet you chose a different path. How obnoxious."

"Do you have any solution?" Wei poured a cup of hot tea for himself and gulped it down, letting the scorching heat burn through his throat.

"I don't. I've never studied Samsara myself. But whatever you did, you'll have to do it with your other clones."

"Then what's the use of using the Samsara Clone Rebirth Art? If I can't merge my clones back into myself, I'm gaining nothing."

No, that wasn't the complete truth. The life he'd had with Fei'er had been worth the effort. Even if he had to discard his clone, he would do it again for a life with Fei'er.

"Then destroy your clone, and start over. It's not like you lack Samsara Rebirth Pills."

Wei nodded. It was better to start over. If he'd known this issue earlier, he might have chosen to go with the flow, but whatever—he'd had a damn good life with Fei'er.

"Des..." He bit his words.

Wei had a premonition that something would go terribly wrong if he muttered the incantation, and the feeling came from deep in his soul, from the fighting will that had always accompanied him in the depths of despair. If it gave him a warning, that meant something bad would happen if he destroyed his wood clone. That made the wood clone a liability, and he couldn't have a liability as weak as the wood clone.

"What are you waiting for? Do you want me to do it?" A knife appeared in Blood Parasite's hand, and Wei flashed forward to stop him.

"Don't. My gut feeling tells me that I shouldn't do this. Let's wait and go with the flow. This is the only option now." Wei stretched his neck, rubbing the throbbing muscle there.

"What are you going to do, then?"

"I don't know. I'll just keep it safe." Wei placed a palm on the wood clone's forehead and absorbed it into him. Strangely, there was no feeling of rejection anymore, and he didn't receive the fatal timer of the absorption limit.

"There is no absorption timer anymore." Wei said, feeling ecstatic. "It can stay inside me forever, and I can use all its powers." A wisp of wood qi materialized on his palm, and it shone brighter than ever with the help of his Yang Wood Pill Clone.

"Problem solved. Do this with your other clones, and you might have an army of clones living inside you."

"I'm not sure if I can call it an army, but let's see," Wei said.

"You can produce more clones that would practice water and fire. It would be perfect—five elemental clones."

"I can, but then I have to increase the level of my divine ability, but I can do it because I've reached the Heart Blood Realm. I know a place where I can increase the level of my Blood Wood Clone Divine Ability."

"Aren't you going to try the next divine ability?" Blood Parasite asked. "Don't waste time going after only a few. You're not a cultivator anymore, so focus on each ability equally."

Wei gave a deep sigh. He'd broken through twice, and he'd gained two divine abilities that came with his breakthroughs, but he hadn't really gotten a chance to practice them.

Blood Metal Siphon and Blood Fire Vortex. As he read through the description, he recognized a pattern. The first one was Blood Earth Force for defense. The second one was Blood Water Healing for healing. Then came the Blood Wood Clones, which dealt with creation. Blood Metal Siphon was for control. It allowed him to form a layer of metal from an external substance around him that could absorb and redirect any kind of energy. Of course, the quality of the metal and the level of his divine art decided how much energy he could absorb and redirect. The final divine art was Blood Fire Vortex, a pure offensive ability that created a vortex of blood fire that could destroy anything in the world—of course, depending on the quality of the fire he had and level of the skill.

This was fantastic. There was nothing stopping him from learning these.

Chapter 58

Xue Qi's Seals

Xue Qi jolted awake from the refinement. The seal she'd placed on Li Wei's clone had been broken.

"Who did it?" She tossed the herb into her control at the corner, letting the juice go to waste on the floor, but she didn't care. Someone had broken the precious seal she'd left on Li Wei's clones, and it was a blasphemy.

But how was that possible? That seal was a Heaven Grade Seal, and she'd felt no resistance other than the fact that it had broken. What kind of unsealing method had Li Wei learned?

"What happened?" The black coin floated at the other end of the room, still working on the sword. He'd been working on it even before the Ancient Constitution Trials had opened for others. After imbuing the essence of thousands of cultivators, he was close to the completion, missing only one pill, which she was creating.

"He broke my seal on his clones," Xue Qi said.

She didn't hide this fact from the black coin. He'd seen her placing the seal on the clones, which was one of the reasons he'd let Li Wei go away. Well, even if he'd wanted to, he couldn't have stopped Li Wei.

Wei had some things even Xue Qi gloated about, and his void pet was one of them. Li Wei didn't know that the pet could break the walls of the reality and take him anywhere. Once it grew into a mature form, it would make him the king of the void.

There were so many good things about him that even he didn't know about, but he didn't have the drive to march forward and conquer everything in his hands. Maybe that bastard Blood Sword Saint was right. He should just embrace his destiny and cleave his way through the heavens, but he was stuck in his mortal relationships, which kept him caught in the lower realms. She couldn't have that happening, and she couldn't let others know about him, so she had to leave him. By choice or by force.

"How did he remove the Soul Cultivation Seal from you? Isn't that a Heaven Grade skill? Did you cheat me?" Xue Qi felt the rage overcome her as she threw a jade slip at the black coin. It contained the half-baked method of the Soul Cultivation Seal.

"Check yourself, and don't doubt me ever again," Xue Qi said. The jade slip floated in front of the black coin before crumbling down in smoke. "What a nasty method to try on your own, friend."

"Do you want me to give up on this?" she asked, the herbs floating in front of her. With a single yes, she would throw them all away.

"Calm down. I'm just speaking objectively. I don't care what your little pupil did or didn't do. I just need our freedom, and you'd better focus on the pill rather than keeping tabs on that mortal. Once Bao Faji and Bao Xiochan emerge from the Devil Rebirth Pool, they will eat your pupil for breakfast."

Xue Qi sighed inwardly. This would be the next challenge Li Wei would face, but could he really overcome it?

Chapter 59

Blood Metal Siphon

Sitting on a chair, Li Wei performed his Soul Tea Ceremony. It had been a long time since he'd made any advancement in the ceremony, and he wondered if he had reached his ceiling. Sometimes it wasn't about the cultivation but about one's intimacy with the skill. Maybe his heart wasn't peaceful enough to make any progress. He was continuously surrounded by violence, fights, and villains, and the tea ceremony required one to have nothing but a peaceful heart. At the moment, he lacked that.

Sighing inwardly, he picked up a Green Fragrant Potato while checking on the people inside the broken treasure ring. The twelve pillars of his formation were cultivating with pills and improving greatly. With Rual'er guiding them, and with the pills his clones had made over the weeks, each had reached the Heart Blood Realm. Whoever was in the Heart Blood Realm had improved by a few layers. Mayor Ling was the strongest among them, and he'd not only broken through into Heart Blood Realm but had also reached layer five of the same, thanks to the Cultivation Sealing Rooms in the palace. Those rooms allowed them to cultivate five times faster, and Wei's pills increased that rate further.

In another room, Rual'er practiced her divine arts and wind-attributed skills. Little Fox just lay in the room filled with fruit, munching on it every few minutes. She was lazing around, and he didn't disturb her. Rual'er floated in the air with her wing only poking out a little. The wind supported her like a mother's grace supporting her child. She had mastered some of the Intent of Wind, and she would be a killing machine once she broke through into the Houtian Realm.

"Maybe they'll change her nickname from One-Shot Killer." He chuckled before pulling his attention toward his wood clone, who was concocting low-tier Gold Grade pills for everyone. With these healing pills, Wei could bring his people to peak condition as long as they had a single breath left and their organs were attached to their bodies.

"Uncle Won, I'll find a treatment for you. I promise." Wei lifted the teacup, glancing at the timer for the Ten-Day Time Chamber. Having the system display the timer in his vision was just fantastic. If everyone could have this ability to see damage numbers and other things, it wouldn't take much time for their lives to improve to the next level. "Three days. It should be enough." Wei finished his tea and accessed the information on the Blood Metal Siphon Divine Art.

Blood Metal Siphon

Control the surrounding metal, giving it an absorbing or redirecting ability on the wish. It can store energy and redirect it based on the divine art level.

Refine One Thousand Metal Pieces into your blood to form a Metal Heart and gain the initial control of the surrounding metal. One needs to refine the metal heart into one's innate weapon for this divine art to work.

Requires One Thousand Silver-Grade Metals to initiate the divine art.

Wei retrieved a few storage rings and poured all their contents onto the ground. They had thousands of swords and other weapons. Perfect for his use.

"Where did you get this many weapons, kid? Did you steal them from a treasury?" Blood Parasite asked.

Wei chuckled. "Don't you remember the treasury of the Three Treasure Auction Hall? Nuan'er plundered them and later gave me these rings for safekeeping. These weapons all came from their treasury. I have so many, so I wonder if I can just reach level three in a day or two."

He scanned the requirements for the next level. By the time he reached the peak-of-level-one description, he wanted to choke himself for laughing at the creator.

"A thousand Silver Grade for initial completion. Five thousand Silver Grade for mid-completion. A thousand Earth Grade for late completion, and five thousand Earth Grade metal pieces for peak completion? Why not just say fuck off and be done with it?"

Where the hell was he going to find five thousand Earth Grade weapons? Even in the treasury of the Heavenly Firmament Sect, he might only find a few Earth Grade weapons.

"This is insane. How am I supposed to collect this many metal items? This is nothing but loot. Even if I plundered all the sects in the Mortal Realm, I wouldn't get this many Earth Grade weapons."

"Are you forgetting the things you obtained from the people you killed recently?"

Wei frowned. He had never looked into the items those people had. Heck, he'd rarely plundered others' storage rings. He focused on people like Fan Tunzi or some supervillains whom he hated. With other people, he just tossed their storage rings into a pile in the corner of his own storage ring.

Maybe it was time to go through them all. But he didn't have to do it himself. His metal clone could do it for him.

He got up, walked to the other room, and emptied his pile of storage rings then let the metal clone sort them out with his divine sense. Back in the alchemy room, Wei picked a thousand Silver Grade weapons to initiate the Blood Metal Siphon. After pulling out the record, he quickly read through the description. With the system, he could store and retrieve anything for reading. Recently, he had also started journaling his thoughts. *Journaling* was a weird word he'd learned from Allen Ming, but it wasn't a completely foreign concept. It was like his diary, in which he recorded his thoughts about Dao of Laziness. With Allen Ming's instructions, Wei had started pouring out his thoughts at the end of each day, and surprisingly, he got a good night's sleep afterward. Whatever shift it brought to him was insanely good.

"This is an excellent ability, but it will be tough to cultivate it in two and a half days." He passed the information to Blood Parasite through divine sense.

"It might even work on the physical attacks," Blood Parasite said. "It doesn't say anywhere that it can only absorb elemental attacks."

"I guess I'll have to try it once I reach the early completion." He had to see if it only worked on energy, like qi and elementals, or if it could absorb physical or melee attacks as well.

"This Metal Heart sounds like your Blood Heart."

Wei nodded. It did have a similar name, but it worked completely differently. By using a thousand Silver-Grade Metal portions, he would have to construct his Metal Heart inside himself. This metal heart would allow him to conjure a thin layer of metal to absorb and redirect the energies with a thought. So he would have to refine a shitload of weapons, using his own essence fire, and turn a mountain of weapons into the Metal Heart.

Essence Fire, or Qi Fire, was a simple technique one could use to light a fire, using qi or essence. Some alchemists even used it to concoct pills, but it couldn't match with the intensity of beast flames or earth flames, so it wasn't a preferred method.

"This will be painful." Wei picked up a common sword and covered his arm with his essence fire. His essence was his blood, so he could even call it blood fire.

Thinking about the blood fire, he recalled that he'd learned a divine ability called Blood Fire Aura, but he'd never had time to use it. That ability was simple to use. In fact, it worked as essence fire only. The main difference was that it used a special pathway to conjure essence fire, and it worked around him as an aura while essence fire was burning the essence at one point.

Moving his blood essence through the predefined path, he conjured the Blood Fire Aura and then accumulated it on his palm. After refining Heart Essence Aura for so many months, he had gained a finer grasp of any aura he controlled. The Blood Fire Aura burned intensely in his palm, and when he refined the metal sword using it, he finished in a mere second.

"Wow, I finished the first part so easily." Wei cheered up. "But the second part will be difficult."

The drop of metal he'd refined from the sword dripped onto his palm but couldn't enter it. His Yin Yang Hands had made his arms harder than an Earth Grade metal, so it couldn't pierce it. Fuck. What was he supposed to do now?

A rune on the back of his palm pulsed with strange energy, and the metal drop got sucked into his palm.

"Integration Rune. How can I forget about this thing?" Wei cried out. In his defense, he'd had no use for it after he dispersed his metal qi cultivation. But it had become useful again.

Spreading his divine sense, Wei scanned his palm, and as expected, the metal drop floated in his palm without harming his meridians or flesh. The Integration Rune had shown its might once again. This was wonderful. Two methods had solved two major problems for him. The Blood Fire Aura helped him increase the speed of the refinement, and the Integration Rune easily absorbed it. It was like someone had gifted him these two things specially to cultivate the Blood-Metal-Siphon Divine Art.

"Kid, when I think I've seen everything, you make me wonder about my resolve." Blood Parasite shook his head. "Come on—offer some better tea to this elder."

"It's boiling in the cauldron. Just take some for yourself."

This guy didn't respect tea, so Wei had no obligation to serve him tea, or even show respect. Ignoring him completely, Wei focused on the pile of weapons in front of him. One by one, he refined them using Blood Fire Aura and then used the rune at the back of his palm to accumulate the refined liquid into his palm. Once he had absorbed a thousand weapons, he would form the embryo of the Metal Heart.

"What a crude tea. In my day, I used to drink Blood Tea, and it tasted the most heavenly of any tea in this world." Blood Parasite sighed.

"Stop chatting, and tell me why you are here," Wei said. Blood Parasite had been appearing frequently, and although Wei didn't dislike talking to him, he had plenty of things to do at the moment.

"I want you to teleport the herb you found in the palace to Xue Qi," Blood Parasite said casually.

"And why the hell would I do that? Why would I give something to the woman who betrayed my trust, our trust?"

Blood Parasite sipped tea from a white ceramic cup. "To ease karma with her."

Chapter 60

Xue Qi's Heart

Xue Qi was flabbergasted when she received a teleportation request from Li Wei. Why was he doing this? And on top of that, how had he found out about the Reverse Teleportation Art? It was an ancient art only a few people in this world should have known about.

Blood Parasite—that fellow must have told Li Wei. Only that bastard would know about this. But why were they doing it? Were they sending a retribution to her end, like a prank or some artifact that would detonate once she accepted it? But they didn't have any skill that would threaten her, so out of curiosity, she accepted the Reverse Teleportation Art.

"Immortal Orchid." Xue Qi shuddered.

A thin sapling, perfectly preserved in the Thousand-Time Wood Box, appeared inside her spirit tool, where she had accepted the teleportation. This plant could produce Immortal Dew, which she wanted for something very precious. All she needed was to dip this plant in Pure Spring Water, and in ten years, she would get the Immortal Dew.

"Why, Li Wei and Blood Parasite? Why are you doing this to me? Are you expecting me to come back to you?" Her heart shook in pain.

Betraying Li Wei hadn't been a simple decision, and she'd believed him when he'd said that she wouldn't die prematurely, sacrificing herself. He could have severed their connection and freed her, but he hadn't, and she was fine with that. The karma she'd planted in him was too much to wipe out, but by providing this simple gift, he had fulfilled one condition she had given him.

"This is complicated. Especially with that bastard Blood Parasite. Why are you doing this to me? What is your purpose?" After so many years, she felt a pain in her heart, which had shredded away after Lord Mayhem had turned her into a Specter. It seemed that not all emotions could be disposed of. Once a human, always a human.***

"Brother Wei, why are you glowing like the sun?" Rual'er asked as soon as Li Wei materialized outside of the Ten-Day Time Chamber. Like the previous time, the palace had booted others out earlier than him. "You are looking resplendent."

Wei chuckled, rubbing the back of his neck. Her choice of words was interesting.

"I cultivated a divine art, and it has this weird effect," Wei said, sighing inwardly.

It was worse than it looked. When he'd cultivated the Blood Metal Siphon to the early completion, a thin layer of liquid metal had formed around him, and he couldn't shake it off. It remained around him like glue, and it shone so brightly that Blood Parasite said it was blinding to eyes. Even Wei couldn't look at himself in the mirror, and it scared the shit out of him. The metal also had this intense smell of the purest form of metal out of the furnace, and although he didn't dislike it, he thought other people might not like it much.

The worst thing was that he couldn't remove the liquid metal until he reached the peak completion of level one, and that meant he needed a lot of Earth Grade metal pieces, and he didn't know where he would get them. The metal clone he set out to sort the storage ring only had a pitiful number of Earth Grade metal weapons, and they weren't even sufficient for reaching late completion.

It was fucking insane. He was afraid to come out looking like that, so he'd taken the pill he used to hide his Yin-Yang Arms and rubbed it along his entire body. He still looked like a glowing metal cube.

"I kind of like this. I can spot you anywhere now." She giggled.

"Li Wei, you look beautiful." Little Fox came near him. "But you smell like metal. Did you do anything to your skin? Come on, give me some fruit, and I'll throw the waste on you, and then you'll smell better."

"Shut up." Wei pushed out his wings and flew away toward Grandpa Ling. "Rual'er, come with me. We have to prepare for the next battle." In a couple of hours, the third wave would come, and he wanted to prepare for it better than the last time.

Grandpa Ling was sitting on a stone, drinking fruit wine from a metal cup. It smelled like Black Wild Grape. It was the same wine Rual'er had offered him, and it tasted fantastic.

"Nephew Wei, you look odd." Grandpa Link scanned him from head to toe. "This nice girl gave me this fine wine, so I can't offer any to you. Please ask her if you want to taste it."

When he glanced at Rual'er, she winked at him. She was already buttering up the old man. Was she really taking the proposal thing seriously? Whatever. He would deal with it when the time came.

"Grandpa Ling, we have to prepare for the next wave. How were your gains in the time chamber?"

"I never felt I could reach Heart Blood Realm in this lifetime, and everyone feels the same. Nephew Wei, you've given life to these old bones, and I can finally see a light for the Houtian Realm."

"That's good. But it will only happen if we survive the next three waves, which seems unlikely. The enemies are growing stronger. I heard they'll send a full team of powerful people in the third wave, and the fifth wave will bring their real firepower." Wei had scanned some memories of the people he'd killed and to learn about what was coming.

"So, what do you suggest? We can always give up on the decree, or whatever thing this is called, and step away from this place."

"Maybe you can, but I can't. I've been chosen to defend this decree, and those enemies won't settle until they kill me for this," Wei answered.

"Brother Wei, don't worry. I won't abandon you. It's just a life, and I'll always come and meet you in the next life." Rual'er smiled.

"I'm not going away either. I'll just smash them to death." Little Fox rubbed her soft head against his palm.

Sonja knelt in front of him. "This servant will accompany you in death, my lord."

"Nephew Wei, we twelve people will protect you. Don't worry." Grandpa Ling joined the others, making Wei's eyes moisten.

"Guys, thank you for your response, but I doubt there's anyone in the incoming wave who can really kill me. I'm more worried about you," Wei blurted. If it only came to him, he could fight thousands, and he had hundreds of things to rely on, but protecting other people while saving himself might prove to be a difficult task.

"Brother Wei, you have the confidence a man should possess. I'm impressed," Rual'er said in a soft tone.

"Of course. He is my Li Wei. He has the strongest confidence of all men, and he will rule the world one day, and I'll be his queen."

Wei frowned. What nonsense this little fox was spurting again. Had she hit her head while visiting the Beast Origin Realm or something?

Wei rubbed his stubble, thinking. "Let's do one thing. I'll teach a forbidden art to twelve of you, which will allow you to reach the peak of the Heart Blood Realm for a short time and should help you save others, but you can only use it once in the Heart Blood Realm, and your cultivation will fall to layer zero of the Heart Blood Realm once you use it, so you've got to use it as the last resort."

Grandpa Ling nodded.

"Teach me that as well," Rual'er said.

"I can't. It only works for the qi cultivators."

Rual'er seemed lost for a moment. "Don't worry. I also know a couple of forbidden arts."

"Are you talking about the Beast Ascension Forbidden Art? If so, no, you can't use it. It will harm your cultivation, and you may never step into the Houtian Realm." Wei had known about this forbidden art, and he couldn't bear to see her use it and ruin her own future cultivation path.

"You even know about that?" she asked, looking confused. "And isn't it better to use it than to die?"

"Don't even think about it. I won't let you die." Wei felt a strong weight settle on his heart. If the information he'd received from Ding Son was correct, they would meet an army from the Destiny Mirror Sect, and he wasn't sure if he could kill them all with his own abilities.

Suddenly, the ten birds he'd caught from various enemies shot into the air, forming a green-lightning barrier among them, and it shone like the sun appearing in the dead of the night. Wei spotted Li Gun standing on the back of one of the birds. Was he trying to attack?

Chapter 61

Stormfeather Guardian Formation

The green-lightning barrier flickered like a dying candle in the gust of night wind and then went out. The fluctuation of the green light had almost blinded everyone, but Li Wei spotted Li Gun falling from the top of the bird like a dead apple.

Damn it. Wei spread his wings and flashed through the air, pushing his speed to the maximum. He caught Li Gun in his arms. Li Gun's face was as pale as a ghost, and a trickle of blood escaped from the corner of his mouth, staining his chin.

Rual'er flew up and hovered next to the ten birds before making a strange sound. The birds replied in a high-pitched noise that scrapped against Wei's eardrums, and he wished he'd worn cotton swabs in his ears to prevent them from bleeding. That intense sound left an irritating taste in his mouth.

"Brother Wei, this brother was practicing a formation with the birds," Rual'er said. "They thought you gave him the order."

"A formation." Wei activated his Divine Vision and scanned the birds.

An invisible current was emitted from their wings and connected with Li Gun's chest. What the hell was he doing? Wei tore open Li Gun's robe at his chest and saw an agate pendant sending green sparks that fizzled out. It was lightning but not something his Blood Lightning Pill Clone wanted.

"What is this thing?" Wei slowly brought Li Gun down and placed him on the ground. He was about to touch the pendant when Li Gun opened his eyes.

"Don't. It's cursed." Li Gun coughed blood, causing Wei to quickly dodge backward to avoid getting any on himself. And thank heaven he did, because the black blood smelled like a decayed piece of flesh lying in the corner of the street.

"Li Gun, are you going crazy? How dare you play with a cursed item? Are you trying to die faster? I can help you with that." Wei retrieved a healing pill and tossed it into Li Gun's open mouth.

"It's okay." Li Gun sat up, the red returning to his face. "My family bloodline has a connection with this item, so it only affects me temporarily. With a quick rest, I'd be fine."

"What formation you were trying with the birds? Were you using this cursed item as a formation eye?" Wei stared at the cursed pendant. He'd never seen anything like it. Generally a cursed item would infect the wielder, who would start losing sanity, health, and rationality. But Li Gun seemed fine.

"Can I trust you, brother Wei?"

"If saving your life and gaining your freedom doesn't count as trustworthy, then no, you can't trust me."

Wei felt like someone had poured a soiled tea into his mouth. What was wrong with people these days? Even after doing so much for Li Gun, the guy still suspected him. Maybe he should have let this guy die and grabbed the treasure robe for himself. That robe was worthless on a petty, narrow-minded person like Li Gun.

"I'm sorry. I'm a hypocrite when it comes to trusting people. I haven't had a good experience other than with my wife." He tossed a book at Wei and then lowered his head.

Wei caught the book with Heart Essence Aura and opened it. Being cautious was better than being an idiot.

"System, scan it and store it as I flip the pages," Wei said in his mind and flipped the pages rapidly. If the system could record the diagrams at the Ancient Runes, then he bet it could scan and store anything. "Beast Formation Compendium. Where did you find this book, Li Gun?"

"In a Void Object."

"No wonder I've never seen this book before," Wei muttered.

Of course, he wouldn't say he knew every formation book in the world, but such a rare one would have at least caught his attention. A dozen formation diagrams appeared in Wei's vision, and as he read through them, he couldn't resist tsk-tsking.

"Li Gun, you are nothing but a stupid brat." Wei tossed the book back to Li Gun.

"What did he do?" Rual'er asked, landing next to Wei.

"He tried out an Earth Grade Formation—Stormfeather Guardian Formation—with ten birds. How insane." He shook his head in disdain. In Wei's previous life, he'd seen many students who loved to jump the levels and try something impossible for their level. They just forgot that a tower was built level by level and never started at level five.

Pushing his wings out, he flew higher and stood in front of the ten beast birds they had captured from the people of the Destiny Mirror Sect. According to Little Fox, these birds belonged to the Beast Origin Realm and had been captured by the Destiny Mirror Sect. With Little Fox's help, they had pledged their allegiance to Wei, and they would help him to eradicate the Destiny Mirror Sect.

"Now, watch how this formation is set up using three birds first." He sent a divine transmission to the birds, and three of them flew out of the flock and gathered around him. "This is a tiered formation, so the grade of this formation is dependent on the number of beast birds you use." He willed his lightning pill clone to imbue him with lightning.

Lightning surged out of his dantian, covering him from head to toe. With his skin already shining, he wondered how eye-catching he had become. Thick arcs of lightning spread across his skin as he carved the formation eye into his left palm. It was a simple formation and used the intricacies of heaven-and-earth energy to form an eye. Generally, such a formation would be built using static poles, but this one allowed a person to use the birds as formation poles. It made the formation flexible and allowed one to protect a large area with a low number of poles.

As Li Gun had already carved the diagrams into the bird's back, Wei didn't have to do anything. Lightning flew out of his right palm and shot over the birds' backs, forming a thin net around them. This was a very basic version of the formation and sufficient to protect a small area, but the main marvel about it was the next stage.

Staring at the sky, Wei performed another incantation. This was the step that Li Gun had failed. Black clouds appeared above their heads by the time Wei finished his incantation.

"Attack." Wei sent a thick bolt of lightning into the dark clouds, and in response, the sky roared and threw a rain of lightning at him. All the lightning was absorbed by the diagrams on the backs of the birds, and the lightning net covering Wei and three birds thickened. Lightning arcs zapped through the net as the birds spread around and formed a tight circle of one mile.

The initial version of the lightning net had originated from Wei's own lightning, but after completing the formation, it gathered the lightning from the heavens themselves, and that was why it was a marvelous formation.

"How did you do that?" Li Gun muttered.

"My Li Wei is a lightning god. He eats lightning for breakfast and drinks it as wine," Little Fox proudly said.

"Very fitting to be my man," Rual'er whispered.

Wei almost coughed blood on that last sentence. The formation fizzled and died down. Shaking his head, he descended. Although he could use the formation, he would need some practice to maintain it for a long time.

"Use this as a formation eye." Wei tossed the Twin-Lightning Book Treasure toward Li Gun. "Start with three birds, and then expand it to ten birds. Do it in the next hour, and you will be responsible for the inner formation that will defend our people."

Li Gun nodded and started carving a diagram on the book treasure without wasting any time.

"Lord, I've finished setting up the traps you asked for," Rual'er said.

Wei nodded at her before staring at the clock. Only one hour remained before the next wave would appear, and with this formation, he was half-confident of saving all the people who had supported him.

Chapter 62

Intent of Time Flow

W hen the light froze, Xin Ba knew they'd entered the proximity of the Five Firmament City. For everyone else, the time froze, but for him and his companion, the time remained flowing as they both had learned the rarest-of-rare Intent of Time Flow. Or at least, their original forms had learned it.

"Cao'er, what are you thinking?" he asked the young woman sitting on the bird next to his own.

Although the time was flowing for them, they had to obey the rules of time. Otherwise, their bodies would be shredded. Once they broke through into the Houtian Realm and learned the intricacies of the Time Dao, only he would be able to move freely through the frozen time.

"Just wondering why they asked us to come here. Others could have finished this task, and yet we were called when I could enjoy my time with my lord husband." She smiled coquettishly, looking like a whore.

She was a whore, in fact. Even he didn't know how many men she'd slept with to get admitted into the Chosen Gold. But did she think she could get it just because she slept with everyone she met? If it weren't for their special bond, he would have killed her already. Sometimes he just wanted to tear apart her skin and turn her into an ugly bitch so she would stop sleeping around.

"Let it go. We'll prove, through this war, that we are no less than those bastards. I heard they'll come in either the fifth wave or the second pulse. As long as we wipe out everyone else, they'll have no option but to concede to our powers." Xin Ba was confident of his own power, and when combined with Xin Cao's, it reached the epitome of anything a peak Heart Blood Realm cultivator could do. They had easily killed ten Houtian Realm cultivators of the Crimson Moon Kingdom using their powers. And if they went further... ha ha... the sky wasn't the limit.

"I wish Houtian Realm bastards could take part in this battle. Killing some chickens of the Five Firmament City is too lowly for my status." Xin Cao licked her lips. Any other time, she would have spent hours adjusting her makeup, but stuck in time flow, they couldn't do anything but twitch here and there and talk. Their powers shone in the real battle.

"Let's just wait. We have four hundred prodigies with us, but none of them are our match. I hope they can at least wipe out some dregs from the Five Firmament City for us."

Sun Nuan glanced at the city through the window on the top of the guard tower built by elder Yen Poe in recent days. It acted as a Formation Pole for a Giant Turtle Formation that Elder Yen Poe had deployed as extra protection. With everything silent, she had a strange peace blooming in her heart, which she couldn't describe in words. The time was frozen for the city, and she had no answer as to why that was.

The strangest thing—she was unaffected by the time freeze. Was it good or bad? She didn't know.

"You'll be meeting your friend soon, little girl." Elder Deimu appeared next to her. He had reached the peak of Heart Blood Realm and then paused his cultivation because the seal would kill him. However, by doing this, he'd regained some of his abilities as a Houtian Realm cultivator, and Spatial Movement was one of them.

"Elder, you're looking much better today."

"The pills you gave me were heaven defying."

Sun Nuan smiled. Those were special pills made from big brother Wei's godly liquid. She'd been experimenting with it under Master Xue Qi's guidance, and she'd had some breakthroughs recently. But she couldn't tell this to the elder. It had to remain a secret between her and Master Xue Qi.

"Elder, do you know why the city is frozen?" She glanced at the streets and once again felt the peace in her heart.

"It's Time Dao."

"Do you know Time Dao, elder?"

"I don't, but I've some tricks up my sleeves, and I've seen this time freezing before. The Ancient Decree has descended, little girl, so be ready to be transported out to the battleground."

"I don't know Time Dao, nor do I have any tricks, so why am I not being affected?"

The elder gave a reassuring smile. Over the days she'd spent with him, she'd realized he had a good heart dedicated to alchemy, and through his stories, she knew he only sought for the good seedlings.

"How can such a trickery affect the descendant of the Primordial Blood Emperor? Little girl, you've a destiny that supersedes that of everyone around you," he said.

"I can't compare to the destiny of one man."

"That kid is—how should I say this? He is not from this world, so his destiny is also not from this world. He may become a god or a devil. But you belong to this world, and your destiny is to rule it."

She smiled, recalling the warmth of big brother Wei's embrace. That was her home, and only there could she feel happy. "I don't want to rule this world. I just want to follow him forever."

Elder Deimu sighed. "That little lass was lovestruck like you, and for the same fellow. I wonder if my destiny is to meet girls like you?" He chuckled.

"Elder, can you tell me why this is happening?" Nuan said, changing the subject. If allowed, the elder would talk about random things for hours, and she didn't have time for that.

"The Ancient Decree has descended, and you will be pulled into a battleground in a few hours."

"Ancient Decree? What is that?"

"A thing that shouldn't exist in this world." He sighed again. "I served the Gatekeepers for a long, long time, and I know a secret or two. This will move everyone less advanced than the Houtian Realm to a battleground, and only one faction can survive. I guess your friend Li Wei will be there. Characters like him don't miss such opportunities."

"Elder, do you hate him?" Nuan had wanted to ask him this question for a long time.

The elder chuckled. "I should hate him for charming two of you, but I can't because both of you love him. Although you didn't accept me as your teacher, I treat you as my disciple, and I can't hate my disciple's husband."

His words tugged at her heart. Big brother Li Wei was her everything, but she wasn't sure what he thought about her. Whatever he thought, she would accompany him to the end of time. This was her vow in the world, and she wouldn't betray it.

Chapter 63

Third Wave

"Brother Wei, I've found something," Kai Shaya said as they watched the new group of a thousand people arriving in the third wave. He'd just returned from his research.

"Tell me, brother." Wei glanced at the formation, sipping tea from a ceramic cup. It was a gift from Nuan'er, and he felt her warmth even though she wasn't here with him.

"As I suspected, there is an inheritance hidden inside the giant clock," Kai Shaya said in a serious tone.

He'd vanished behind the clock after they came to this barren world with no sun and a dusky atmosphere. If it weren't for the sweet taste of his tea, Wei would have been irritated to death by the dry taste this place left in his mouth.

"Let's talk while we finish these people." Wei flew forward, and Kai Shaya followed him on a flying tool.

Winds whipped around Wei as he stopped above the thousand-odd people. Half of them stood to one side, and half of them were scattered. So there was a single group and indecisive people. Wei didn't want to kill everyone without giving them a chance.

He sent a divine transmission that covered everyone. "Guys, I'll only say one thing. If you want to take me as your enemy, then be ready to die. Otherwise, take a heaven-and-earth vow, and join my side." Some seemed shocked, and some bellowed at him.

A tall girl sitting on a giant bat flew up. "Are you Li Wei?"

"I am."

"Then fuck off!" She laughed before looking back and making some action with her fingers. In a swift and brutal motion, his sword swiftly severed her neck.

"Fantastic. I can summon a single sword with just a thought."

Wei cheered up, staring at the sword image hovering around him. It was the Wood Sword Tornado, a self-created skill from the Wood Creation Sword. After the wood clone merged into him, he could use his martial skills once again with the help of wood qi.

"Brother Wei, how did you do that? That woman was an early Heart Blood Realm cultivator. I don't believe she served you her neck on a platter," Kai Shaya stuttered.

"Oh, that. She didn't," Wei said. She'd had a defensive qi guard set up around her, but his sword had moved like wind and cut through her neck without any resistance. "I guess my skill level has improved. Let me try something new." Wei channeled the wood qi into the main sword, and ten sword images appeared around it. No, he didn't want sword images but sword rays.

Closing his eyes, he channeled the Yang Wood Pill Clone's pure energy into his wood qi, bringing the quality of the qi to a new height, and as expected, the sword images changed into ten sword rays instantly. With a thought from Wei, the sword rays shot through the crowd and cut ten people before coming back to him.

"Was that really a sword ray?" Kai Shaya asked, shivering. "No wonder you could cut her like a tofu. You're getting scarier day by day, brother Wei."

Wei nodded. The power of Sword Intent increased with each level, starting with Sword Flash and Sword Image and then Sword Ray. As Sword Ray was much more powerful than Sword Image, he could cut early Heart Blood Realm cultivators like cabbages using the Sword Ray, but upgrading his Sword Images to the Sword Rays took everything out of him.

"One more warning. Who wants to join my group? Step out, or die," Wei said in a grim tone, not letting anyone have a second thought about his intentions. In the midst of this brutal war, he had no time to reassure those with lingering doubts.

A couple hundred people stepped out, their faces full of worries but their hearts clear.

"Brother Shaya, let's finish this and go training." Wei unleashed his Heart Blood Aura, Wood Sword Tornado, and started cutting through his enemies.

Whoever hadn't stepped away was swept in his attacks and died. It exhausted the fuck out of his wood qi, but he had no other option. Along with those two skills, he also used Blood Sword Tearing through the Earth to cut large masses. These were three of his best group-wiping skills, and he didn't shrink from using them to the fullest.

Kai Shaya also joined him, a thousand-hand buddha unleashing a flurry of punches at the enemy. Although he couldn't kill as much Wei could, he still managed to kill a few dozen people in no time.

The two hundred people who had separated from the group joined in the battle and finished Wei's enemies, and in less than an hour, the entire place was filled with dead bodies of the enemies. Out of the two hundred who'd joined him, only ten people had died, and that was because of their foolishness and Wei's inability to save everyone. Seeing them die had pained him deeply, but Nuan'er had once told him that a general couldn't save everyone in the chaos of battle. The general's toughest and most important job was being there, providing moral support.

"Sonja, make sure everyone takes a vow of heaven and earth, and only then admit them into the bigger group." Wei wiped his sword on a dead man's clothes as he walked away from the battlefield.

"I understand, lord." Sonja bowed down then went on to do her job while Wei faced Kai Shaya, who looked eager to speak.

"Say it, already." Wei handed him a cup of wine Rual'er had given him. This monk hadn't drunk wine before Wei met him, but after tasting the wine Wei had brought from the other world, he'd grown addicted to the drinks of the gods in the Mortal Realm.

"Brother Wei, I've found an inheritance site." Kai Shaya stared at the ancient clock stabbed in the ground a few dozen miles away from them.

"Are you sure about this?" Wei asked. "Let me say one thing. Inheritances are no free lunch. If you accept them, you'll create karma with the inheritance creator, and trust me, this is not a good thing. I wouldn't recommend accepting any inheritance."

Kai Shaya smiled sheepishly. "Brother Wei, it's too late for that. When I won first place in the sect tournament, I accepted the inheritance from a similar clock, and this will be just an addition to that."

Wei sighed. He couldn't blame Kai Shaya. In fact, he himself had been ecstatic when he'd first received an inheritance. He'd only known about it after Xue Qi told him, and later, Blood Parasite had confirmed it. An inheritance was a big, big trap.

"It will also help me learn Intent before breaking through into the Houtian Realm."

"If you're going only for that, I've some other ways to help you. I helped Rual'er." Wei shrugged.

"There is one more thing. I might get a chance to create that resurrection pill after all."

Okay, that made sense. When they'd first met, this bald monk had been creating a resurrecting pill and attracted tribulation lightning, which Wei had absorbed without knowing.

Tribulation lightning. Wei thought about another treasure he'd gotten from one of the lightning cultivators. It was a small needle but packed a lot of tribulation lightning. Just touching the needle made his Blood Lightning Pill Clone stir in excitement. Before the next wave appeared, he wanted to study it and see if he could work on the Lightning Emit and Lightning Sea of Taichi skills he'd learned.

"Fine, go, do what you want to do. I'll protect you."

"Thank you, brother Wei. I'm glad that I found a friend like you. I must have done something good in my previous life."

"The pleasure is mine." Wei patted Kai Shaya's back.

System: Information Interface detected.

The third wave is finished.

Chapter 64

The Heavens' Decree – Fourth Wave

"**B**rother Wei, you've trusted many people this time." Rual'er floated next to Li Wei's clone on a training ground.

They were in the palace, where a hundred core people from Wei's group trained with various skills. The palace was the perfect environment for all sorts of training for different types of cultivators. It also had multiple meditation chambers that increased their training speed by five times. If he'd access to this palace earlier, he could have developed his army in no time. Well, better late than never.

"This is fine. I bound them by a special vow, and they only think you're exploiting a time rift on the battleground." Wei's clone smiled. "I'll concoct some pills while the main me is practicing some new moves."

"Brother Wei, make sure you don't end up unconscious this time." Rual'er winked, making Wei blush. It was embarrassing. He'd gone overboard the last time and almost lost face in front of everyone.

"Absolutely not. I'm only practicing some moves for the fifth wave. The information I gathered indicates that the fifth wave would be the most difficult. To win the Ancient Decree, the Gatekeepers have enlisted the help of numerous prodigies. It will be tough."

"Don't worry. We'll win."

"Let's hope." Wei pursed his lips and walked into an alchemy chamber in the mansion.

The main body sat in the Ten-Day Time Chamber, drinking a salty wine Rual'er had given him, which helped him stay focused. He wondered if it was the salty taste of the wine, reminiscent of ocean air, that made it difficult to concentrate on anything else but the thing he wished to focus on.

He had plenty of things to practice, and while his Blood Lightning Pill Clone absorbed the tribulation lightning, he focused on increasing the number of swords he could conjure through the Wood Sword Tornado. When he pushed with Sword Images, he could easily reach number twenty, but Blood Parasite stopped him at nineteen and converted all to Sword Rays. After spending a day converting nineteen Sword Images to Sword Rays, Wei stopped to eat something.

"Blood Parasite, what will happen when I add the twentieth Sword Ray?"

"It will be fun." Blood Parasite appeared. "Give me some tea, and I'll tell you."

Wei frowned. This guy had been asking for tea more and more. Was he also trying to use Tea Soul Ceremony to improve his soul?

Whatever. Wei offered him one of the finest teas he had.

"It's the Will of the Skill. When you created the ten Sword Rays, I felt the heavens stir, and that only happens when a skill is about to get the Will of the Skill. I could sense it because I've created my own Will of the Skill."

"Is that good? Can I create it just by pushing the Sword Rays to the maximum number?" Wei felt excited. Then he remembered where he was.

The heavens wouldn't know anything was happening in here. "It's no use. We'll never get to hear what will happen here."

"Not if you perform the skill in the Intent Room. The Infernal Fire Palace has merged half with you, so you can access the third level of the Primordial Blood Palace with a cool-down period between."

"Can I really do that?"

"Let's go." Blood Parasite patted Wei's shoulder, and they materialized in the familiar space with Intent Energy present everywhere. If he could let his people practice here, wouldn't they learn the Intent much faster?

"This place is connected to the heavens. So add the twentieth Sword Ray, and you'll hear the Heavens' Decree," Blood Parasite said.

Wei didn't waste time asking about the Heavens' Decree. He calmed his mind and moved the nineteen Sword Rays around him. Maintaining every wave took a toll on him and his wood qi. If he didn't have the support of his Yang Wood Pill Clone to control the wood qi perfectly, he wouldn't be successful in this.

"A bit more." Wei pushed his will to the maximum and extracted the final wood qi from his dantian then used it to create the twentieth Sword Ray.

The sky rumbled, and a ray of light cut through the muddy clouds and shone upon him. A large scroll appeared in the heavens with his name transcribed on it in silver lines.

System: Information Interface Detected.

Heavens' Decree

The Heavens bestow Li Wei the first Will of the Skill. The power of the skill will be quadrupled when used with the approval of the heavens.

The words washed over him and made him realize the profound power the heavens controlled. The words were enough to send him shivering in awe. People always said the Violet Palace Realm cultivators were closest to the heavens because they learned the Creation Concept, but now he realized it wasn't the truth. There were many realms above that, and heaven was unfathomable, so a tiny Violet Palace Realm cultivator couldn't be closest to the heavens.

Just thinking about it excited him. Houtian was just the first step in the cultivation, and he was so close to reaching it. This was going to be thrilling.

"Let's see if I can push my Sword Rays further." Wei pushed the wood clone out and made him cultivate the wood qi alongside him.

A few days later, Wei and a hundred people stepped outside of the time chamber, and the fourth wave was on the horizon. However, with the boost in his power, Wei knew he would crush it easily. A thousand people appeared in the fourth wave. They were from the Destiny Mirror Sect, and each one possessed a rare artifact like the ones Li Wei had fought before. However, they were no match for the guardian formation Wei had set up using the ten people he had trusted with the help of Rual'er. Out of those thousand people, two hundred agreed to joined Wei's side. And after scanning them with his divine sense, Wei let them join and easily eliminated the remaining eight hundred with his Wood Sword Tornado.

"Lord, there is good news and bad news." Sonja appeared next to him when he killed the last person from the Destiny Mirror Sect. "There is a bigger plan in motion, and I suspect the Five Firmament City is in danger."

Wei rubbed the back of his neck. "What's the good news?"

"The Five Firmament City will probably be in the fifth wave."

Wei smiled. This was really a good thing. Even if he didn't get any help from his city, just seeing them would raise his hopes. And if Nuan'er came here, it would be the best thing that happened in the last day.

Chapter 65

Everyone Appears

When Xin Ba appeared in the battlefield, he looked around and frowned. The place he had teleported to looked barren, devoid of any life. Along with two thousand of their people, two thousand more people had appeared, but no one gave him any sense of danger. It meant everyone who'd arrived only had cultivation levels below the Heart Blood Realm. They were nothing but trash.

"Cao'er, quickly use the Cultivation-Sensing Talisman, and see where the people from the Five Firmament City are." If they'd teleported with the trash, the Five Firmament City's people must have teleported somewhere else.

Cao'er retrieved a compass-like object and poured her qi into it, and as the time passed, her brows twitched. "We are scattered, and I don't see them anywhere in a hundred-mile radius. I think they went to the other decree node," she said after a brief pause.

Xin Ba cursed inwardly. There were four nodes of the Ancient Decree, and each had a five-hundred-mile radius. People from one place could get teleported to one place only, but accidents did happen, and it wasn't unheard-of for people to be teleported to a totally different node. If they couldn't kill everyone from the Five Firmament City in the fifth wave, it would become a big issue.

A raspy voice played in his mind and told him that someone named Li Wei owned this decree node, and they would have to defeat him to win it.

"What should we do, brother Ba? There are three other nodes, and the Five Firmament City people must have teleported to another node. Should we search for them?" Xin Cao asked.

Xin Ba's forehead throbbed with pain. This was fucking insane. They were right outside of the Five Firmament City, so shouldn't they be put together? How was he supposed to search for the brutes from the Five Firmament City now?

"What do you think?" he asked her.

"I think we should divide. Half of us can look for those bastards from the Five Firmament City, and half of us will wipe out this Li Wei. I recall seeing his name in the Gatekeepers' most-wanted list."

Xin Ba also recalled seeing that name in the Purple Frame. It was third highest list of must-kill individuals, and Li Wei's name was at the top. Killing him would fetch a good number of sect points.

"If we do this, we can control two decree nodes, and sect elders will be happy about us," she said.

"Let's do it. Take five hundred with you, and I'll wipe this trash with five hundred people."

"What about the thousand that came from other sects?" she asked.

"If they don't pledge allegiance to us, kill them. They're all trash, after all."

Xin Ba stared at the dot that represented Li Wei's group. and there were around eight hundred people with him. It should be easy. In fact, he could send more people to Xin Cao's help, but it would leave this place sparse for the next wave, and he didn't want to take the risk. In all his battles, he'd learned one thing, and that was to never look down on the people of the Mortal World. No one knew when some powerful person would appear and destroy everything they had planned.

"Elder Deimu, where are the others?" Sun Nuan scanned those who had teleported along with her and only saw a thousand people. They had a five-thousand-strong army of peak of Boiling Blood Realm cultivators, and only a thousand had come here. But their powers weren't less than those of peak of Heart Blood Realm cultivators, due to their dual body-and-qi cultivation.

"I told you I'd choose four thousand people to stay behind."

She recalled that he'd said something like that when the time had been frozen, and then he'd gone somewhere and reappeared here.

"I concealed them from the Ancient Decree. They are in the Five Firmament City along with the main army of Heart Blood Realm cultivators. So if the Gatekeepers attack while we're stuck her,e they can protect the city."

Nuan felt gratitude toward Elder Deimu. If everyone had come here, she would have been worried to death for the city big brother Wei loved. There were so many people he cared about, and she couldn't let them suffer because of some trial.

"Thank you for putting that narcissistic fellow at a distance from the ones who have entered," she said.

"Wang Purang can be sometimes a nuisance." Elder Deimu chuckled. "Who knew he would take a liking to you? Keeping him in the city might prove useful."

Nuan clenched her fists on recalling that detestable fellow's methods and his typical ways of wooing her. If he hadn't been Elder Yen Poe's pupil, she would have killed him. But that seemed impossible. He'd had multiple mechanical puppets with him.

Anyway, she could forget about him, as she had things to take care of. Sighing, she scanned the crowd. Only a hundred Heart Blood Realm cultivators had appeared with her. So they had a six-hundred-person army and a few generals, and out of them, only Nuan, Elder Deimu, and Tun Hu had appeared.

Then she saw her father, along with a few of his generals. The State of Zin had a pitiful one hundred Boiling Blood Realm cultivators and ten Heart Blood Realm cultivators, including him, and those were because of the pills she'd sent him.

"Daughter, you're here as well." Her father, King Sun Xaohua, walked forward with a big smile on his face.

She shook her head and looked away. There was no father-daughter love between them. All she could remember was how he'd hit her badly in her childhood and how her mother, who was still missing, had suffered because of him.

"General Duanz, please bring everyone in the formation," she ordered.

A message played in her mind from someone with a deep growling voice. They were supposed to fight Jim Cam, who owned this node of the Ancient Decree.

"Elder, do we have to fight this Jim Cam? Big brother Wei is not here?" she asked, frowning. If big brother Wei were here, he should be holding the node, not some Jim Cam.

"This is just a single node. Li Wei could be anywhere on the other three nodes."

"Then what should we do?"

"Do you have anything you can use to connect with him?"

"Yes." Sun Nuan tapped on the earrings, but nothing happened. "Why isn't this thing working?" She removed them and checked them carefully. She wasn't an array cultivator, so for her, they were only jewelry given by her beloved.

"Let me check." Elder Deimu held the earrings in his hand and chanted something, and then he pointed to their right. "I sense a connection coming from that side. Let's go and check that node."

Nuan ordered her army to mount on their own flying tools.

Her father rushed to her. "Daughter, please take us with you. I can only trust you in these brutal times."

Nuan signaled General Duanz to help her father. Although she hated him, her mother had loved him once, and she couldn't just break the ties her mother had built.

"Big brother Wei, I'm coming to you." A smile played on her lips as she rose in the air.

Jim Cam watched the big group of cultivators who'd appeared in his node walk away, and he felt a deep peace. He had already gone through a brutal fight, and he didn't have any army left to fight again, but this damn Ancient Decree wasn't allowing him to go away. It wouldn't settle until he died, and he didn't want to die. But at least he was safe from the fifth wave.

Whatever the future held, he would have time to prepare his Undead Army once again. Thousands of people had died on the battlefield, and he would raise them again when they got out of this place.

"Little girl, if we meet again, I'll go easy on you, and if you are willing to be my bride, I might even convert you into an undead to live next to me forever."

Chapter 66

Welcoming Xin Ba with a Slap

In the middle of the formation created by twelve human poles, Li Wei sat cross-legged in front of a golden furnace while his divine sense spread and watched the big team of newcomers massacre a few hundred people and then leave.

Green smoke wafted out of the cauldron, pulling his attention back toward it because of the little fox trying to jump into it to devour the bunch of fragrant fruit he'd tossed into it a moment ago.

"Little Fox, that fruit doesn't taste good. Those are two-thousand-year-old Vile Poleň Fruit. You'll burst if you eat them raw."

"You waste so many good things," Little Fox growled.

Shaking his head, Wei glanced in the direction of the newcomers. The three-thousand-odd people separated into two groups. A thousand people made their way toward their left, led by a beautiful girl. The other team of the two thousand people headed in his group's direction, led by a bulky man on a giant bat—an Earth Cave Bat. It spanned a dozen feet. The other members flew on a Yellow Feather Peacock, another beast from the Beast Origin Realm.

Seeing those birds treated like mounts, the beast birds at his side squealed in anger and wanted to rush out, but the little fox's single growl forced them to stay put.

"Nephew Wei, there are almost two thousand people, and each one has a cultivation base higher than the Boiling Blood Realm." Grandpa Ling stood next to him, his face full of worry.

"What are you worried about? You've already enhanced your defensive formation, and everyone in our team has at least reached the peak of the Boiling Blood Realm. Are you still not sure about their battle prowess?" Wei asked, mixing cold liquid in a metal bowl. He had to keep stirring it counterclockwise for a minute to let the heaven-and-earth energy pour into it perfectly. It was tedious work, but alchemy wasn't a simple profession and required the utmost attention. Herb processing was the biggest part of the puzzle.

"There must be a few hundred Heart Blood Realm cultivators among them."

Without looking up, Wei covered the incoming people in his divine sense.

"A hundred peak of Heart Blood Realm. Five hundred in the early Heart Blood Realm, and the others are mostly at the peak of the Boiling Blood Realm," he said calmly. Normally, this number would put fear into anyone's heart, but he wasn't afraid. "Li Gun, how is your progress?" Wei threw a White Blade Grass into the cauldron, and his wood clone sitting next to him tossed in Qi Water at the same time.

Having a second hand while concocting an Earth Grade pill was heaven-sent. Earth Grade pills were very complex in nature, and this was his first time trying to concoct one. This Limb Enhancing Pill was the simplest and most essential. However, even this one required him to process seventy-two ingredients, and he was only preparing them to last one hour. The more he practiced the Alchemy Clone Art, the more miraculous he found it to be. It wasn't just a pill clone cultivation art—it also had profound alchemy principles he'd never seen before. Xue Qi was right. The more he practiced the alchemy, the easier it became.

A burning smell wafted out of the cauldron, and it shuddered violently. Then, with an intense thump, the lid shot into the air, and black smoke covered his face.

"Much better than you, brother Wei." Li Gun chuckled as he used the Twin-Lightning Book to control the lightning and formed a net with five birds. Although he hadn't achieved success in the ten-bird formation, he was doing well.

"Don't increase the bird count. We have our friends coming for us." Wei got up and slapped his robe to shake off the fine dust. So far, he had processed twenty-three ingredients. He could do the others later.

Sonja stepped forward and wiped his face with a wet cloth. Her feminine fragrance aroused his memories of the time he'd spent with Ki Fei in his reincarnation—the nights of love and the cuddling and teasing.

"Lord, you seem worried about something," Sonja said in a soft voice.

Wei sighed hard. "Nothing. Just thought about a friend."

"Another girlfriend?" Rual'er teased him.

"Aren't you afraid I'll marry a few girls?" he snapped. She called him her man and talked about how they should get married, but then she teased him about having a few girlfriends.

"Why would I? An accomplished man always has ten wives and a hundred concubines. As long as I'm your principal wife, I don't mind sharing you with some more sisters."

Wei felt his blood revolting in his chest. What kind of thinking did this girl have?

"Even if I marry you, you won't be my principal wife," Wei muttered. He wasn't sure about marriage, but he surely loved more than one girl, and he didn't want to think about it right away. He would just let things take their natural course.

Suddenly, green smoke covered the horizon, and a few wails echoed. They came from the incoming party. It seemed like the group had triggered the trap set by Sonja. A few more wails resounded, and a few hundred people who were running toward them dropped dead.

"Li Wei, bastard, what have you set up here?" the hulky man on the giant bat shouted, pointing at Wei's group. "I, Xin Ba, will shred you and fuck your woman."

He shouldn't have said that.

"Teleport." Wei teleported next to Xin Ba and bent the man's finger backward while slapping him with his other hand.

"Intent of Time Flow. I've got you, Li Wei. Now, die." Xin Ba's twitching face curled in a smile, and the time around Wei slowed to a crawl.

Fuck. This was an Intent of Time. The surrounding space had turned into a gel-like substance, and Wei couldn't do anything to get out of it.

Chapter 67

Second Slap

X in Ba couldn't believe his opponent was so naive. When the sect had described him in the Purple Frame, they'd called him a cunning snake who would use his wits, brains, and powers to get things done. He would use any despicable means to torture a person before killing them. They called him a devil specializing in dark arts who could come and go like the wind and whip others from a large distance. Xin Ba had even been given a soul artifact to prevent any soul attack.

It must have been a joke. Whoever had fought with him before had to be a couple of cultivation realms lower than this guy. Either those people were stupid, or they'd described the wrong guy.

Xin Ba had provoked him with a single sentence. How could Li Wei be called "a cunning snake" when he couldn't even control his anger? In fact, he, Xin Ba, was as a cunning snake because he knew how to play with others.

Of course, it had cost him a finger and a slap on the face, which he would take revenge for soon enough by playing with Li Wei until he died with regret.

Li Wei struggled inside his water ball.

"I've got you, Li Wei. How dare they call you a cunning snake? You're nothing but a frog at the bottom of a well." Xin Ba chuckled, pushing his water qi into his broken finger.

The deformed finger quickly healed back to normal. His Infant Water Qi Cultivation Art was one of his specialties, and unless someone cut his head from the torso, he could heal instantly. He was unkillable.

"Intent of Time. Interesting," Li Wei answered, the panic on his face vanishing. He eased up and stopped struggling with the water bubble imbued with Intent of Time Flow.

Xin Ba squinted. This guy wasn't that bad. The water bubble enclosing Li Wei was infused with the Intent of Time Flow, twisting the natural flow and turning it into a prison. The more one fought against the confines, the tighter their prison became. However, Li Wei had adjusted his breathing and settled down as if he knew how Xin Ba's special skill worked.

"Don't boast as if you've seen anyone using the Intent of Time. It's one of the rarest Intents of this world. Unless you have Intent of Null, like that guy, it's useless. Just give up, and I might send your corpse back to your lover."

"Bao Faji?"

"You know him?" Xin Ba asked, his heart beating a little faster than usual. He'd fought with Bao Faji, whose Intent of Null could cancel out Xin Ba's Intent of Time Flow, and that bastard was a layer-one Houtian Realm cultivator, so Xin Ba couldn't beat him in a straight match. Of course, if he fought along with Xin Cao, no one could stop them.

"I whipped his ass with my sword once. Anyway, are you done playing?" Li Wei vanished from the water bubble and appeared next to him, his arm moving in a flash and leaving a handprint on Xin Ba's face.

Xin Ba roared in fury, and his Intent of Time Flow surged out of him, covering a hundred feet area around him. A few of his people got caught, and they squirmed in pain, but Xin Ba didn't care if he killed a few to teach Li Wei a lesson. This bastard had slapped him again, and it hurt his soul and his pride. No matter what, he was going to kill him.

Li Wei floated in the air, a cunning smile playing on his lips. Then smile vanished, and he looked toward a group of outsiders, those who'd been teleported along with Xin Ba's group. Xin Ba turned around and saw that Li Wei was looking at a girl, a petite bitch who couldn't even carry shoes for Xin Ba's sweetheart, Xin Cao. Why was Li Wei staring at her? Did he like ugly, flat girls? Or did he like an old woman who looked like a teen girl? This girl would fit that profile. She had dark-brown hair tied in a perfect ponytail, and if he hadn't known she was at the Heart Blood Realm, he would have thought she was a fifteen-year-old.

"I'll see you soon, Xin Ba," Li Wei said in a wry tone before teleporting back to his own group.

"You—who are you?" Xin Ba pointed at the flat girl.

"Sir, I'm Hui Ma, just a stray cultivator, but I've already pledged my allegiance to the Gatekeepers, so please don't kill me." The girl shuddered in fear under Xin Ba's gaze.

So Li Wei liked flat, ugly girls. Or maybe he was scared of Xin Ba, so he'd pretended he was meeting an expert and then run away.

Chapter 68

Giant Killing Bow Divine Art

"Good job, Li Wei," the little fox said as soon as Li Wei teleported back to his camp.

Using his essence, Wei quickly evaporated the water, and only then did he feel normal again. The water was imbued with some Intent of Time and made his movements sluggish, as if he were stuck in sticky mud.

Little Fox moved around him like a proud cat, but Wei couldn't share the joyous feelings of her heart. Instead, he felt wary of his opponent. Wiping the sweat from his forehead, he glanced back at the enemy camp. They'd lost a few dozen people because of Sonja's trap, but it didn't put a dent in their rankings because only low-level cultivators had died. Wei suspected those people belonged to non-Gatekeepers and Xin Ba didn't even care about them.

"Brother Wei, you look tense. Come and drink some wine." Rual'er offered him a glass.

Every time she met someone new, she would offer them a glass of wine. Was she trying to socialize or get people drunk? Wei had seen one guy continuously approach her for wine, and he was already sleeping like the dead in a corner.

"Try it. It's made of Tree Soul Flower, which only grows inside a hundred-year-old tree and sucks away all of its vitality. The wine is quite spicy, and tastes like melon."

"Spicy melon?" Wei took a swig, and the spicy taste burned his throat and the digestive pipe. When it settled in his stomach, a vibrant wood qi rushed out and eased into his organs, rejuvenating them.

Although it had no effect on Wei, it would be useful for his wood clone. In just a few days inside the Ten-Day Time Chamber, he had pushed his wood clone cultivation to layer nine of the Bone Baptization Realm, but the clone had gotten stuck and couldn't break through into the Marrow Cleansing Realm. Wei knew the reason. It was a pill overload. Eating too many pills in a short time would be detrimental to anyone, including his clone.

"Isn't this good?" Rual'er brought her own glass toward her nose and inhaled deeply.

A seductive maiden flashed in Wei's mind when he looked at Rual'er's small-dragon figure. Once she broke through, she would be an absolute beauty who could topple a nation, yet he'd foolishly declined her in his previous life.

"Li Wei, why didn't you kill that bastard?" the little fox asked naively.

Rual'er glanced at her before shaking her head.

"Little Fox, if killing a peak of Heart Blood Realm prodigy was this easy, the world would be much peaceful," Wei said, inhaling the aroma of the wine before sipping it. "There's someone else among them who gave me goose bumps."

He recalled the feeling when he'd sensed the gaze of the petite girl in the red robe. If he wasn't wrong, she was a Blood-Colored Assassin. It had been a while since anyone had given him a threatening feeling. She wasn't someone to be taken lightly.

"There's a Blood-Colored Assassin girl I don't want you to engage with," Wei said.

Rual'er's eyes filled with killing intent.

"Am I clear, Rual'er?"

"I can take care of her."

Wei shook his head. He couldn't let his friend die because of some stupid enmity from the past. "Don't act like a child. You're a grown woman. When I said you can't handle her, I meant it."

"Brother Wei, I can do this. Trust me," Rual'er said.

"If you value our friendship, don't act like the stupid fox."

Little Fox growled in complaint but said nothing. He guessed her ill-fated attack still weighed on her soul.

"What is our next plan, nephew Wei?" Grandpa Ling walked toward them with a wine cup in his hand.

"We wait," Wei said, sipping his wine. Rual'er really had a talent for wines. Every one she gave him had some use or other. "Sonja's traps should work somewhat, but our key strategy will be to defend and launch sneak attacks on them."

"Let me do it. I haven't shown the power of my treasure robe yet. With my improved cultivation, I can kill a few." Li Gun dropped from a bird, looking exhausted. After his constant playing with lightning, his long hair had frizzed out like a bird's nest.

"No. We don't have the number, nor do we have teamwork. We can't risk our main defense person for some kills." Wei shook his head. "When the offense is not strong, we can only rely on defense. I, Sonja, Little Fox, and Rual'er would be the main vanguards to tear them apart. I can attack their back with my teleport, and you guys can attack their sides."

"But I want to fight," Li Gun complained.

"Don't you take pride in your array formations? You can't even pull fifty percent of the formations' might with the sloppy act of your power. Look at the fifth bird on the right. Its formation diagram is flawed, losing twenty percent of the lightning on its wings. Its wings are already scorched black, and it will fail when it comes to depend on you."

Li Gun lowered his head and rushed to the fifth bird. Wei didn't want to look down on him, but if he kept doing such sloppy work, Wei couldn't take it.

"Li Wei, can I really attack?" Little Fox asked, her voice shaking.

"Yes, from the middle fire, straight into their ranks once they close in. Don't hold back."

"If I go all out, I can only attack five times before I need to rest."

"It should be enough." Wei rubbed her soft head. Her presence was like a soothing wine, easing his worries and bringing him peace. "Rual'er, how was your archery training?" He'd seen Rual'er training in archery, along with her Intent of Wind, in the palace training rooms, but he wasn't sure how confident she was.

"I can't match Wi Vistara—that bitch." She snorted, not hiding her anger. "Are you thinking of letting me attack with arrows? You'd better let me shout at them, as it has more of a chance of killing a few."

Wei chuckled. She was right. Her roar might scare away half of the beasts the enemy used, and it might kill more than her arrows would.

"I have a divine art that will suit you perfectly. In fact, it's made for you and you alone."

Rual'er stared at him with doubtful eyes. Chuckling, Wei transferred Giant Killing Bow Divine Art to her through the divine sense. He only had three levels of it, but that should be enough.

"This." Rual'er's breath sped up as she accepted the transmission. "Brother Wei, please tell me clearly. Have we met before? How do you know I can breathe five hundred times a second and three of my Wind Acupoints are already open?"

Wei smiled. This divine art was quite hard to practice, but Rual'er could skim most of the things and practice it easily. When they'd been roaming together in his previous life, she hadn't only taught him three levels but had also told him how she'd encountered a Wind Missionary in her childhood and how that had opened up three of her Wind Acupoints—namely Wind Pool, Wind Gate, and Wind Screen. This divine art was one of the reasons she was known as Goddess of Blood Rain.

"Will you believe me if I say I met you in my previous life, and you told me everything about yourself?"

Rual'er squinted, doubt clearly visible in her eyes. "Even if I don't, I can't see any other reason you'd know this much about me." She shook her head. "Did you push me to learn archery because of this divine art?"

Wei nodded.

"Is it really that good?"

Wei smiled and retrieved a Gold Grade bow he'd found in the Three Treasure Hall. Then he pulled out some arrows made from Green Metal Bamboo Trees, an excellent material he had found in the Beast Origin Realm.

"These arrows are amazing." Rual'er touched one, her voice becoming soft as if talking with her lover.

"Watch how my Sharpshooting Arrow tears through their defense." Wei nocked the arrow and pulled the bowstring, using his divine sense to lock onto an early Heart Blood Realm cultivator.

Zoom! The arrow cut through the air like a lightning bolt and pierced the cultivator's heart before he even noticed it.

The woman who gave Wei goose bumps moved like air and retrieved the arrow. She stared in Wei's direction. Her eyes had a hint of red, and as expected, the person Wei had killed was one of the Blood-Colored Assassins.

Suddenly, multiple people retrieved a thin layer of armor and put it on. It was done so fast that no one around them seemed to notice.

"Thirty-three. Not bad," Wei whispered.

"Wow. You didn't even use your full power, nor have you learned the Intent of Wind Push. How did you do it?"

"My divine sense helped, but with your wine acupoints opened and your Intent of Wind proficiency, you can do much better than me."

Rual'er gave him a dreamy look. "It is awesome. I'll practice it, but I don't have enough time to learn it before the battle." She sounded sad.

"You have enough time." Tapping on her shoulder, Wei activated the Ten-Day Time Chamber and sent her in.

It should be enough time for her to master at least the first two levels. He just had to make sure he defended their position for the next hour.

Chapter 69

Xin Ba's Strategy

Xin Ba was furious. No, not just *furious*. He was incensed that Li Wei had slapped him twice and then run away. He'd provoked Xin Ba further by killing one of the outsiders with a bow and arrow. What a cheap motherfucker.

"Bastards, activate defense runes on your armor, and if you don't have them, attack those fuckers. Do I need to tell you something so simple?" Xin Ba shouted, keeping an eye on the enemy.

If more arrows came, he would have to use the Intent of Time Flow and slow them down. Letting the enemy wantonly kill his people would only demoralize them. Even if he only killed outsiders, it won't be good for the entire team.

In a show of leadership, he retrieved a thin piece of armor and fastened it onto himself, feeling its presence on his body, even though he knew it wasn't necessary. It was an artifact, and no metal below the high-tier Gold Grade could pierce it. With his healing abilities, no arrow could kill him.

"Leader, what should we do? The enemy has set up hundreds of traps surrounding us, and they even have an archer who can kill a Houtian." Xio Da, his reserve deputy, stepped forward, his gaze jumping everywhere.

Generally, Xin Cao handled everything like this, but in her absence, Xio Da performed the deputy role.

Taking a deep breath, Xin Ba suppressed his itch to slap this bastard to death. He understood the situation. Witnessing a leader being slapped around didn't build confidence in his troops.

"Calm down. Divide the team into scouts, vanguard, and main body. Use the outsiders as scouts, and let them charge forward and disable the traps, and then use all of our Earth Qi cultivators to send avalanche attacks on them. The main body will mainly consist of long-range attackers."

This was embarrassing. How could Xio Da not understand basic things? Had he, Xin Ba, made a mistake by choosing him as deputy? He missed Xin Cao. She handled all such things, and she could have done much better than this bastard.

"Xio Da, these are basic war tactics, so how the fuck did you forget them?"

"Leader, please forgive me, but outsiders are pissed off. We didn't let them ride on our beasts, so they're complaining."

Xin Ba glanced at the bloody motherfuckers who were demanding things from them. He'd done them a mercy by letting them join his group. If he combined forces with Xin Cao, no one among them would be a match for the two of them, and the outsiders would fall to their knees and beg for their lives.

"Kill whoever complains, and later give the group twenty beasts and ask ten to charge from the front and five from each side. We have to eliminate all the poison traps the enemy has set. Do I have to do it myself, or can you do this simple thing?"

Xio Da nodded and then busied himself with arranging things. After a few loud shouts and a dozen deaths, the outsiders jumped onto the low-level beasts Xio Da gave them and charged in a predictable manner.

To Xin Ba's surprise, the ugly flat girl was sitting on one of the beasts, heading forward. She'd looked cowardly a few minutes before, and now she was charging out with a happy smile. What was wrong with her? Had she agreed to collude with Li Wei? Was this a legendary flatbed love story?

Shaking his head, Xin Ba focused on his people and ordered them to make a tight-knit formation to charge out. They were going to use the Falcon formation, taught in the Martial Realm, to trap the eight hundred people and kill them all in one go.

Chapter 70

News of the Five Firmament City

When the petite woman from the Blood-Colored Assassins sat on the beast bird, Li Wei's face twitched into a frown. Why was she coming as a vanguard? It didn't make sense for an assassin to charge at the front lines unless she had an ulterior motive. Was she trying to sneak in and kill his people who acted as formation poles?

Wei licked his lips, moistening them. Something was odd about her move, and it left a bad taste in his mouth, like the bitter taste of leftover tea powder in the bottom of a cup.

Anyway, it didn't matter. Pushing that thought away, he sipped tea from a new cup to avoid the bitterness. Sonja had prepared this tea, and she wasn't proficient in brewing. Other than Li Niya and himself, he didn't trust anyone to make tea.

"That assassin girl is among the ones attacking." Rual'er's body tensed up when the giant birds flew close to their camp.

"It doesn't matter. With our formation active, she can't sneak through. And even if she does, I can spot her," Wei said confidently.

"Your odd divine sense. Someday, you've to tell me all your secrets."
Rual'er winked.

Sneering, Wei focused on the opponent. Xin Ba had used a basic crude
strategy. He'd sacrificed the outsiders, who had joined his team after they'd
been teleported onto the battlefield. Wei had no issues with that. It was a
common tactic to use people as cannon fodder. Those people had joined
Xin Ba by choice, and they would be responsible for their own deaths.

And they died like cabbages. Their pained wails filled the battlefield. The
poison traps set by Sonja could draw a dragon to death. He felt bad about
killing a few beast birds, but in a war, casualties would always occur.

The ten beasts targeting the sides of his camp died miserably. Not even
their flesh could escape. The poison cloud corroded it and left nothing
behind within a few seconds.

The people coming from the front were a little prepared, and they had
used some form of antitoxin pills to survive a bit longer, but when they
were exposed to the constant assault of the poison, their pills' effectiveness
vanished, and they died in excruciating pain.

Except two of them. One was a tall guy with a long beard, who wore
glittering armor that protected him from the poison. The other was the
petite girl, who'd vanished in the thick black smoke of poison.

"Damn it." Wei flashed out of the formation and checked the spot where
she'd disappeared. Even with the divine sense of a Xiantian cultivator, he
couldn't spot her within a five-mile radius. This was bad.

Divine sense, while not all-encompassing, worked on everything and
anything. Although some people could conceal themselves from divine
sense, he bet no one in the Realm could do it. A sense of silvery dread covered Wei's spine. An assassin hiding in the shadows was the most dangerous
thing in this world, and even he shuddered at remaining in the open.

"Senior Wei, please save me." The glittering-armor man was sprawled on the ground, his face twitching. Despite his armor preventing poison from entering his body, he was crying in pain.

"Who are you?" Wei scanned him carefully, but he couldn't recall seeing this tall man anywhere before. The guy looked like a rotten potato. With just the peak of the Boiling Blood Realm cultivation base, why had he come to the battlefield and volunteered in a suicide attack?

"Senior Wei, I came from the Five Firmament City and worked for Kang Tu. You must not remember me, but I was there when you first fought with young Master Kang in the streets of the Five Firmament City, and Elder Yen Poe intervened."

"The Flowery Hero, Kang Tu?" Wei frowned. He didn't like it when Nuan'er had allowed that bastard to work in their alchemy firm. For her sake, he hadn't killed him.

"Yes, senior." The glittering man lowered his head. "Young master has changed now, and he is a better man."

"Why are you here? Shouldn't you be in the Five Firmament City?"

"I was patrolling the outside area when this happened. The entire Five Firmament City has also been drawn in the battle."

Wei's frown deepened.

"Senior... I..." The man's face turned black. It seemed his armor had an expiry.

Dropping next to him, Wei absorbed the poison from him and the surrounding area. It didn't reduce his pained wails, so Wei tossed a healing pill in his mouth. Although Wei wasn't sure if this guy was telling the truth, he couldn't discard any chance to get information about the Five Firmament City.

Grabbing the guy with his Heart Essence Aura, Wei flew back to camp and tossed the man into a small defensive formation he'd set up beforehand. That should prevent him from doing anything to sabotage Wei's defensive formations. Even if he detonated his cultivation base, it wouldn't blow a single hair from the people standing next to the formation.

"Tell me, what's going on?" Wei sat on a chair, and Sonja came forward to serve him tea.

The guy retrieved a leather skin and drank a lot of water. He smelled like poison and decay. Even after absorbing all the poison from him, Wei could sense his internal organs slowly shutting down. He couldn't be saved easily.

Without warning, the glittering-armor guy began coughing uncontrollably, and a stream of blood spewed from his mouth. His cough intensified as if he wanted to throw all his internal organs from his mouth. The poison was acting, and there was nothing Wei could do here.

"Sonja, do you know him?" he called to the voluptuous woman standing next to him.

Every time he looked at her, he found a new colored veil on her face. When was she changing it? Even after spending so much time with her, he had never once seen her face. The Fairy Moon Race had some bullshit law about only husbands being able to see their women's faces.

"He is Kang Rurang, and he worked for Kang Tu before, but Princess Nuan put him in the patrolling team for his good concealing abilities," Sonja answered.

"Give him an antidote."

Nodding, Sonja pierced Kang Rurang's neck with her nail and poured a yellow liquid into it.

"What are you doing?" Wei asked, flabbergasted by this unique method of giving the antidote.

"If I infuse the antidote into the blood, it works thirty percent faster."

"How do you know?"

"I experimented."

"On humans?" Wei asked.

Sonja didn't reply, but Wei understood.

"Sonja, unless you get a dying man like him, do not experiment with humans," Wei said. "Not even on prisoners or our enemies. I'd prefer killing them in one go."

Wei inhaled deeply. She had crossed his bottom line. He didn't approve of human experimentation with poisons.

"This servant understands, lord."

"Kang Rurang, now speak up. What's going on, and why were these people outside the Five Firmament City?"

"I didn't hear much, but I heard someone telling how they'd traveled from the Crimson Moon Kingdom in two days to take part in this battle, along with the Five Firmament City. Half of them have already gone to fight with Princess Nuan."

"Nuan'er is here?" Wei felt a thud in his heart. Part of it was happiness, and the other part was worry. He felt an urge to teleport to where the people were led by the girl with Xin Ba, but then he realized the giant clock would kill him if he left this place. Rual'er had been pretty clear about that, and he trusted her.

"Yes, senior. The princess is here along with the army. I was outside the city, patrolling the area along with four of my brothers, and got pulled in with those bastards. All of them died, and I survived." Tears streamed out of his eyes. "I should have died, too, but I thought I should at least inform you." He coughed another mouthful of blood.

"Will he survive?" Wei asked.

"He will, but he will require time to heal."

"That's fine. Just make sure he survives." Wei squatted down. "What is this armor? How did you get it?"

"Princess prepared it for all the army. It has an antipoison paste of herbs applied. It even has a construct that lets you survive without air for a few minutes, but I ran out before you came to me."

"Interesting. Where did she get someone to make these exquisite pieces of armor?"

"I heard it was young Master Wang Purang who was infatuated with the princess's beauty and vowed to court her fair and square."

"Court Nuan'er?" Wei coughed. What was going on?

Chapter 71

Smashing through the Enemy Lines

A hiccup slipped out of Sun Nuan's mouth.

Tang Sia stepped forward and rubbed her back. "Sister Nuan, are you all right?"

She had teleported to this battlefield along with them, and Nuan had only found out after she'd changed into her regular appearance and they were on the flying tools.

"I'm fine. I thought someone called me." Nuan looked at the desolate barren land. They'd been flying for a few minutes. With the flying tools' speed, they should have gone five hundred miles by that point, but they were still over the ominous gray land. "Elder, why haven't we reached it yet? Didn't you say we only have to cross five hundred miles?"

Elder Deimu opened his eyes from their meditative position. "Little girl, time works differently in this place the farther we go from one of the nodes. We would at least need a couple of hours to cross this distance."

"Why didn't you tell me this earlier?"

"I thought you'd grasp it when you couldn't communicate through your little array device."

Nuan rubbed her earrings.

"What a beautiful pair, sister Nuan. Do you have more of these?" Tang Sia asked, her blue eyes sparkling. She, too, had recently reached the peak of Boiling Blood Realm, but she'd had to leave her home when the Destiny Mirror Sect attacked them.

"I'm sorry. This is a gift from big brother Wei, and I don't have any more," Nuan said, brushing her fingers against the grooves in the earrings. They were a gift from her beloved, and even if she had a few more, she would never share them with anyone. Except for sister Ki Fei.

"The same big brother Wei who used to be a toddler in diapers." Tang Sia sighed.

Nuan giggled. Tang Sia had some history with big brother Wei, but it wasn't a romantic entanglement. Instead, Tang Sia used to be a proud elder in the Divine Fragrance Sect, and big brother Wei had been no one at that time. Tang Sia had taken sister Ki Fei as her disciple and taught her. Who would have known things would change this much? Big brother Wei was no longer a nobody. He was like the sun now, shining in the sky and looking down on the earth, and she would be his moon. They might not ever meet each other, but they would be content with each other's existence.

"What is he like now?"

"He is a sun to me, lighting others' lives forever," Nuan answered, saying what she had just thought.

"Strange thing. Even that lass once said he was like the sun to her and she was his moon."

Nuan felt a twinge in her heart. "Did she really say this?"

"Why do you think the same way?" Tang Sia asked, her beautiful eyes staring at her.

Nuan nodded. This was ironic—two sisters thinking the same about a man in their lives. She hadn't known sister Fei for long, but their hearts were connected through big brother Wei, and they must have thought alike too.

"You two were the oldest women in his life, but I don't know how many more he would have found. Are you really sure about this?" Tang Sia teased, a smile popping onto her thin lips.

"Does it matter? A strong person will always have ten wives and twenty concubines, but that doesn't mean he would forget us," Nuan snapped. She didn't like when someone bad-mouthed big brother Wei. Even if it was a good sister.

"Girls, get ready." Elder Deimu opened his eyes and got up from his position. "There are people heading toward us, and I know one of them—Xin Cao, that evil woman, is leading the charge, and if she is coming to this place, that can't be good."

Nuan tensed. Did she have to fight before meeting big brother Wei? Well, it didn't matter. Let anyone come at her. She was ready with her sword.***

"Lord, my traps are exhausted," Sonja said as Li Wei checked on the Stormfeather Guardian Formation with Li Gun.

Li Gun couldn't comprehend a few small things, so Wei was helping him fix the flaws in his formation. A simple thing could alter the efficiency of the formation, and Li Gun had too many flaws. He was only able to draw in sixty percent of the formation's might. However, he was getting there, and Wei had to admit that this guy was damn good at comprehending new formations.

"Shall I use that poison?" Sonja asked.

"No." Wei turned to face her. He stared straight into her multicolored eyes. "Sonja, get it in your brain correctly. You're not to use that poison unless you're about to die. Do you understand?" There were implications he couldn't tell this girl.

Nodding, she stepped back.

"Li Wei, that guy has arranged his forces in a strange formation," Little Fox said, fruit juice leaking from the corner of her mouth.

Wei turned back and instantly recognized the formation. It was a classic one.

"That's a Falcon formation." Grandpa Ling joined them.

Wei had made some changes in the defensive formation and made Grandpa Ling the main formation eye, so he could move around, and when the time came, Li Gun would protect him.

"Yes. He is not stupid as he looks. It's a good formation," Wei said. This human formation was based on the old beast formations Wei had studied in his previous life.

Xin Ba was standing at the eye of the formation, and a few weird-looking people were taking the helm—or the beak—of the falcon, while the outsiders were spread as the wings. This was going to be a three-pronged attack, but Wei had no qualms about losing his calm.

"They've already exhausted the traps by sacrificing a few dozen people, and they will strike harder and faster this time." Wei focused and saw Xin Ba showing him a middle finger. In fact, all the weird men were shaking fists at him. "Let me teach them a lesson before they even dare to attack. Teleport."

Wei rubbed Purple's soft fur and teleported next to the falcon's head, where the weird-looking men stood. Upon getting close, Wei noticed their helmets were designed to look like a bird's beak, and they had a strange construct attached to the beaks of the metal armor.

"You really came." An evil chuckle spread across Xin Ba's face as a water bubble encompassed Wei on all the sides.

"You haven't learned your lesson." Wei was about to activate the teleport when he sensed a few gazes focused on Xin Ba.

Blood-Colored Assassins had marked him. They would attack whenever Wei teleported next to Xin Ba. This was a trap.

Wei sensed a number of people vanishing from the Falcon formation and appearing next to his camp. Everyone looked like giants and had giant axes in their hands.

"Formation-Piercing Talisman on the Earth-Sharp Metal."

Wei gasped. He knew that metal. It wasn't the strongest, but it was very sharp, and when carved on the top with a Formation-Piercing Array, it became a deadly device to break through the formations. The main flaw with the metal was that it could only create an opening, but as long as one could clear the formation poles through that opening, it could break a mighty formation.

Winds hurled, and the ground shuddered as they attacked the formation line.

"Twenty body cultivators." Wei squinted. "Earth attributed, and they're accumulating power from the earth. Nice one, Xin Ba. You're really not as stupid as you look."

"What the fuck? Whom are you calling stupid?" Xin Ba flared up, but a man standing next to him patted his shoulder, and Xin Ba calmed down. "Anyway, you're trapped, Li Wei. Your people are doomed. With the combined forces that can even crush a mid-Houtian Realm cultivator into ground, how are your people going to survive?"

Wei chuckled. If this bastard thought he could cut through Wei's formation like this, he would be the biggest fool of this battle. Ignoring the battle behind him, Wei focused on the front and activated his blood clones while teleporting to Xin Ba. This bastard had insulted him, and Wei was going to play him to death.

"Water Domain of Time." Xin Ba chuckled, giving Wei an *I got you* look.

The world turned sluggish when Wei appeared next to Xin Ba, and five intense auras locked on him. The intensity of the Time Intent around him was so strong that he had to exert a lot of power even to lift his arm, and five red daggers were coming for him from behind.

This was a good attack. Xin Ba had caught him in a nice trap. Wei's friends were in danger, and he could only think about saving his own ass. Normally, Wei would be hard-pressed for time, but not at this moment.

Chapter 72

Slapping Xin Ba Again and Again

The five daggers entered the Water Domain of Time, but they didn't slow down even by a fraction. They continued their path like a bull, unchallenged by the fierce wind. Unlike them, Li Wei had to face all sorts of resistance when he tried to lift his arm. It was like moving against a heavy stream of water smashing on him from the heavens.

"Break for me!" he shouted, burning a few dozen blood pearls.

An acidic taste of blood pearls filled his mouth as he funneled the power toward his right arm. After breaking through the Heart Blood Realm, he had thousands of blood pearls, and the power they brought him through burning them was unbelievable. Unfortunately, he rarely had a chance to use them in a physical fight. In most of his fights, he depended on martial skills and divine arts rather than his hands and feet. If he could have used the Intent of Arm, he could have broken through this barrier in no time.

Wait—he could use something else.

"Dragon Fist of Pain." A dragon roared behind his elbow, and Wei's arm moved up like a cannonball, smashing through the wooden walls. In the final moment, he spread his fingers from a fist into a slap and crashed it on Xin Ba's bewildered face.

Xin Ba couldn't even fathom what had just happened before he was sent flying away like a rock thrown by an immortal. He crashed into a beast bird right behind him and then dropped to the ground with his head down.

Wei's muscles were torn up, and blood splattered through the cracks on his skin because of forcefully changing the nature of the fist attack into a slap. Pain radiated through his muscles, but he chuckled in joy—the same chuckle he enjoyed after drinking warm tea in fine weather. He could even feel the fragrance of the tea leaves from the imaginary tea.

Unfortunately, the threat was far from gone. With a sudden, vicious attack, five daggers, their blades as red as blood, plunged into his back, injecting a poisonous substance that quickly seeped into his bloodstream. It was blood poison. If he wanted, he'd could have pushed his wings out to block them, but when they closed on him, he smelled a thick scent of blood poison and felt a faint yearning from his Yin Poison Pill Clone, and he just let them stab him.

"Ha ha." Xin Ba chuckled as he tried to get up but failed and fell back.

A few blasts sounded from behind Wei, and his camp was drowned in smoke, dust, and wails. The thick curtain of dust engulfing the battleground made it impossible to identify the source of the wailing. The water bubble around Wei vanished, and he felt an ease he hadn't felt in a while. Inhaling deeply, he burned his blood pearls to heal his right arm.

Xin Ba chuckled once again, this time getting back up to his feet.

"Are you laughing at yourself?" Wei asked calmly, dropping to the barren ground.

"No." Xin Ba pushed his broken chin upward, and a water membrane covered it, instantly healing it. "I'm laughing at you. With my Blood-Colored Assassin friends, it was so easy to kill you. I shouldn't have given your intelligence any merit."

"Am I dead already? Are we in yellow spring, Xin Ba?" Wei chuckled sarcastically.

"You will be soon. That daggers were coated in special Blood Necro Poison. It will eat your flesh out and then your skeleton. You will feel a pain worse than death and will beg for it while I slaughter your people. In fact, half of them must be already dead. My Heaven-Shaking Guards have immense power, and they will cut through them like chickens."

Wei smiled and then grabbed his chest and dropped to the ground, convulsing in a fetus position. Laughing, Xin Ba walked close to him. Wei was waiting for this moment. A smile crept onto his mouth, and he sprang to his feet and slapped Xin Ba so hard that his arm rang like a bell. Xin Ba was sent crashing through his pedestal army, smashing a few to death.

He ended up in a deep pit with his head on the ground and legs in the air. It looked funny as hell. Of course, he wasn't dead, but he wouldn't be able to show his face to his people anymore.

"Impossible!" someone shouted.

Aha—the Blood-Colored Assassins. Wei had marked them with his divine sense. Moving with lightning speed, Wei left the people behind and materialized in front of a small-framed man with had an intriguing mark on his throat.

"A Blood-Colored Assassin. Don't you like sneak attacks?" Wei chuckled as he smashed a punch through his opponent's heart. He'd caught the opponent in shock, so his fist just went through to the assassin's back.

"Why are you coating your fists in wood qi? Are you afraid of the blood staining your hands?" Blood Parasite cried in his mind.

"Shut up!" Wei shouted as he teleported in front of a man with a thin neck.

"That's impossible. The Blood Necro Poison should have killed you already," the guy cried before trying to leap back. But Wei was too fast for him, and his arm clapped around the guy's neck and squeezed it, like squeezing a melon.

"Li Wei, you bastard. I will kill you and your mother." Xin Ba dug himself out of the ground, and he looked a sorry figure. His left eye was missing, and blood leaked from the broken socket. His entire left ear had caved into his jaw. He looked like an undead creature.

Nonetheless, he healed rapidly with the weird water skill he had used previously. His healing ability seemed to be more heaven defying than Wei's own. Killing him would be tougher than Wei had expected.

Wei teleported to another man and killed him. Surprisingly, these people were not the ones who wore the armor, along with the petite woman who called herself Hui Ma. He wondered if they were really Blood-Colored Assassins or just a prop.

After killing the third person, Wei teleported next to a woman with a weird smile on her face, and she dropped dead even before he could do anything to her, but her words before death echoed in his ears: "Our leader will avenge our deaths, maggot."

Shaking his head, Wei teleported next to Xin Ba and slapped him again. As he didn't use Dragon Fist of Pain, Xin Ba only got black eyes and a deformed chin, along with broken teeth.

"Li Wei, if you dare, then fight me like a man!" Xin Ba shouted, his eyes going red.

"I will soon. Wait until I kill every one of you." Chuckling, Wei teleported next to another man, who smiled at Wei as soon as he appeared.

"I was waiting for you, Li Wei. You can die in peace." His cultivation level shot up and smashed past the Heart Blood Realm, and then he exploded.

Rual'er had warned Wei that anyone who broke through in the trial would explode, and it would be heaven defying.

A divine sense locked on Wei from somewhere, and it had a strange power to hold him in the space for a moment. An attributed divine sense? Fuck. Wei couldn't even teleport away as the explosion had twisted the laws of space. How was he supposed to make his way through the explosion?

Chapter 73

Hui Ma Makes Her Move

The explosion that engulfed Li Wei sent dread through his heart. The inside flipped out, and he activated the Blood Earth Force Divine Art when he realized his body was shining brightly under the yellow-and-red light of the explosion.

Blood Metal Siphon. How could he have forgotten about it?

The glitter he'd painstakingly hidden with the help of the pill burst out as the energy of the explosion poured into him. The thin layer of metal around him crazily absorbed the energy. It rushed over his skin, and he could feel his internal organs shaking violently as the blood rushed to his throat, ready to burst out. He couldn't hold onto this much energy, and he had to spit it out fast. Otherwise, he might just burst along with it.

And he had the perfect target. A dark sneer played on his lips as he teleported a few dozen feet away from the old man in a dark-green robe who had locked him with attributed divine sense. Some cultivators would be born with a strange soul, and once they broke through into the Houtian Realm, they would gain an attributed divine sense. This attribute could take any form and would be insanely hard to defend against. However, they gained a flaw along with it—they couldn't reach the Violet Palace Realm anytime. These people would be stuck at the early Xiantian Realm. In fact, breaking through into the Xiantian Realm was so hard that many stayed at the peak of Houtian and became elders of the various sects.

But how could a Houtian Realm cultivator enter the Ancient Decree? It made little sense.

Whatever. He would just kill that bastard. Closing his eyes, Wei pointed the target at the source of the divine-sense attack from earlier. Then man in the dark-green robe was so old that it would be difficult to find smooth skin among the wrinkles.

The old man's face twitched when he noticed Wei's divine sense locking onto him.

"Got you. Bye-bye." Wei sent a divine transmission, and the power of the explosion shot out of him as a pure energy beam and hit the old man.

The old man conjured some kind of shield in the nick of the time, but it wasn't sufficient to defend against the explosion, and he burst into specks of smoke, along with dozens of beast birds around him. Even from a few dozen feet away, Wei felt like a mountain had smashed into him, and if weren't for the Blood Earth Force Divine Art in full action, he would have suffered some injuries too.

Wei glanced at the pit the explosion had created. The twelve early Heart Blood Realm cultivators were nowhere to be seen. Not even a piece of cloth remained, nor any storage rings. Sweat trickled down Wei's lower back. If he'd tried to defend them, he might not have survived.

Damn it. If he'd known this could work this way, he would have targeted Xin Ba. It would have been interesting to see if the guy could heal his way out of this power.

Upon turning, Wei found Xin Ba shaking in fear.

"Teleport." Wei flashed away as he sensed something amiss on his side of the camp. His heart slumped to the bottom of his stomach. It seemed that Hui Ma had made her move.***

Won Lian watched the play of the children from the corner of the thousand-strong army. He was sitting on the ground amid the army of outsiders, trying to connect with nature amid the chaos. After he'd met that madman who didn't tell his name and just followed him for ten days, it had been harder for Won Lian to connect with nature. Ten days of torture had pushed him to the brink of madness, and he'd joined the vanguards of the sect and come here.

And thank heavens, that guy had left after he'd mixed with others and hadn't come here. Won Lian might have killed himself if he'd had to face that guy again. However, another guy reminded him of the mechanical-winged bastard, so he couldn't concentrate anymore.

Sighing hard, he watched the criminal Li Wei flapping his metal wings. They looked similar to those of the mechanical-winged bastard. Was Won Lian going to meet another bastard like him? No way.

He should just kill Li Wei and let this end, but then he would be attached to the Ancient Decree, and he didn't want to expose his presence. He was a reserve member of the Chosen Gold—what a shitty name—and he wasn't supposed to be here. All he wished for was peace amid the chaos, but this Li Wei had disturbed him with the wings.

Rubbing his face, he wondered what he should do. If he couldn't kill Li Wei, he should at least leave him half-dead and let that kid Xin Ba kill him. About that Xin Ba—he was a prime example of how foolish one could be. He was practically extending his face to be slapped around. Who the fuck stood in that position while the enemy was in front of them? He was losing face with the Destiny Mirror Sect. Not that Won Lian cared about it. The

Destiny Mirror Sect was nothing but a toy in the Gatekeepers' hands, and once his assignment was over, Won Lian would just go back to his empire.

"It's none of my business. Those Chosen Gold should handle this. I'm just a reserve member." Using his left arm as a cushion, he closed his eyes, but then the bastard Xin Ba almost crashed into him. If it hadn't been for his senses picking up on that and redirecting him elsewhere, he would have been indirectly slapped by that Li Wei.

Damn it. Half opening his eyes, he stared at Li Wei. Should he at least slap that bastard?

It wasn't worth it. He'd decided to go back to sleep when he saw Li Wei using something interesting. He had somehow redirected the explosion of a Houtian Realm cultivator and even absorbed some of it. The explosion that should have killed Li Wei a thousand times was forced back onto a heretic.

Won Lian hated those bastards, who used a cheat to lower their cultivation level and join such trials. Only the Gatekeepers used guys like that to win trials like these. If Li Wei hadn't killed this weed from their ranks, Won Lian himself would have killed him. If one cheated with artifacts or used some abnormal skills, that was fine. Every skill was a person's strength. But when someone cheated in such a derogatory way, Won Lian couldn't restrain his anger. This behavior was condemned in the Empire, and he would condemn it everywhere he saw it.

"Ahh, she also came." He frowned when he sensed Hui Ma appearing on top of Li Wei's gang of criminals. "Why is she here? The Blood-Colored Assassins shouldn't be sending their own Chosen Gold. Does she want a piece of pie for herself? Li Wei, you are doomed. That girl has mastered the Intent of Void. You'll be dead before you can even grasp anything."

He shook his head. This girl was trouble. Rumors were that she challenged every man or woman who excelled in speed and concealing art, and no one could touch her.

But he had nothing to do with this, so he just went back to sleep. Peace amid chaos. Only then could he grasp the Concept of Peace in this world.

Chapter 74

The Alchemy Way

The water river spread across the horizon and covered everyone on Sun Nuan's side. It was corporal and noncorporal at the same time. One could feel it but couldn't grab it in their palm. It was an odd feeling, and the worst thing was that it made everything sluggish. Even breathing became a drag for everyone around her. They couldn't stay in this hell for long.

"Who are you?" Nuan asked the mysterious woman standing on a giant bird a few hundred feet away.

She had opened up this river as soon as they locked gazes. She was more beautiful than any marble statue Nuan had admired, and her cultivation robe exposed her lithe figure at the right spots. Nuan bet many men would be courting her. Thinking about men, she hoped Wang Purang would stop trying to woo her. Despite telling him dozens of times that her heart belonged to someone else, he kept pestering her.

"Xin Cao. Your humble death. I've captured you in my mysterious power, and you will only suffer your death. Open up your arms to receive the lord's punishment for your crimes."

"Nonsense. This is Time Dao," Nuan snapped, moving her bloodline ability to counter the effect of the water river around her.

"You know Time Dao, bitch?" Xin Cao squinted.

Nuan frowned. This woman had gone from talking nonsense to cursing. Nuan activated her bloodline ability by burning a fraction of her life force. It was a tiny payment, but the sluggish feeling evaporated like a drop in the desert.

"You practice the Intent of Time as well. But what can you do alone? My men will wipe your army in no time, and then they will play with you. You mother-whore, they will fuck you until their balls are blue." She chuckled as she signaled a few of them to enter the river water.

"Xin Cao, don't go overboard. Your death will be unbecoming of you!" Nuan shouted, her fury reaching her bones. No one dared to talk with her in such a way, and this woman would pay the price for it.

However, it wasn't easy. Her own army was in trouble, and the opponent's army rushed into the time river and attacked them.

Nuan bit her lower lip. Xin Cao was right. She couldn't take this lightly. The people at her side were struggling to get out, but the opponent's army was like fish in the water. While Nuan's army faced a mountain of pressure, the opponent moved effortlessly. They were just reaching her army, who already had experienced a few causalities.

This would not work. She retrieved her sword. It had been a while since she'd used this move, the Wood Emperor's Strike. Considering everyone's cultivation levels, it might not be enough to face the opponent. Nuan had control over some form of time, but she'd received a higher version of the same move from Master Xue Qi, and it could make up the difference between their cultivation levels.

"Wait, little girl. This is a Time Dao, and you are an alchemist. You can't brandish your sword to deal with these fools. That would be an insult to your alchemy roots." Elder Deimu stopped her from charging her wood qi into the sword.

"Elder Deimu, I know you don't enjoy fighting, but I don't have any choice. If I want to save my people, I have to act like their leader and fight it out with this woman," she said, pushing her wood qi into the sword. It hummed with a strange noise that eased her heart, but the others around her didn't seem to like it.

"Little girl, trust this old man. When I helped you refine the Forest Elemental, I told you one thing: trust its power, and you will find the means to do anything."

Nuan rubbed her stomach. Inside her dantian, the new Forest Elemental had been giving her an endless supply of the wood qi. Despite her refining it constantly, she couldn't absorb everything, so she'd had to seal the power with the help of the original Forest Elemental who resided in her body.

"I don't get it. I'm constantly using it to refine pills, and I can see the quality has improved, but how can it help me fight with this woman?"

"Didn't you create Wood Soul Pills for this purpose only?"

"You mean...?"

Elder Deimu chuckled. "Isn't this the perfect condition for the means to the end, little girl?"

Nuan sneered. He was right. At his directions, she'd created many Wood Soul Pills and handed them to her army. Elder Deimu had only told her it would allow her to sense their life force, but after a few people consumed them, she found out the reality—it was a unidirectional sharing pill, a marvelous wonder that allowed her to share her unbound wood qi with her people. Of course, she was limited in how much she could share, but she could choose the output at her whim.

Sitting cross-legged, she closed her eyes and activated the connection between her and the Wood Soul Pills. With those pills, she could gauge the situation of the battle. One thin person was attacking one of her commanders on the far-right side. With a thought, she covered him with the time energy she could muster, and the commander broke free and instantly ducked and dodged. He caught the opportunity and stabbed his sword through his opponent's throat, killing him in one shot.

Then she sensed another person from her side who was on the verge of death, and others couldn't reach him in time. Pushing her wood qi into the injured person, she helped him to dodge the attack and leap back toward the others, and he was saved by another soldier. They all had lifesaving pills with them, but if they didn't get a chance to eat them, it would be futile.

This situation repeated everywhere, and in just ten minutes, she'd saved countless lives. Elder Deimu was right. Alchemists didn't fight until it was necessary. This was much better than fighting it out alone with Xin Cao.

Chapter 75

Xin Cao's Weapons

Xin Cao squirmed in agony. How had it happened? When an opponent had shed the shackles of her skill, she'd felt like a fire ant was biting her under the skin. Maintaining the Intent of Time river was exhausting, so when someone fought and shook it off, she felt a throbbing pain. It wasted a lot of her Intent energy, and she could only use so much of it.

"Fuck, how is she doing it?" Xin Cao stared at the elegant woman. Sun Nuan had done something and helped her people fight against her Time Intent.

"That bitch. I want her dead!" Xin Cao shouted, hatred rushing through her mind like lava moving in a volcano.

Xin Cao hated these women who looked down on her just because she was more beautiful and knew how to present herself. She hated the woman who hid their breasts in the daytime only to expose them at night and put them on sale in the market. They would pretend to be righteous, but they were whores of this cultivation world.

Sun Nuan wasn't any different from them. She wore a full robe that hid everything, showing her people how righteous and elegant she was. Xin

Cao could read the reverence in her followers' eyes, as if they were looking at their goddess.

"Nonsense. I know you sell every part of your body in the dark of the night." Xin Cao cursed and strengthened her Intent of Time river.

However, it didn't work as well as she wanted it to. The opponents had gained some secret power, and when things were turning in her side, the opponent would change stance, throw the shackles of her time and Intent away from their bodies, and fight a fair battle. With her side going in to devour the dogs, they ended up losing most of the battles. In just ten minutes, two hundred of her people had fallen while only thirty casualties appeared on the other side. And the worst part was that she was losing her control on the Intent of Time river. If this continued for a few more minutes, she would lose the effect and maybe the battle as well.

That was when she noticed Sun Nuan, the righteous bitch, sitting in a meditative position all the time. She hadn't pulled out her weapon again. Only she had some way to tackle Xin Cao's Time Intent.

"Wan Za, what are you waiting for? Use your move already." She cursed the short man standing next to her. Just a few hours before, she'd let him play with her so he would fill his yin powers to the fullest and use it to grasp their victory.

If she could finish the Five Firmament City in one swoop, she might get invited to the reserve Chosen Gold and get an artifact to go with her Intent of Time river. Once that happened, she wouldn't have to sleep with the narcissistic bastard Xin Ba and appease his every foolish decision. That fatty couldn't even eat a single lunch properly. She could just tear his manhood out and hang it outside as a doorbell. It was useless anyway. He couldn't even hold on for five minutes. She sometimes wondered if he really belonged to her race. She was the supreme being here, and she should have been put in charge of the original form.

"Don't shout at me, Xin Cao. I'm not your servant or your husband's servant. Don't forget, I was on top of you, so act like my bitch." Wan Za chuckled and pulled out his giant axe. He was a body cultivator, and when he used his artifact axe with his Intent of Earth, he was unstoppable.

"Kill that one for me." She pointed at the righteous Sun Nuan sitting on the flying tool. Once Sun Nuan died, everything would be settled. Then she would take her revenge on this bastard Wan Za for insulting her. She would show him who was the bitch.

Wan Za smashed into the enemy lines, and before anyone could react, he had killed a dozen people from the opponent's side. With his Intent of Earth Gravity, he could glide over the earth as if flying. He was invincible as long as he was connected to the earth.

In just a few minutes, he'd reached the core of the battlefield. No one could stop him. The death count mounted on the opponents' side, and she couldn't stop smiling.

Suddenly, a woman stepped in front of Wan Za. "Stop there for me." Her sword cut down through the air like a hell storm, and Wan Za had to stop and defend himself. That woman looked familiar.

"Tang Sia—that bitch. What is she doing here?" Xin Cao cursed. On the other side of the Gatekeepers, she'd had heard the news that the Tang Kingdom had been conquered, but the royalty had put up a lot of resistance, and she'd been transmitted this bitch's image.

This was going to be troublesome. If Tang Sia intervened, Wan Za couldn't cut through the crowd in the time needed, and casualties were happening on Xin Cao's side. The people on the righteous Sun Nuan's side were miraculously shedding her Time Intent and fighting back, and she couldn't hold the Intent for too long.

Turning around, Xin Cao ordered fifty of her guards to charge ahead and target Sun Nuan, the righteous troublemaker. Only if she died would the tide of the battle be reversed.

Chapter 76

Rising Through the Desperation

L i Wei was late. Before he'd arrived, a cultivator—who also acted as a formation pole—had dropped dead under the assault of a blood-colored dagger. The assassin had found a perfect gap to kill him before he could defend himself.

Fuck. How had she done it?

Wei teleported again and materialized next to her, only to see her vanish into thin air. Despite spreading his divine sense and scanning the place multiple times, he couldn't sense her. All he found was the unwilling expression on the dead cultivator's face.

He wasn't ready for death—no one was—and this death would be on him. Because Wei had failed. He'd boasted that no one under the Houtian Realm could break the formation, yet a girl had broken it like a wall of clay, leaving a nasty taste of defeat in his mouth.

"Attack! The formation is down!" Xin Ba's shout echoed, and a thousand-strong army rushed toward his eight-hundred-person group.

Although Wei had used every means he had to increase their cultivation base, he couldn't make them invincible in a few short hours. This was true especially for the people who'd joined him in the third and fourth waves. Those remained a weak link in his formation. The enemy would cut them like cabbages, and he could do nothing.

A weight settled on his chest, and he felt like he was drowning in the expectations of everyone around him. It had happened before, and it was happening again, and it might happen again in the future.

First was the Li clan. He couldn't save them or his grandfather. Then the Chang clan had suffered, and Wei couldn't save them from catastrophe. He'd been left with a few people and a mangled Uncle Won. Heck, he couldn't even save his brother's fiancée.

These were only the major calamities. He couldn't even count how many individuals he'd made suffer because of his inability. Fei'er, Nuan'er, Fang'er. The list would go on. Fei'er was missing just because he'd asked her to join the Divine Fragrance Palace. Nuan'er had suffered so many near-death situations just to support him, and Fang'er had lost her life just to preserve his dignity. She'd died in his arms, and he couldn't do anything to save her.

Wei coughed hard as if someone had put a stone in his windpipe. "I'm sorry." He lowered his head, saying sorry for everyone he'd affected by reincarnating again in the same life. How was he going to answer them when the day of reckoning would be upon him?

"Li Wei, wake up. Why are you dillydallying? Kill that woman." Little Fox slapped his wrist with her claw and pushed him forward. Her nails scratched his arm but couldn't penetrate his skin.

He was a selfish bastard who only worked on himself to become indestructible while his friends remained fragile and mortal. That was always his goal—chasing the sun and moon while leaving his friends behind. His limbs went limp, and he sprawled in the middle of the battle, losing all hope in himself.

"Lord, get up and fight." Sonja squatted next to him, supporting him to get up. "If you give up, then what would we do? Fight, lord." Sonja's words echoed in his ears as she ran into the enemy, putting her life in danger for him.

"Brother Wei, you have to hold on—for me and for all those who trust you from the bottom of their hearts," Fei'er's voice echoed in his heart.

"Fei'er, why did I wake up?" he asked the phantom of her in his mind. He got it. He was missing her. He was missing the joyous life he'd spent inside the reincarnation.

"Because you have friends waiting for you," she said softly, tears in her eyes.

Wei broke into tears. While in the reincarnation, he'd told her about his life outside of the reincarnation, and she'd been happy because he had so many friends he could trust and who trusted him.

"Husband, you still have me waiting for you somewhere else, and you've got to preserve it so the other me will find peace in your arms," the phantom said in his mind, giving him goose bumps.

Wei pushed his palm against the rough ground as he got up. "You're right, Fei'er. I can't let this bog down on me. No matter what, I have to save as many as I can. This is a war, and there is no end to it until I stop it. Someday, I will make the entire Mortal Realm a war-free zone. If it's the Gatekeepers, I'll remove their roots from the Mortal Realm and toss them away."

Determination floated through his veins, and unknown to him, the purple light in his heart shone brightly.

Inside Li Wei's soul space, a man on a red throne smiled, staring at the far-off purple light while peacefully drinking tea. He feared that light, so he always kept a safe distance from it. If he had to count the things he feared about this kid, then this light would take first place.

"Kid, you always amaze me. Once again, you suppressed your heart devil effortlessly." Blood Parasite chuckled. When he realized the heart devil had struck Li Wei, he'd thought of helping the kid, but he wanted to see how the kid did on his own. Li Wei had done splendidly. "Xue Qi, you bitch. If you hadn't betrayed us, you could have seen his growth. You'll cry foul when we meet again."

"Stop disturbing me, old fool," a voice said, and he almost spit out the tea.

"Did you really hear me? I thought you couldn't communicate with me."

"I can't, but his heart devil startled me, and I thought I would help him one last time. For the Immortal Dew he gave me," Xue Qi replied.

"Fuck you, old bitch."

"You can only dream about that, old fool. Even when I get my body back, you'll still be stuck inside this damn soul of the kid, and then I'll laugh at you."

"Fuck! I should just possess this kid after all." He sipped more tea. This tea was good.

The kid really made good tea, but he was too fixed on how to make tea and then how to drink it. He even performed a ritual every time before he drank a cup. What the hell was wrong with this generation? If you liked something, you should just drink it until your stomach burst.

"Blood Parasite, what do you think? If I can't scan that assassin, how can I find her?" Li Wei asked, startling Blood Parasite.

A.P. GORE, PATRICIA JONES

"Goodbye, old fool, and thanks for the gift. I'll repay the debt whenever I can," Xue Qi said.

Blood Parasite sighed. That old bitch still cared for the kid, so why did she even leave? Wasn't it better to bet on this kid than on the half-dead artifact of that bastard emperor?

"Wait, I know why I can't sense her. She's using Void Intent. Damn, why didn't I think this before?" Wei said.

Blood Parasite chuckled, seeing the enthusiasm of the kid after he'd been almost suicidal. Suddenly, the world around the kid changed as he grabbed the woman's attacking hand and was pulled into the void.

"Void..." Blood Parasite chuckled. This was a home ground for the kid. That girl had made a mistake by bringing him here.

Chapter 77

Hui Ma's Crisis

H ui Ma couldn't believe it when Li Wei caught her hand like a farmer catching a chicken. Her heart fluttered at his touch. It was the first time anyone had touched her after she'd become a level-seven assassin. In fact, no man had ever touched her since she'd joined her master, who kept men away from every assassin in her all-woman group. If a lecher tried to touch them, her master would cut his manhood off, so no one at the organization had touched her in many years, and as to her prey—well, not even their dead bodies could touch her.

Yet Li Wei had touched her with ease. In panic, she activated Shadow Escape, turned her hand into smoke, and slipped into the void. She placed her palm on her heart, suppressing the strange feeling boiling inside. This was impossible. She was invincible in the Houtian Realm. Her master had told her that only a person in the Violet Palace Realm could catch her by using their Void Intent or brute power. Or a person who had gained Void Intent could catch her. Others could only give up.

However, not a single soul in the entire Martial Realm could do that. As a Blood-Colored Assassin, she had details on everyone and their so-called Intents, but she had yet to know someone who could catch her in the void. She had detailed information on this Li Wei. Although an impressive man, he had only gained the Intent of Earth, and there was no mention of Void Intent.

Had he learned Void Intent since they had last collected information about him?

Impossible. It wasn't a Void Intent. It was a fluke. Technically, Li Wei hadn't caught her in the void, but he'd somehow managed to do it right after she'd sneak attacked him.

A fortunate event and nothing else. It had happened once, but it wouldn't happen again. He would die as the only man who'd touched the queen of the assassins.

This time, she appeared before him and stabbed into his back, yet he twisted and grabbed her hand. She used Smoke Escape again and vanished into the void.

No, it wasn't a fluke. He had caught her twice. His senses were quite powerful, and he had detected her presence with a divine sense. This wasn't mentioned in his information, but Li Wei had somehow gained divine sense.

Was he a heretic bastard who had lowered their cultivation using pills? No. The information said he'd raised his cultivation level one step at a time, and there were records of his battle with the Du clan, in which he'd just been a tiny Foundation Realm cultivator. There were many odd things about him, and this must be one of them.

No matter what, she had to kill him now. No man had touched her twice, and if he touched her thrice, she would have no option but to give up on killing him. This had been her vow in front of her master. It was her pride, and she would be ashamed to live like this.

Through the void, she watched his actions. He was a powerful body cultivator, and he smashed many people into pulp by just depending on his fist attack. She liked such people. Too bad she had a mission to kill him today. If she'd known he looked so handsome when he killed someone, she wouldn't have taken on this mission. Handsome killers were rare in this world, and she'd never met one before today.

Was this the man of fate her master had talked about? But she felt nothing from him. After living with her master for so many years, she could sense their fate lines, and this man didn't have any fate with her.

"Li Wei, you've touched me twice. But I dare you touch me a third time. If you touch me the third time, I'll give up killing you, and if you manage to touch me again, I'll become your woman." She giggled as she stepped out of the void. This time she had picked a moment when he was under a barrage of attacks and couldn't focus on all of them.

She was right. He didn't notice her sneak attack, and her dagger had reached deep into his gut before he turned and smiled at her. A killer smile. One could die for that smile.

And then he touched her.

"Void Escape," she whispered.

This was it. She was going to give up on him. Assassins were killers, but even they had their pride, and her word was law for herself. If she couldn't carry out her own promise, she had no place in this world. With one more touch, she would have to marry him, but she'd used the void escape before that happened.

Wait... no.***

The battle was turning bloody, and they were losing people. Li Gun was facing tremendous pressure from the enemy's strong cultivators, who were thrashing the formation like it was a whetting stone.

Fuck. Li Gun looked around and saw lightning energy pulsing out of the treasure, providing support to the giant birds. They were doing their best to hold up the formation, but without the main formation, it was getting difficult to hold on. Especially from the berserk cultivators of the enemy.

There were five of them in the early Heart Blood Realm, but each one hit like a mountain. If he had two more minutes, he could use the treasure robe and amplify this defense formation, but he didn't have that much time

.

Li Gun didn't want to say it, but he had to. "Mayor Ling, if we don't deal with those five, I can't hold on much longer."

Mayor Ling looked around and sent a bunch of people out of the formation. They were early Heart Blood Realm cultivators, and they charged toward the five brute heads who were dealing the most damage to the formation. Behind them, Mayor Ling walked out of the formation, instantly boosting morale. Wyan Jim hailed him. They both were heading into their deaths, and Li Gun didn't like it, but they had no other choice.

"Just give me a minute more, friends." He clenched his teeth and poured more qi into the treasure robe. The battle was ferocious, and many of their people had died. Every dying person increased the burden on his chest because he was betraying the trust of brother Wei.

Li Gun lost his breath. A brute was attacking Mayor Ling at a close point, and the mayor was engaged with another brute. That meant he would die.

For a moment, Li Gun felt like dropping everything and saving Mayor Ling, given the man's closeness to brother Wei, but when he looked at the five-hundred-plus people inside the formation, he couldn't do it. Was he going to lose Mayor Ling? How would he face brother Wei after this?

Suddenly a light flashed on the battleground, and the brute who was about to end Mayor Ling's life was cut in half. Wyan Jim had used his sword to cut through the enemy, but then he, too, bled out and died. Wyan Jim had sacrificed his life to save Mayor Ling.

A power burst out from Li Gun's robe and covered the birds with a new radiance.

"Mayor Ling, please rush in. I can't hold on for long until brother Wei returns." He blew out a long breath. Finally, he could save a lot of people. Maybe this wasn't a complete failure.

Chapter 78

Picking up Girls Like a Big Flirt

L i Wei was waiting for this moment. Every time he caught the woman, she slipped into the void, and no matter what he did, he couldn't stop her. She was a danger to everyone around him, and he had to kill her.

But for that, he had to catch her. She was too slippery. Even with Purple helping him teleport, he couldn't do it. She always escaped his clutches.

No more. When she appeared to his left, he knew she was coming for his gut. He let her stab him and then caught her hand, and then her shoulder, so she wouldn't escape him again.

He found himself in a darkness. The woman had brought him into the void, and she was emitting a faint light. The familiar scent of nothing hit him, making him reminiscent about the old times. It was as easy as walking into the garden.

He had suffered so much in the void that it felt like home. All his pores opened up and greedily absorbed the void energy through them. After painstakingly cultivating the Void Body Cultivation Art I, he had rarely visited the void. In fact, he'd avoided it so as not to go somewhere random. Purple could teleport him through different worlds, and he didn't want to get stranded in a hostile world again. However, by not visiting the void, his void body skill had been stuck at level one, and now he felt he was making leaps and bound in ability.

"You—how could you do it?" She broke into tears. "You wronged me, Li Wei. You wronged me."

She slapped his chest repeatedly, and in panic, he let her go and leaped backward. There was no landing point in the void, so he had to use his wood qi to resist the free flow. Void was dangerous, and without a proper anchor, a person could lose their way completely.

Wei floated in the void, a few dozen feet away from her, tensed up and waiting for her attack. Nothing happened. She just kept crying like a small girl.

Wei felt his heart pounding a little. Although she was an assassin, he felt sad when he saw a girl crying. She reminded him of the Tun Hu, that flat girl who'd spouted nonsense day and night. She'd been tough to talk with, and he'd always had a headache whenever she opened her mouth.

"You. How dare you touch me four times, bastard!" Hui Ma pulled the rubber band from her perfect pony and threw it at him.

Her dark-brown hair flowed over her shoulder like sea waves, transforming her from a teen into a mature woman with big watery eyes. She was attractive and looked pitiful when she cried.

"You fool. Why did you touch me four times? Answer me right away," she demanded.

Wei arched his brows. What had just happened to this woman? Was she half-crazy?

He activated his Void Eyes and watched the void lines around them. The lines were beautiful when he looked at them from the void's side. He'd been to the void many times, but he'd never had time to study these lines. Could he study them?

"You big pervert." She stomped her feet in the void, pulling his attention back to her.

Yes, it wasn't good to ignore her. Who knew when she would go mad and attack him like a dog?

"Wait, when did I touch you like that? Don't slander me. I'm not a pervert, and I already have many... friends." Wei had almost repeated the lie spread by others. No, he didn't have many girlfriends. He only had friends. Period.

"You caught my hand two times, then you caught it again, and now you hugged me. How are you going to take responsibility for this?"

Wei gulped hard. What was wrong with this woman? Was this another of her tactics? If it was, then she was very good at it. He'd almost fallen for her tactics and melted into her watery eyes. Damn it.

Wei put his guard up, both emotionally and physically. Blood Earth Force Divine Art was activated around him, ready for any mishap.

"Let's go back. You will die if you stay here," she said, wiping her tears, her tone sincere.

Wei stared at her, trying to probe her intention. She might attack anytime, so he readied his blood pearls to burn up and heal him. He even readied One Recharge Qi and One Rebirth Qi for the worst case. This woman was an assassin, and his senses kept warning him about her whenever she came close to him.

"Come on—come to me." She waved her hand as if calling a street puppy closer.

Wei laughed. "Woman, you must be naive to think I won't see through your ploy. Let's fight it out." He charged up. "I'm not falling for your tricks."

If they fought here, he would be fifty percent certain of the victory, and outside, he would be only twenty-five percent certain. The martial skills she'd displayed were beyond his current capabilities. If she hid in the void, he had no chance of killing her, but here, he could try some of his moves. Void was like a second home to him, but he had no means of entering it by himself. One could only probe it after reaching the Violet Palace Realm, and only if they'd learned some Intent of Void.

"Li Wei, are you crazy? Why are you doubting my intentions? If you act like a child, then forget about our marriage." She gave him a disdainful look.

"Wait, who wants to marry you?"

"You, of course. I've said it already. You touched me four times, so you have to take responsibility for your actions. Didn't I say it already?" She tied her hair with a new cloth band, transforming from a woman to a teen girl. Something was odd about those cloth bands.

"You must be crazy. All assassins are crazy." Wei didn't know what he should feel. Hui Ma was beautiful, but that didn't mean he would marry her.

"Don't insult my profession, or I'll carve out your tongue while you sleep."

Wei pursed his lips. Assassins were crazy, and if he couldn't kill one, he didn't want to anger one.

"Come hug me." Hui Ma spread her arms like a spider spreading its legs to catch prey.

Wei floated backward. It would be better if he just stayed away from this crazy girl. Forever.

"What's difficult in this, Li Wei? Do you the brain of a twelve-year-old?"

"You're a twelve-year-old."

"I'm twenty-seven. A perfect woman. Do you want to sleep with me?"

Sweat dripped along Wei's lower back. This girl wasn't an ounce better than Tun Hu.

"Come on. This is the void. If you're exposed to it for too long, you'll die." She sounded concerned.

"The void won't kill me, but you will. So either fight with me, or leave me alone."

"You're pissing me off, so I'll just wait until you become a piece of rot and decay," she said furiously.

Wei sat cross-legged and waited for the woman to take some action. For him, living in the void for one minute or ten minutes was the same. The woman should be worried about her own timing in the void. Once again, he activated the Void Eyes and started studying the void lines. They were beautiful, and the more he stared at them, the better he could understand them.

After a while, he found a strange rhythm in those lines, and an idea started forming at the back of his mind. Could he really use these lines to enter the void?

Should he ask her? No way would she answer him.

"Li Wei, come on. Let's go." Hui Ma stepped forward, watching him like a spider with too many eyes.

The sweat on his lower back dripped like a river flowing down a mountain. Without a word, he stood and retrieved his sword. "Young woman, don't blame me for attacking you without warning. I will absolutely do it." Heck, why was he telling her this? Who warned their opponent?

"Li Wei, I'm going to marry you. I take a heaven-and-earth vow I'll marry you only. Shadow Escape." She burst into shadows, a hand touched his back, and he was out on the battlefield in front of a beast bird.

The beast bird opened its mouth and gulped Wei down before he could react. Wei stabbed his sword upward to cut through the bird, but before he could even touch the inner line of the beast bird's giant mouth, a ray of red cut through the head and opened a wide enough gap for him to walk out.

"I'm sorry, husband. I put you in danger. I'm a shy girl, so I'll meet you afterward. Kill all your enemies, okay?" She brushed her lips over his cheek before vanishing into the void.

What the hell had just happened? Had she just kissed him?

Chapter 79

Power of Constructs

Li Wei was still in shock after the girl disappeared. Her wink had sent goose bumps through his entire body, as if he'd stepped into a cold bathtub after a hot and sweaty day. Fuck. What was wrong with that woman?

"Brother Wei, please take me as your apprentice once we get through this war," someone called from behind him.

When he turned, he saw Li Gun standing on a bird's back, wearing tattered clothes. Lightning zapped around him, and he looked like a lightning angel. With his Stormfeather Guardian Formation, he was holding up well.

"What apprentice? Do you finally want to learn arrays from me, brat?" Wei chuckled, spreading his divine sense widely. If that assassin girl appeared again, he would kill her before she spouted any more nonsense about taking responsibility and marrying her. She was crazy, and he hated crazy.

"No. Please teach me the art of picking up girls. You even wooed an assassin in a mere five minutes. Are you the legendary Silk Pants everyone keeps mentioning in those stories?"

Wei almost coughed blood. He'd read the stories in his previous life. Those guys with a big hundred-plus girl harem were called Legendary Silk Pants.

"You did good, brat." Wei nodded at Li Gun. He could see Li Gun had used his robe to power up the formation, and it had stabilized the battlefield.

"I was already impressed with the large number of girls following you, but this tale is epic, brother Wei. I can't resist bowing to your godly power." Li Jun bowed deep in the middle of the formation.

Wei coughed blood. Once the battle was over, he would definitely beat Li Gun half to death. There would be no stopping him.

"Li Wei, I've got you." Xin Ba's laugh echoed in Wei's ears.

When he turned, he saw a dozen mechanical constructs hovering around him. They looked like humans, but they weren't. They exuded no aura, so he hadn't been alarmed through his divine sense when they'd encircled him. A good tactic.

He was probing them when a cultivation aura burst out of the ten constructs, matching the cultivation aura of a peak of the Heart Blood Realm. It was as sharp as a needle, and it wasn't organic. Sharp wings burst out of the constructs' backs, and they circled around him.

"You were hiding something. Not bad, Xin Ba." Wei nodded.

"This is just a start. I was waiting for enough people to die to raise them."

Wei realized the battlefield looked kind of empty. Out of his eight hundred people, only six hundred had survived, while out of two thousand opponents, only eight hundred had survived. Dead bodies and blood littered the ground.

Two hundred people had died on his side, and it made him sad and speechless. Those people had trusted him with their lives, but he couldn't save them. When he recalled what had happened with the help of his five blood clones hiding in the battlefield, and his metal clone helping Li Gun, he knew that those hundred people hadn't wasted their lives but had fought with multiple people at a time, killing many.

They'd died to protect others, and Wei wouldn't let them down. Yet Wei felt dejected. He was processing that when one of the constructs shot an energy beam at him.

Dropping a few feet, he dodged the beam, which attacked the opposite side of the circle. Another construct shot a beam at him, and then another. Soon, he was dancing between the energy beams. Against all expectations, it was a simple endeavor. Anyone with decent speed could dodge them. What were these constructs playing at?

The constructs abruptly stopped shooting beams, and an energy net of the same beams appeared around him, covering him on all the sides. Then it started shrinking, and he felt a deep sense of danger. This net wasn't a simple thing.

Dragon Fist of Pain. Wei charged up and attacked the energy net with the full power of his skill. A dragon's roar echoed behind him, and he smashed his fist into the energy beams, making a hole in them. However, Wei had paid an immense price, and his hand was riddled with holes that he couldn't heal with just his blood pearls. And the worst thing was, the hole he'd created filled up, and the net shrank rapidly.

Fuck. If he let the energy net touch him, he might get out, but his body would fall apart without any protection. What was he going to do now?

Chapter 80

Fate Lines

Hui Ma watched Li Wei getting battered from the sidelines. He was going to be her husband, and she should help him. In fact, she could get in and get out easily from that net, as nothing could stop her when she used the Intent of Void.

However, she stayed in her pocket of the void. If this man wanted to marry her, he had to prove that he was worth the effort. If he couldn't even beat a single dreg from the Gatekeepers, he would have to die in this battlefield, and she would live the life of a widow. In fact, that would be a good thing. A guy who was ready to lose his life in the void just for the sake of his pride wasn't worth her.

When she thought she would see the end of Li Wei, he grew a pair of wings. Metal wings. They shone with a translucent light, and when they touched the energy barrier created by the mechanical puppets of Xin Ba's artifact, they absorbed it.

Wait—what? It was the same light she'd detected when she was in the void. Hui Ma hadn't been able sense it, because it hadn't broken into the void, but she'd felt the impact. Li Wei not only absorbed the energy beams but also sent them back at one of the constructs and destroyed it in one go.

"This guy. Not bad. Our fate is not that weak. But can you do it again for nine more of them?"

Void Escape. Hui Ma vanished from the battlefield and traveled toward the giant clock that was stabbed into the ground not far from the battlefield. She saw Won Lian heading toward the clock as well. The disturbance she sensed was real, then. Something had happened.

From the corner of her eye, she saw Li Wei, too, looking in that direction. A woman wearing a lot of clothes shot out of his camp and headed toward the clock. Hui Ma raised her speed to the maximum and reached the clock first. A strange aura enveloped it, leaving her bewildered.

"Why are the fate lines so disturbed at this place?" She tried to look beyond the aura and saw a bald monk meditating under the clock.

"He is gaining some inheritance, and we can't let that happen," Won Lian said grimly.

"Stop it there, or don't blame me for not showing mercy to you." The veiled woman, in multiple layers of clothing, leaped in front of them. Her body had a peculiar scent of poison. Hui Ma knew it very well because most assassins dealt with poison.

"Woman, fuck off, or I'll kill you." Won Lian placed his palm on the ground, and an Earth Giant rose from it. That was his signature move—Earth Guardian. "Hui Ma, help me, and the Gatekeepers will owe you a little."

"I don't care what little scheme you've got there. She is my husband's woman, so I won't go against her. I'll just watch it from here." Hui Ma had no interest in whatever inheritance the bald monk gained. She was only curious if this bald monk was the guy she was supposed to marry as exuded the fate lines her master always talked about.

Suddenly, she was happy. Compared to this bald monk, Li Wei was a much better prospect. He had looks, power, and the killing Intent. This was great.

She'd always believed that a person wrote their own fate, and she was going to write hers by marrying Li Wei. Li Wei could not escape this marriage.

Chapter 81

Reverse Sword Ray

"You don't have time to be distracted, Li Wei." Xin Ba's roar awakened Li Wei from his stupor. An axe came down on him while gravity became heavy, pulling Wei down.

Fuck. Wei retrieved his sword from the storage ring. It had been weeks since he'd used this sword, and it smelled like life and nature. He'd missed it.

Xin Ba had applied his water bubble while attacking him from the front. The energy net surrounded Wei on all sides, so there was no area to dodge this attack. Wei's frown deepened. The axe in Xin Ba's hand had a weird effect—it exuded an aura pressure when it attacked. That pressure, added to the muddy Time Intent, made it impossible for Wei to move. Wei had faced it twice already, and he'd had to teleport away at the last moment so the axe wouldn't cleave through him.

However, he had a few charges of teleport left in the Primordial Blood Palace, and Purple was exhausted because of the Time Intent. Teleporting wasn't a solution. If he continued it, Xin Ba might just charge into the Stormfeather Guardian Formation, which was still holding up, mostly, and then Wei's side will be in deep trouble. There would be a massacre.

Wei couldn't let that happen, and Sonja was busy. A fatty had appeared from Xin Ba's side, and when he exploded with intense Earth Intent, Wei had known he wasn't an easy opponent, so he'd had to send Sonja away to defend Kai Shaya. Whatever Kai Shaya was doing inside that inheritance bubble seemed important to him, and Wei would protect him as long he could.

Hui Ma also had moved in that direction, but thank heavens, she'd stepped away after spouting some nonsense about marrying him. That was enough for Wei. If Hui Ma wasn't going to attack, he believed Sonja would hold the fort.

"I owe you one, Hui Ma," Wei whispered.

"Your dead body will owe nothing to anyone." Xin Ba chuckled as his sword descended on Wei, light reflecting over the sharp edge of his axe.

Water Sword of Flow. Wei poured his wood qi into the sword, and it moved like a fish in the water and intercepted the axe. The recoil forced Wei back, but Xin Ba's face held an expression of awe. Wei had counterattacked him under the immense pressure of time, water, and the axe.

Wei sneered. Licking his lips, he tasted the blood on his lip. It tasted as sweet as honey. Water Sword of Flow allowed him to maneuver his sword as he wished, even inside the time-flow Intent from his opponent. Five Elemental Way Qi Cultivation Art was awesome, and he regretted not being unable to practice it. When he'd separated his clones, his sword skills had turned into basic stabbing and swooshing, but after the wood clone broke through and perfectly merged with him, he'd sensed the affinity with his sword skills once again. This could have been the effect of the rune he'd carved into his sword, but nonetheless, he felt good about it.

Xin Ba adjusted his bearing, his axe growing in size. "Li Wei, what kind of artifact are you using to move freely in my water bubble?" he roared,

A.P. GORE, PATRICIA JONES

the veins on his neck bulging. "You won't be able to do it again. Intent of Water and Intent of Time Flow, merge."

The water around Wei became denser, and his sword became extremely heavy. Nine beams of energy shot at him, and although he could absorb them, he wasn't sure he could fend off the axe coming at him at the same time.

It was time to test whether he could use the other sword skills, or Intents, as he had gained some portion of his qi cultivation back. In the depths of his mind, he had a feeling that the Intent would work perfectly to counterattack another Intent.

He rotated his wrist, pointing the sword tip toward his thighs. Then he closed his eyes and covered the incoming axe with his divine sense.

Reverse Sword Flash. Wei's sword moved in an arc and cut through the water and time Intents together as if they were tofu. He moved along with the sword, merging with the world. The sword and Wei vanished into the air, instantly materializing next to the axe, and the sword continued cutting through the artifact that gave Xin Ba immense power. It cut through the axe and then through Xin Ba's left arm.

Wait—this wasn't Reverse Sword Flash. It was something more than that.

Xin Ba wailed in pain. If he hadn't leaped back after Wei's sword cut through his left arm, he would have been cut in two.

"Aaaa..." His wails echoed in the battleground, bringing the chaotic battle to a standstill. "Merging with the world using Reverse Sword Ray. Li Wei, I will kill you." Xin Ba's arm grew back instantly, but his face turned pale, and another axe materialized in his hand.

"Li Wei, you keep surprising me." Hui Ma appeared next to him, clapping her hands.

Wei readied his sword to attack once again. It wasn't the Reverse Sword Ray, but he could sense he'd almost comprehended it.

"Blood Parasite, it makes little sense. I couldn't even use normal Sword Flash properly, and now I could almost use the Reverse Sword Ray. How did I learn it without practicing a million times?"

"Kid, who said you can learn the Intent only by practicing? A unique opportunity, combined with peace of mind, can change things. You hadn't practiced it, and you'd forgotten about it, and under the merged Intent of Time and Water, you had a perfect opportunity to break through your shackles. But now you have to practice it ten thousand times to actually break through it."

Wei nodded. He understood. He hadn't used the Reverse Sword Flash for so many days—or months, if he considered the time in the time chamber—and when Xin Ba had locked him in a unique merge of Intent, he'd just trusted his gut feeling.

"The good thing is you don't have to rely on your qi cultivation anymore. You've broken through the shackles without using your qi, and this is beneficial to you."

Wei chuckled. He felt weirdly satisfied. It was time to cut through his enemy with the same feeling.

Chapter 82

Xin Cao's frustration

Xin Cao watched her army getting decimated one by one by the bastards from the Five Firmament City. Now she understood why the sect wasn't sending powerful people less advanced than the Houtian Realm to capture it. There were hundreds or thousands of abnormal people stuffed inside that city.

"Fuck it. Why do they have so many powerful people?" she asked to herself.

"Lady lord, their people have practiced both qi and body cultivation," one of her guards replied.

Her slap sent him flying away. "I can sense that, bastard. I don't need you to tell me this."

Her gaze drifted toward the enemy camp, and she gulped down her anger. Why did they have around a hundred peak of Heart Blood Realm experts who could very well fight with a Houtian Realm expert? Though she also had many such experts, they were lacking when compared to the enemy. The bursts they received in their qi and blood from the bitch in the middle were especially powerful. She was using some unorthodox method to lift their power in the dire situation, giving them an undue advantage.

Rubbing her face, she looked back, wondering if she should use the reverse army. Those were old heretic cultivators who had eaten pills to enter this place and refused to obey her orders. Fucking useless oldies. Especially their leader, the fat woman who sat on a giant bird and sipped some drink as if it were a fine wine from her house.

"Elders, why aren't you responding?" she asked again, leaving her ego buried in her stomach.

"Are you asking us twenty-five to fight with weak enemies? Are you looking down on us, Xin Ba?"

Fuck them. She had twenty-five such heretics, and Xin Ba had seventy-five, and she had no doubt that Xin Ba was in a worse position. But then, he'd gotten a weak enemy, and he had to be done with his fight already.

This was insane. Why had she gotten the tough enemy? She hoped Li Wei had some balls and would put up a good fight.

Wan Za roared, his hair flaring as he charged at Tang Sia. The defeated princess of the Tang Kingdom was holding out well in front of the crazy cultivator. The fifty guards she'd sent to kill Sun Nuan were down to twenty-five.

Then a dozen of her guards fell to a bizarre attack of a body cultivator who conjured ten clones and exploded them. Fuck.

"Do you think of them as weaklings? Kill her already!" she yelled. "If you don't act, I'll be the only one remaining from this group."

"Old gents, can I ask you not to take any action?" An old man appeared overhead, floating. He had a sickly face, as if he'd just gotten over a long-lasting disease. If he could fly, did that mean he'd taken the heretic pill?

"Alchemist Deimu, why are you here? Did you also...?" one of the old men asked gravely.

"I didn't. But I know a way to solve your issue. In return, I only ask you to not participate in this fight."

"Old man, who are you, and what are you doing here?" Xin Cao growled, sending a stream of Intent of Time river toward him. How dare he step into her matters? Was he trying to buy her people right under her nose? Impudent bastard.

"Xin Cao, hold your attack. You don't know who this respected old man is." A tall old man from the twenty-five floated up and attacked with his palm, deflecting her Intent of Time river.

"Damn you, bastard!" Xin Cao shouted, her anger flaring. If she hadn't been busy controlling this big time river, she would have smashed the tall old man out of the battlefield.

"Alchemist Deimu, can I know what's going on here? Have you defected the Gatekeepers?"

"I have, unfortunately," the sickly old man said in a grumpy tone.

"See? That old bastard is a sinner of the Gatekeepers. Attack and kill him!" Xin Cao shouted, sneering. By agreeing to this, the old sickly man had signed his death warrant.

"Lady Xin Cao, if you don't shut up, don't blame me for slapping you hard." The fat old woman, leader of the twenty-five floated up. "Alchemist Deimu, do you realize the consequences of your actions?"

"I know, and I also know the Gatekeepers have tossed you away. You guys are no longer useful to them. You will die after this mission, but I can save you and guarantee your breakthrough into the Houtian Realm."

"We are at the end of our rope. Why would we be concerned about this?" The fat old lady shook her head.

"If you break through again, you will gain three hundred years of life. I can vouch for that on my own cultivation base."

Another old lady floated up. "Are you talking nonsense, old man Deimu?"

"Sister Wuha, I'm heartbroken to see you here," Deimu said.

"And I'm heartbroken to find you with the enemy."

"How about we come to a consensus and just stay away from this fight and let the kids fight?" old man Deimu said confidently.

"And in return, you will give us pills to break through again? Can you take a heaven-and-earth vow?"

"Fair enough." Old man Deimu said the vow, and the heavens rumbled in agreement.

"Lady Xin Cao, we can only guarantee your escape to young Master Xin Ba. The rest is on you," old woman Wuha said.

"Fuck! I'm going back." Xin Cao ordered the remaining two hundred people to move away from her side and then turned back.

She had lost this battle, but she wouldn't lose the war. She would combine her power with Xin Ba and then would show these fucking bastards what the Dao of Time really meant. Their original form would triumph over them, and they wouldn't even find time to beg for their lives.

Chapter 83

Undying Xin Ba

Li Wei's sword cut through Xin Ba's gut, cleaving him in two, yet the result didn't satisfy Wei. The blood sprayed from the two halves of Xin Ba, but Wei knew he would patch himself back together. Maybe Wei should just roast him, leaving him as charred as a burnt chicken. But he doubted even that would kill him.

This Xin Ba was like an undying cockroach. No matter how many times Wei had cut him—five, to be precise—he still survived. Two halves of Xin Ba stuck together as if glued.

Before Wei could try something else, an energy beam came at him, forcing him to leap back. The combined energy beam of six constructs could send him to the yellow river, but he wanted to live on, have children.

"Should I just finish those bastards first?"

"Your normal attacks are useless—unless you can pull another Reverse Sword Ray," Blood Parasite said.

"I need practice for that. I've grasped the feeling, but something is stopping me from completely comprehending it."

"Then use the third move of the Blood Sword Tearing through the Heavens. But I forgot—you can't."

"Let's use the second level." Wei retrieved his blood sword and channeled his Intent of Earth into it. The surrounding ground cleaved as he sucked in the Intent from the earth and stored it in his sword.

As if sensing his intention, the six mechanical constructs moved closer to each other, creating a strange formation with three on top, one in the middle, and two at the sides. Energy arcs buzzed between them, forming a mesh-like pattern. When they'd used it as an offense, they had formed one formation, and now they formed a different one. Wei would have loved to study them, but he didn't have time for such things anymore.

Wei's hair flew up and down like earth pulses as the earth surrounding him gave the essence happily. While he hadn't noticed this before, now he could notice by using the Heart of the Skill the nature gave him happily, and when he used a common Intent of Earth, he had to fight with the nature for the same essence.

"Blood Parasite, why do I feel like nature is giving me the essence with a happy smile on her face?"

"It's the Heart of the Skill. You attuned it with the help of nature, so it's giving you its everything."

"Does that mean...?"

"Yes. There is no limit to this. As long as you have enough earth around you, you can keep charging it to the fullest. If you take more than necessary, you'll just blow up."

Sweat trickled down Wei's lower back as he stopped absorbing more of the Intent of Earth. He was already feeling full of power, but he pushed himself to cut through the enemy in one go.

Blood Sword Tearing through the Heavens. A giant sword floated above his head, but it wasn't the usual red. Instead, the image had dark brown mixed in and running along it like veins on the earth, pulsing with sheer power.

The ground shook, and the air became turbulent as Wei attacked with all his power. A long crack started from his legs and spread outward as the attack descended on the mechanical constructs. They forced more power into their shield, and it shone like an evening sun exploding with orange and red.

However, it wasn't enough. The energy shield cracked like paper, and the mechanical constructs were blown to smithereens. The sword attack continued toward Xin Ba, whose face lacked any substantial color.

"Damn it. Are you nuts, child?" A hulky man who looked to be in his seventies charged in front of Xin Ba.

Raising his arms, he made an X-like symbol in the air, and a wind shield appeared in front of him, covering him and Xin Ba on all the sides. The shield collapsed under the sword, but it also forced the sword to lose its luster.

"Break for me." The old man punched hard at the sword, shattering it.

But he had to pay a price for that—his life. Wei had teleported at the last moment and had run his sword through the opponent's heart, killing him in one go.

Xin Ba staggered back, fear flashing through his eyes. "You. How did you kill him in one shot?"

Wei chuckled. "I learned it from my friend." Turning back, he smiled at Hui Ma. "Thank you."

She'd pulled him into the void by accident, and he'd used that opportunity to see through the Intent of Void with the help of his Void Eyes. It allowed him to see the lines of void running across the reality of the current realm. So when he stabbed his sword through the old man's heart, he activated one of the lines and sent half of the old man's heart into the void.

"That's Void Transfer. Did you really learn the Intent of Void, my husband?"

"That's a secret, my friend," Wei sneered, but he was feeling exhausted.

This attack had been intended for Xin Ba. The flashy attack that tired Wei deeply had been meant to pull him out. He'd succeeded, but he'd failed to kill Xin Ba with his trump card. Now Xin Ba would be guarding against this move, and it would become impossible to kill him.

Damn it. This was the first time Wei had needed to expose so many trump cards to take down a single ant in the Heart Blood Realm.

Chapter 84

A Trap?

Ten men jumped in front of Xin Ba, forming a circle of protection around him. They all had an aura similar to the man Li Wei had just killed.

"Kid, they all have the powers of Houtian," Blood Parasite said in answer to his question. "They've forced their cultivation base to drop into the Heart Blood Realm by some forbidden technique. They might have sacrificed something, but here they are more powerful than anyone else. And dozens of people like them are mixed in with the enemy lines."

Ten new mechanical constructs popped up out of nowhere and surrounded Wei once again. Fuck. Did Xin Ba have an unending supply of them? If so, Wei had no chance of winning this unless he killed Xin Ba in one go. Which seemed impossible at this moment.

"Li Wei, give up, and put your neck under my blade. I have an undying body." Xin Ba chuckled. "Look at your army. They're suffering. Soon their formation will fall apart, and then I'll chuck them out like roasted mushrooms from a street vendor."

"Go! Is this threat not enough for you to act?" Xin Ba shouted, and ten old men charged at Li Gun's battlefield. They all had an aura of Houtian, and Li Gun wouldn't hold on for long.

Wei's frown deepened. Xin Ba was right. If he let those five people smash Li Gun's formation, he would have no option but to give up on the ones who trusted him from their hearts. Seven hundred people depended on him, and he couldn't let them die like this.

Rubbing his face, he looked at Li Gun then at Sonja's battlefield and then at Xin Ba. "Send five people toward that other bitch. I will kill every one of his friends." He sent a divine transmission to the pretty girl sitting on a couch in the middle of the battlefield, eating some nuts: "Hui Ma, you'll want to hide in the void if you don't want to die."

Wei bet those nuts tasted good and it felt awesome to watch the battle as if it were a show. She was annoying. She clapped whenever he performed a new move. When he used his blood clones, she was so happy, like a child finding a hidden candy, which baffled him. Was she an assassin or a clown? Her behavior made no sense, and every time she showed up, she declared her undying wish to marry him.

A timer flashed in his vision, and a smile played on his lips. Someone was coming out soon, and he would have the matter settled. However, things at Kai Shaya's side looked bad. Sonja was holding up against five old people and the fatty who cultivated the Intent of Earth. She was using every poison possible to keep them away, but she was losing her momentum.

"Do you see now, Li Wei? If you give up and surrender your head, I might let your friends live for some time, and I promise I'll make your women my concubines. It's better than being a plaything. I wish your mother was here too..." Xin Ba's chuckle deepened.

"What did you say, motherfucker?" Anger rose in Wei's throat as if a volcano had erupted in his stomach. How dare he insult Wei's mother and his women?

"I said if your mother was here, I would have played with her as well. I bet she would be beautiful."

Wei let go of the anger, and the world turned silent for a moment. "If you don't protect him now, you won't have him alive after a few seconds," he said calmly.

This was it. He was going for the strongest skill he had in his arsenal.

Lightning Emit.***

Hui Ma sensed the change in Li Wei's mood, and she frowned. This guy was too sensitive to the words of his opponents. It was easy to anger him. Her man should be an emotionless killer, not an emotional fool. It seemed like she would have to work on him a lot after she took him back to her master. Her master would be happy. She would get two pupils who were born to kill.

But why would he warn her?

Suddenly, lightning burst out of Li Wei and covered a thousand feet area around him. It was so fast that Xin Ba didn't have any time to run away and the heretic old men in front of him could only protect him with their lives.

"Tribulation lightning. Li Wei, my husband, you keep surprising me with every new move. Although we might not have fate lines between us, you are the best choice for me. You'll be the killer no one has seen in this world. Together, we'll create a team of a dozen little killers. They will massacre the world, and we will watch while eating nuts."

A lightning sun appeared in the middle of the battlefield and then exploded, leaving only a big crater and a few charred bodies behind. The charred bodies belonged to the old fools who had used pills to recess their cultivation, and out of ten, eight had died. Xin Ba had turned into a piece of roasted chicken.

That Li Wei cultivated a very rare water qi art, and he couldn't die unless someone took his life in one shot.

"Li Wei, you bastard. You'll pay for this!" Xin Ba shouted as he got up, and forty more old people leaped in front of him.

There were around a hundred of them with this army, but only sixty or seventy stayed behind. So there were too many for Li Wei. How was he going to kill them?

And why had he asked her to hide in the void? Was he trying to show off, or was he still afraid of her?

Li Wei chuckled, a trickle of blood leaking from the corner of his mouth. "Xin Ba, that was just the trailer. The next skill I'm going to use will be a hundred times more powerful than this. Can they really save you this time as well?"

"You're bluffing. You can't produce such a powerful skill again."

"Let's try it. Lightning Sea of Taichi!" Li Wei shouted, and his hair flew upward.

Lightning arcs zapped around him, and every single one was made from tribulation lightning. Hui Ma sensed a danger she'd only felt from her master. Now she understood why he'd asked her to hide in the void.

That bastard husband. The first use of power was just to bring more people into his impact area. The real explosion would happen now.

Genius. He would become one of the greatest killers of this world. He not only had brawn but brains as well.

Smiling, she hid in the void, watching the fireworks outside, and it was the most beautiful fireworks she'd seen in her entire life. The lightning dragon spread like an avalanche and gulped down everything within a few hundred feet, grumbling, roaring, and churning it to death. Going forward, all she had to do was to gather all her targets in one place, and then Li Wei could kill them all.

Chapter 85

Lightning Seed to the Rescue Once More

The world burst open, and colorful lightning crushed his world. Xin Ba felt blinded before the lightning sea washed over him. Lightning invaded every inch of him, leaving nothing behind. If it hadn't been for the thirty old heretics protecting him, he would have died. Every inch of him felt like fried bear meat. He was drowned in the sea of lightning for a few breaths only, but it was enough to make him fear for his life. Even his healing power would have failed if he'd to stay in the lightning sea any longer. The attack had come out of blue. He'd never thought Li Wei could be a lightning cultivator as well as everything else.

No one had fucking told him Li Wei had something like this. If thirty heretic old bastards hadn't covered him in defensive layers, he would be dead. But he wasn't good either. The thirty people around him had turned into pieces of charcoal. If he spread some spices on them, he might be able to eat them as evening snacks. Forty old heretic people had died under Li Wei, and if the remaining bunch of people didn't take this seriously, he didn't know what they would.

Slowly, his limbs healed back to their normal condition. In the previous attack, he'd used most of his healing powers, and if he had to suffer another such attack, he would be dead.

"Little Ba, you look toasted." An old fogey leaped next to him, sending a bolt of lightning into Xin Ba's body that sucked out the lingering lightning from Xin Ba. "Holy fuck, this is tribulation lightning. Why didn't you say so?"

The old man's face contorted with agony, his features etched with lines of suffering as he transformed into a charred remnant, joining his heretic friends. Forty-one heretics had died. Xin Ba had really underestimated his enemy this time. And now he regretted it badly.

"Xin Ba, this mission is really suicidal." A tall old man stepped next to him but kept a few feet between them. He was afraid of Xin Ba, and he should be.

"Yes, I underestimated this bastard. I shouldn't have sent my wife away." Xin Ba sighed, staring at Li Wei, who was holding his knees a few hundred feet away. "He is spent. Look at his condition. I don't think he's got any of that attack in him, so this is our chance to finish him."

He spread his time bubble once again. However, Li Wei flashed back to his camp, escaping Xin Ba's sneak attack.

"Li Wei, you couldn't kill me, and something that can't kill me only makes me stronger." Xin Ba chuckled.

Li Wei was at the end of his rope, which meant Xin Ba would have the victory secured quickly. With these old heretic men as his witness, his charisma in the sect would be lifted. If he could kill the guy who'd killed forty-one heretics, maybe he could even join the Chosen Gold team. This was his chance.

"Old seniors, this is our chance. Please shred him. I don't need to beg you to join the battle anymore, and I assume you know the cost of not joining the battle."

Seventeen people surrounded the formation and attacked in unison.***

Li Wei expelled blood from his mouth, one mouthful after another. If his Yang Wood Pill Clone hadn't reacted in time, along with all his healing skills, he would have coughed out his internal organs instead. When he'd absorbed the tribulation lightning from the twin treasure of lightning, he'd never thought it would be this big. He'd kept it aside for a big move like this, inside his Blood Lightning Pill Clone, and it had proved useful.

Moreover, the path through which the lightning surged out of his dantian had opened up completely, and the next time he used this move would be easier than before. Of course, he didn't wish to use it again, nor did he have enough lightning stored to do that. Unless...

"Li Wei, are you all right?" Little Fox walked to him, looking exhausted. She'd used a lot of her apocalyptic attacks on the enemy and had drowned a chunk of their people with her gale balls, but she lacked stamina and raw energy, so she had to lie down after a few attacks.

"I'm fine, and you all did well." Wei glanced at everyone.

Although he wasn't able to catch the action when he was in the void, he'd seen everything through his clone. They'd attacked, retreated, and defended in a timely manner. They'd sacrificed their lives to save other people. Within a matter of hours, they had formed a tight-knit bond and demonstrated their team's value. Wei couldn't have been any happier for them.

"You killed so many with your lightning ball." Little Fox rubbed her soft head against his palm.

"Yet I couldn't kill everyone." Wei clenched his fingers. Killing Houtians wasn't easy, and he had failed once again.

"I loved that skill. Why didn't you use it earlier?"

"I couldn't kill Xin Ba, so does it even matter?"

"Li Wei, just watch how I decimate your formation!" Xin Ba called.

Twelve people charged at the formation, including a few from before. Then the attack on the Stormfeather Guardian Formation tripled, and whatever Li Gun had done to increase its defensive power didn't seem to be enough. If this continued, the formation would collapse, and then Wei would have no way of saving all the lives.

No, he couldn't let that happen. After retrieving a wooden piece from the Lightning Wood he'd found inside the Beast Origin Realm, he poured a few drops of the Yin Yang Liquid on it and instantly turned it into a Lightning Seed.

"Li Gun, don't worry. We have so much lightning here that everyone will be brought to their knees before they can even touch us."

Chapter 86

Rual'er Shows Up

Xin Ba coughed blood. It just came out on its own. First, he'd been slapped around by Li Wei, and those seventy-five old fogies had watched, laughing in their hearts. Then Li Wei cut through his mechanical constructs, and cleaved him in half, and they did nothing, laughing at him and calling him pussy. And when the time to fight came, they'd died like cabbages.

Now they couldn't even break a formation for him. Either Li Wei was a god, or he, Xin Ba, was too weak to fight with him. The formation that was about to crumble turned tougher than metal, and their attacks were like hitting it with wooden sticks.

"Senior, what the hell is going on?" he asked the fat heretic next to him. These were people already in the Houtian Realm, and they acted lofty and powerful after eating the heretic pill. They were powerful, but they were failing miserably against a guy in the Heart Blood Realm.

"That Li Wei is the problem," the fat man said. "We should have killed him when he slapped you, but it was so funny we couldn't resist lying dormant and watching it happen."

Xin Ba coughed another mouthful of blood. How could this old fatty say something like this? A funny thing? Was it funny seeing his own comrade slapped by an enemy?

"Senior, what should we do now?" the fat heretic asked. "I don't have a way to break this formation, and if we let him recuperate, he might use the same ability as before. With his teleportation power, we won't survive next time."

Xin Ba was afraid of Li Wei like he was afraid of the Chosen Gold. Even the people at his side were freaks. A single poison girl was holding out against five heretics and one powerful guy without sweating a lot.

Why did he meet so many freaks? And where the fuck was Xin Cao? Shouldn't she be done with her task and be back here?

"Senior, I have a way. This guy is very sensitive about his friends, and we have one who is not hiding under a turtle formation."

"You mean...?" Xin Ba asked.

"Yes. Let's pressure him and force him to go help her, and then we can use that chance to attack the formation. Once we kill a few of his friends, he'll make a mistake, and we can win this war despite losing a battle."

"Good thinking. You learned a lot from me in a short time," Xin Ba said.

The fatty gave orders, and ten old heretics moved toward the poison woman fighting toe-to-toe with other people.

"Li Wei, what will you do now?" Xin Ba chuckled. It was an evil chuckle, but he liked that. Evil suited him. "Your girl will be trapped in no time, and then I'll enjoy her in front of you. Do you like watching your girl getting enjoyed by another man? If not, then get the fuck out of there, and fight like a real man."

An arrow snapped through the air and pierced his heart, and a beautiful girl appeared in the sky. "Who allowed you to wag your tongue against my man, you filthy worm?"***

Li Wei was infuriated. Xin Ba, that bastard, had used a despicable option Wei hadn't been ready for. He was hitting under the belt, and Wei didn't know what to do.

Six hundred people depended on him. He needed to stay with Li Gun for a few minutes before he could refine the Lightning Seed and move away. However, if he didn't help Sonja, he might lose her along with Kai Shaya. These bastards who possessed the power of Houtian would shred them. He couldn't even teleport as he only had two teleport charges remaining, and even if he used them, it might not be enough.

Sighing, he separated his blood clones. He could only detonate them and kill everyone who attacked Sonja and Kai Shaya. It would be an enormous loss, but what else could he do?

"Xin Ba, you're making me do this." He stared at the ring on his finger.

Wait—he could do something else as well. If he could let someone else bind the ring and pull the people in, then he could send that person to Ten-Day Time Chamber. But Rual'er was there, and he couldn't send people in back-to-back. Damn it. The timer still had a few minutes before Rual'er came out, and he didn't have that much time.

A message from Kai Shaya popped up in his mind. "Brother Wei, I'm fine. Send your companions in. I can protect them."

Wei's face lit up. This was good.

Out of nowhere, a mysterious ripple emerged beside him, unveiling a graceful woman with a captivating smile on her radiant face. A golden robe flowed over her curvy body, and the mark of wing was clear on her gentle forehead. Her aura was as fierce as the wind, and her smile was calm like a river.

"Rual'er, you transformed. Did you...?"

Her smile unfolded like a delicate flower, brightening her face as she shook her head. "Brother Wei, thanks to you, I learned the Concept of

Wind. It allowed me to transform beforehand. Do you like it?" She gracefully twirled, showing him her exquisite beauty.

"You look amazing," Wei said, completely flustered.

"Li Wei, wait till I transform. I'll be a hundred times lovelier than her." The little fox growled.

"Rual'er, I can't believe you look the same."

"It's as if you've seen me in this form before." She giggled, a smile blooming on her face.

"Did you...?"

"Just watch how I tear them up." With the grace of a queen, she floated in the air and then elegantly shot out of the formation. She wasn't a princess anymore. She would be hailed as a queen once she went back. Only a rare few could transform before becoming a Houtian Realm cultivator, and whoever did so was treated like a deity.

"Rual'er, you are as beautiful as one could get." Wei sighed, regretting his choices from his past life.

Wang Zia was beautiful, but she lacked the grace of Rual'er or the innocence of Fei'er or the loveliness of Nai Fang or the loyalty of Sun Nuan. Heck, she couldn't even match the craziness of that girl Hui Ma. He looked around and saw Hui Ma smiling at him with crazy eyes as if she knew he was thinking about her.

Rual'er shot a Sharpshooting Arrow from the Giant Killing Bow Divine Art. He didn't know what she'd done in the time chamber, but whatever it was, she'd gained a lot from that time.

"Rual'er, leave them to me. Can you help Sonja and Kai Shaya?" he asked, steadying his resolve. If he wanted to save his people, he would have to take some strong steps.

Chapter 87

Two-Headed Hydra

Xin Ba retrieved an arrow from his heart. Thanks to his water qi, his heart healed rapidly, yet the storm of fury inside him remained unquelled. Who was she, and where did she come from? She'd attacked and pinned his heart even though seventeen heretics surrounded him. All of these bastards had divine sense spread around, yet they could do nothing.

"Who are you, bitch?" he roared, wanting to leap up and tear apart her clothes and fuck her head.

"Do you want to die, moron? Who are you calling bitch?" The winds around her turned fierce, and they formed sharp blades that came for him.

Wait. How could she fly? He didn't recall seeing her in Li Wei's camp.

What was going on? Had Li Wei hid her in a disguise? That sly bastard. If he survived this, he would take vengeance on Li Wei by tearing him into a thousand pieces and feeding each fragment to dogs from every country he knew.

A panic settled in his heart. Someone close to him rapidly approached him, and she didn't seem to be in a good mood. Her panic was infectious, and he could feel her unsettling thoughts. Xin Cao. She'd suffered a heavy defeat in her endeavors, and her anger was about to reach the heavens.

He and she had both faced defeats in their journey. It again proved they were better together. They not only shared time dao, but they were bound by their yin and yang as well, and although he hated her cocky attitude sometimes, she completed him. She was part of him, and he couldn't deny that.

"Honey, you're back." He spread his arms and welcomed the woman leaping into his arms as if she were coming from a thousand year-long journey.

"Xin Ba..." Tears rolled down her cheeks.

"We need to merge. We can't do this alone," he said calmly. When they were separated, the master had told them not to merge until things became dire, and if they merged, they had to kill everyone around them.

"Are you sure? Once we merge, we can't use our Time Intent effectively, and we may not separate for a few years."

"I almost died three times," Xin Ba said, his throat choking with emotion. "We'll merge and try the Epic Twister Form. We have to kill them all."

"I'm not sure. I lost everyone, and if we merge, we'll be the only two people alive in this node."

"If we can still make it through this, we can give a proper answer to the Gatekeepers, and in the worst case, we'll just run away. With the two of us combined, nothing can stop us from running away."

"No one can go against the descendant of an Origin Beast, can they?" Xin Cao sighed, a sigh of helplessness.

He understood her. He plotted to kill her and gain the supremacy over the time dao they shared, but this wasn't the time for that. This was the time to kill, and they could think about killing each other once they separated again after a dozen years.

Xin Cao reluctantly offered her essence blood to him, and he offered the same to her. They stuck a pin into their foreheads and pushed the blood into the wound.

Time froze. The yin and yang separated from them, merging, swirling around each other, and a storm gulped them down. An eternity of pain echoed through the battleground, spreading currents through the air. The ground cracked, lava burst out of the cracks, and a gloomy atmosphere gripped the hearts of the twenty-five heretic cultivators who followed Xin Ca o.

The storm was the end of everything, and for everyone.***

Li Wei had a bad feeling the moment Xin Ba and his female companion exchanged their essence blood. Something felt odd about the entire thing, but he couldn't put his finger on it.

"Blood Parasite, can I use a Time Grain to create an ad hoc time chamber here?" he asked, unable to hide his desperation.

"Yes, you can, but you don't have six hundred Time Grains to send six hundred people in."

"Not six hundred, but I have to save one thousand five hundred people." Wei glanced at the side from where Nuan'er was coming, and she brought a powerful army of nine hundred people with her.

"That's impossible."

Xin Ba and Xin Cao were undergoing a strange transformation, twisting around each other. When their bodies merged, Wei's divine sense was cut off from the process, and a storm engulfed twenty-five old people who followed the female, Xin Cao. They vanished as if they'd never existed in this world.

Wei's sense of danger pulsed intensely. He had little time left. "Not when I can use this ring. I'll only need one Time Grain." Wei teleported to Rual'er.

"Do you really trust her?" Blood Parasite asked.

"I do." He handed the ring to Rual'er and asked her to bind it to herself. If he hadn't known her from his previous life, he wouldn't have trusted anyone but Nuan'er and Little Fox with this ring.

"Brother Wei, do I take it as a betrothal gift? Are you proposing to me already?" Her cheeks turned bright red as she averted her gaze.

"Rual'er, bind it, and cover everyone inside the ring." He pushed her toward the six hundred people by his side. "Sonja, abandon everything, and walk into the energy pulse. I can sense Kai Shaya has gained some control of it, so you'll be safe inside." Before Rual'er appeared, he had received a weak message from Kai Shaya, who said he could protect himself and a few more people. "Little Fox, join Sonja. I might need you, but don't come out unless I ask you explicitly."

He teleported once again, using the last charge from his Primordial Blood Palace and materializing next to Nuan'er. "Nuan'er, go with Rual'er. This battle is going to be tough, and I don't want you harmed at all." He rubbed her forehead, wrapped everyone in the wind, and increased the flying tools' speed as he flew them toward his base camp.

The storm settled down, and a two-headed dragon appeared out of it. Golden runes were marked on its foreheads, and they had facial features similar to Xin Ba and Xin Cao.

"Brother Wei, this is the legendary Two-Headed Hydra. Although this one looks like an infant, I feel threatened," Rual'er said, shaking.

The elder behind Nuan'er spoke, his voice cracking as his aura rose suddenly. "Little girl, give him the main pill you've prepared, and stay with him. I'll go out and distract this nasty creature. I never thought they would leave the key with the children. Are they going to destroy the world or what?"

"Li Wei, I'll help you this one time." Hui Ma appeared next to him and covered all the people around him, pushing them into the void. "You have five minutes before I'll have to pop them out of the void," she whispered before she vanished.

Now only he, Rual'er, and Nuan'er remained on the battlefield. They looked at each other. Nuan'er and Rual'er had strange expressions on their faces.

"Big brother Wei, who was that girl?" Nuan'er asked before handing him a pill that smelled nicer than the sweet wine Rual'er kept feeding him.

Wei stared into the void, trying to figure out where Hui Ma had taken all the people at his side. "A friend whom I owe one." He was going to believe her despite her crazy batshit claims of being the love of his life. Whatever came, he would meet it head-on and fight for his friends. Five minutes was all he needed to take down this monster.

Chapter 88

Concept of Wind Shows Its Power

The Two-Headed Hydra roared at them, sending out a jet of water. It cut through the air with such intensity that a whizzing sound followed its path. The hydra was larger than Rual'er in her full beast form and even the largest snake beast Li Wei had seen in the Beast Origin Realm. The sheer physical force from that attack could shred Heart Blood Realm people to death. It was a good thing that Hui Ma had taken his people away from this place.

"Brother Wei, let me handle this." Rual'er floated in front of him and waved her hands, commanding the winds.

The winds obeyed her command as if she was the mother and they were her children. Good children. They formed a revolving shuriken in front of her, expelling black smoke that filled the air with a pungent smell of rot and death. Before Wei could push it away, a fragrance as pure as holy water from the heavens covered them. It instantly turned the surrounding area into a place devoid of filth. It was like sitting under a world tree that exuded only a saint form of air from its branches. Wei had a feeling that if he cultivated in this air, he would have greater benefits.

"Rual'er what is this Concept?" Wei couldn't resist asking. This had to be a Concept. A simple Intent wouldn't be able to do this.

"Brother Wei, I've learned the Concept of Wind called Concept of Quintessence of Celestial Winds. It's the most primal form of wind, and it can expel every impurity. The quintessence form of wind will bow to my command and do whatever I want. I show you what you've bestowed on me, brother Wei. I'll remember this graciousness of yours in my heart and serve you until eternity."

"I did nothing." Wei smiled. This lass—she looked so beautiful that his heart almost fluttered.

"Big brother Wei, your abilities to woo women are heaven defying. I didn't think you'd find many sisters." Nuan'er smiled, almost teasing, but her eyes exposed a hint of fear.

Sighing inwardly, Wei pulled Nuan'er close and rubbed her forehead, making his affection known to her. "No matter what, no one can take your place in my heart," he whispered and watched her bloom like the Blood Lotus on a full moon night. Poets in the Martial Realm described the blooming Blood Lotus as the most beautiful thing on earth. "By the way, what was that pill?" He sensed the aftertaste of Holy Cicada Life-Sharing Fruit. It was bitter and sweet like a grapefruit.

"It's a formula given by the elder who came with me," Nuan'er said. "Let me show you something." She closed her eyes and sat cross-legged on her flying tool.

Wei felt a stream of pure wood energy entering his body through a mysterious connection. It was refreshing and healing and warded off evil.

"Core energy of a Wood Elemental." He activated his Void Eyes and saw the world turning black and white. Everything was gray, and a pure white energy line connected him and Nuan'er.

However, when he looked at her carefully, he saw a strange mark on her soul, shimmering with a hint of red. It was so minimal that he wondered if he'd seen something else. But with the system, he could replay what he'd seen and confirm that it was the red. This was first time he'd seen a color in the black-and-white world. The red mark pulsed with a dim intensity and vanished into Nuan'er's stronger-than-average soul.

"Interesting. There's someone hiding in her soul," he said in his mind. "Blood Parasite, can you see that thing?"

"I don't share your Void Eyes. They are exclusive to you."

Wei looked around and detected a pocket of bright energy inside the void, and Hui Ma was looking out from it. Wei met her gaze .

"Li Wei, how many cards are you holding? Can you really see me? I feel like you are everywhere," Hui Ma whispered.

Wei sent a divine sense message into the void: "Girl, we must have a good chat after this all ends."

"So, you really can see through the void. I love it." Hui Ma smiled. "But you should look at your other girlfriend. She's doing well against that monster."

Wei turned and saw the water jets shooting out in front of Rual'er's celestial wind. Her celestial winds were the purest white while the water jets were the darkest black. The mesmerizing sight of the black and white striking each other held his gaze.

Pain tingled across his forehead, and he shut down his Void Eyes. Although they didn't disintegrate him at the cellular level anymore, his forehead hurt when he activated the void eyes for a long time.

"Bitch, I'll kill you," Two-Headed Hydra said in a mix of a woman and a man's voice. One of its mouths opened and spat a giant water ball at them. The water spun rapidly, resembling a black hole that devoured the air and energy before launching outward like a pouncing tiger.

"You must be dreaming, monster." Rual'er made a cutting motion with her right arm, and the celestial winds turned into a giant arrow that pierced the water ball, tearing it apart from the inside.

Rual'er descended like a stone dropping from the sky, and Wei had to leap forward and catch her in his hands.

"Thank you. I can't float while using the full power of my attack. That water attack was brutal," she said, blushing, adjusting herself in his arms before floating back up.

"If I support you to fly, can you try out your full attack?" Wei asked.

"Do you want me to?"

Wei nodded and flew upward before slipping his arm around her waist to support her. In such proximity, he could perceive her body quivering and detect the alluring aroma wafting from her, yet he controlled his longing and soared to greater heights.

"Let's do it. Let's see what that monster can handle," he said.

"Celestial Winds, hear my command and come to me." The swirling winds created a colossal bow that shimmered with a blinding intensity, right in front of Rual'er.

Wei's heart skipped a beat as an arrow materialized on the bow string, emitting a powerful force that could send the earth shattering and heaven collapsing.

"Nova of Arrows." The words that escaped her lips seemed to possess an otherworldly power, resonating through the air like a deity delivering cosmic decrees. Then she released it, and he felt her losing control. Her face turned pale, and her body reverted to her beast form. "I'm sorry. I couldn't remain in that beautiful form." She sounded sad.

"You look beautiful in every form, and your skill is equally beautiful," Wei said, watching the giant arrow piercing the air and turning into five giant arrows that targeted the Two-Headed Hydra. It might just kill the two heads this time.

Chapter 89

Big Sister Nuan'er

Sun Nuan felt like her heart would break when big brother Wei hugged the beautiful princess from the race of the dragons. The beast princess's loveliness was overwhelming compared to her own. Looking at them unleashing skills in the midair made her feel depressed. A strange sensation spread through her heart, making her want to destroy everything she held dear to her heart. It was telling her to undo the bindings of this world and cast the ultimate ability that came with her bloodline because big brother Wei was hugging another woman.

Rubbing her face, she watched the nova of arrows shred the hydra's two heads. The skill was so powerful that she felt helpless. Once again, she'd failed to help her big brother Wei in any capacity. She was nothing but a nuisance.

She was useless. She couldn't even count on being his silent follower. Was she doomed to remain alone in this world forever? Couldn't she at least remain in his shadow?

All she wanted to do was stay by his side, attending to his wishes, but every time she tried to get close, a new girl popped up, stealing her position.

"Nuan'er, are you ready? I may need your qi supply to destroy this monster." Big brother Wei's voice echoed in her ears, lifting a weight from her shoulders. The darkness that had consumed her heart disappeared, replaced by a glimmer of hope emerging from the end of the tunnel.

"Big brother Wei, do you really need my help?"

"Who else would I ask for?" He frowned. "Aren't you ready to help me anymore? Did I hurt you?" he asked, sounding a little down.

"Not at all." Sun Nuan cheered up like a little girl. "Take it as much as you want. Even if you take my life, I'm willing."

"And why would I take your life? You know how much I like you, so get to business quickly. Stop talking nonsense. Don't forget, you are my strongest support, and no one can match you."

If she could have hidden in the earth, she would have. Had he just said he liked her?

"Big brother Wei..."

"I'm going in." Big brother Wei flapped his wings and shot into the shredded parts of the Two-Headed Hydra, which were wiggling toward each other.

She sensed a life force greater than anything she had experienced before. That thing was tough to kill, and big brother Wei needed help from his favorite. That meant her.

"Big brother Wei, don't worry," Sun Nuan said.

"Sister, you're gorgeous." The dragon princess transformed into a beautiful girl once again, but Nuan didn't feel any jealousy from her.

"Thank you, sister. Call me Nuan'er."

"Big sister Nuan'er, I'll protect you with my life."

Nuan closed her eyes, but she couldn't keep the warmth from reaching her cheeks. She'd called Nuan big sister. Wow. It couldn't get any better than this.***

When Nuan'er gave Wei a burst of healing wood qi, a smile played on his lips. This was interesting. He knew where he could use this much wood qi.

"Nuan'er, you came at a perfect time." He gave her a thumbs-up.

His wood clone breaking through into the Marrow Cleansing Realm had given him access to all the sword martial skills he'd missed before, including the Wood Sword Tornado, one of his self-created skills. After practicing it in the time chamber, he'd even developed a Will of the Skill. He was limited by the wood qi he had, but with Nuan'er's help, that restriction could be lifted easily.

Cutting through the barrage of the water curtains, Wei charged at the hydra's shredded body, but as he got close, he became slower while the hydra healed faster and faster.

"Damn it. What's going on?"

"This is a legendary beast, brother Wei. It has higher healing power than its human forms," Rual'er said.

"Even the time power is a bit stronger." Wei sensed the waves of wind washing over him, forcing him to slow down. If he hadn't spent so much time in the time chamber and experienced the fight between the time cultivators, he would have been helpless in this place. Apparently, every tribulation had its own benefit.

By the time he was close to the hydra, it had healed back to its previous self. Two sets of red eyes stared at their prey. The fight had just gotten more difficult.

"Li Wei, you're going to die now," Xin Ba said directly into his mind. Wei could hear a feminine tone hidden in his words. The hydra's mouths opened and shot a glimmering ball of water through both its heads.

"Wood Sword Tornado." Wei sent his swords out, and they transformed into the afterimage of multiple swords that revolved around each other, forming a tornado.

Every moment, a new sword was added. Soon he broke past his previous limit of twenty-five sword rays, and the air hummed with a divine chant when the thirtieth sword materialized. The divine decree appeared and announced that the Will of the Skill has pushed past level one.

Wei felt a lingering pain in his forehead. Creating thirty Sword Rays wasn't difficult, but controlling them with his mind was quite taxing. He was at his limit.

"Nuan'er, now."

An unbinding power rushed into him, easing his pain. Wood qi rushed through his meridians, and the wood sword tornado got bigger and bigger. The swords kept increasing, and the fortieth sword appeared.

The divine decree descended once again, and this time, he could feel it resonate with his soul. Something had broken through, and he felt a wave of healing energy washing through his Soul Palace. The world froze, including the hydra. Time hadn't stopped, but the world had lost its meaning for a moment. Only Wei existed, and the divine decree.

System: Information Interface detected.

Host's soul has broken through a new shackle. New Soul Art available. New system functionality is available.

Wei felt ill when he looked at the Heavens' Decree. Through it, he detected a threatening gaze locking him down. Something was odd, and he had a gut feeling that if he pushed his Wood Sword Tornado any further, he might not survive this. Anyway, he could feel he had drained Nuan'er, and he couldn't ask more from her, so he just unleashed his forty Sword Ray Wood Sword Tornados on the hydra.

Boom!

Chapter 90

Inside the Hydra

The Wood Sword Tornado shredded the Two-Headed-Hydra like a knife cutting through a piece of paper. The void itself was cut into pieces, and the hydra's wails echoed for a few seconds.

Li Wei coughed a mouthful of blood as the sword dissipated. That third level of the Will of the Skill had cost him a lot of blood essence. The power that rushed through him when Nuan'er poured all of her wood qi into him took a large toll on him, and even with his Muxi's Blessing, he couldn't heal it instantly.

The hydra was shredded into pieces smaller than what Rual'er had done before. However, he knew the hydra wouldn't be dead by one move. Even before turning into the hydra, Xin Ba had shown impossible healing powers, and Wei bet they'd only multiplied after he merged with Xin Cao.

"Li Wei, you bastard. I will kill you," an evil voice echoed in his mind, and time slowed down.

No. It had accelerated for the hydra monster. The small pieces zoomed past his eyes and merged, forming a giant Two-Headed Hydra once more. In front of that monster, Wei floated in the air like a tiny ant trying to fight a dragon. As the sky-covering monster loomed overhead, he felt an immense weight pressing down on him, making it hard to breathe.

"I've got you, Li Wei." The evil chuckle made its way into his mind again, sounding more sinister than before.

Sweat dripped down Wei's lower back, and he felt an itch to back down growing in his heart.

"Break from it." The jarring sound of Blood Parasite shattered Wei's trance, bringing him back to reality.

Wei sliced upward with his sword, blocking a sneak water attack. "What the fuck was that? How did it bypass my divine sense and put me in a trance?" Wei shuddered. If Blood Parasite hadn't woken him up, he would have been cut in two, and there was no coming back from that.

"It's a wave-based illusion. It used the vibration of the time to control your mind. Even if I didn't wake you up, you would be fine. The thing slipping into you wouldn't let you die in a parlor trick like this."

Wei nodded. The purple light in his soul had never failed him. It had shown up and helped him when he needed it the most.

"Li Wei, listen. This hydra is a descendant of an Origin Beast, and you can't kill it from outside. If you want to win, you have to enter its body and cut through its heart. That's the only way to take it down," Blood Parasite said.

Wei knew something like this would be needed. Rual'er and Nuan'er had done the best they could, and now it was on to him to cut down this behemoth.

Steeling his mind, Wei charged through the waves the hydra was constantly generating. It was insulting him so it could capture him in the trance once again. However, it couldn't budge Wei anymore. His wings danced through the curtain of water. He flashed past the water attacks and then zoomed close to the huge body. The size that gave the hydra the advantage proved to be a weakness as well. It could lose Wei, but Wei couldn't lose it.

Wei's sword landed on the hydra's skin, cutting through it easily. Using that opening, Wei drove into the hydra's body. He'd thought about it. Even if he cut the hydra for a hundred years, he wouldn't be able to cut it into pieces, and the hydra would continue living, but he could always cut through the hydra's heart a hundred times and win this battle.

The inside of the hydra was different from what he'd thought. It wasn't made of flesh and blood vessels. They were there, but they only occupied a quarter of its body, and the remaining space was empty, like a vacuum. Darkness gave the vacuum an eerie feeling that would make even a strong heart doubt their decision twice.

As a strong suction force pulled Wei toward the walls of the hydra's body, he saw something that shouldn't have been present there. Tens of thousands of mini hydras guarded the internal organs of the hydra. They were tiny when compared to the original beast, but they were bigger than Wei.

"What abomination is this?"

The hydras attacked him from all the sides. They were simple water-based attacks, something he wouldn't be bothered with if he only faced a few. But when facing hundreds of attacks at the same time, he had no option but to push his Blood Earth Force Divine Art to maximum power to prevent them from destroying him. Along with the skill, he had to use his Sword Rays to cut through them and prevent them from reaching him.

But Wei wasn't a Sword Saint or someone who could cut through the air a thousand times in a fraction of a moment. He was a mere mortal when it came to swordplay, and between every two slices of his sword, a dozen water attacks hit him, weakening his defensive divine art.

Numerous cuts appeared on him, and he bled like there was no end to it. The more he attacked, the more wounds he received, and even with his

Blood Essence Body Cultivation Art, he knew he would end up bleeding to death. It wasn't going to work.

"Intent of Expansion." Wei tossed a few metal balls around him and covered himself on three sides with metal walls, using the Intent he'd learned through Brah Gansha's Life Blood Weapon. It was a fairly low-level Intent, but it was useful against the common attacks. They had the advantage of numbers. He wanted to reduce that and give himself a breather.

It worked like a charm, and only a few attacks reached him from the front, which he easily parried with his sword.

Slowly, he made his way through the hundreds of small hydras until he finally reached a giant organ that looked like a kidney. It was enveloped in a golden energy dome and a few hundred golden hydras that were bigger than the mini hydras he'd been facing before. The mini hydras were like soldiers, and now he was facing the guards.

The hundred golden hydras charged at him, shooting water arrows through their two heads. The golden water arrows blasted the metal walls he'd built around him and easily pierced his skin. Their damage wasn't sufficient to heavily injure him, but as with the mini hydras' attacks, he would bleed or be shredded to death if he didn't cut down their number.

"Li Wei, I've got you again. Now you're trapped inside, and I'll let my blood clones play with you forever."

Hundreds of golden hydras moved in unison and formed a tight-knit circular dome around him. There wasn't even an inch-wide gap through which he could escape. The hydras laughed hysterically, some sounding like Xin Ba and others like Xin Cao. They opened their mouths to reveal golden balls of water swirling inside them. Even if he'd had a body of stones, he would not survive if they attacked together.

Yet Wei gave an evil smile. "Did you say blood clones, Xin Ba?" He chuckled. "Blood Control!" he shouted into the vacuum in the hydra's stomach.

Chapter 91

Burning the Hydra from Inside

The golden hydras squirmed in pain when the water balls burst in their mouths. From a distance, Li Wei watched them cry. He gave a snort. They deserved it. Who'd asked them to gang up on him?

Some of them tried to resist his control, but how could they when Wei controlled their blood? It would be impossible for him to control the blood of any person with the same cultivation realm as his, but these were not real cultivators or beasts. They were blood clones, and he could do whatever he wanted with them. It was time to prove his supremacy over blood.

Wei chuckled evilly before tossing a ball of fire made from Blood Fire Aura with a hint of his Hell Flame added to it. The first golden hydra didn't even notice before it caught fire and burned into puffy smoke, leaving a disgusting stench behind, like a forest of farting animals. The next few also burned into nothingness without anyone realizing what was happening. When a few of them figured it out, they tried to run away, but Wei selectively targeted them with Blood Fire Aura balls.

In less than thirty seconds, the space they occupied became devoid of anyone. However, their wails continued echoing in the walls of the vacuum. Finally, they died down.

Wei turned to face the tens of thousands of the gray hydras that had left off chasing him when he'd entered this place. They gave him a pleading look before trying to run away, but how could Wei let them do as they pleased? He conjured a few hundred balls of Blood Fire Aura and tossed them into the stampede. The mini hydras were so close to each other that they couldn't avoid the flames spreading through them rapidly like a forest fire.

"What the hell are you doing, Li Wei?" a deep voice boomed through the vacuum before a giant wave of water washed over the gray hydras and saved them. Despite the healing wave, it was too late for the gray hydras—half of them had turned to smoke.

"Why didn't you do it earlier?" Blood Parasite asked.

"I didn't know they were blood clones. Their attacks hurt so much." Wei burned a few dozen Blood Pearls to heal his fleshly injuries. "I don't get it. I can't breathe in this space, but this doesn't seem like a vacuum."

"It isn't," Blood Parasite said. "A common beast has a stomach, but this one is a descendant of an Origin Beast, which don't have stomachs in their bodies—they have worlds. It's complicated, but know that you have to destroy at least three organs to kill it, and it would have thousands of such sentries protecting their energy cores."

"A world in itself. That's interesting." He wondered if the beasts he'd faced in the strange trial through the Dark Forest also had worlds inside their bodies.

A Two-Headed Hydra formed out of the inner lines of the main hydra's internal body. A thick film of water swirled around it, making Wei's fire useless, so he kept it away. This hydra had a faint-blue body color. It wasn't even as powerful as the golden hydras.

"Li Wei, you are dead. How dare you kill my generals?"

Wei chuckled, sensing the panic in the hydra's voice. "Xin Ba, I'm just starting. I won't settle until I slap all of your heads." He flashed through the vacuum and slapped the newly formed hydra's heads one by one.

"Damn you, motherfucker," Xin Ba said, and one of the hydra heads burst into a giant storm of water that charged at Wei, trying to gulp him down in one go.

"Wood Sword Tornado." Wei let twenty sword images cut through the remaining hydra's head and slice it into pieces. It didn't heal back, and the hydra soldiers had run away from him, leaving a small-hut-sized kidney floating in the vacuum, connected by blood vessels that an average human could easily pass through.

"Li Wei, that kidney has a strong connection with the metal. This might be useful for you through the Integration Rune."

"Why don't I feel anything?"

"Your cultivation realm is still low to understand some things."

An idea played in Wei's mind as he cut apart the blood vessels and sucked the kidney into his storage palace. When Hui Ma had shown up, Wei hadn't given the ring to Rual'er but had kept it with him. It proved useful now.

"Li Wei, I'm going to tear the two girlfriends of yours." Xin Cao's voice echoed through the space.

Wei entered one of the blood vessels. Of course, he'd covered himself in a thick armor of wood qi. The last thing he wanted was the hydra's disgusting blood coming in contact with his skin or clothes, so he kept a safe distance.

"Absorb some blood for me as you go along. It's not useful for you, but I can use it to create a body for me in the future," Blood Parasite said.

With a shrug, Wei created a small opening in his wood qi armor, allowing the blood to seep into the enormous barrel tucked away in his storage ring. He and Blood Parasite were partners now, and if he needed something and it didn't harm Wei's friends and family, Wei would do anything for him.

"Li Wei, I've caught the little beast. She smells so good. I'm going to fuck her tight and nice. Do you want to watch? I bet you haven't touched her yet."

"Do as you like," Wei replied.

His metal clone remained hidden underground, ready to act at the required time, and Wei knew both of his friends were fine. In fact, the giant hydra wasn't in good condition and had lost a dozen feet of height after he'd stored away its kidneys. His plan was working perfectly. All he had to do was tuck away a few more organs so he could kill the so-called Origin Beast descendant.

Chapter 92

Surprise at the Heart of the Hydra

Entering the blood vessel was the right choice as Wei reached the hydra's spleen in a mere thirty seconds. Swimming through a giant river of blood wasn't his favorite option of transportation, but he'd nonetheless done it. When he reached the spleen, purple hydras stared at him—a new type of small hydra. They were surrounded by thousands of golden hydras, trying to drown him in angry gazes. The purple hydras exuded an intense aura of slaughter.

"Li Wei, you came. I was waiting for you." The ten purple hydras shot out of the inner circle and appeared next to Wei.

Wei felt an intimate connection with these hydras, and a particular pill clone inside his dantian was stirred up like a kid asking for food. Poison. Had this hydra's body been made for him?

"We are made of the poison expelled by the Water Dao, able to kill anything we touch. Once we touch you, you will burn in hell for eternity," one of them said.

"Anything new, guys? Come quickly. I'm desperate." Wei charged ahead, spreading his arms to get bitten by those hydras all over himself.

Twenty mouths latched onto his entire body, leaving nothing but his pubic region intact. Even his ass was bitten by two heads. Their sharp teeth sank into his flesh and poured a ton of poison into his bloodstream.

"Wow! I never thought I would love the taste of poison." Wei moaned

He hated himself for doing it. Yes, he was angry at himself for even thinking like this. After living with his pill clones, he'd developed some weird habits, including getting naked under the lightning and letting big snakes bite each of his ass cheeks.

"Heavens. What am I turning into?" he muttered.

"Cry, Li Wei. Soon you will die." A chuckle echoed from the mouth of one of the hydras, who had stopped biting him in the hand.

Wei's free arm, which protected his pubic region, moved like a sword and slapped the head. "Fuck off. Just bite, or I'll bite you instead."

The hydra's head made a wronged expression and sank its teeth into the existing position.

"Now it feels good." Wei enjoyed the ecstasy of his Yin Poison Pill Clone. It had been months since he'd filled its stomach, and this was the best way. Maybe a degenerate one, but the best one indeed.

After a few seconds, one of the hydras pulled its head away. "Why aren't you dead already?" it shouted.

"Shut up, and keep biting." Wei slapped it so hard that it ripped apart from the other head and rolled away.

The other head wailed and tried to bite Wei's head, but Wei grabbed its mouth and tore it open. His Yin Poison Pill Clone swirled inside his dantian, and the poison from all the ten hydras got sucked into his skin. The hydras wailed and pulled their mouths out of him, but he couldn't let them go, could he? After conjuring twenty Wood Sword Tornado swords, he stabbed through nine hydras and a headless hydra and into his skin.

They stuck to him like a pill ingredient stuck to the bottom of a cauldron after the pill had gone bad.

"Let them go, Li Wei. How dare you blaspheme my head generals?" A big hydra appeared in front of him. It was a miniature version of the main hydra.

Wei was annoyed at hearing this bastard, so he stabbed two of his swords through its head. "I'm sorry, but I can't raise my arm to slap you. So just stay happy with a piercing."

After sucking all the poison from the purple hydras, Wei tossed a Blood Fire Aura onto the golden hydras that had accumulated in hordes around him. They didn't dare attack him when the purple hydras were biting him, so they just ran for their lives.

"I don't have time for this shit." Wei charged toward the spleen of the giant hydra.

This organ was bigger than its kidney, and he guessed it might be useful in the future, so he cut the blood vessels connecting to it and kept it in his palace. The giant hydra shrank once again, almost reaching half its original size.

"Li Wei, if you dare touch one more of my organs, I bet you will lose your lovers. Fuck, I will get out of this place and raze your entire family and fuck every woman in your clan."

Ignoring the bastards, Wei dashed through another blood vessel. It was time to aim for the main organ of this descendant of the Origin Beast—the heart. However, he knew it wouldn't be an easy fight. So far, he'd faced golden hydras and purple hydras, and fortunately, he had a countermeasure for both of them, but he knew the next fight would be the real heads of the hydras.

He never expected to meet two humans tied by a thick thread, waiting for him at the heart of the hydra. It was really a surprise.

Chapter 93

Mark of the Origin Beast

After traveling through the blood vein for a minute, Li Wei faced a dead end, so he cut through the wall and entered a space near the giant heart of the hydra. It was a strange world. A mansion-sized heart was suspended in the space, hanging by thick human blood veins connecting it to the remaining body of the hydra. Two people, Xin Ba and Xin Cao, hung below the giant heart, connected by the two thin blood vessels.

"Li Wei, you came. But you shouldn't have," Xin Cao said, but her mouth didn't move and her eyes didn't open.

"I'm here, and I'm going to slap you to death," Wei said, disgusted by the stench coming out of the black heart. It was rotten to the core, and it didn't look healthy. Was the hydra dying?

"Yes, she is dying, but unless we are dead, she can't die. She is sucking the blood and vitality out of us," Xin Cao said once again, her tone devoid of hatred or malice.

"Shut up, bitch." Another Xin Cao walked out of the giant heart and slapped the one hanging below the heart. The new Xin Cao wore golden robes, but the gold couldn't hide the hideous skin hidden below it.

"What the hell is going on here?" Wei asked.

"They've been sacrificed to conjure an Origin Beast," Blood Parasite said. "I was wrong. This is not a descendant of an Origin Beast but a sacrifice to control the shell of a dead Origin Beast."

"You're not making any sense," Wei said.

"I'll explain," the first Xin Cao said. "We were siblings, Xin Ba and I, who shared a rare bloodline of World-Devouring Hydra. Our clan found a shell of a dead hydra and used our essence blood to resurrect it. It's a rare necromancy technique that had been long lost in the annals of time."

"But we fought a few minutes ago," Wei said.

"We've been in this suspended position since we were children. The experiment was unsuccessful because we were teens, so the consciousness of the dead hydra sealed us inside her two heads, which you fought. They grew in this world, and so did we along with them. The plan was for them to gain their original memories over the time, and they would have merged back once the time was ripe, but a dire situation forced them to merge, and we ended up gaining our consciousness back."

"Stop it, bitch," the hideous Cao said. "You all are going to die anyway. Although we haven't gotten our full power back after devouring you all, we will have enough force to rule the Mortal Realm."

"Li Wei, if you have means to run away, then do it," the first Xin Cao said. "Find a way to get out of this world, because you don't know how dangerous this creature is. My clan sent us here to experiment, but even they don't know that when the hydra gains full power, it will devour them all because they hold the bloodline of the hydra."

"In that, you are right," the hideous Xin Cao said. "We were destroyed because we posed a great danger to those cultivators, but they don't know we have planted the seeds of our resurrection throughout the cultivators.

Those fools will only give rise to more and more of us in the coming time. Once we regroup, we'll take our revenge on the cultivators."

"She's telling the truth," Blood Parasite said. "I've read about the Origin Beasts and their destruction. Give me control, and let me destroy this filthy creature."

"Do you think, you, a soul slave, can destroy me, the World-Devouring Hydra?" A hideous Xin Ba suddenly appeared, his voice sounding like a bitter melon was being scraped. His head flickered between that of a hydra head and that of a human.

An army of red hydras poured out of the rotten heart, covering the entire space in mere seconds. They all emitted an intense pressure of a peak Heart Blood Realm cultivator. Wei couldn't control their blood as they were made of something else.

"You see? Your tricks can't work on them. They are born out of decay and rot, and you won't be able to absorb them either."

"You're right. I can't do anything to them." Wei shook his head, dejected. "Xin Cao, I guess you still hold some part of the humanity. So if I destroy this heart, will you die along with it?"

"Yes, but death is better than remaining a prisoner forever in this filthy creature's consciousness." Tears rolled down from her closed eyes. "You don't know how torturous it was to see the memories of this creature destroying worlds after worlds."

"Then I'm sorry for your death."

"Li Wei, do you have a way to destroy this creature?" Blood Parasite asked.

"Of course. I always had it, but I've never gotten a chance to use it before. One Recharge Qi."

A powerful energy burst out of his pill clone and rushed into his dantian, filling his Blood Lightning Pill Clone with the power of tribulation lightning.

"Lightning Sea of Taichi." Wei let loose the lightning as soon as he sensed the pill clone had become full. It was his ultimate attack that could destroy anything.

"Impossible. You can't have that thing again..." Hideous Xin Cao and Xin Ba tried to charge at him, but they were too late. A lightning sea covered the entire space, destroying everything in its wake, including the shell of Xin Cao.

A moment before the lightning reached her, Xin Cao opened her beautiful eyes, and Wei saw a pure joy flashing through them. "Thank you." Her words lingered in the air as her body disintegrated.

Cries followed the lightning sea and the army of red hydras incarnated inside the lightning sea. This was the most powerful attack Wei had, but he hadn't expected it to be this strong. In fact, he was ready to put up another brutal fight for his life.

"How...?" The mangled body of Xin Ba remained behind, half-hydra and half-human.

"You are a creature of death, and lightning is the bane of the darkness. Die forever." Wei used the remaining tribulation lightning to char the remains of Xin Ba into nothingness.

System: Information Interface Detected.

Mark of Origin Beast is planted on the host's body. This mark will pulsate whenever an Origin Beast is in proximity.

Fuck. This bastard hydra had cursed him before dying. Now he would be facing a horde of origin beasts descending upon him.

Chapter 94

News of Ki Fei

T he Ancient Decree hadn't finished doling out its final results, so Li Wei sat on a large stone with beauties all around him. To his left, Sun Nuan prepared tea for him, while Rual'er sat to his right pouring glasses of wine for everyone. The scent of the wine wafted in the air, recharging everyone's battered mood. They'd lost many friends and brothers, and Wei felt weary, so he'd asked Rual'er to give everyone a soul-calming wine.

The sky was as gloomy as before. After spending a few hours in this place, Wei missed the sun and the bright rays of hope. Although he had his beauties next to him and a fox who lay with her soft, furry head resting in his lap, he didn't feel content. Something was missing.

"Brother Wei, you should drink some wine too. You exhausted most of your powers in the last fight," Rual'er whispered.

"I'm fine." Wei smiled sheepishly.

He longed for a good tea. There were many things he had to go over, including the system upgrade and the Mark of the Origin Beast, but he just sat there among his people, chatting. It felt good to have this human connection after so many months of solo traveling and fighting enemies. While relishing the delicious taste of meat loaf, he found himself laughing heartily at the jokes exchanged by the military individuals from the Five Firmament City. He'd missed these things.

"Big brother Wei, your tea is ready." Nuan'er handed him a ceramic cup filled with a piping-hot tea. It smelled like butter and honey, the way he liked it.

After giving him tea, she stood behind him like an obedient maidservant. Of course, he disliked it, so he grabbed her soft hand, pulled her forward, and forced her to sit next to him. Then he poured a cup of tea for her as well.

"Big brother Wei, I want..."

"Brother Wei, are you going to forget me just because your old girlfriend showed up?" Rual'er elbowed him lightly and sat next to him, holding a cup in front of him.

Chuckling, Wei poured tea for her as well. In her human form, she was stunning, and he found himself unable to peel his eyes away from her.

"Brother Wei, aren't you going to introduce the sister to me officially?" Rual'er asked, her eyes dancing between him and Nuan'er.

"I thought you connected when I fought with the hydra." He pulled Nuan'er closer to him. "Look, this is my most trusted partner, Sun Nuan, a princess from the State of Zin. I can't do a single thing without her, and I trust her with my life."

Nuan'er shuddered, and he sensed her emotions through the warmth her body exuded.

"She is very special to you," Rual'er said.

"Of course she is. In fact, I'm proud of her. Without me helping her in the slightest, she raised an army of dual qi-and-body cultivators." He glanced at the army trained in the Five Firmament City, sitting in a neat formation. They were ready to tackle any challenge, and he doubted he could have done any better than to have them helping him.

"It was the master's recipe," Sun Nuan said.

"And you improved it. I couldn't have done this without you, Nuan'er." He pulled her closer, letting her soft body melt into his embrace. Allen Ming had taught him many things, but one thing he remembered perfectly—he'd said if you care for someone, then show it with touch, talk, and h ugs.

"Big brother Wei, please let me go. Everyone is looking at us."

"Let them."

"Sister Rual'er will be jealous," Nuan'er whispered.

Laughing, Wei turned toward Rual'er. "She's saying you'll be jealous if I hug her. Are you?"

"I'm not. Until you propose marriage to me officially, I won't say a single thing." Rual'er shook her head.

"But I don't like it. If you don't leave her, I might kill her," a cold voice said, striking his ears through the void. He instinctively released Nuan'er, who ran away like a scared rabbit and hid amid a group of female warriors.

"What happened? Afraid of showing your affection?" Rual'er asked.

Wei touched the back of his neck, feeling the cold sweat trickling down his lower back. This girl Hui Ma was dangerous. Although he wasn't afraid of her, he couldn't stop her from killing his friends.

"Nothing." Wei shook his head. "Let's discuss the Incursion. This thing is not over yet, right?"

"I only know there are three more Pulses, which will settle the final Incursion winner."

"I can fill you in those details, junior," the elder who accompanied Nuan'er said. When Wei first met this elder, a nasty poison had infected him, and Wei had cleared it out using the Yin Poison Pill Clone.

"Tell us, elder. What is next?"

"Next will be the second pulse, where all of you and the winners of the other nodes will be transported into a different realm and given an opportunity to search for treasures. It will be a month-long treasure hunt, but only a day will progress in real time."

"Another time manipulation."

The elder nodded. "In the third Pulse, you will be facing Outerworld champions, and you'll undergo individual and group battles."

"Outerworld champions? From other Mortal Realms?"

The elder shook his head. "I don't know. I only know there's a war happening between the world we live in and the monsters from the Outerworld, and these Incursions are the precursor to them."

"Then what is the bullshit everyone is spreading about Void Objects as a reward?"

"In the second Pulse, you may find a Void Object."

"So, what will happen in the fourth Pulse?"

"I don't have any idea. There were ten Incursions in the Martial and Mortal Realms, and out of ten, Gatekeepers have won two and two are undergoing Incursions."

"Wait, I heard only four Incursions were there."

"The other six are won by the Outerworld champions, and it's taboo to talk about them. The one we're in right now and the one happening in the Evil Host Empire are the last ones, and once those reach third Pulse, we will know what will happen in the last Pulse."

"Elder, how do you know all of this?" Wei asked. This was the most correct information he had obtained, and he had a hint of its truth because Xin Cao had said the same thing.

"I must apologize before I can say my identity." The elder slightly bowed to him.

"Elder, please. You helped Nuan'er. Why would you apologize?"

"Because I wronged you indirectly by keeping Ki Fei as my disciple. She kept begging me to let her go, but I couldn't let her waste her talent on any other trivial things, so I forced her to stay back, and then that guy came and took her."

"Who took her?" Wei got up, his hands shaking.

"Wang Fantai."

As if a quake had was happening inside him, Wei trembled violently. "What did you say?"

He grabbed the elder by his neck and raised him into the air. Today he would kill this elder no matter what.

Li Wei is coming back in the next thrilling adventure. Grab it now!

Finding Dao (Path of Lazy Immortal Book 11)

Chapter 95

Cultivation Index

R ealms of cultivation in the Mortal World (Body and Qi cultivation share the same names)

Mortal Realms (Where a person's body is still considered a mortal body.)

Refinement Realm

Foundation Realm

Blood Baptization Realm

Marrow Cleansing Realm

Boiling Blood Realm

Heart Blood Realm

Houtian Realm

Xiantian Realm

Violet Palace Relam

...

Meridian List for the Blood Essence Body Cultivation Art

Lower body Constellation

Refinement Realm (Earth Constellation) -   1) Yangming of stomach 2) Taiyin of spleen

Foundation Realm (Water Constellation) -   1) Taiyang of bladder 2) Shaoyin of kidney

Bone Baptization Realm (Wood Constellation) - 1) Jueyin of liver   2) Shaoyang of gallbladder

Grades of everything (Divided into three tiers. Low, mid, high)

Bronze

Silver

Gold

Earth

Human

Heaven

...

Array Realms

Array Carver Realm

Array Apprentice Realm

Array Adapt Realm - 9 Stars

...

Alchemist Realms

Pharmacist

Pill Apprentice – 3 Stars

Pill Adept - 6 Stars

...

Martial skill completion levels

Early Completion

Middle Completion

Late Completion

Peak Completion

If you like cultivation novels, don't forget to check below facebook groups to find out more books in cultivation genre.

Western Cultivation Stories

Cultivation Novels

Made in the USA
Las Vegas, NV
23 February 2025